UNIDENTIFIED
FUNNY
OBJECTS
6

Edited by

Alex Shvartsman

UFO Publishing
Brooklyn, NY

WITHDRAWN FROM
RAPIDES PARISH LIBRARY

c.1
RAPIDES PARISH LIBRARY
Alexandria, Louisiana MN

PUBLISHED BY:
UFO Publishing
1685 E 15th St.
Brooklyn, NY 11229
www.ufopub.com

Copyright © 2017 by UFO Publishing
Stories copyright © 2017 by the authors

Trade paperback ISBN: 978-0-9992690-0-8

All rights reserved. No part of the contents of this book may be
reproduced or transmitted in any form or by any means without the
written permission of the publisher.

Cover art: Tomasz Maronski
Interior art: Barry Munden
Typesetting & interior design: Melissa Neely
Graphics design: Emerson Matsuuchi
Logo design: Martin Dare
Copy editor: Elektra Hammond
Associate editors: Cyd Athens, James Beamon, Frank Dutkiewicz,
Nathaniel Lee, James A. Miller

Visit us on the web:
www.ufopub.com

TABLE OF CONTENTS

FOREWORD

ALEX SHVARTSMAN

T his year's installment of the annual Unidentified Funny
Objects series features cranky goblin cooks and lecherous
space pirates, soul-searching snot elementals and disagreeable alien
symbiotes. New characters from fresh voices in the speculative
genre appear alongside iconic stalwarts of humorous SF/F such
as Alan Dean Foster's Mad Amos and Mike Resnick's Harry the
Book. Wacky settings and unusual characters are the norm for the
series, but there's something else commonly present in each UFO
volume, and that's an abundance of epistolary fiction.

The traditional definition of an epistolary story is a literary work written in the form of letters. (Think Bram Stoker's
Dracula.) Over time the definition has expanded to include
all forms of documents, such as Charlie's progress reports in
Daniel Keyes's *Flowers for Algernon* or the alien invasion tale told
through a Twitter feed from Jake Kerr's story in the inaugural
volume of UFO.

This book includes a higher-than-usual percentage of such
stories. Our authors spin their tales through advice columns,
chat transcripts, Craigslist posts, footnotes, and, of course, actual
letters—be they correspondence between giants or an entreaty
to an ascendant AI overlord. I've often wondered whether the
prominence of epistolary stories in my anthologies is due to
personal preference (I enjoy unorthodox storytelling both as
a reader and as a writer) or because such formats are especially
well-suited for humor, and more so for the unusual, unidentifiable
sort of humor I seek for this series.

1

I'm of the opinion that the story format is just another tool in the writer's arsenal. It can enhance the story as much as a unique voice or an unexpected setting. Will you reach a similar conclusion? I invite you to delve right into this book and find out for yourself.

Happy reading!

A GAME OF GOBLINS

Jim C. Hines

G olaka never intended to marry. She certainly never intended to marry a human.

She was in the midst of slow-roasting a halfling with peppercorn and chunks of wild apple when the screaming began.

Cries of "Humans!" and "Kill them all!" and "Run away!" echoed through the obsidian tunnels beyond the lair. Golaka ignored them. If the goblin guards killed the humans, it meant more meat for her stores. If the humans killed some goblins, it meant fewer mouths to feed.

The humans won. Like they usually did. Golaka heard panicked goblins retreating into the cavernous lair. They slid a heavy door of lashed-together pine logs to block the tunnel behind them. Mild curiosity made her swivel her ears to listen.

"These humans are terrifying," gasped one of the guards who'd presumably survived through the proud goblin tradition of running away and leaving his companions to die. "Grim and dark, with eyes like fire and hearts of ice."

"I thought it was the other way around," said another.

A new voice, this one human, thundered from the tunnels. "I seek the lord of the goblins!"

"Seek quietly," Golaka yelled back. "Some of us are trying to cook!"

After a brief pause, the human continued. "I am the Wolf of the

Winterlands, heir to the Onyx Throne."

"They have a talking wolf," whispered a different goblin.

"Someone tell the chief a wolf wants to talk to him," said the guard.

Golaka grabbed her cleaver from the counter, just in case.

"Open this door, and I will spare your miserable lives," the human continued. "Refuse, and suffer a massacre to rival the morning every man, woman, and child of House Brionnen was slaughtered over poached quail eggs. Even you savages must have heard stories of the Red Brunch."

"What's a brunch?" the guard retorted.

Axes thunked into the makeshift door.

"Wait!" screamed at least a half-dozen goblins. Being goblin-built, the door wouldn't have lasted long anyway. Wood scraped over stone as they struggled to open the door again.

Golaka tested the edge of her cleaver and stepped forward for a better view. Five humans stood at the entrance to the lair. Trail dust and weariness darkened their faces. Four held heavy crossbows ready to shoot. The fifth stood with sword in one hand, a flickering torch in the other.

Goblins backed away, their own shoddy weapons shaking. One flattened his ears in fear as Golaka stood on her toes to try to see past the humans. "Where's the wolf?"

"I am Samuel Loncaster, Wolf of House Loncaster, bastard son of Ryan Loncaster, the Shadow Viper of the north." The human with the sword was tall and meaty, dressed in black leather and black furs. His black hair was shaggy and windsnarled, his young, stubbled face callused like bad leather.

Another goblin cocked her head, her blue face crinkled with confusion. "If your father's a snake, how can you be a wolf?"

Samuel ignored the question. "I would summon your leader to the Conclave."

"Our leader's sleeping off a klak beer hangover," said the goblin guard.

"Is a Conclave like a brunch?" asked another.

The humans muttered amongst themselves. Samuel rubbed

his brow. "Once every ten years, the lords of the north gather at Conclave to try to choose a high king to sit upon the Onyx Throne and rule the Army of Immortals."

"An onyx throne?" Golaka muttered. "Sounds like a bad case of arse blisters waiting to happen."

The human was still going on. "For a century, each vote has ended in stalemate. My father would have been the first Loncaster to sit upon the throne, but he was betrayed and murdered on the Night of Twelve Blades. I mean to fulfill his destiny and restore our House."

"Goblins aren't very good at building," said a goblin. "If you want to fix a house, you should talk to the dwarves."

The human stared, like he was trying to decide whether the goblins were mocking him, or if they were simply idiots. Golaka could have answered that one.

"This was a mistake," Samuel said at last. "The Conclave will never take these blue-skinned imbeciles seriously."

"A suggestion, my lord." One of the guards, a scarred man missing several teeth, stepped forward to whisper to Samuel, too quiet even for goblin ears to overhear.

Whatever he said made Samuel's face turn red. "Are you mad?"

"It would give the delegate legitimacy."

Samuel growled and studied each goblin in turn, until his gaze fell on Golaka. Those tiny human eyes widened. "You, old woman—" He hesitated. "You *are* a woman?"

Golaka bared her fangs. The goblins skittered back in alarm.

"You will come with me," Samuel continued. "As delegate of the goblins."

"I will garnish tonight's dinner with your liver is what I'll do." Golaka raised her cleaver.

"You don't frighten us, monster," said Samuel, though the way the guards shifted and pointed their weapons at her gave lie to his words. "I fought and killed the Boulder himself in the Courts of Farathun. My men can kill you where you stand—and slaughter your fellow goblins for good measure—or you can accompany me to the Conclave. Once I sit upon the Onyx Throne, you'll be free to return to this dark, filthy cave you call home."

Golaka narrowed her eyes. Four crossbows and a sword against one cleaver. "That's it? Cast a vote and go?"

Samuel's thin lips twitched. "There's also a minor ceremony..."

THEY RODE THROUGHOUT the day—the humans on thick, meaty horses, and Golaka on a mule whose spine seemed honed to split a goblin's backside. Dinner was tasteless jerky, tasteless bread, and cheese that made her wish for tastelessness.

Afterward, the scarred guard pulled Golaka aside while the other humans made camp. With him was Samuel and a thin, bare-faced human with clenched fists.

Samuel pulled a length of white rope from a pouch at his belt. "This is Chale Loncaster, the Hummingbird of House Loncaster."

"Hummingbird?" asked Golaka.

"He likes to hum." Samuel knotted one end of the rope around Chale's wrist.

"Father would behead you himself for this insult," hissed Chale.

Samuel merely smiled and extended the rope toward Golaka.

"Try to leash me to that human, and I'll pull out your intestines and hang you with them."

Now it was Samuel's turn to scowl, while Chale smirked. The guard whispered something to Samuel, who shoved him away.

"Very well." Samuel dropped the rope, letting it hang like a snake from Chale's hand. "Let this betrothal mark the alliance between House Loncaster and the goblins. Thomas Smoke, will you witness this contract?"

The guard squared his shoulders. "I so witness."

Samuel pulled a knife and cut away most of the rope, leaving the loop knotted around Chale's wrist. "You'll sleep there tonight," he said, pointing to a small tent the color of human blood.

Golaka shrugged and ducked through the tent flap. Two battered sleeping mats lay on the ground. She sat down on one and scratched. The journey had left her stiff, sore, and sweaty in any number of cracks and crevices.

Chale and Thomas followed her in. Chale pulled a knife, watching Golaka closely.

"You think that toy would stop me if I wanted your guts for a late-night snack?" Golaka shifted to one side, farted loudly, then raked her hair back from her face. "I'm not going to kill you, human. Least, not while we're surrounded by your brother's guards."

Slowly, he lowered his weapon. "What makes you think the knife was for you? *I'm* the one Samuel betrothed to a goblin."

"You're not exactly a prize for me either, Human." Golaka lay back on the mat.

He sighed. "This is but the latest insult my brother has heaped upon me."

"So go out there and stab him in the face."

"That's not how things are done, Goblin. This is a *civilized* gathering."

"Fine, stab him in the back." Golaka shrugged. "All this fuss over a stupid chair."

"Whoever is chosen to sit upon the Onyx Throne will command the Army of Immortals," Chale said stiffly. "The houses have played this game for centuries, but none have gathered enough votes to claim the throne."

"Humans always complicate things." She closed her eyes. "I assume your brother plans to kill me when this is over? Or is it more 'civilized' if this guard does it?"

"Thomas is only here as part of the betrothal ceremony. To..." Chale's voice sounded strained. "To protect the virginity of the bride-to-be."

Golaka opened one eye. "That meal was eaten years ago."

"What a vulgar figure of speech," Chale said.

"What makes you think it's a figure of speech?" With a chuckle, Golaka rolled over to sleep.

THEY ARRIVED EARLY the next day at the Wall of the Dead, site of the Conclave. The wall was a once-mighty edifice of dark stone, thirty feet tall, encircling what Chale described as a plain of petrified trees and a lone crypt.

Gray drizzle turned the ground to mud. A large, open pavilion had been erected outside the wall, near an enormous rusted gate. Golaka counted at least thirty humans gathered in small groups, some within the pavilion, others standing close by. A stout man with a round face, curly gray beard, and flat cap was cooking porridge—burning porridge, from the smell—over a fire.

"Each House can send up to six people," explained Chale. "Advisors, guards... assassins. More Houses will arrive throughout the day."

Golaka rubbed her arms against the chill. She was used to the rippling heat of the cook fires back home.

The cook looked up at their contingent and shouted, "Gorge!"

Golaka stopped. "I don't understand."

"That's Gorge. It's all he ever says. He's damaged in the head. He has no loyalty to any House, so he's the only person everyone trusts to cook for them."

Golaka sniffed again. "You call that cooking?"

Samuel strode ahead, calling greetings to some, while pointedly ignoring others.

"That's Marguerite of House Crowley," whispered Chale, pointing to a short, brown-skinned woman. Tufts of white down clung to her hair and cloak. "She was flung naked from the cliffs of Saint Ives for unlawful fornication. She returned two days later atop a hippogriff. The hippogriff bit off her husband's head. She married her lover the next day, naming her queen at her side. She's called the Hippogriff Queen, Mother of the North, and the Bringer of Stormclouds."

"That's a mouthful," said Golaka.

Chale gestured next to an older man, pale with a wispy white beard. "Laurence of House Ashcroft, known as the Night Dagger. He's a member of the ancient Night Bears sect. Six years ago, he orchestrated the Blood Moon Massacre that led to the downfall of House Whitlatch."

"You humans collect names like ogres collect lice." Golaka shut him out, mentally renaming each human things she'd remember: Feather Lady, Graybeard, and so on. The head of House Hollister was One Eye. She'd killed her predecessor by forcing him to drink molten lead. Her husband was Nose-Picker. House Larch was led by Gap-Tooth, who was known for using hunting ravens with poisoned talons against his enemies.

All Golaka cared about was keeping them from killing her. Judging from the way they stared, that might be tricky.

"What is this, Samuel?" demanded Feather Lady. "If you've brought this creature to feed to my pets, I'm afraid it will take a higher quality of snack to earn my favor."

Samuel puffed up like a lizard-fish trying to mate. He'd obviously been planning for this moment, probably practicing exactly what he'd say once the eyes of the Conclave were upon him. "This is—"

"Golaka," she cut in. "Called the Goblin Chef. Cooker of Humans."

"She is the delegate for her people," Samuel continued, with a glare at Golaka. "The House of Goblins may be small... and foul... but—"

"Should House Larch now give a vote to our messenger ravens?" scoffed Gap-Tooth. "Perhaps the rats who raid Ashcroft's grain stores would like a say as well?"

Samuel's hand went to his sword, a movement that caused the rest of the humans to step back and reach for their own weapons. "She is my future sister-in-law, and I demand you apologize for your insult."

It was amusing to watch the humans' attention turn back to Golaka, then shift to Chale and the white rope around his wrist. Some smirked or chuckled. Others looked like they'd tried to get a bite of stew, only to find they'd dipped their spoons in the chamber pot by mistake.

"You'd tie your House to that *creature*?" asked Nose-Picker.

"Gorge!" added Gorge.

"The Army of Immortals has slept too long," Samuel said firmly.

"They will awaken soon, with or without a ruler. If we don't end this stalemate—"

"House Hollister will never kneel to a Loncaster," pronounced One Eye. "We remember your grandfather's betrayal at the Battle of Four Fleets."

"Hollow words from a descendant of the Mantis," snapped Feather Lady.

Soon everyone was shouting, too loud and angry for Golaka to follow. She let it drag on until everyone was good and riled, then bellowed, "Whoever wins this vote becomes high king and sits on the rock throne and rules the dead army, yes?"

"Yes, that's so," snapped Samuel.

Golaka cocked her thumb at Samuel. "I'll vote for whoever kills this pile of pig dung."

The reaction was instant, but not what she'd expected. Whereas goblins would have immediately swarmed Samuel, the humans simply looked... bemused. All save Samuel, who was turning a vivid shade of red.

"You fool!" he shouted. "Do you realize what you've done?"

Golaka had expected Samuel to be furious, but why were the others so happy? Happy humans were never a good sign.

"Gorge," the cook said sadly, shaking his head.

"There are laws," Chale whispered. "The Conclave is a place of truce. To openly plot betrayal and murder..."

"This monster is your responsibility, Samuel," said Feather Lady. "Take her away and behead her so we can get on with our business."

Right. These were humans. Betrayal and murder were fine, but you had to be sneaky about it. She should have remembered. Golaka bared her fangs and flexed her arms. Too late for regrets now.

"Wait," shouted Chale. "You can't execute her."

"Quiet," snapped Samuel. "Unless you wish to join this monster on the block."

"Would you kill a bride on the day of her wedding?" Chale asked.

"What are you babbling about, brother?"

Golaka was equally confused, but said nothing. If Chale kept everyone distracted, she should at least be able to snatch Samuel's knife and plant it in his neck.

Chale took Golaka's hand, ruining that plan. "The goblin and I mean to be wed. You may have seen her only as a step toward power, brother, but I've come to respect and love Golaka."

Samuel had gone from red to purple. Golaka hadn't realized humans could turn that color. "It's an obscenity," he hissed. "You would make a mockery of our House."

"Only its lord," Chale shot back, in an equally low voice.

"You're the one who defended the goblin, moments ago," One Eye pointed out with a chuckle. "Looks like you're trapped in your own snare. To deny the boy's wedding would prove your own words hollow. Would you dishonor House Loncaster in front of all assembled here?"

"Very well," said Samuel, through gritted teeth. "Tie her up and lock her in the crypt for now. She can be wed tonight and executed in the morn. Since my brother is so protective of his betrothed, throw him in as well. Let him enjoy what time he has left with his beloved."

THE CRYPT SMELLED of old blood. Golaka swiveled her ears, tracking the scratching footsteps of rats in the darkness. To her right, Chale grunted as he struggled with his bonds.

"Why the crypt?" asked Golaka.

"It's the only building within the Wall of the Dead that's still standing. I'm sorry. I hoped for more than a day's reprieve..."

Golaka tested the ropes knotted around her wrists. The humans knew their rope craft. Nothing short of a blade would free her hands from behind her back.

The thinnest sliver of light pierced the crack at the edge of the door. As her eyes adjusted, she made out Chale hunched on the floor by the wall.

A series of stone tables stood in the center of the room, each with a body upon it. Other corpses had been shoved headfirst into open chambers in the rear wall. She leaned over the closest table and sniffed. "Doesn't smell dead. Just dusty. This is the army everyone's worried about?"

"The Army of Immortals." Chale whispered like he feared to wake them. "Centuries ago, they served the Winter King during the Three Day War. They're sworn to obey the high king, and to defend him against all enemies. But if they awaken without a high king, they might decide *everyone* is an enemy."

"So chop them up and be done with it. Or burn 'em. Lots of ways to dispose of dead humans."

"You think it's not been tried? Burn them, and they reform. Lock them in chains, and the links rust and fall away. Cut one up and seal the parts in a chest, and they break through the chest to return here. Every midnight, they recover from whatever has been done to them. They're unstoppable."

"Humans. Bad enough you want to control everything that lives. Now you have to control the dead, too." She walked over to kick the door. It was like kicking a mountain. All she got was a sore foot and an angry shout from one of the guards outside. The air passing through the narrow crack smelled of badly overspiced meat from the cook fire. "You humans don't *like* that man's cooking, do you?"

"We hate it," Chale admitted. "But nobody dares say so to Gorge's face. In his day, he killed more people, in more horrible and gruesome ways, than anyone can count. They called him the Red Reaper, though I'm told his real name was Martin."

"And the 'gorge' thing?"

"Some say he was struck with the gift of prophecy, and it's a warning of future threat, one even he doesn't understand. Most Houses avoid gorges and canyons and valleys, just to be safe. I say he was struck one too many times to the head."

"Or one time too few," she muttered. "Why'd you try to get your brother to spare me?"

"Because it was the right thing to do. Some Loncasters still believe in honor."

She snorted. "Try again, human. You think you're the first to try to lie to Golaka?"

"I wanted to humiliate my brother," he said with a sigh. "Bringing you to Conclave was a desperate gamble. Your betrayal made him a laughingstock. For that alone, I'm in your debt."

"Good to know. Do any of these dead humans have weapons? If not, maybe we could use their bones for clubs, or break them to stab with."

"That's... disturbing. Even if we could, you'd be lucky to kill even one before they cut you down." He sighed. "If only we could persuade the other Houses to intervene on your behalf. If you were pardoned, it would be another slap to Samuel's smug face."

Golaka sniffed the air again, a new idea beginning to form. "Human weddings usually involve a feast, yes?"

"That's right."

"As bride-to-be, I think I ought to prepare my own feast."

"You mean to poison them? You can't. They use silver plates and cups to detect—"

"Poison wastes a perfectly good meal," Golaka snapped.

"Wait, you claim to be a *good* chef?"

Golaka shoved him to the ground and stepped on his chest. "How about I roast you and we find out?"

Chale tried to squirm free. "I believe you!"

Golaka removed her foot from his chest. He hurried to the door. "Guard! I need to speak with my brother about my wedding preparations." To Golaka, he said, "If you're to impress the other houses, you'll need to prepare a meal worthy of kings and queens."

Golaka smiled, a smile that had been known to make other goblins wet themselves. Fortunately, it was too dark for Chale to see. "It will be fully worthy of them. I promise you that."

SAMUEL ONLY AGREED *after* Chale pointed out the additional shame that would fall on House Loncaster if the wedding lacked a palatable feast.

"She can't do any worse than Gorge," Samuel had grumbled.

"But she's to be accompanied by guards at all times."

That worked out well. Golaka pointed to the clump of brown mushrooms growing in the shade of the wall. "You with the beard like a rat's nest, grab those mushrooms."

The guard hesitated. "I don't think I should—"

"You'd rather help clean boar kidneys? Fine." She spun without waiting for an answer, stabbing her finger at the second guard. "We passed a stand of nettles yesterday on the way in. I need some. Gather more wood, too. Long, thin branches for skewers, and logs for the fires."

"Fires? More than one?"

"That's right—one with flames chest-high to start. Another burned down to the coals. And you, get me a bucket."

"Why do you need a bucket?"

Golaka threw up her hands. "To piss in. Unless you expect me to drop my drawers and go right here?"

To her left, Chale muffled a laugh. Golaka's mouth twitched, but she stifled her own amusement and whirled. "Why are you just standing there, my betrothed? Someone's gotta finish butchering that boar, and these idiots won't give me a knife. Get to work!"

"But... but Gorge already started roasting it," Chale protested.

The cook stood with folded arms a short distance away. Touched in the head or not, he watched the proceedings like a hawk.

"Started burning it, you mean," said Golaka. "The skin's ruined. It'll taste like ash. We need to cut the burnt meat away and start over."

Gorge shrugged. "Gorge," he said apologetically.

Golaka snatched the bucket from the guard and stomped toward the crypt.

"You can't go in there," the guard called after her.

"It's the only private place inside this wall, and I don't think Samuel wants me wandering loose among the trees outside, do you? I'm sure the dead humans won't mind. Now get to work!"

IT WASN'T LONG before the smell of roasting meat began to overpower the humans' skepticism.

"More wine," Golaka bellowed. Chale slapped a half-empty bottle into her hand. He was turning out to be a halfway-competent helper, though the humming was annoying. She downed several swallows, then poured the rest over the chops, making them sizzle. Tossing the bottle aside, she moved to the bed of coals. She used a blackened stick to flip the long strips of meat she'd laid out. Judging them done, she scooped them up onto the silver platter held by one of her guards. "Get those skewers ready. Rat-Beard, have you finished grinding the marrow paste yet?"

"It smells... *good*," whispered one of the humans—Feather Lady, the one with the hippogriffs. Golaka wondered briefly what hippogriff tasted like.

"Probably poisoned," sneered Samuel.

Golaka grabbed a strip of meat and bit off the end. Chewing happily, she said, "If you're afraid, don't eat it. More for the rest of us."

Several humans chuckled. The cook smirked and added, "Gorge."

"Keep that platter covered," Golaka barked at one of the guards. "Chale, dig the roots out of the coals. Those need to be mashed, then mixed with the marrow and chopped thistle leaves. You, the fire for the roast needs more wood. No pine, though. The smoke's wrong for boar." She marched over to to another guard and sniffed his work. "What this paste really needs is a garnish of fire-spider eggs..."

The crowd had grown. Golaka wiped her hands on her shirt and scowled. "Staring and drooling won't make the chops cook faster."

Chale cleared his throat. "It's almost sunset. Traditionally, weddings are performed while the sun shines. Preferably outdoors.

Without any hiding places for assassins or ambushes. With all weapons peace-bound." He shrugged. "We've had issues with weddings."

"Gorge," agreed the cook, stroking his beard.

Samuel tugged his brother from the cook fires. He spoke low enough to prevent human ears from overhearing. "You truly mean to marry this beast? You'd tarnish our house out of spite? What would father say?"

Chale swatted Samuel's hand away and whispered back, "I imagine he'd order you imprisoned for assassinating him."

"So be it." Surprisingly, Samuel didn't appear angry. "You'll see him soon, brother. While you sullied yourself with the goblin, I've negotiated a new alliance. I'd prefer not to share the Onyx Throne, but this is better than seeing the Army of Immortals under someone else's control."

"Which House?" Chale demanded.

"You won't be around long enough for it to matter." Samuel turned away to shout, "Friends of House Loncaster, let us gather for the union of the Hummingbird, Chale Loncaster, son of the Shadow Viper of the North, with... Golaka."

The humans formed a large, loose circle around Samuel, Chale, and Golaka. A circle with plenty of room between groups.

Samuel grabbed the bit of rope hanging from Chale's hand. "By my authority as head of House Loncaster, I give Chale to this woman. Who gives this goblin to Chale?"

The scarred guard, Thomas, started forward, but a glare from Golaka stopped him. "I give myself," she snapped.

"Very well." Samuel stepped back. "Who witnesses this contract?"

As one, the gathered humans shouted, "We so witness!" All save the cook, who shouted, "Gorge!"

Samuel nodded. "I pronounce you wed. Kiss your bride, brother."

"Try it and I'll bite your lips off." Golaka glanced around. "That's it?"

"The longer the wedding, the more opportunity for treachery."

Chale swallowed, took Golaka's hand, and planted a quick kiss on the knuckles. "Samuel means to kill us both," he whispered. "We should try to escape tonight, before—"

"Back to work, Goblin." Samuel pointed to the cook fires. "After the feast, you and my brother can celebrate your wedding night in the privacy of the crypt. Behind locked doors, with guards to ensure you're not disturbed."

Chale sagged, his eyes dull with defeat.

"Cook now. Pout later." Golaka shoved her way toward the fires. "Where are my guards? Those mushrooms won't slice themselves!"

GOLAKA STABBED A boar chop with her nails and brought it to her lips. She tore a generous bite from the edge, chewed, and nodded. "It's ready."

She grabbed another piece of meat and tossed it to Chale. She watched with amusement as the humans struggled between revulsion at the idea of eating goblin-cooked food and the craving of their empty bellies. As it always did, hunger won out. One by one, the humans brought their silver plates and helped themselves.

Chale started to go back for one of the paste-coated slabs of boar, but Golaka caught his shoulder. "I don't want my husband tasting like marrow-salt on our wedding night. Or wild onions, so avoid the skewers as well."

Chale paled. "You don't mean to..."

Golaka laughed and punched him hard enough to knock him to the ground. "Like you'd survive a night with me."

"Gorge," added the cook, laughing.

Golaka stiffened as one of the humans—Nose-Picker—approached her. But the human was beaming as he tore meat from a skewer with his teeth.

"This is... quite good," he said, his words muffled.

"Delectable," called Graybeard.

"And this paste," added Feather Lady. "You *must* share your secrets before your execution."

"Samuel Loncaster, it would be a crime to kill an artist of such skill," announced One Eye.

Chale grabbed Golaka's hand, seemingly without realizing what he was doing. "It's working."

"You'd petition to save a *goblin*?" Samuel demanded.

"Eat one of these chops before you decide." Nose-Picker shoved his plate in Samuel's face. "I insist."

Golaka finished her own meat and absently sucked grease from her fingers.

"All are in agreement," said Feather Lady. "Don't look so glum, Samuel. House Crowley will happily buy this creature from you."

"House Ashcroft's coffers are deep enough to match any price!"

"Think of your grandfather's long friendship with House Hollister. Give the goblin to us as a gift."

"Shut your gobs," Golaka bellowed. The humans fell silent, their mouths round with shock. "You're saying either the bastard here executes me in the morning, or else I spend the rest of my days serving humans, is that it?"

"What are you doing?" whispered Chale, trying to tug her back.

"That's right," said Feather Lady. "Though you'll have to learn to mind your—"

Golaka cut her off with a loud, drawn-out belch. "I'd sooner cut out my own liver and fry it up in lizard-fish oil than live as a slave to you spoiled, scheming, power-mad *humans*." She pulled away from Chale and started toward the crypt. "Enjoy the feast."

"ARE GOBLINS SO proud they'd rather die than cook for humans?" Chale asked from the darkness of the crypt.

"Goblins? Proud?" Golaka laughed. "We're monsters. The difference between us and you is that we know it. You humans have spent centuries finding new and gruesome ways to kill each other. You've turned it into a game."

"Goblins are no better," Chale snapped.

"We don't pretend to be. Why haven't you killed your brother yet?"

"It's not that simple. I can't just—"

"Exactly. Because human games have rules."

Chale moaned. "This place smells like death."

"That was me. Human wine gives me gas."

A piercing scream made Chale jump. Golaka simply leaned against the wall beside the door.

"Where is this Onyx Throne, anyway?" asked Golaka.

"It's said it will appear when the high king is chosen."

A growling, gurgling sound came from the other side of the door. One of the guards groaned and whispered to his partner. "Too many of them skewers." Hasty footsteps signaled his departure.

Golaka stretched her shoulders the best she could. Samuel had bound her arms again, more out of spite than any real fear of what she might do. "What time do you think it is?"

"How should I know?"

More screams filled the air outside. The remaining guard hurried away. "One of the Houses must have plotted betrayal," said Chale.

Golaka yawned. "Did you notice how much burnt boar we had to throw out? There wasn't enough meat left to feed all of you humans. So I fetched some extra."

"How?"

"From the crypt. A couple of those dead soldiers stacked up in back."

"You... you what?" Chale sounded faint. "You had no knife, no—"

"I had fangs and a bucket. Remind me, what happens to these dead soldiers if you chop them up? Or chew them up?"

"The pieces return at midnight," Chale whispered. "Through any barrier. Merciful god, you'll kill us all. We have to vomit before—"

"Quit whimpering. I made sure to prepare a couple of untainted pieces for us. The rest, well, anyone who smeared marrow paste on their meal, or ate one of those skewers, or tried the stew..." She tried the door, but it didn't budge. "Maybe you can call this one the Night of the Bloody Privies."

Chale didn't answer. He didn't speak at all for the next hour, though he moaned when small shapes like ragged, bloody caterpillars began crawling beneath the door to rejoin the bodies Golaka had taken them from.

Only when the last of the screams had died did he stir. "We're trapped in here. If the Army of Immortals doesn't awaken and destroy us, we'll starve to death."

"Not me," said Golaka. "Not while I have you around."

Chale moaned again.

"You think I *want* to eat raw human? Besides, we're not trapped. The first thing every goblin learns is to always have a plan for running away. If I'm not mistaken, you're now head of your house, and the only other survivor of this Conclave."

"Most likely," Chale admitted.

"In that case, as delegate of the goblins, I vote for Golaka as high king." She paused. "The way I see it, you can vote for me, and I'll order these dead bastards to break down the door and escort us home. Or vote for yourself, and it's another tie, meaning we're stuck in here and I rethink the idea of eating uncooked human."

"I vote for Golaka as well."

"Right." She looked around. "Dead humans. Get your arses up and break open that door."

For several moments, nothing happened. Then bodies rustled. Footsteps shuffled across the floor. Golaka and Chale backed away as dead fists assaulted the door.

None of the dead humans spoke. The quiet was a nice change from the past day or so.

The door cracked and fell away. Moonlight and fresh air flooded the crypt. Golaka shoved past the dead humans and stepped outside. A few bodies lay scattered across the ground. Most had died near the privies and latrines.

Chale began to laugh. It was the kind of laugh that brought to mind the shattering of glass, or the breaking of ill-tempered steel. "You... you're High King of the Winterlands. A goblin! You could conquer... everything!"

Golaka scowled. "Sure, but where would I put it?" She took a knife from one of the bodies and awkwardly sawed through her bonds. "These dead bastards have caused you humans more than a century of grief. You think I need that kind of headache? I've got a whole lair of goblins for that. Goblins who've probably made a bloody mess of my kitchen by now. Stuffed themselves on my stores, swiped all my best knives..."

Golaka jabbed a finger at the closest of the immortal army. "You, guard Chale and see him home. Do whatever he tells you." Her finger moved to the next group. "You four, find that silly throne. The rest of you? Drop dead, and this time, stay that way."

The Army of Immortals collapsed, all save the ones Golaka had indicated.

Chale stared at the bodies, then at Golaka. "They're really dead. The army. My brother... the Conclave."

"Every one," agreed Golaka. "Seems fitting that the greedy bastards gorged themselves to death."

"I'm head of House Loncaster now. I'll need advisors of my own. And a chef. I... you could be both, if you wanted. Not as slave or servant, but—"

"I don't think so." Golaka started to walk away. "You know, you've decent skill at the cook fires. I could use a helper back at the lair. Do a good enough job, and the other goblins probably won't eat you."

Chale shuddered. "No, thank you."

Beyond him, the other dead soldiers had returned, staggering beneath the weight of a gleaming onyx chair, black with long, wispy clouds of white stretching through it. They set it in the dirt in front of her.

"Now that I look at it, that would go nicely with the rock of the lair," Golaka said. "Needs a cushion, but it's about the right height for when I'm stirring the stewpot."

"You mean to use the Onyx Throne as a *kitchen stool?*" Chale laughed again, but the madness was gone. "I think I understand your lesson. Thank you, Golaka. Farewell!"

What lesson? Idiot humans, always digging for lessons and layers of meaning in everything. Still, the young human was a step up from most. Maybe he'd even survive the bloodbath of human politics for a while.

Golaka ducked into one of the tents to grab a bedroll. It wasn't like the previous owner needed it anymore. She draped it over the throne for padding and sat down. "All right, humans. *Lift!*"

The four immortal soldiers raised Golaka and her throne smoothly into the air.

High King of the Winterlands? Who needed that? Golaka was perfectly content to be Unquestioned Lord of the Goblin Kitchen. "Let's march."

Jim C. Hines

Jim C. Hines' first novel was *Goblin Quest,* the humorous tale of a nearsighted goblin runt and his pet fire-spider. Actor and author Wil Wheaton described the book as "too f***ing cool for words," which is pretty much the Best Blurb Ever. After finishing the goblin trilogy, he went on to write the Princess series of fairy tale retellings and the *Magic ex Libris* books, a modern-day fantasy series about a magic-wielding librarian, a dryad, a secret society founded by Johannes Gutenberg, a flaming spider, and an enchanted convertible. He's also the author of the Fable Legends tie-in *Blood of Heroes.* His short fiction has appeared in more than 50 magazines and anthologies.

Jim's forthcoming *Janitors of the Post-Apocalypse* series marks his first foray into science fiction. Book one, *Terminal Alliance,* comes out in November 2017. You can find him at www.jimchines.com or on Twitter as @jimchines.

THE BREAKDOWN OF THE PARASITE/HOST RELATIONSHIP

PAUL R. HARDY

PAUL R. HARDY

RESEARCH VESSEL *WISPFOLLOWER* CHATLOG PARTICIPANTS:
Life Support System CHEN SHI
Mission Captain UCHELL

UCHELL: Good morning, Chen. You joined us quite recently, so I wanted to see how you were settling in.

CHEN: I regret to inform you that I am settling in very poorly, Captain. I had no idea that working as a Life Support System to a florungus could be so degrading! I was prepared for the sensation of having a sentient parasite wrapped around my spine, but not for their carelessness in using my body.

UCHELL: I'm sorry to hear that. Kirireg usually gets on well with their LSS—has there been a specific issue?

CHEN: There have been several, but I can supply an alarming example from just this morning. When Kirireg finished their engineering shift and returned control of my body, I was immediately struck by an urgent and unpleasant sensation. They had not troubled to urinate once during their entire work shift! I had to float through the transit tubes to the nearest bipedal toilet facility in an extremely undignified pose. I barely made it there in time!

UCHELL: I see. Have you spoken to Kirireg about this?

CHEN: It is difficult when we cannot both be awake at once, but I have made several attempts nonetheless. I have used the interpersonnel chat system. I have left voicemails. I have asked other crewmembers to pass on messages. I have placed post-it notes in Kirireg's workspace. I have written memos on my hands. I even held a large noticeboard in front of myself as I handed back control so that he would have no excuse not to see it. He has ignored me every single time! Surely a civilized parasite should be more accommodating than this?

UCHELL: You didn't try any other methods? Although to be honest, I'm not sure if we have any...

CHEN: Captain, I would be grateful if you took this matter seriously.

UCHELL: Yes, of course. I'll have a word with Kirireg and see if we can't sort this out. They've been working flat out to prepare for our dark matter observations, so I imagine they've just been busy.

CHEN: Captain, I shall look forward to the results of your intervention. Thank you.

RESEARCH VESSEL *WISPFOLLOWER* CHATLOG PARTICIPANTS:
Mission Captain UCHELL
Gyroscopic Engineer BELIK-EMMIK-KIRIREG

UCHELL: I know you're busy, but what's all this I hear about not letting your LSS go to the toilet during your shift? I don't recall you having issues like this on the last mission. I can't have my crew backbiting each other once we're halfway out of the galaxy with six cycles of dark matter observations ahead of us. Especially when it's the same back they're biting.

KIRIREG: Ha-ha. Very funny. But seriously, you have no idea what I'm putting up with! This guy Chen was forced on me at the last minute—my previous LSS decided to retire without telling me, so I had to take whoever the agency had available. They said Chen was compatible and willing to work, but I think they were just trying to get rid of him.

UCHELL: Why, has he turned out to be incompatible? Have you spoken to Dr. Lallimore about that?

KIRIREG: Nah, it's not the physical side. It's the everything-else side. He's insufferable! The only thing that could make it worse is if we were awake at the same time and actually had to talk to each other. Do you know what the first thing I found was, when I wrapped myself round his spine and woke up in his body? A list of rules!

UCHELL: What's wrong with a few rules?

KIRIREG: You haven't read the list he gave me. I should put it on the shipwide boards so everyone can have a laugh. I mean it's just ridiculous:

• *Toilet break to be taken for fluid waste (urine) every TWO HOURS. DO NOT DRINK THE URINE! It may seem efficient to recycle but it is DISGUSTING. Use the correct facility for disposal!*

• *Handwashing to be undertaken after every toilet break. Use the alcohol cleaner (in the tool belt I have provided). DO NOT INGEST THE ALCOHOL CLEANER! You will get my body drunk and I will have to report you to the captain for alcoholism.*

• *Do not defecate solid wastes unless it is ABSOLUTELY NECESSARY to do so. DO NOT SAVE THE FECES. I am aware that florungal species require soil to germinate their seeds and I do not want my feces used as fertilizer!*

...And it goes on like that for another six pages. See what I mean? Seriously, I wonder why Chen signed up for this if he's such a xenophobe that he thinks I'm going to want to use his piss and shit for anything.

UCHELL: Okay, so he's a bit humorless, but that doesn't change the fact that his species needs to urinate regularly. Humans haven't been out in space for all that long, so they haven't made a full adaptation yet.

KIRIREG: I didn't know you were an expert on humans.

UCHELL: That is literally on the first page of their species wiki.

KIRIREG: Really?

UCHELL: I take it you haven't looked that far.

KIRIREG: Well, I've been busy. Calibrating gyroscopes. You know, the thing I'm being paid for.

UCHELL: Kirireg, I know we have a lot to do and your work schedule is stressful, but I can't have you damaging your LSS through neglect. Do some research before you decide it's okay to ignore his requests. And please, respond to his messages and find a solution that works for both of you.

KIRIREG: Fine. I'll sort something out.

RESEARCH VESSEL *WISPFOLLOWER* CHATLOG PARTICIPANTS:
Life Support System CHEN SHI
Mission Captain UCHELL

CHEN: Captain, I am still very unhappy with Kirireg. I had hoped your intervention would prompt it to address my concerns in an honest manner, but instead they chose to play a disgusting practical joke! Rather than simply use the toilet facilities as I requested, they wore an adult diaper! And of course they left it to me to clean up. It was absolutely filthy, soiled with both forms of waste! And worse than that, the diaper was not designed for human physiology and therefore did not fit me correctly, leading to leakage which caused a rash. This is a medical issue which will only grow worse if their behavior is repeated. Indeed, it may result in Kirireg having to miss work shifts while it heals. I do not wish to insist on taking medical leave, but I will have little choice if this continues.

UCHELL: I'm very sorry to hear that this situation is continuing. I will speak to Kirireg again to impress upon them the importance of regular urination breaks.

RESEARCH VESSEL *WISPFOLLOWER* CHATLOG PARTICIPANTS:
Mission Captain UCHELL
Gyroscopic Engineer BELIK-EMMIK-KIRIREG

UCHELL: Come on, Kirireg. A diaper? Seriously?

KIRIREG: I did exactly as you asked! I looked it up on the species wiki, and this is how they dealt with the urination problem when they first started getting into space. It's certainly efficient! And anyway, it's not like I had a choice. Chen's put me in a position where I have to maximize the amount of time I spend around the gyroscopes.

UCHELL: Explain.

KIRIREG: I think he's deliberately starving himself to get back at me.

UCHELL: I think you're deliberately testing my patience.

KIRIREG: I'm serious! It's as though he doesn't realize he's eating for two. I keep finding that I don't have the energy to get through the shift—I have to work more slowly to keep up my concentration, and the only way I can do that is to cut out anything that's not work-related. Like following Chen's stupid rules.

UCHELL: Kirireg, I don't have time for this. I know he's annoying, but you two need to work together. So this is an order: take the piss breaks as he requests and stop messing about.

RESEARCH VESSEL *WISPFOLLOWER* CHATLOG PARTICIPANTS:
Mission Captain UCHELL
Life Support System CHEN SHI

UCHELL: I've spoken to Kirireg about the urination issue. Please let me know if there are any further problems. There's another issue I'd like to just check on—are you having any difficulties with nutrition?

CHEN: Thank you for your help, Captain. I am indeed having difficulties, and again it is Kirireg who is the source of the problem.

I've been trying to eat as healthily as I can so that I do not put on weight, which can be an issue for those working as Life Support Systems. But Kirireg has been compromising my efforts by eating during their work shifts. And their choice of food is simply disgusting! I keep finding pieces of fermented algae and candied spiders in my pockets! The taste in my mouth is frequently vile—I am sure they do not brush my teeth and floss as I politely requested. I certainly provided detailed enough instructions!

UCHELL: I see.

CHEN: I sent three copies by three different methods, each one enclosing a toothbrush, toothpaste, and an adequate supply of dental floss. Therefore I am, once again, certain that Kirireg has deliberately chosen to ignore me.

UCHELL: Clearly.

CHEN: In summary, I have gained a hundred grams in weight over the last ten days despite the fact that I bear the burden of eating for two. Therefore I have reduced my own calorific intake to compensate, and increased my exercise schedule to counter Kirireg's slovenly habits—I don't think they have performed the stretches I requested even once!

UCHELL: And how many ways did you send those instructions to Kirireg?

CHEN: At least four. Kirireg continues to ignore me, and I sense you are not taking this entirely seriously either.

UCHELL: I'm sorry. Go on.

CHEN: I am afraid to say that the experience of working as an LSS has fulfilled my worst fears. If this kind of behavior continues, I will have no choice but to ask Dr. Lallimore to separate us.

UCHELL: I would strongly advise against that. The penalty clauses for breaking your contract would be very serious indeed—you would be charged for the cost of postponing the mission while we find a replacement LSS. Paying off the debt could take the rest of your life.

CHEN: Forgive me, Captain. I will of course do everything in my power to fulfill the terms of my contract. I can only hope that Kirireg does the same.

RESEARCH VESSEL *WISPFOLLOWER* CHATLOG PARTICIPANTS:
Mission Captain UCHELL
Gyroscopic Engineer BELIK-EMMIK-KIRIREG

UCHELL: Please tell me you've sorted this thing out with Chen. He's talking about getting the two of you separated.

KIRIREG: Seriously? But what about the penalty clauses?

UCHELL: It doesn't matter. He'll never be able to pay off the debt and the mission will be postponed for space knows how long while we find more funding.

KIRIREG: Well, I've been trying to work with him. But he's completely inflexible! It's all rules, rules, rules! He wants me to put any snacks I eat on a chart along with calorie content and time and how much they weighed when they came out the other end. Seriously, he wants me to weigh his shit! I'm here to calibrate gyroscopes, not study the human dietary system!

UCHELL: Can you please just put up with it for one mission? If this goes to litigation, you might get hit in the fallout as well.

KIRIREG: Fine. But I'm going to have to do something about the food issue.

UCHELL: I really don't care how you do it. Just sort something out, for the love of space.

RESEARCH VESSEL *WISPFOLLOWER* CHATLOG PARTICIPANTS:
Life Support System CHEN SHI
Mission Captain UCHELL

CHEN: Captain, I have to report a grave abuse upon my person by the parasite Kirireg.

UCHELL: What is it?

CHEN: When I awoke after their last shift, I felt uncommonly tired. I suspected foul play, and I turned out to be right. When I returned to my quarters and removed my worksuit, I found leaves!

UCHELL: You're complaining about Kirireg's snacking habits

now? This is really none of my business. Frankly, I'm fed up with all of this petty nonsense.

CHEN: I apologize if I was unclear. Kirireg has not been eating leaves. They have been growing leaves! There are now more than a dozen stems bursting from my spine and wrapping around my body, bearing variegated leaves in enormous quantity—no wonder I felt so tired when I came off shift! I look like I'm covered in ivy! Kirireg has been using all the energy they claim they need for work to grow foliage instead. Heaven only knows why. If this continues, I will have to activate clause 17b in my contract, "Permanent Physical Harm to the Host," which permits separation without penalty.

UCHELL: Very well. I'll have a word with them. Again. But my patience is very nearly at an end.

RESEARCH VESSEL *WISPFOLLOWER* CHATLOG PARTICIPANTS:
Mission Captain UCHELL
Gyroscopic Engineer BELIK-EMMIK-KIRIREG

UCHELL: Explain the leaves now before I fire your florungal ass.

KIRIREG: I didn't have a choice!

UCHELL: That is not an explanation.

KIRIREG: Seriously, I had no control over it. You know how it is for my species—if we don't get enough nutrition from the host, we put out foliage and photosynthesize. I couldn't help it!
UCHELL: Kirireg, I do know your species, and I know very well that it's the flowers you can't control, not the leaves.

KIRIREG: Ugh, don't say that about flowers. Don't even joke about it. That's the last thing I need. And yes, I can usually restrain the foliage but I'm in a weakened state. It's a starvation adaptation, and he was starving me! Do you know what he did when he found out?

UCHELL: He re-read his contract and found that you were giving him a way to get out of it without penalty?

KIRIREG: He started trimming! He got hold of some pruning shears from the hydroponics bay and hacked them all off!

UCHELL: Kirireg, I'm serious. You're just giving him a reason to break his contract. Any physical harm—like, say, putting holes in his skin with your stems—will give him an excuse for separation.

KIRIREG: What about the physical harm to me??? That's my flesh he's cutting into! And the more he cuts, the more I'll grow. Trimming just triggers the growth reflex. I can't help it!

UCHELL: Kirireg, I've had enough. You're putting the mission at risk.

KIRIREG: How is this my fault?

UCHELL: I really don't care whose fault it is. Here's what you're going to do. Send him a present. A peace offering. Something nice that he'll like. Maybe a card as well. Send a groveling message to go with it. Apologize to him. Explain that he has to stop cutting before you can withdraw the stems. Negotiate a solution. Got it?

KIRIREG: Got it. Humiliate myself. Right.

UCHELL: Kirireg, I swear that if the next thing I hear from you two isn't a report about how you've sorted it out, I'll put you off the ship in a lifepod together and let you make it back to civilization by yourselves.

KIRIREG: You wouldn't!

UCHELL: Try me.

KIRIREG: Fine. Whatever.

RESEARCH VESSEL *WISPFOLLOWER* CHATLOG PARTICIPANTS:
Life Support System CHEN SHI
Mission Captain UCHELL

CHEN: Well, Captain, things have taken a turn for the better! I must congratulate you on your diplomacy. Kirireg has presented me with a gift to apologize for their behavior, and I am minded to come to a compromise with them.

UCHELL: Seriously?

CHEN: Yes, absolutely.

UCHELL: Huh. Okay, that's good to hear. To be honest, I was starting to think the two of you were never going to see eye to eye (so to speak). What did they give you?

CHEN: Flowers! The most remarkable and delicate kind of orchids. Well, I suppose they are not actually orchids, but they are quite similar in many ways! And the stamens are nicely concealed in a pouch so that the pollen does not trouble my allergies. So thoughtful!

UCHELL: Chen... did Kirireg grow these flowers themself, or did they come from hydroponics?

CHEN: Kirireg grew them! Of course, I am aware that florunguses cannot consciously control the growth of flowers, so I can only guess that they are an unconscious signal of friendship.

UCHELL: That sounds unlikely. You're absolutely sure they're meant as a gift?

CHEN: Certainly! They left a very polite message via the chat system telling me I would soon find a gift—the message was a little grudging, perhaps, but they seemed honest and I think we can come to an arrangement. Meanwhile, I have placed the flowers in water and they cheer the cabin up nicely!

UCHELL: Please tell me you did not cut them off.

CHEN: Yes, of course I did—why, what else would you do with flowers?

Excuse me a moment. I think the internal postal system has something for me.

UCHELL: Are you still there? Please reply.

CHEN: Captain, something strange has occurred. I have just received a package in the internal post which contains a small glucose bar and a card that reads 'sorry if I did something wrong.' It is signed by Kirireg. I am not sure what this means.

UCHELL: Chen, the flowers were not a gift.

CHEN: I do not understand.

UCHELL: Kirireg hasn't bloomed in all the time I've known them. If they have, then it's probably something to do with the foliage and the stress. Do you know what flowers are, to a member of Kirireg's species?

CHEN: The same as on my world, surely? A way of attracting pollinators?

UCHELL: That's part of it. They have both male and female organs. They make seeds. The seeds grow into baby florunguses. Flowers are for reproduction.

Chen, you just cut off Kirireg's genitals.

CHEN: oh my god

UCHELL: Kirireg would have self-pollinated and saved the seeds for later planting, but that won't happen now. They'll grow new flowers in time but that could be years away. You're going to have to make an apology.

CHEN: I think I might throw up

UCHELL: It was clearly a misunderstanding, but a very serious one nonetheless.

CHEN: This is not a misunderstanding. This is a deliberate insult.

UCHELL: ??? Please explain.

CHEN: Kirireg has tricked me into decorating my cabin with genitalia!

UCHELL: What?

CHEN: It is another practical joke. On me, as always! These so-called flowers are nothing more than private parts sent to humiliate me!

UCHELL: Oh, for space's sake...

CHEN: I am putting these disgusting efflorescences into the trash at once!

UCHELL: Chen, don't do that—they're delicate!

CHEN: THE FLOWERS BURST

THERE IS POLLEN EVERYWHERE

MY ALLERGIES

I CAN'T STOP SNEEZING

RESEARCH VESSEL *WISPFOLLOWER* CHATLOG PARTICIPANTS:
Gyroscopic Engineer BELIK-EMMIK-KIRIREG
Mission Captain UCHELL

KIRIREG: I just woke up with a pain in my head. In Chen's head, whatever! I think he hit it on something. And there's slime dripping out of his nose! What the hell?

He had an open chat with you. It just closed itself. Were you talking? What's going on?

UCHELL: Now don't get too excited

KIRIREG: Ugh his lungs just spasmed and sprayed more of that slime everywhere! It's disgusting! Why the hell has he done that to himself?

UCHELL: I need to tell you something and you aren't going to like it. Please be calm.

KIRIREG: Wait—what's this in the trash?

UCHELL: Kirireg, I need you to listen to me.

KIRIREG: Flowers? They look like...

THEY'RE MY FLOWERS

HE CUT THEM OFF

THAT BASTARD CUT OFF MY FLOWERS

I DIDN'T EVEN KNOW I'D GROWN THEM

UCHELL: Stay calm, Kirireg. This is not deliberate.

KIRIREG: Are you telling me that SHEAR-HAPPY BASTARD didn't cut my flowers off on purpose? I'LL CUT HIS FLOWERS OFF AND SEE HOW HE LIKES IT

UCHELL: It wasn't on purpose! That's what I'm telling you!

KIRIREG: WHERE DID HE LEAVE THE PRUNING SHEARS DAMMIT

UCHELL: Kirireg, please don't do anything rash! I've alerted Dr. Lallimore and she's on her way, we'll see if there's anything she can do.

KIRIREG: The flowers are DEAD dammit and I can't find the shears so MAYBE I'LL JUST PUNCH HIM IN HIS FLOWERS INSTEAD

UCHELL: Kirireg, please just wait!

KIRIREG: HOW DO YOU LIKE THAT? YEAH? WELL TAKE ANOTHER ONE IN THE STAMEN THEN

UCHELL: Kirireg, just stop!

KIRIREG: OW OW YEAH YOU BET THAT HURTS

UCHELL: This is just stupid!

KIRIREG: YOU'RE REALLY GOING TO FEEL THIS IN YOUR OVULES WHEN YOU WAKE UP OW OW OW

UCHELL: You're only hurting yourself!

KIRIREG: ow ow ow ow YOU'RE DAMN RIGHT I AM what what what is happening

UCHELL: Kirireg? What was that?

KIRIREG: it hurts it hurts WHY WON'T THESE FINGERS DO WHAT THEY'RE SUPPOSED TO I don't understand my hands keep moving by themselves STOP IT JUST STOP IT what is happening YOU'RE NOT SUPPOSED TO BE AWAKE JUST STOP IT

UCHELL: Okay, Dr. Lallimore is there, she's going to give you a hypo, just hold still

KIRIREG: well I am awake and I've had enough I want you out SHUT UP SHUT UP GO BACK TO SLEEP I won't I want you out JUST GO BACK TO SLEEP I won't ow something stung me what is happening WHAT IS HAPPENING doctor is that youuuuuuuuu

RESEARCH VESSEL *WISPFOLLOWER* CHATLOG PARTICIPANTS:
Mission Captain UCHELL
Medical Officer DR. JUHN LALLIMORE
Life Support System CHEN SHI
Gyroscopic Engineer BELIK-EMMIK-KIRIREG

UCHELL: Is there any option other than separation?

LALLIMORE: We're at the last stage before that becomes necessary. It's up to them, really. They need to come to an agreement.

UCHELL: Any sign of that?

LALLIMORE: Well, they can't talk—they fight over control of the larynx when they try. But they both have pretty good control over one side of the body. So, I've set them up with a keyboard each.

UCHELL: Okay. How is it going?

LALLIMORE: Not well. I'll let you observe their chat session so you can see for yourself.

CHEN: *GET OUT OF MY BODY*

KIRIREG: *GO BACK TO SLEEP! We can't survive with both nervous systems going at once!*

CHEN: *I DON'T CARE IF YOU DIE*

KIRIREG: *You IDIOT it won't just be ME that dies!*

CHEN: *You will if I kill you first!*

KIRIREG: *Oh, what are you going to do, beat me to death? I'M INSIDE YOU YOU CAN'T GET AT ME*

CHEN: *OH CAN'T I?*

KIRIREG: *Argh! What was that?*

UCHELL: What happened?

LALLIMORE: They spasmed. I think... oh my. They're growing leaves again. That's not good.

KIRIREG: *how are you doing that*

CHEN: *nervous systems linked I just have to concentrate and I can make you grow. Hah!*

KIRIREG: *WHY ARE YOU MAKING ME GROW LEAVES YOU HATE IT WHEN I GROW LEAVES*

CHEN: Because this is how weedkiller works and *YOU'RE A WEED*

KIRIREG: *What?!?*

CHEN: Weedkiller makes the weed grow so fast it starves to death *NOW GET OUT OF MY BODY UNLESS YOU WANT TO STARVE*

LALLIMORE: Goodness. They're really sprouting now.

KIRIREG: *You IDIOT I get my food from YOUR BLOODSTREAM we'll both starve!*

CHEN: *NOT IF I GROW THE LEAVES FAST ENOUGH*

KIRIREG: *Stop it or I'll—damn it damn it damn it I don't want to do this but you're making me*

LALLIMORE: Oh my. One side—I think it's Kirireg—has ripped off a handful of the new growth and shoved it into their mouth! They're eating the leaves!

CHEN: *STOP THAT*

KIRIREG: *Hah! Bet you didn't know I could reabsorb the leaves, did you? And you can't stop me eating when you're concentrating on growing them, can you?*

CHEN: *I'LL GROW THEM FASTER SO FAST YOU'LL CHOKE*

UCHELL: I think I've seen enough. They're never going to agree on anything. Separate them and I'll turn the ship around. Damn it.

LALLIMORE: I'm not sure I can. Their vital signs are all over the place—it might kill them. Wow, they're really shoveling the leaves in! The stems are getting thicker as well...

KIRIREG: *Well then I'll just have to MUTATE YOUR BODY so you can EAT MORE*

CHEN: *what the hell does that mean OWOWOWOW WHAT ARE YOU DOING*

LALLIMORE: I can't believe what I'm seeing!

UCHELL: What? What are you seeing???

LALLIMORE: I'm not even sure I can describe it! Chen's body is growing somehow, it's bending round, his mouth is getting bigger, they're eating more...

CHEN: *you're not supposed to be able to do that they told me you wouldn't be able to do anything like that*

KIRIREG: *I didn't know either BUT IT'S WORKING AND YOU CAN'T STOP ME*

LALLIMORE: It just keeps on! I don't understand this...

UCHELL: Don't understand what? What's going on down there?

CHEN: *THEN I'LL KEEP GROWING I'LL MAKE THE STEMS COME RIGHT OUT OF MY BOTTOM*

KIRIREG: *THEN I'LL KEEP EATING THEM I DON'T CARE WHAT IT TASTES LIKE*

UCHELL: What the hell is going on?

LALLIMORE: I don't know!

KIRIREG: *I'LL KEEP EATING*

CHEN: *I'LL KEEP GROWING*

KIRIREG: *EATING EATING EATING*

CHEN: *GROWING GROWING GROWING*

KIRIREG: *EATING*

CHEN: *EATING*

KIRIREG: *GROWING AND EATING*

CHEN: *GROWING AND EATING*

KIRIREG: *EATING AND GROWING*

CHEN: *EATING AND GROWING*

LALLIMORE: Their vital signs! Something's happening! They're... I don't believe this...

UCHELL: Don't believe what? Doctor, just tell me what's going on!

KIRIREG: *GROWING AND EATING AND GROWING AND wow suddenly I feel kind of relaxed*

CHEN: *GROWING AND EATING AND GROWING AND wow suddenly I feel kind of relaxed*

LALLIMORE: They're completely in sync! The readings are exactly the same!

KIRIREG: *it's like I'm spinning in place*

CHEN: *it's like I'm spinning in place*

LALLIMORE: They're typing in unison! And they're still eating!

KIRIREG: *but I'm perfectly calm*

CHEN: *but I'm perfectly calm*

LALLIMORE: This is incredible! I've never seen anything like this!

UCHELL: Can somebody tell me what just happened?

RESEARCH VESSEL *WISPFOLLOWER* MESSAGE TO THE CREW FROM:
Mission Captain UCHELL
Gyroscopic Engineer KIRICHEN

UCHELL: I would like to ask you all to welcome our newest colleague to the *Wispfollower.* Engineer Kirichen has asked to assume the duties of former engineer Kirireg. Dr. Lallimore has certified them to be in a stable chimeric state, so I see no reason to object. I'll ask them to explain a little more so you know what to expect when you meet them.

KIRICHEN: Hello, everyone! Please don't be alarmed when you see me—I know I appear to be have transformed into a ring-shaped monstrosity with a florungal stem bursting from the anal region which is constantly being consumed by a slobbering overgrown mouth... but you should see what happened to the other guy.

Just kidding! I am the other guy!

The good news is that the weird physical stuff is distracting all the negative aspects of my personality(ies) and leaving me feeling very calm and able to do my job with no trouble at all. As long as I can see and type, I can calibrate gyroscopes.

So let's get on with this thing!

UCHELL: We'll be continuing with our observation mission as planned—please do everything you can to make Kirichen feel like part of the crew of the *Wispfollower*.

After all, there's a sense in which they were born here.

Thank you.

Paul R. Hardy

Paul R. Hardy has not yet built up a long enough list of credits to mention in a biography; but he was in last year's UFO anthology, so he's off to a good start. He resides in the United Kingdom and has a non-mysterious past as a maker of short films and corporate video. Thanks to recent surgery, he now makes an audible ticking noise with every heartbeat, while his sternum is held together by several loops of metal wire which are clearly visible on x-ray. He does not plan to use commercial air transport in the near future.

FROM THIS SHE MAKES A LIVING?

Esther Friesner

T he town of Chelm enjoys a dual existence, both on the map of Poland and in the heart of anyone who appreciates a good laugh. Like England's Gotham and Denmark's Mols, the Chelm of Jewish folklore is reputed to be a place entirely populated by fools. It is not the first (Cumae's membership in the Chowderhead Chamber of Commerce goes back to the fifth century, B.C.E., in spite of being home to the all-knowing sybil.) and a quick glance at any newspaper will tell you that it is far from being the last[1].

But fools or not, what did they ever do to deserve dragons?

REB[2] NACHEM WAS the first to be devoured. It could have been worse. He was not a well man and Dr. Zoydmacher gave him only two weeks to live. The dragon gave him less.

"It's for the best. He was suffering terribly," the respected healer said, holding forth among those worthies seated on the Chelm town council. "You could almost call it a mercy eating."

---

1   Other fool-centric communities of the world include Lagos in Mexico (for those who prefer to do silly things in a better climate) and the Italian town of Montieri in Tuscany (for those fools smart enough to realize that the worst blunders are most happily forgotten with a glass of the best wine.)
2   Mister. Not a rabbi.

Pinchas Draykup, the town's butcher emeritus, sighed deeply. "Still... !" he said. And that was all he said, for the honorable Draykup was a man of more implications than words.

"What you say may be true, Dr. Zoydmacher, *in this case*," said Rabbi Elfundtvelf. "But suppose Reb Nachem is only the first to be devoured?"

Which he was. You read it here first, don't deny it. It's right up there at the start of this thrilling narrative. Yes, it is! How dare you lie in front of a doctor *and* a rabbi?

I'll deal with you later.

At that very moment *Tanteh*[3] Ruchel Zalman came bursting into the council chamber, tearing her hair and yowling like a sackful of cats with appendicitis. (Tanteh Ruchel was a woman who stretched the definition of *zaftig*[4] almost as far as the waistband of her yoga pants, so she could encompass a *lot* of cats.) "My Beynish! That rotten beast ate him in one bite!"

"Impossible!" cried a horrified Mottel Elimelech-O'Connell, Chelm's chief economic advisor and freelance reader of entrails.

Tanteh Ruchel shrugged. "All right. So it was maybe two bites instead of one, so sue me. The animal was eating my husband and I was running for my life. Excuse *me* if I didn't count so good."

There was a general susurrus of alarm and speculation in the council chamber. The intense *continuo* of rhubarb-rhubarb-rhubarb was punctuated by periodic offers from Pinchas's son Leib, Chelm's attorney general, to go ahead and sue the widow Zalman. She'd asked for it, hadn't she? Her late husband was one of the town's richest citizens. If she settled out of court, they'd collect enough to more than cover the budget for the annual council picnic.

Pinchas responded as any proud father might, by giving his son a hefty *klop* in the head. "*Shmendrik*[5]! Who cares about picnics? We've got dragons!" It was the longest string of words anyone on

---

3   An affectionate term meaning "Auntie," whether or not you're related.
4   Describes a female of generous proportions; pleasingly plump; *very* pleasingly. Hubba-hubba!
5   A jerk.

the council had ever heard him utter. Truly our children inspire us to accomplish extraordinary things.

"All the more reason to live well, while we still can," Leib countered. "I'm talking caviar and craft beers!" He got another *klop* for that.

The rabbi rose to his feet, shaking his head slowly. "Dragons. Oy. It gets worse every year," he said with a sigh. "It's almost as if the Holy One, sanctified be his name, is testing us to see if we are worthy to continue living in this blessed state."

Dr. Zoydmacher, that notable man of science, blew a scornful breath through his thick mustache. "How do you call our situation blessed?" he demanded. "We're not a town; we're a laughingstock! Look up the name of Chelm anywhere you please. Nine times out of ten you'll see us called the village of fools!"

"What about the tenth time?" Mottel asked.

"That's when they're talking about the *real* place, the one in Poland."

"*That* Chelm is why I call *this* one blessed," the rabbi maintained. "There, we Jews were half the population until the war and those filthy fascists, those runny droppings from a rabid dog's syphilitic behind, came and—"

"You want I should write all that into the record, *rebbe*[6]?" Yona Esseppis, the council secretary, was a speed demon at shorthand but a snail at making judgment calls. "Or you want me to say nothing of the dog?"

Rabbi Elfundtvelf took a deep breath and subdued his righteous wrath. "No, Yona, let it go." He turned a contrite gaze to his colleagues. "Sorry. I didn't mean to talk politics. I only wished to remind you that there are worse things our people have had to deal with than dragons."

"True, true," the doctor opined. "I admit that there are advantages to our situation." A murmur of agreement went up from his fellow council members. There was a general atmosphere of having accomplished enough for one morning. Someone

---

6 Okay, *this* one means rabbi.

suggested adjourning for lunch, but when they tried to leave the council chamber they found the doorway blocked and then some by Tanteh Ruchel.

"Where do you think you're going?" she demanded. "Didn't you hear me? My husband was eaten!"

"Well, that's no reason the rest of us should starve," Leib pointed out. The widow's reaction to this remark cinched the lawyer's claim to the title *Attorney General and Klop-in-Kupf*[7] *Magnet.* He had new business cards printed the following day.

"*This* is why they call us a town of fools! Seriously, what are you *yutzes*[8] waiting for?" Tanteh Ruchel gave her spiritual leader a brief look and an automatic "No offense." Before the rabbi could respond, she was off again. "What's it going to take? For that scaly beast to gobble up someone from *your* family?" She pointed at Leib. "Your mama, maybe?" She pointed at Dr. Zoydmacher. "Your sister?"

She pointed at Mottel, but that gentleman preempted her by volunteering a hopeful: "My mother-in-law?"

"All right, all right, we'll think of something." *Rav* Elfundtvelf made *shah, shah*[9] motions with his hands, seeking to placate the irate widow, or at least get her to button her lip. Everyone drifted back to his place at the table. "Perhaps the same phenomenon that brought us this dragon has also brought us the means for dealing with it."

"Ah yes, the Lint Brush Corollary to the *Shvartse Shtreimel, Veise Katz*[10] Imperative," Leib said, looking as owlish and insufferable as anyone compelled to show off knowledge that everybody else already knew.

Well, perhaps not *everybody* else.

"Um, excuse me?" The doorway that the widow Zalman had just vacated was now occupied by another woman. Blond, blue-eyed, and built like a runner-up from America's Next Top Model, she clutched an iPad to her #*Thanks Obama* T-shirt. "Could you help me? I'm *really* lost. One minute I'm heading for the L train,

---

7   Such a smack in the head!
8   Plural form of *yutz*, also meaning a jerk.
9   Shhh, shhh, for heaven's sake shush already!
10 Black Hat, White Cat, the specifics of said hat being described further along in our story. Go, read, enjoy!

the next I'm here. Like, *here*-here, out in this hallway, eavesdropping against my will. I'm normally not a nosey person, but now I'm kind of curious. Can you forgive me for overhearing your conversation and give me directions to the L and tell me what's that you were saying about a black shtreimel and—"

"A new one!" Leib exclaimed, joy writ large upon his countenance. He rushed forward to take the bewildered lady's hand. "What year is it?"

"Y-year?" She regarded him as one might any casually encountered madman. "You mean now?" Yogi Berra's ghost smiled as the visitor stammered out a date belonging to the twenty-first century of the Common Era.

He frowned to hear it. "Isn't that a little late for dragons?"

This remark was more than she cared to process in such proximity to someone clearly a few wontons short of a Jewish Christmas dinner. She jerked her hand free of his clasp and made a break for it. Her flight was intercepted by Tanteh Ruchel's daunting person and impressive speed. The council's unexpected guest was soon forcibly seated at the table. There Rabbi Elfundtvelf briefed her on the present situation and reassured her that all was *somewhat* well.

"This is well?" said an incredulous Barbi King (for thus she had introduced herself). "I'm stuck here? Forever? In *Chelm?*"

"Ah, so she's heard of us," Dr. Zoydmacher remarked sardonically. "Yet another newcomer horrified to find herself trapped in a community of fools for the remainder of her days. *This* is our reputation! A *shayna shanda*[11]!"

Barbi glowered at the doctor. "You think that's what's got me upset? I once worked as a Senate page. When it comes to stupid, this Chelm of yours is Wannabe City next to *that* hive of scu—My *gosh*, I'm not going to get to see the next Star Wars movie!" She bawled like a nerdy baby.

The rabbi gave her his handkerchief and swallowed a couple of aspirin. "Daughter, our reputation is for foolishness, not stupidity. Some of our citizens are highly intelligent and learned. Many of those who arrive here as you did have a strong grounding in

---

11 Literally, a "pretty" scandal or embarrassment, with "pretty" used ironically, as in "a pretty kettle of fish." Fish kettles are not as attractive as you'd think.

science, mathematics, and technology, though how useful their skills are depends on the era whence they came. Still, you never know. We owe our WiFi access, limited though it be, to a hacker from twentieth century Pinsk and an alchemist from thirteenth century Pisa. Perhaps one day we will even learn how to reverse the process that brought you here."

"Which brings me back to the Shtreimel-Katz Imperative," Leib said, with much satisfaction. He edged his chair closer to Barbi's and tried to emulate the roguish charm of an iconic movie heartthrob. His efforts fell short of Cary Grant's charisma and just barely reached the allure of Ulysses S. "Now, a shtreimel, sweetheart—"

"You're talking about the big, round, fur hat that Hasidic men wear on *Shabbat*[12] and other special occasions," she broke in. "I know that. I'm from Brooklyn. And I know what a white cat is, too," she added, deftly cutting off any further Chelmsplaining Leib was likely to do. "What I don't get is the Imperative part. Or the lint brush reference. Or why you're calling me 'sweetheart.' Are you looking for a lawsuit?"

"As a matter of fact—"

"You'll have to excuse Leib, Miss King: he's a jackass," Tanteh Ruchel said in a grumpy tone. "The answers you want are simple enough. The hat can be in a box in a closet in a sealed room in a locked house in a town that is a hundred miles from the nearest cat. No matter: when you open the box, white hair! All over the black hat, white cat hair! It's *imperative.*"

"I still don't understand—" Barbi began.

"Chelm is the shtreimel." The rabbi stepped into the discussion. "And believe me, in my whole life, I never thought I'd say a sentence like that. But yes, Chelm—*this* Chelm—is the black hat that can't help but attract the white cat hair from the ordinary world. Our scholars have made a study of the singularity that is this Chelm's existence. As far as they can determine, there came a point in history when the stories about our citizens', ah,

---

12   The Sabbath, from sundown Friday to sundown Saturday.

unique way of dealing with problems acquired so much power in the telling and re-telling that they overwhelmed and abducted reality. And us! Since that time, centuries ago, we dwelt separate from mundane existence, though we still are born, live, and die exactly as you do."

"What, her people also die from dragons?" Yona quit scribbling long enough to pose his question and be roundly shushed for it.

The rabbi raised his index finger, a quirk of his when expounding everything from Talmud to why it was impossible for his daughter Miri to adopt a puppy. (She got the puppy.) "Sometimes, however, our world and the world you come from brush up against each other and things from your reality are captured by our own."

"So I'm not the first person to—to cross over?" Barbi's eyes widened.

"It's not only people, my dear. I don't think any of us will forget the Year of the Yoga Pants." As one man, the council turned disapproving eyes on Tanteh Ruchel.

The lady was unfazed. "And the Time of the Velour Track Suits was a bargain?"

"In any case—" The rabbi cleared his throat loudly to cover his embarrassment. (His track suit had been purple. He believed it complemented his eyes.) "In any case, there is thus far no way we can control the timing or quality of the figurative cat hair our shtreimel attracts. We accept the good—"

"Vaccines," said Dr. Zoydmacher.

"Sudoku," said Pinchas.

"Pocky," said Yona.

"Yoga pants," said the prodigiously stubborn Tanteh Ruchel.

"—with the bad."

"Mullets," said Pinchas, giving his son a meaningful look.

"Pet rocks," said Dr. Zoydmacher.

"Fanny packs," said Yona.

"My mother-in-law," said Mottel.

"Yoga pants," said Leib, making a face at Tanteh Ruchel. She reached into her fanny pack and threw her pet rock at him. She missed by a solid yard, but it's the thought that counts.

"In sum, that's how it is for us, and now for you, too," the rabbi said. "It's *beshert*[13], fated, nothing to be done about it."

The widow Zalman eyed the council members coldly. "Just like these *schlemiels*[14] are doing nothing about the dragon that ate my Beynish!"

Rabbi Elfundtvelf pinched the bridge of his nose, a man at the end of his rope. "Ruchel, what do you want us to do? Go running after the beast and get eaten ourselves? Will that bring back your husband?"

"It's worth a try," said the aggrieved woman. "But why bother? It's not like you have a reason to help a poor widow, all alone in this world. No, why should you, when you could be chatting up a pretty, skinny little *shiksa*[15] who dropped from the sky! It's all right. Ignore my heartbreak. I'm used to it. Don't worry, I won't trouble you for much longer. I might as well just march out of here and find that dragon so he can gulp me down in who cares how many bites?" She rested one hand on her bosom and raised the other heavenward as she turned from the council members and declaimed, "You hear that, Beynish? I'm coming to join you. It'll be in a dragon's *kishke*[16], but beggars can't be choosers. I don't want to live anymore!"

She continued in this vein, indefatigable, and without showing any sign of running out of material. The councilmen conferred in whispers, debating how they might achieve their squad goals of getting her to stop *without* promising to hazard their lives by confronting the dragon. All of them agreed that the latter was non-negotiable.

"*Gevalt!*[17]" A mighty shout of exasperation rang out in the council chamber. Barbi leaped to her feet and folded her arms in the least nonsensical of no-nonsense poses. "*Nudniks! Genug, shoyn! Ich bin krank fun diese narishkeit.*[18]"

---

13 Meant to be, predestined. Not to be confused with *borschtshert*: "We are having cold beet soup for dinner. You'll eat it and *like* it!"
14 Would you look at that? Yet *another* way to say "jerk"!
15 A non-Jewish girl or woman.
16 Gut. Also, Jewish haggis. Like we haven't suffered enough.
17 OMG!
18 "You P.I.T.A.s! [or pests, if you will] Enough, already! I'm sick of this foolishness!"

The utterly shocked silence that answered her outburst lasted long enough for Yona to deem it worth memorializing in the minutes.

Tanteh Ruchel took it upon herself to restore communications. "Sooooo... you're not a shiksa?"

"Sorry, I left my bat mitzvah certificate in my other reality." Barbi smirked. "Now that I've got your attention, let me *really* get your attention. While you've been staging the first Yiddish *telenovela*[19], there's a monster on the loose. No one is safe. If I have to live out my life in Chelm, I want it tallied in years, not minutes. We've got to do something about that dragon *now!*"

"Young lady, we will not be rushed, certainly not by you," the doctor said sternly. "As a newcomer, your duty is to watch and learn, not to dictate."

"I don't want to dictate; I want to help. I overheard that guy—" she indicated Leib "—mention something called the Lint Brush Corollary. I'm guessing that means a way to clean up the whole hat-cat mess?" Everyone nodded. "Okay! I've got some ideas we could use." She threw her arms open and nearly lost her grip on the iPad. "Let me be your Lint Brush!"

Dr. Zoydmacher puffed himself up like an inflatable walrus. "You will be *nothing* without the council's approval. We will follow protocol and honor due process. Chelm has established ways of dealing with emergencies."

"I know. I've read the stories.[20]"

Wait. Was that sarcasm?

What do *you* think, Einstein?

The physician fumed over this insolence, but did not step down from his invisible lectern. "As far as we know, the dragon might be gone by now, flown away to some distant part of our world."

---

19 This is not a Yiddish word. Nothing to see here. Move along.
20 Such as the one where every time it snows, the synagogue beadle messes up the pristine whiteness by making his rounds to wake people for morning prayers. Everyone complains that they want to enjoy the beauty of an unspoiled snowfall. No problem! The sages of Chelm prevent the beadle's feet from touching the snow by having four strong men carry him on his rounds in a chair. Eh, good enough for government work.

"Is Chelm even big enough to have *distant* parts?"

Barbi's question was plowed under. "There's no need to get hysterical, little lady." If Dr. Zoydmacher stooped to further condescension, he would have been stuck with permanent curvature of the spine. "I'm only pointing out that so far, we have but two instances of the beast devouring anyone. If he were a more widespread and immediate threat, the streets would be full of people screaming—"

"—*a dragon stole my child!*"

For the second time that morning, the council chamber was invaded by a frantic woman. "My Fishel! My precious little son is gone!" She collapsed, weeping. Barbi hurried to kneel by her side, hugging her close while Tanteh Ruchel gave the council a look that would reduce steel to ashes.

A slowly swelling wave of sound came from the street below. The people of Chelm were gathering, having had their day's routine interrupted when the bereaved mother came running down the town's main thoroughfare, proclaiming her woe. The civic clamor covered every possible reaction to the news of a dragon in their midst, from confusion to terror to demands for action by their community leaders.

Tanteh Ruchel peered into the street pursed her lips. "*Now*, they care! But when it was *me* yelling about that *fershtinkina*[21] dragon, did they listen? No. What am I, chopped liver?" She re-launched her litany of grievances, distracting the council from their deliberations on how to deal with the dragon, since deal with it they must.

Meanwhile, back on the floor, Barbi was multi-tasking, comforting and questioning Fishel's mother at the same time. She helped the poor lady back to her feet, said, "So he *wasn't* eaten, just taken?" and walked out while the rabbi was still trying to make the widow Zalman calm down.

"Hey!" cried Pinchas, the first of the council to notice Barbi was gone. He spread his hands to indicate her absence from the room.

---

21 Stinking. Did you really need me to translate this? Stink, shtink, po-*tay*-to, po-*tah*-to.

"What happened? Where'd she go?" Mottel asked.

Yona checked his notes. "I don't know. It's not in the minutes."

"She's gone after the dragon," Fishel's mother said, in a small, miserable voice. "She asked me where—where the beast struck. I told her that I was walking with Fisheleh[22] at the edge of the woods by the old, abandoned mill."

"Picking mushrooms?" Tanteh Ruchel asked. Everyone in Chelm knew the site in question was the best place for that. "Exactly why my Beynish and I were there! He didn't trust me to tell the difference between good and bad ones. Look where it got him!"

"That's also where Reb Nachem's housekeeper told me they'd gone when he was taken," Dr. Zoydmacher said. "She ran away as soon as the dragon sprang on him."

"But that young woman's not from here," Yona interjected. "How would she know which road would take her to the mill?"

"She asked me for directions," Fishel's mother replied.

The council members took a moment to marvel over this unheard-of method for getting from Point A to Point B without a lot of cursing.

"Enough talk," the rabbi decreed. "Summon every able-bodied man in Chelm. We're going after that monster!"

"*Finally*," Tante Ruchel said, with bitterness abounding.

The mustering of the village *shtarkers*[23] took longer than expected. Where dragon-removal was concerned, most of them preferred to raise their voices rather than risk their necks. Ultimately, a grudging posse of six additional heroes was assembled thanks to diplomatic tactics that included pleas, flattery, some shaming, and a tad of outright blackmail. (This was Dr. Zoydmacher's specialty. Physicians know the *darndest* secrets!)

The road to the abandoned mill was unshaded and the sun was hot. Unwillingness slowed the mission even more. The only souls in a hurry to reach the beast's supposed hunting ground were

---

22 Adding -*leh* is how Yiddish creates the diminutive form of proper names and other words. So *mama* = mother while *mamaleh* = mommy. It is usually done to express affection. *Usually.* Wait until you get to footnote 39. Just wait.

23 Tough guys.

Tanteh Ruchel, Fishel's mother, and a stray dog of mixed ancestry and ill repute who also liked to crash weddings and funerals. By the time the group reached the part of the path that led into the shade of the forest, their collective pace had slowed to the point where they were up to their ankles in metaphors involving tar, taffy, molasses, sloths, and slugs.

"We're almost there," Leib said in a hushed voice. "It's so quiet! Do you think the beast ate her already?"

"It makes no difference." The rabbi was grim. "Whether or not that poor girl has met her death, we still have to do something about the dragon."

"Oh, I agree, I agree!" the lawyer exclaimed, lying. "But... in case she was devoured, would it be okay if I took her iPad?"

Really, they should have sold tickets to *Give Leib a Klop in Kupf.* It would have paid for *two* council picnics.

"Shh!" Pinchas put a halt to the crowd-pleasing *zetz*[24]-fest his son had provoked. "Listen."

The sound of three voices wafted through the trees. The first was deep, gravelly, and unknown. The second was calm, upbeat, and immediately recognized by the council and Tanteh Ruchel.

"*Gott sei dank*[25], she's alive!" she cried.

The third voice was a high-pitched wail, as grating on the ears as it was miraculous to hear. "*Fisheleh!*" The child's mother raced toward the sound, oblivious to the chorus of frightened men behind her, begging her to stop, come back, be careful. As if that would hold her! She was into the trees and out of sight. They had no choice but to follow.

All right, so they had the choice to turn tail. As if! *You* try *mishegas*[26] like that with Tanteh Ruchel watching, I dare you! More proof that the men of Chelm might be fools, but they weren't stupid. (Yes, I know: Leib.)

---

24 Like klop, a healthy smack upside the head. You will notice there was no footnote for the first mention of klop. Given the delectable onomatopoeia of the word, I thought you had the *sechel* to get its meaning. (sechel: intelligence; brains; smarts.)
25 "Thank God!"
26 Madness.

They burst from the forest *en masse* [27] and saw the abandoned mill before them, on the far side of a pond. There on the grassy bank sat Fishel, half-smothered in his mother's arms, but no longer yowling. There, too, sat Barbi. And there, three, sprawled a green-scaled, blue-winged dragon as big as the town hall.

"Hey, hi! What took you so long?" Chelm's newest citizen waved to her would-be rescuers and urged them to come closer. "It's safe, honest! This guy promised to stay on his best behavior, or else." She smiled at the dragon.

"Or else what?" asked a Doubting Tevye in the posse.

The dragon blew yellowish smoke from his nostrils. "The lady has had occasion to prove to me her expertise in the Israeli martial art of Krav Maga. It is not an experience I wish to repeat." He shifted uncomfortably on the greensward.

"It *talks*?!" said all the men at once.

"Yes, *he* does," Barbi shot back.

"It—I mean, *he,* understands us?" the rabbi asked.

"*I* understood *you* when I first arrived here," Barbi said. "No big deal—*ich ken Yiddish*[28]. But you also understood *me* when I was speaking English. Unless you've got really good ESL classes in Chelm, I bet there's some kind of *meshugga*[29] hoodoo turning what we say into words the other person can comprehend."

Rabbi Elfundtvelf shrugged. "The truth is, we've lived with that miracle for so long, we don't even think about it."

"I figured that if it worked for people, it might work for dragons. Not that I've ever met a dragon, but in some stories they *do* talk. It was worth a try."

"A *successful* try!" The rabbi was so pleased, you would have thought he'd been the one to do it.

"But if we heard everything she said as Yiddish, how come it was such a shock to hear her when she was *actually* speaking the *mama loshen*[30]?" Tanteh Ruchel asked.

---

27 What are you looking here for? If you can't tell the different between French and Yiddish *vous avez besoin de plus* sechel, *voyons donc!*
28 "I understand Yiddish." And now so do you, a *bissel*. (See if you can figure this one out on your own. I believe in you!)
29 Crazy.
30 The mother tongue, i.e. Yiddish.

"That is a very good question," the rabbi replied. "And I have a very good answer: who knows?" He turned his attention back to the monster. "So, Mister Dragon, if you're going to stay here in Chelm, we're going to have to set some conditions. Number one, no more eating people. This is also numbers two through infinity. We have plenty of nice goats, sheep, cattle, plus whatever wild beasts you find out here in the woods. Agreed?"

"Who are you to set conditions for *me*?" The dragon lifted his chin.

"Me? I'm nobody; just the rabbi, although I believe I'm speaking for the entire town council on this." The council immediately moved, seconded, and enacted into law the Desist Eating Humans Edict, though Mottel did attempt to attach a rider concerning his mother-in-law. It was a nice change of pace to have someone besides Leib earn a klop in kupf.

"Come on, big guy, don't be like that." Barbi nudged the dragon in a chummy way. "You know you want to be accepted here and make a new life."

"I should accept the beast that ate my Beynish?" Tanteh Ruchel had a prodigious ax to grind.

"What choice do you have? What comes to Chelm, stays in Chelm," Mottel reminded her. Everyone waited for him to tie this remark to his mother-in-law. He left them hanging. For a freelance reader of entrails, he was kind of a jerk[31]. For an economic advisor... mnyeh.

"Um... that's not quite true," Barbi said. "The dragon didn't get sent here. He came voluntarily. He can leave the same way."

"We creatures of unfathomable enchantment travel where we will," the dragon informed all present grandly. "You ought to feel honored that your world attracted us. We suffered far too much persecution in our original home—"

"Look who's talking persecution," Leib muttered.

"—and wish to lead a peaceful life. If not eating one's neighbors is the rule here, we will abide by it. As a token of good faith, I herewith return the one called Fishel to you, uningested and

---

31 Yutz.

untouched." He gestured with one huge claw at the child. Barbi elbowed him a second time. "You big poser," she said, with a good-natured laugh. "You told me you *never* intended to devour that kid. Don't lie to your new *landsleit*[32]. Let them know why you *really* grabbed Fishel."

"We wanted to adopt him, to add to our family." The dragon lowered his eyes. "We can't have children of our own."

"Wait, what, 'we'?" said Yona, who had brought a memo pad and was desperately trying to make the record keep up with events. "There's more of you? Oy! And why would two dragons want to raise a human child? He'd never fit in. There's more family resemblance between a gopher and a waffle iron!"

"Family resemblance isn't an issue," Barbi told him. She stuck two fingers in her mouth and blew a shrill whistle.

Right on cue, a dazzling ray of sunlight lanced into a nearby grove of evergreens which suddenly decided to grow both pinecones *and* cherry blossoms. As the pink and white petals tumbled to earth, they provided the only carpet lovely enough to welcome the dainty golden hooves of a milk-white unicorn. With a majestic gait, the ineffably lovely creature came to stand between Barbi and the dragon. Every human present felt the power of mystic glamour emanating from that vision of grace and starlight.

"Hi, baby. Daddy's home." He nuzzled the dragon's snout. "Everything okay here?"

It is said that the boom of so many jaws hitting the forest floor at once could be heard echoing above Chelm for days. One of the town's top entrepreneurs decided to capture the explosive sound in bottles and sell them to people who wished to jazz up their summer fireworks displays. He would have made a fortune if not for a batch of faulty corks.

What followed ushered in a fresh era for Chelm. Beyond the initial shock, there were no negative reactions to the new couple's relationship. Living in a town located within a fragment of folklore was not an orthodox situation, so neither were the main

---

32 Fellow townsmen or even countrymen. Singular: *landsman*.

spiritual practices of the populace. Some were more ready to welcome the pair than others, but no one had a selective memory lapse when it came to recalling the words of Deuteronomy 10:19.[33] The dragon kept his word and did not eat any more human beings. He submitted himself to the judgment of the court regarding an appropriate punishment for his three initial crimes, namely one count of kidnapping and two of manslaughter/mandigestion.

Luckily, like all reputable fire-wyrms, he possessed a vast treasure hoard which he had transported to Chelm with no respect for the laws of physics because ooooh, *MAGIC!* He was allowed to atone for his crimes by giving each of the plaintiffs enough riches to render even Tanteh Ruchel speechless.

Justice having been done, nothing prevented the dragon and his unicorn partner from becoming an accepted part of Chelm society. The latter was a homebody, but didn't mind if his beloved maintained separate interests. The dragon proved to be a gregarious creature who enjoyed a heavy philosophical discussion as much as any college sophomore. He debated law with Leib Draykup, discussed feminism with Barbi, and spent his happiest hours in conversation with the rabbi on the subject of faith.

This led to... complications.

"Oy, how do you circumcise a dragon?" Leib groaned.

"Carefully," said Pinchas, master of the deadpan delivery.

"Rebbe, are you one hundred per cent sure that he wants this?" Yona's hands were shaking so badly that when it came time to translate the minutes from shorthand, it appeared that the dragon was a candidate for circumnavigation.

"He wants to convert. He said so. I rejected him three times, as one must, but he was adamant. He has studied our ways and can read Hebrew better than many of you. He has attended services at our synagogue *conscientiously.*" He gave Dr. Zoydmacher a hard stare. "On my head be it. I will be the one performing the procedure since our previous *mohel,*[34] Reb Nakamura Kenshin passed away last month, *olev hasholem*[35]."

---

33 Look it up.
34 A man who performs ritual Jewish circumcisions. A person my Dad used to refer to as "the Yankee Clipper." I miss you, Dad!
35 "May he rest in peace."

"We're going to need a bigger *mikvah*,[36]" Mottel said, referring to the ritual bath that was part of the conversion ceremony. "We can't afford to build something like that!"

"So we'll use a lake."

"Who will be the *sandek*[37]?" Yona asked. "Who could possibly hold a dragon on his lap?"

The rabbi sighed. "That would be a difficulty only if we were discussing an infant's *bris*[38]. Sandek means 'companion to the *child*.' Which you'd know if you studied as much Hebrew as our dragon, who is *no* child."

"He's a reptile," the physician said. "I kept a pet snake when I was a lad. There's a very interesting detail about their male generative organs: they have hemipenes."

Look it up.

Oh, never mind. It means *eyn shmekeleh, tzvey tsveygn*.[39]

Now look it up![40]

"I looked it up," Dr. Zoydmacher continued. "As far as I could learn, it's the same for all male snakes and lizards. Which of the two gets—?" He made snipping motions with two fingers.

"Dealer's choice," said the rabbi dryly.

"He can't convert!" Leib was losing it. "He's—he's—he's a reptile! He's *trayf*![41]"

"Were you planning to eat him?" newly appointed council member Barbi King asked archly. "That would end the transportation service he's been running for us."

(The service to which she alluded took advantage of the dragon's ability to shuttle between Chelm and the commonplace

---

36 *Again*, you're looking down here? It says "ritual bath" right in the same sentence!

37 A person (usually male) who either passes the infant (male; d'uh) to the mohel or in some cases holds the child on his lap throughout the circumcision. In which case, give that man a *drink*!

38 Jewish covenant of circumcision, also called *brit milah*.

39 One male generative organ, two branches. In this case, the Yiddish word for the male generative organ is not just a diminutive, but a diminutive *of* a diminutive! Used to affectionately describe said organ when it belongs to babies, toddlers, and very young boys. Weaponized to describe said organ when it belongs to a teenaged or adult male who has ticked you off.

40 By which I mean *See footnote 39, above.* (I'm spoiling you, amn't I?)

41 Not kosher.

reality of Terra. With Barbi on board to deal with the hands-on part of their visits, they were able to bring back gobs of the latest merchandise. No longer did the people of Chelm need to await the random contact of their shtreimel with earth's cat hair! It also allowed Barbi to tidy up her personal finances, pay her bills, break her lease, and let friends and family know her new address, though future correspondence would be email-only.

Why didn't she choose to get off the dragon and stay in the world of her birth, you ask?

To which I answer: have you *seen* this place lately? Better a home where the fools mean well than one where the "wise" mean wickedness.)

"Ha, ha, very funny." Leib was as petulant as a thwarted toddler. "That's no solution to the *big* problem, namely circumcising—"

"All it will take is drawing one drop of blood. It's an acceptable practice where the convert can't be circumcised in the usual way, for whatever reason." Barbi stood up from the council table. "And *I'll* do it."

"You? But you're—you're—"

"—a mohel." She smiled. "Actually, a *mohelet*[42]. I'd just gotten my certification when I was *shtreimeled*[43] here. I would have said something sooner, but I didn't want to step on anyone's toes if you already had a mohel."

The dragon's conversion went without hitch or glitch. The event became a double celebration, with many a heartfelt *mazel tov*[44] for the guest of honor and his unicorn partner as well as for Chelm's new mohelet. The whole town was present, as were a number of beings from the dragon's original world. Although the hostile atmosphere of that place had driven the heterogeneous couple to leave, not everyone from back home was a *schmuck*.

Oh, so *that* word you know?

Rabbi Elfuntvelf was watching Tanteh Ruchel doing the Chicken Dance with a pixie when Barbi found him. "Having a

---

42 A female mohel. They exist! And why shouldn't they? Who are you to decide?
43 Neologism ahoy!
44 No. Absolutely not. I refuse to believe you don't know this one. Do something yourself, for once, you nogoodnik!

good time, rebbe?" she asked.

"We all are, thanks to you," he replied. "I've been having the most fascinating conversations with some of our visitors. That gray one with the wings over by the punch bowl said he wants to learn more about Judaism, too, maybe consider conversion. He'll be coming to see me for lessons. Even if he doesn't turn out to be dedicated, at least he'll be educated! And if he *does* hang in there when I try to turn him away—" The rabbi chuckled. "How do you feel about circumcising a goblin?"

Barbi stared at the creature Rabbi Elfundtvelf was talking about. She blanched. That was no goblin: that was a gargoyle. Every step it took left a six-inch deep depression in the ground, as you might expect from a grotesque, animate statue whose body was one hundred per cent solid granite.

"We're *really* gonna need a bigger mikvah," she muttered. "And a chisel."

Esther Friesner

Nebula Award winner Esther Friesner is the author of over 40 novels and almost 200 short stories. She is also a poet, a playwright, and the editor of several anthologies. The best known of these is the Chicks in Chainmail series that she created and edits for Baen Books. The sixth book, *Chicks and Balances,* appeared in July 2015. *Deception's Pawn,* the latest title in her popular Princesses of Myth series of Young Adult novels from Random House, was published in April 2015.

Esther is married, a mother of two, grandmother of one, harbors cats, and lives in Connecticut. She has a fondness for bittersweet chocolate, graphic novels, manga, travel, and jewelry. There is no truth to the rumor that her family motto is "Oooooh, SHINY!"

Her super-power is the ability to winnow her bookshelves without whining about it. Much.

TWENTY-NINE RESPONSES TO INQUIRIES ABOUT MY CRAIGSLIST POST: ALIEN SPACESHIP FOR SALE. $200, YOU HAUL.

TINA CONNOLLY

1. No, I don't know what "galaxy far, far away" it's from. This isn't Star Wars, dude. I just woke up and found it crash landed in my backyard. That's literally all I know about it.

2. Sorry, no pictures. It's got some kind of force field that makes my phone go wonky. Like, when I went out last night to see if it had damaged my climate-controlled greenhouse I swear my phone said 1:11 am, and I remember because I thought that was a funny time for weird things to happen. And then a few minutes later my phone said 3:15. So I dunno, weird force field.

3. No, it won't fit in your roadster.

4. Nor your cargo bike.

5.   Don't you know anyone with a pickup truck? Or maybe two pickup trucks and like a lot of rope?

6.   Yeah, you might need a crane. BUT I'm not letting anyone in my backyard with a crane. I am a master horticulturist with a very important garden experiment that this damn saucer crash-landed into. I lost three of my best specimens and the remaining dozen are really agitated.

7.   Look, maybe get twenty friends to help you lift around the saucer edges? I'm spitballing here.

8.   IDK, maybe you know a bunch of frat boys or something. I don't know your life.

9.   If that's the way you're going to be, I'm moving onto the next responder. Don't come over here or I'll sic my ten-foot Venus flytraps on you. Next!

10. No, I won't take $50.

11. Nor "$55 and some really killer weed."

12. I do think $200 is reasonable, actually. It's going to cost me twice that to repair the damage to the flytraps' greenhouse. Next!

13. I *guess* you could turn it into a Tiny House??? Good luck getting a permit for it without any windows though.

14. No, I didn't call the police, the FBI, or the CIA. I don't need the government poking around my backyard, thank you very much.

15. I didn't say I was on the run from anybody or that I might be wanted in several states for bio-engineering giant man-eating plants. I don't care what you googled.

16. Look, do you want it or not?

17. Everyone so far is a flake. Are you a flake? Because if you're a flake you can flake off right now. My Venus flytraps are going nuts snapping at this thing and I really want it gone. It's time for their steak dinner.

18. Of course they eat steak. Who doesn't like steak? I mean, obviously I started them on offal from the butcher counter but they find red meat preferable to viscera. The fresher the better, in fact. Can't say I blame them.

19. Well, no one asked you to come over here anyway, with or without your toddlers. I never said, "Oh hey, my backyard is fun and safe for all! Bring the whole family!"

20. Look, I don't need any lawsuits. Forget we talked.

21. OMG isn't anyone going to take this thing away? My Venus flytraps are licking it like it's covered in something tasty. If this thing poisons them I'm going to strangle somebody.

22. No, I don't know if it has "psychick emasculations." I'm a horticulturist, not a... whatever that is. You are welcome to come look for yourself.

23. No, I won't take a check.

24. Ugh. I'm taking a break from email for 20 minutes. My plants aren't interested in their perfectly normal and not at all weird dinner menu, which is stressing me out. Maybe they want some Worcestershire... anyway, you're next on the list, so LMK if you want a genuine real alien spaceship, no questions asked, no stupid questions answered.

25. NO I HAVEN'T GONE INSIDE TO SEE IF THERE ARE ANY LIVE ALIENS IN IT! YOU PEOPLE MUST THINK I'M AN IDIOT!

26. Of course it's a spaceship!!!!! It is a freaky looking flying saucer that makes my phone go crazy!!! Why else would I have a missing gap of 2 hours from my memory last night!!!!

27. No, I DON'T think anything in particular happened in those 2 hours, like I went out at 1:11 am and found 3 dead Venus

flytraps and 4 dead aliens, and while the last alien lay dying on the ground we had a touching heart to heart where they showed me how to pilot the ship back to their home planet with my gigantic Venus flytraps to save their people from being eaten by giant alien flies, and I repressed that memory because I couldn't yet deal with it!!!

28. I mean, you must think I'm a moron, I mean, surely those five dead aliens would still be strewn around my greenhouse instead of twelve snappy, happy Venus flytraps with no interest in their steak dinner—oh wait. let me just check on something. brb.

29. AUTO-GENERATED REPLY: This posting has been deleted by its author. The title on the listings page will be removed in just a few minutes.

Tina Connolly

Tina Connolly is the author of the Ironskin trilogy from Tor, and the lighthearted Seriously Wicked series from Tor Teen. Her novels have been finalists for the Nebula and the Norton. Her stories have appeared all over (including in UFO3 and UFO4) and her collection *On the Eyeball Floor and Other Stories* is available from Fairwood Press. She is one of the co-hosts of *Escape Pod,* and runs the Parsec-winning flash fiction podcast *Toasted Cake.* Find her at tinaconnolly.com.

TYLER THE SNOT ELEMENTAL SCOURS THE NEWSPAPER, SEARCHING FOR CHANGE

ZACH SHEPHARD

Guarding a largely forgotten lighthouse is not exciting work, even for a snot elemental. At first I was a vigilant sentry, always keeping an optoplasmic orb out for trespassers, but no one ever came. When I got bored, I tried whale-watching. When the local humpbacks got eaten by a kraken, I tried kraken-watching. When the kraken left a note at the lighthouse calling me a pervert, I tried bird-watching. Birds are boring.

I was not happy with life.

My existence didn't feel as meaningful as I knew it should, but I wasn't sure why. So I went to Madame Gozlag's Daycare and Fortune Tellery for advice. Madame Gozlag was an orc who read dirty diapers the way others might read tea leaves or glass shards. I asked her what was wrong with my life.

She pulled a diaper off a baby troll, releasing green fumes into the rafters above. A bat squeaked in the darkness and fell to the floor, dead.

"Hoo-boy," Madame Gozlag said, holding the diaper at arm's length and pinching her nose. "It's time for a change."

She was right.

I thanked her and left a handsome tip. As I slithered away she insisted she hadn't done anything, but I think she was just being modest.

The next morning I woke up ready to make a change. I left my apartment feeling like a new mound of phlegm.

I stopped by my boss's office on my way to the lighthouse. Kabra the Goat-Slurper sat at her desk, filling out paperwork and stirring a cauldron with her tail. I couldn't tell what she was cooking, but it was red and chunky and occasionally let out a pained bleat. Probably spaghetti.

"Excuse me," I said.

My spiral-horned supervisor looked up. "Tyler!" she said, still scribbling and stirring. "What can I do for you?"

"I'd like a change."

"Good thinking. I've got a satyr wizard who can turn you pink as a petunia. You'll blend right in with that fungus outside the lighthouse." She opened a day-planner. "How's Tuesday morning sound?"

I told her I didn't want to be pink. Also, on Tuesday mornings I played my bagpipes.

"Okay," she said. "Then what kind of change did you have in mind?"

"I'd like a new job."

Kabra stopped working, which I'd never seen her do before. We stared at each other in silence. The cauldron let out one last, strained bleat.

"I think your spaghetti's done."

"We need you at the lighthouse," she said. "You're a valuable part of the team."

I tried to respond but couldn't get a sneeze in edgewise. Kabra went into a long pep-talk, saying the lighthouse was an important responsibility that only a snot elemental of my viscosity could handle. At the end of the speech she tried patting me on the head, but squished my left aural sac instead. I didn't say anything because it wasn't really her fault. Not many schools teach snot elemental anatomy anymore.

I spent the rest of the day thinking about how I might improve my life. Maybe my job wasn't the problem. Maybe there were other ways to make myself a better booger.

The next morning I stopped at a newsstand and bought a paper, hoping the advertisements could guide me in my quest. I found my first opportunity on page twelve.

A local gym was offering free trial memberships for a limited time. It must have been a really special deal because they even put a small star after the word "free."

At the gym all I had to do to get started was provide my signature and three major credit cards. The succubus running the counter gave me a free* sweatband as a welcome gift. The band stretched over my head-dollop and constricted back to its original shape, making me feel thinner already.

In high school I'd been in much better condition, thanks to four years of track and field. I'd never won a race because apparently you actually have to hurdle the hurdles, but I always gave it my best and slithered under them as fast as I could. It was time to feel like an athlete again.

I went to a treadmill and asked the nice succubus to start it for me. She smiled, pressed a button and walked away.

I got sucked into the belt and spent the next twenty minutes riding the loop.

A flattened snot elemental looks a lot like a sweat stain, which is why no one found me until a minotaur got on the treadmill and slipped, hurting her calf. When I finally got free I apologized to the calf, even though it wasn't my fault the little fellow had been standing so close in the first place. He threw a tantrum, stomping around with a moue on his face until his embarrassed mother picked him up and left.

I thanked the succubus and slithered away. On the sidewalk the minotaur berated her calf, telling him the gym was her one place of peace and now he'd ruined that, too. If I'd been in her type of physical condition I wouldn't have complained, but it sounded like the treadmill incident was not her first annoyance of the day. She told him that after dinner he was going straight to bed with no cud.

I wouldn't let the gym experience deter me. Just because I was an out-of-shape snot-glob didn't mean I couldn't be happy. I checked the newspaper again.

A classified ad presented a good dating opportunity. USLFHSE: Unmarried Siren Looking For Handsome Snot Elemental. I answered the ad with a brief email and went to the Harborview address that evening.

My date was waiting at a restaurant table by the water. She looked less like a siren and more like a zombie-squid wearing a tarnished crown. Also, she was a he.

"Tyler?" the small squid asked, as I slithered up.

"Otto?"

Otto was an old bowling buddy of mine. I'd never been good

at the game because it's hard to grip anything when you're slimy and amorphous. Otto had the opposite problem: his suction cups would stick to the ball after the throw, pulling him down the lane with the sound of a flat tire rolling along the highway. He usually came to a stop about halfway to the pins, then crawled back for some nachos. The alley served great nachos.

I climbed into the empty chair across from Otto. As it turns out, USLFHSE actually stood for Undead Squid-Lord From Harborview Seeking Escape. Common mistake.

"Escape from what?" I asked.

"My wife."

"I thought you loved Loretta."

"I do! But I miss my free time. Before marriage I was my own squid. I could do whatever I wanted. Now, it seems like the calendar is already full whenever I want to ink something in. I miss bowling."

It was true that we hadn't been to the alley in months. The memories gave me a craving for nachos, but there weren't any on the menu so I ordered calamari instead. Otto was quiet the rest of the night and I don't know why.

The next morning I was sad. I'd spent a whole day looking for change and nothing good had come of it. Maybe I needed to try focusing on my professional life again. I opened the newspaper and searched the employment ads.

A group called Expeditions Incorporated was putting together a cave-exploration team in the northern hills. I didn't have any experience spelunking, but decided the time I'd spent gestating inside the dark cavern of a cyclops's nose might give me an edge over the competition.

I slithered into the building's waiting room and took a chair. Sitting beside me was a bark-skinned tree-nymph with one arm missing. I tried not to stare at her stump.

"Here for the cave job?" she asked.

"Yes."

"Be careful what you wish for. Not all the trips are smooth operations." She held up the remainder of her arm.

"You lost that in the caves?"

"Lost it on the journey over. I didn't get along with the expedition's cook, and she ended our argument the hard way."

"Axe?"

"Beak. She was a seven-foot woodpecker goddess."

"Oh. So why are you back here?"

She sighed. "Exploring is just where my talents lie. Ever since I was a sapling I wanted to be an artist, but I was never good enough to pay the bills. I kept thinking I'd get better some day, but that dream died along with my hand."

She looked away, an amber tear dripping from her eye. I reached out to comfort her, but decided she might not be ready for the soothing touch of a stranger's snot.

"I'm sorry about your art," I said.

"It's fine. Just don't end up like me. No sense wasting your life on a stupid dream."

I looked at the tree-woman's silvery hair and wondered just how much time she'd spent pursuing her passion. I decided it would be rude to ask her age, and even more rude to cut her in half to check.

The office administrator called my name. I said goodbye to the tree-nymph and slithered through the door.

The horned figure behind the desk scribbled away at some paperwork. While tending to that, she also stirred a bubbling cauldron with her tail.

"Kabra?"

"Tyler? What're you doing here?"

I'd never realized Kabra the Goat-Slurper worked in the private sector, but I supposed there was no reason she couldn't have multiple careers. I climbed the chair across the desk. "I'm here for the job."

"You already have a job."

"I want something more fulfilling. Like what you have."

Kabra sighed, dropping her face into her hands.

"My life's not as great as you think," she said. "No matter how hard I work, it's never good enough."

"I think you're good."

"Thanks, but unless you're my parents, that doesn't help."

She seemed upset, so I didn't point out I couldn't possibly be her parents. We weren't even in the same genus.

Kabra explained she'd come from a long line of successful demonkin, all of whom had made significant contributions to monster society. She started crying partway through, which was especially awkward because she didn't seem to notice her hellfire tears had ignited a corner of the desk. I casually leaned over and smothered the flames with some of my snot rolls, continuing to nod like a good listener.

When Kabra finally ran out of steam I told her she was doing important work, whether she knew it or not.

She sniffled. "How so?"

"You help people with their careers. It may not be the life you want, but you're giving others a chance at happiness. That's the next best thing."

Kabra ran a tissue over her nose. "You really think helping people is that important?"

"I do."

"Thanks. You're a good friend, Tyler."

"Sometimes, that's all you need."

The moment I said it, an idea sparked.

"Ready to talk about the job now?" Kabra asked, composing herself.

"No, thank you. I think I've found something better."

I slopped out of the chair and headed to the newspaper office, ready to place an ad.

I WAS BUSY refilling the snack bowls in the lighthouse when I heard a knock at the open door.

"Kabra," I said. "Come in."

The Goat-Slurper stood in the doorway, smiling shyly. In her clawed hands was a lidded cauldron the size of a laundry basket. She set the bleating batch of spaghetti near the food table.

"Do you think anyone's going to come?" she asked.

"They already have. The others are down by the water. Let's head that way."

We went to the sandy strip of beach, where a tree-nymph, undead squid-lord and minotaur-mother sat on a blanket, eating nachos and playing cards. The tree-nymph had painted the cards herself, and we all agreed they were very good for someone with only one arm and a minor case of termites.

I introduced Kabra to the others and we joined the game. Everyone was happy: the minotaur-mom, who'd been so frustrated with her calf, had hired a babysitter to gain some free time; Otto the squid-lord, whose days had often been scheduled by his wife, was available now that Loretta had taken a part-time job watching someone's child. It was a nice coincidence that they could both attend the party. I wondered if Loretta and the minotaur's babysitter knew each other.

Kabra and I sat down for the next hand of cards. As Otto dealt, something huge erupted from the water, blotting out the sun. It waved its many tentacles and let out a long, gurgling roar.

"Hi," I said.

The roar cut off. The tentacles froze.

"I... hello," said the kraken, water dripping from its suction cups. "I saw an ad in the paper. Is this the support group?"

"It is."

"Can anyone join?"

"Anyone who needs a friend," I said, smiling.

The kraken scooted closer, careful not to splash our blanket. We dealt it into the game. It examined its cards.

"Got any sevens?" it asked.

"Go fish."

We spent the rest of the day playing cards and enjoying each other's company. I may not have had a perfect body, an exciting job, or a loving wife, but as long as I had friends who needed me, life wouldn't be so bad.

Zach Shephard

Zach Shephard's fiction has appeared in places like *Fantasy & Science Fiction, Galaxy's Edge* and *Intergalactic Medicine Show.* He spends a lot of time taking and teaching kickboxing classes at his local gym, mostly because he spends even more time eating foods he probably shouldn't. For a full list of his published stories, check out zachshephard.com.

AGENT OF CHAOS

JACK CAMPBELL

Were this one of her stories, Suzanne reflected, she would be writing about rain falling in what seemed to be solid sheets, flung by a cold wind from the north which was not quite icy enough to numb exposed skin but plenty chilly enough to leave a body shivering. The battered leather armor covering her upper body didn't seem any better at protecting her from rain than it could against weapons, though it did trap a fair amount of frigid water between the leather and her shirt. Her stomach growled occasional complaints about the lack of food, her throat had the icky scratchy feeling that portended a nasty cold, her sword, Guardian, kept banging against her leg, and whenever she tried to shift in the saddle the pen in her pocket dug into her thigh. It could have been worse, Suzanne consoled herself. At least all of those other things helped distract her from the pain in her butt after riding her horse, Inconstant, for a day and a night across the bandit-infested plains outside the city and into the wild mountains that lay to the east.

Not that she had had any desire to ride out of the city and across the plains and into the mountains. But, as Suzanne had learned, a writer had to follow her muse. Whether she wanted to or not.

As if summoned by the thought, her muse, Calliope, popped into existence, floating in front of Suzanne at eye level, drifting at a pace that kept her ahead of Suzanne's horse as he slogged through the storm. Suzanne, feeling the unwelcome tug inside

that pulled her after the muse, gritted her teeth.

Her muse, untouched by the storm, was smiling.

"The goddess Inspiration has been kind to us!" Calliope announced. "You're getting some wonderful experiences to help with your writing. Just think of how colorful your descriptions of travelers suffering miseries in storms will become."

Suzanne clenched her teeth tighter, her mind filled with colorful thoughts about what she would like to do to her muse.

"It's a pity we haven't encountered any more bandits," Calliope sighed. "Adventure presents many opportunities for plot devices and exciting prose. Perhaps we'll have better luck after the sun rises. Unfortunately, in this weather you are almost invisible to anything that might want to try to kill you!"

Her muse was drifting just outside the reach of her sword, Suzanne estimated. Perhaps if she swung the blade and simultaneously leaped forward over Inconstant's head...

"Any good story ideas coming to you?" Calliope asked.

"I'm considering a few ideas," Suzanne replied, her voice quavering as her body shook with cold. "I don't suppose the powers of a muse include any way to start a fire in this weather?"

"A writer must suffer for her art," Calliope declared airily. "How would your character find shelter in such a storm?"

Suzanne winced as a fresh sheet of rain hit her. Shaking off the frigid water, her hand so tight on her sword that she could feel the hilt biting into her palm, Suzanne glared at her muse. "I'm not a character! I'm a writer!"

"Then listen to your muse. Be creative."

"Go away! I don't want a muse anymore! I want to go back to the city!" Suzanne tried to turn Inconstant's head around, but found herself unable to as the pull of her muse dragged on her.

"A writer must follow her muse," Calliope chided, as she drifted ahead of Inconstant. "And you can't make me go away. The goddess Inspiration's priest-editor warned you about that."

"Since when do writers listen to priest-editors?" Suzanne grumbled.

"They rarely do. That's why they need the help of their muses."

Calliope paused dramatically, still floating in mid-air just out of Suzanne's reach, and raised one hand to her chin as if thinking. "I wonder if there are any *caves* in these mountains."

Suzanne glowered into the storm, wondering how badly her soaked trousers were chafing her thighs as she rode. She had lost feeling in them a while ago and dreaded discovering the answer.

"Caves," Calliope repeated. "*Dry* caves."

That last penetrated through Suzanne's misery. She glared suspiciously at her muse. "Would these caves happen to be the homes of bears? Or bandits?"

"Unknown perils in the dark! Wouldn't that be wonderful?"

"No. Can you at least tell me—" Suzanne broke off the question as Calliope vanished like a soap bubble bursting.

Muttering curses, Suzanne tried to turn Inconstant around again, only to find herself still unable to do so. Praying to the goddess Inspiration for aid, she aimed Inconstant off the path to one side and uphill through the trees. They hadn't gone far before a wall of bare stone that marked the steep side of a mountain rose out of the rain-lashed darkness. Turning Inconstant left, Suzanne rode slowly along the flank of the mountain, thinking dark thoughts of mudslides and avalanches.

Inconstant jerked to a halt, pitching Suzanne forward onto his neck, then stood unmoving as she muttered curses into his ear. Kicking didn't get the horse moving, so Suzanne dismounted, keeping a firm grip on the reins, and walked forward so she could pull her mount ahead.

Instead of advancing under Suzanne's tug, Inconstant jerked his head to one side. Suzanne's feet went out from under her as her boots slipped on the wet grass and mud, causing her to flop backward into more mud and lose her grip on the reins.

By the time she struggled to her feet, Inconstant had once again lived up to his name and vanished into the storm.

Suzanne considered sitting back down in the mud, then began trudging along the mountainside, one hand running along the slick rock as she went to help keep her balance on the slippery grass and mud under her feet. This worked well for a little while, even though walking close to the mountainside meant she was constantly stumbling over talus fallen from above. It was while carefully stepping over a pile of stone fragments that the supporting rock wall vanished from under her hand and Suzanne fell again, sideways this time.

It took her a moment to realize she wasn't being rained on anymore. Suzanne looked around, unable to see much in the gloom except for the lighter patch of black which marked the entrance to the cave into which she had fallen. She couldn't smell any bears or hear any bandits, so Suzanne cautiously searched for the cave wall. Finding it, she huddled on the ground, listening to the rain pour down outside.

A glow lit the cave as Calliope reappeared. "That's no way to find adventure," Suzanne's muse scolded.

"All I want to find is a fire and something to eat."

"You are so easily discouraged! A writer must suffer for her art! But perhaps some unexpected plot development will occur despite your character's lack of motivation."

"What? Plot development? I don't want to be motivated!" Suzanne's head came up in alarm as Calliope vanished again. Worried, Suzanne stood up, drew her sword and eyed the pitch black around her. She almost dropped the weapon when a deep voice rang out from the depths of the cave.

"It is death to enter here!" the voice bellowed in tones too loud and too deep for even a troll.

"I was just going," Suzanne answered hastily, groping for the entrance to the cave.

"Too late. Are you ready to die?"

"No, not really." Suzanne backed away from the voice, trying to move silently.

"Hold still!" Suzanne froze as the voice continued almost peevishly. "What kind of fool disturbs me? Are you an adventurer in search of wealth or glory?"

"No, I'm a writer, not an adventurer, and I've kind of given up on the whole wealth thing because the priest-editors of Inspiration don't pay all that much, and as for glory no one really knows who I am and—"

"You're a writer?" the deep voice interrupted.

"Yes. Yes, I am."

"How do I know you're telling the truth?" Now the voice sounded suspicious. "That was a run-on sentence just then, wasn't it?"

"Sometimes in dialogue you have to—"

"You could be a writing instructor. Or a priest-editor who doesn't know what she's doing. How do I know you're really a writer?" the voice demanded in tones that slightly deafened Suzanne and shook the walls of the cave.

"Uh... I'm not wearing much make-up. And I have on sensible shoes, and..." Suzanne reached quickly into her pocket and pulled out the object she kept there. "I have a pen."

"Anyone can have a pen," the deep voice grumbled. "Maybe I should just kill you."

"And I have a muse," Suzanne added desperately. "I followed my muse into these mountains."

"A muse?" The deep voice pondered that for a while. "Come."

To Suzanne's horror, the one-word command resulted in her being seized by some unseen force that felt like a huge hand. She was rapidly dragged by the invisible grasp deeper and deeper into the cave, fighting off a dizzying sensation of being pulled at great speed far beneath the surface, until she came to an abrupt halt in a large cavern dimly illuminated by the glow from a massive creature in the center of the space. The invisible grasp fell away, but Suzanne felt her legs lock with fear as she stared at the creature, which looked like what would happen if a giant human had been haphazardly combined with pieces of other giant creatures.

The monster gazed at Suzanne impassively for a moment. "Where's this muse?" it thundered in a voice that echoed from the walls of the cavern.

"She's... she's not here," Suzanne quavered in reply. "She never comes when I want her to but when I don't want her she's always there and—"

"Silence!" Fragments of rock fell from the top of the cavern in response to the roar from the creature. "You have just proven to me that you are a fellow writer! Only we understand how fickle a muse can be."

"A... fellow writer? You have a muse?" Suzanne gasped.

"Had. I ate it." As the monster picked at his fangs in memory, a cobra rose from the gloom along the floor and spat venom into its face. The creature flicked away the steaming venom and sighed. "Try not to step on the cobras."

Suzanne's hair rose on end as she saw that the floor of the cavern was writhing with snakes. She watched another cobra spit a dose of venom at the monster. It wiped the latest assault away as Suzanne found her voice again. "I didn't know a muse could be eaten."

"*You* couldn't eat one," the creature rumbled. "I could because I'm a god. Gothlack. I assume you know the name. The only things I get to eat are whatever wanders into this cave, and my muse. Lucky for you, I'm in a good mood today."

"G-Gothlack? The god of chaos? B-but you're supposed to be—"

"Confined by the other gods beneath a mountain with snakes spitting venom at me," Gothlack finished in annoyed tones as he waved one hand around to indicate his surroundings. "You didn't notice? And I didn't even do anything to deserve this fate."

"You tried to destroy the world," Suzanne pointed out.

"And I'll try again! That's my job. Chaos. I destroy things." Gothlack flinched as another cobra spat into his face. He hefted a thick pile of vellum on which words literally burned with tiny flickering flames. "But sometimes even I create things. Like my novel here. That's why I'm in a good mood. I finished it today."

Suzanne stared at the manuscript, wondering why the flaming words didn't consume the vellum.

"My masterpiece. *The End of Everything.*" Gothlack laughed like a pile of rusty metal falling. "It's a great title, isn't it?"

"A wonderful title. Is there any chance I could go right now to tell people about it—"

"Because," Gothlack continued with a hard look at Suzanne, "that's exactly what it is. The whole manuscript, all one thousand pages, is a very carefully crafted curse. The first time anyone finishes reading the whole thing the entire world goes poof. Get it? *The End of Everything.* What is that? Irony?"

"I'm not sure. I could go look it up—"

"But to be read, the manuscript has to be given to my agent and my publisher, and as you see, I can't deliver my manuscript in person." The god of chaos gestured again, this time toward the tremendous chains of orichalcum holding him prisoner. "That's why you're going to deliver it for me."

"Me?" Suzanne tried to back away, but the unseen force held her in place. "I was actually planning on—"

"Did I mention that I'm a god? So this isn't a request. It's a waddayacallit. A geas. You've got to do it."

He held out the manuscript and Suzanne felt her legs carry her forward through the cobras, which fortunately remained focused on spitting venom at Gothlack. Suzanne's hand rose of its own accord to take the vellum. The god of chaos frowned as he measured Suzanne's hand against the tall stack of vellum, then compressed the manuscript between his palms until it was thin enough to fit into her grasp. Suzanne winced in anticipation of being burned, but the cold flame of the words left her untouched.

"Where am I going?" Suzanne asked as her legs tried to walk her out of the cave. With a tremendous effort she held herself still for a moment.

"To my agent. Mani the Agent in Nwe Yerk. Say hi to him for me."

"Nwe Yerk?" The largest city in the land. Suzanne had never dreamed of actually visiting it.

"Yeah. My publisher is there, too. The Temple of Inspiration in Nwe Yerk. Nothing but the best for the god of chaos. You've heard of them, right? 'We treat our writers like gods, because some of them are.' One of their priest-editors visited me here once. I ate him, too." Gothlack shrugged. "Inspiration wasn't too happy with me about that, but who needs Inspiration or editors to write a thousand page novel? Have a nice trip." He gestured a final time and Suzanne felt herself yanked backward at tremendous speed again through the utter black of the cave's passages until she came to a sudden stop right at the entrance.

Outside the rain was still falling in sheets. Suzanne gazed out into the storm. Maybe by morning the rain would've stopped and she could—

"Get moving," Gothlack's voice rumbled behind her, and the unseen force kicked Suzanne out into the downpour.

Suzanne stumbled several paces, gasping against the renewed drenching, then came to a halt as she ran face first something wet, hairy, smelly, and fairly solid. Blinking away rain, Suzanne realized it was her horse Inconstant, who stood unconcerned as if nothing had happened.

Snarling a few curses, Suzanne stuffed Gothlack's flaming manuscript into one of the saddlebags, then mounted Inconstant, her soaked pants settling into the wet saddle with a squishy *thump*.

A small glow marked the reappearance of Calliope a short distance away. "Did you have any interesting experiences?" the muse inquired. "Something you could include in a story?"

Suzanne yanked Guardian from its sheath and kicked Inconstant into a gallop toward the muse, who vanished just before Suzanne's sword cleaved the air the muse had once occupied.

NWE YERK OCCUPIED a long island just off the coast, a few weeks' travel from the mountains where Suzanne had left Gothlack. Forced along by both her muse and the god's geas, Suzanne had gotten fairly adept at quickly grabbing food and dealing with other necessities during the brief stops she was permitted. At least Inconstant had stayed on the right roads so Suzanne had been able to sleep in the saddle.

Suzanne slumped wearily in the saddle as Inconstant plodded through the crowds moving across one of the great bridges connecting Nwe Yerk to the mainland. The lines outside the city sorely tested the patience of her geas, but eventually Suzanne reached the gate guards.

The guards, who looked remarkably like close relatives of

the gate guards in Suzanne's home city, studied Suzanne with worried expressions as they took in her bedraggled appearance, sword, leather armor, shirt, and pants. Finally their leader spoke up. "Are you a crazed but unusually modest-dressing barbarian swordswoman?"

"No. I'm a writer."

"But you have a sword," the guard noted accusingly.

"I've also got a pen." Suzanne hauled out her pen for the guard's inspection.

"It's been used, sure enough," the guard announced, after examining the pen closely. "What brings you to Nwe Yerk?"

"I'm under a geas from the god of chaos."

The gate guards stared.

"And I'm following my muse."

The guards broke into understanding smiles. "Oh, that's okay, then," the leader announced as he waved her inside the gate, Suzanne following the tug of her geas through the teeming streets of Nwe Yerk.

Calliope appeared, smiling benignly. "Nwe Yerk. The queen of cities, where Inspiration can be found on every street corner."

Suzanne cast a glance at the scantily-clad women occupying the nearest corner as they waved invitingly at passing males, doubtless inspiring many ideas in those men. She wondered for the thousandth time—in the last couple of weeks—whether Gothlack would eat Calliope if Suzanne begged hard enough. "Go away."

"But this adventure is just beginning."

"I'm about to be forced to deliver a manuscript to the agent of chaos, who will read it, and then the world will end. What about that classifies this as the beginning?"

"Try to think of another plot twist," Calliope suggested. She vanished again as Suzanne felt the geas' tug abruptly yank her sideways toward a modest three-story building.

Suzanne took advantage of the geas' power to help jerk Inconstant's stubborn head in the same direction, then dismounted, her entire lower body screaming with chafing and aching from the long trip. Tying up her horse and grabbing the saddlebag containing the manuscript, Suzanne ran one hand through her hopelessly-tangled hair, settled her sword in its sheath, then staggered into the building as passing women desperately tried to shield their children from her.

The geas tugged Suzanne up two flights of stairs, then down a hall to a door bearing a sign reading Mani – Literary Agent to the gods and other Writers. Shoving open the door, Suzanne stared at the short, rumpled man seated at a desk. "I'm looking for an agent."

Mani groaned. "Send me an outline and the first three chapters and I'll try to get back to you within three or four seasons. Maybe five."

"Really? You'll look at three chapters? I've got—" Suzanne stiffened as the geas locked on her. "No, it's not about me. Gothlack says hi."

This time Mani sighed elaborately, waving Suzanne inside. "He wants another extension, right? Tell Gothlack if he wants Deadline to grant him more time, then he's in a lot better position to talk to another god than I am."

"No, he finished the manuscript." Suzanne pulled the vellum from her saddlebag. "But there's a problem."

"Sweetheart," the agent of chaos assured her with a grin as he grabbed the document, "if he turned in a manuscript, there's no problem."

"Terrible things will happen if anyone reads it!"

"Let me assure you," Mani stated solemnly, "that no matter how bad Gothlack's novel is, I've read worse. You'd be amazed."

"I'm not talking about quality! The manuscript is a curse for destroying the world!"

Mani drooped in his chair, grimacing. "Writers never listen. You need a series, I tell Gothlack. That's the way to go. Set up a sequel. What does he do? Write a book that destroys the world. How much sequel potential does that have, I ask you?" He frowned at the manuscript. "Is it any good?"

"I haven't read it!"

"Want to be a reader?"

"I—" Susan hesitated. "How much does it pay?"

"Pay? You want me to pay you for the privilege of being my intern? For the honor of being the first to see the submissions from hopeful writers?"

"The slush pile? You want me to read your slush pile and not get paid?"

"That's right," Mani beamed. "What an opportunity to break into writing!"

"But—Look, I can't. Anyone who reads that manuscript will destroy the world."

The agent of chaos flipped through the pages rapidly. "A thousand pages long and you say it'll destroy the world. Maybe I'll let the priest-editors at the temple worry about reading it."

"But..." Suzanne cast around desperately for the right motivation for an agent. "If the book destroys the world, you won't get paid."

Mani smiled. "Wrong. Gothlack is a celebrity author. Not only does his book not have to be any good, but he gets a huge advance, payable on delivery of the manuscript, so I get my fifteen percent upfront. I get paid, and if you're right, *then* the world ends. Not a problem." The agent of chaos peered at Suzanne as she fidgeted under the pull of the geas. "You wouldn't happen to be going in the direction of the temple of Inspiration, would you?"

"Gothlack's geas forces me to deliver the manuscript to the publisher, too," Suzanne admitted.

"I get the advance for the novel and I save on a delivery fee?" Mani exulted. "Gothlack, you are one great writer," he told the ceiling.

Suzanne pointed to one side and down. "He's more in that direction."

"Hey, you can deliver his advance to him! Minus my fifteen percent and offerings to the gods for the manuscript to be finished and all other associated costs and expenses, of course."

She glared at him. "No! Don't you care what happens to the world?"

"Would you want me to work against my client, who has his

faults but does nonetheless have a contract with me? Do you know what would happen if I broke my contract? There are forces in this world who love chaos. Lawyers, for example. They love it when no one else can figure out what they're doing, and if they heard I'd gone against Gothlack they'd all descend on me waving swords and subpoenas. That's a certainty, whereas I have only your word for it that this manuscript will destroy the world." Mani shrugged again as Suzanne stumbled out the door under the force of the geas. "Don't forget!" he called after her. "Three chapters and an outline!"

Inconstant had managed to loose himself and wander into the street, where he was blocking traffic and was surrounded by angry wagon drivers debating the most painful way to kill him. Suzanne (who had had those same feelings about Inconstant more than once) tried to walk toward the temple, but found herself yanked toward Inconstant by the geas. As she resignedly started to climb into the saddle, a wagon driver who was easily twice Suzanne's size grabbed her arm. "Is this your horse?"

Inspiration came to Suzanne's aid. "No. I'm stealing it."

The drivers backed away, grinning, as Suzanne viciously kicked Inconstant into motion again.

The huge temple of Inspiration in Nwe Yerk occupied most of a city block, rising upward for several stories. Its façade was covered with carvings representing various famous tales and writers, as well as the goddess herself and the lesser deities in her pantheon such as relentless Deadline and proud Contract. Suzanne had thought Inspiration's temple in her home city was impressive, but that seemed almost a hovel compared to this structure.

A long line of hopeful writers waited to enter the temple, clutching the manuscripts they would place in the offering trays for the priest-editors of Inspiration to judge for worthiness.

Unable to wait with Gothlack's geas tugging at her, Suzanne trudged up the steps alongside the line of hopefuls, trying to ignore their scandalized looks. The priest-editor at the entrance frowned at her, pointing to the rear of the line, then froze with his mouth open as Suzanne thrust the flaming manuscript at him.

"Are... are you a goddess?" he gasped.

"Do I look like a goddess?"

The question made the priest-editor pause, his appalled gaze studying Suzanne's appearance, but caution won out over candor. "Inspiration has been known to take many forms—"

"I'm a writer! Just take the manuscript!" Suzanne yelled, tossing it at him.

The priest-editor caught the flaming manuscript, juggling it frantically until he realized it wasn't burning him.

Suzanne almost collapsed as the force of the geas finally vanished. "That's from the god of chaos, Gothlack. You have to destroy it."

The priest-editor looked from Suzanne to the manuscript. "But it's an offering to the goddess—"

"It'll destroy the world if anyone reads it! I only delivered it because Gothlack put me under a geas to bring the manuscript to his agent and to his publisher—"

"His publisher?" The priest-editor straightened and nodded. "Then this manuscript is an offering to Contract and Inspiration. I'll deliver it to the senior priestess-editor immediately."

"But—"

"Thank you on behalf of the goddess." The priest-editor vanished into the temple, leaving Suzanne standing in the entrance.

Calliope appeared, beaming happily, causing a chorus of awed and envious sounds from the waiting line of would-be writers as they saw Suzanne's muse. "How's your character's storyline doing?"

"It sucks. Why did you help Gothlack deliver that manuscript here?"

"I didn't help him, I helped *you*," Calliope said. "My writer."

"Thank you so very much. Your writer won't be writing much more after the world is destroyed. You do realize that, don't you?"

The muse nodded. "That would be a problem. I can't really help you with it since I have to pay my respects to Inspiration, but I'm sure you can plot out a satisfactory ending to the story."

"No!" Suzanne yelled. "No! This is not a story!"

Calliope smiled. "Of course it's a story. It's your story, filled with adventure and peril. What more could a writer want?"

Romance popped into Suzanne's head, but fortunately she managed to avoid saying it. There was no telling what kind of situations Calliope would get her into if the muse decided to try adding her idea of romance to Suzanne's life. Instead, Suzanne swung a fist at the muse as it vanished. She glared into the inner precincts of the building, shifted her sword, settled her armor, grasped her pen, and marched into the temple of Inspiration.

She paused to let her eyes adjust to the dimness of the vast nave, gazing at the tiny cells spaced along the sides of the area where the priest-editors awaited offerings from hopeful writers. The senior priestess-editor wouldn't be in one of those, Suzanne guessed, but would be much higher up somewhere in the sacred ivory towers where writers were never allowed.

Bracing herself for a blast of divine displeasure, Suzanne nonchalantly strolled to the staircase leading upward as if she had every right to go in that direction. She didn't encounter anyone else as the staircase went higher, growing broader and grander, letting out onto progressively nicer landings. Reaching the top landing, Suzanne stared anxiously down a magnificent corridor with a vaulted ceiling high overhead. At the far end she could see a door massive enough that Gothlack could have walked through it.

Inspiration still hadn't struck her witless, nor had the lesser god Block appeared to steal her writing ability, so Suzanne started down the hallway, only to almost run into a young priestess-editor hurrying out of a side door.

The priestess-editor halted and stared at Suzanne. "What are you doing here?"

"Uh... Inspiration led me here. So did my muse," Suzanne added.

"Your muse? Are you a writer? I'm sorry, but your offering doesn't meet our current needs," the editor recited rapidly.

Suzanne smiled in what she hoped was a winning way despite her general crazed appearance. "I didn't bring an offering. I had to come here because I was following my muse."

The priestess-editor sighed. "Every once in a while a new acolyte will come to me and ask why a writer did something that we can't understand. I just tell them not to worry about it, that the writer is just following their muse. Do you writers like following your muses?"

Suzanne shook her head. "Actually, I want to kill mine."

"Isn't that difficult? Our senior priestess says the only way a writer can kill a muse is if they don't want to do it."

The full extent of her problem finally became clear to Suzanne. "Really?"

"Yes." The priestess-editor glanced around with a guilty expression. "The senior priestess-editor will become very upset if she sees me talking to a writer. She'll probably make me do penance by copy-editing. I should go back to my cell."

"Wait, please! I need to kill a book."

That statement bought Suzanne a frown from the priestess-editor. "You want to kill a book and your muse?"

"Yes, though I'll settle for the book right now. But I'm not sure how to kill it."

The priestess pondered the question. "I'd try Marketing if I were you. Usually when a book dies everyone says Marketing is responsible, so they must kill a lot of books."

"But it can't be at Marketing, yet," Suzanne insisted. "I just delivered it to the temple. It was written by Gothlack, the god of chaos. Can you help me find the editor who has it?"

To Suzanne's surprise, the priestess-editor laughed. "No editor in their right mind would touch a god's manuscript. What do you think happens when you copyedit a god's writing? At the very least you annoy the god, at the worst you get cursed, and very likely it's all for nothing anyway because the god just creates a new rule of grammar rather than change their manuscript. How do you think we ended up with the fourth-person prepositional infinitive phrase rule?"

"I've always wondered about that."

"Then you understand why we don't want Gothlack, of all gods, creating new rules of grammar so he wouldn't have to agree to a copyedit. I guarantee you that manuscript was sent straight down to..." The priestess-editor glanced around nervously and whispered the rest. "To the guy in Marketing."

Suzanne gazed up and down the hallway. "Which way is Marketing?"

"I told you." The priestess-editor pointed straight down.

The grand stairway dwindled again as Suzanne headed back down without seeing any sign of Marketing. She passed ground level and kept going, the stairway getting narrower, the steps steeper, and the torches set at greater intervals so that Suzanne was soon creeping down through patches of darkness. The walls had become rough stone, covered with wet patches and pockets of slime. Suzanne became aware of rustling sounds, then came to a total halt as she spotted something like a giant rat's shadow crossing the staircase below her. Drawing her sword Guardian, Suzanne crept forward, her eyes and ears straining for any sign of danger.

Finally, the stairs ended facing a battered door with 'Marketing' painted on it in faded lettering. Suzanne, whose worries about the guy in Marketing had grown as her surroundings got more dismal, took a firm grip on her sword as she pushed open the door.

A very large room filled with desks met her eyes. Most of the desks were covered with piles of manuscripts and artwork, as was most of the floor space. Only one desk had an occupant, a man of indeterminate age blinking at her with large, dark eyes set in very pale skin. A carved wooden sign on his desk read Borgul - Marketing.

"Ready tomorrow," Borgul assured Suzanne in a hoarse voice, eyeing her sword.

Suzanne glanced around for danger, then sheathed her sword. "What will be ready?"

"Whatever the nice person with the sword wants."

"Actually, I want the manuscript which the god of chaos just delivered to this temple."

"Nasty swordmistresses can't have it!" the guy in Marketing replied, clutching a thick file folder to his chest.

"I can't let you read that manuscript!"

Borgul squinted at her, his expression baffled. "Read it? Why would we want to read it?"

Suzanne gazed back at him, also perplexed now. "I thought you chose the cover art and how to promote the book and—"

"Yes," Borgul interrupted in irritable tones. "What do those things have to do with reading the book?" He leaned back and sighed happily, still clutching the folder. "We have already chosen cover and tag line, so now nice manuscript just needs to go back upstairs to divine printers."

"Do the printers read it?"

Borgul looked at Suzanne as if trying to judge whether she was serious.

Suzanne reached out tentatively. "Is there any chance I could see the cover you—"

"No!" the guy in Marketing insisted, gripping the folder tighter. "It's *mine*."

Suzanne eyed Borgul, trying to think up a way to gain access to the manuscript. What could influence this... person? What did he like? Praying silently to Inspiration, Suzanne studied the room for clues.

Aside from the piles of manuscripts everywhere, the dominating features were illustrations on the walls of young women with impressive bust measurements and well-rounded rear-ends, all of them clad only in extremely inadequate amounts of chain mail armor. Each woman also carried a sword. Suzanne looked down at herself. She couldn't do anything about her bust or her rear end at the moment, but she still had her sword.

Pushing her chest and her sword forward, Suzanne smiled at the guy in Marketing. "You wouldn't be interested in going out with me somewhere, would you?"

Borgul's mouth dropped open. "Where does the nice swordswoman want to go?" he finally asked.

"Where?" Expertise honed in countless blind dates came to Suzanne's rescue. "There's a bar eight blocks west from here. I'll meet you there."

"Why not come now?"

"I... need to change into my chain mail first."

Borgul's eyes widened, then he grinned and darted out and up the stairs.

Suzanne waited only until the door closed, then lunged for the folder containing Gothlack's manuscript. The first thing she pulled out was the manuscript itself. While under the geas she hadn't been able to do anything to it, but now she tried holding it to a candle flame. The manuscript didn't burn. Neither would it rip, tear, cut, or be smeared by water or ink. Suzanne strained mightily to yank the last page free but only succeeded in pulling a muscle.

Breathing heavily from her efforts, Suzanne dumped Gothlack's manuscript back into the folder and drew out the cover art. She wasn't all that surprised to see the picture was dominated by a barbarian swordswoman from the Double-D Cup Clan, her chain mail halter top covering only a small fraction of her straining breasts. Suzanne squinted at the picture, trying to figure out if the woman was supposed to be grimacing with battle lust or in response to having her boobs pinched by the chain mail of the halter top.

Dropping the picture into the nearest trash can, Suzanne rummaged through the cover art files, stopping only when she came across one showing an indistinct image of a man sitting at a desk, gazing blandly into the distance, the background a flat, dreary expanse of land. The color scheme of the picture seemed to make use of every available shade of beige.

Replacing the original cover art with her own selection, Suzanne studied the Marketing sheet, on which her recent acquaintance had scrawled *An epic adventure of amazing exploration*. That sounded not only generic but entirely too interesting. Suzanne drew her pen, crossed out the words, pondered for a moment, then wrote carefully: *An exhaustive interpretation of the philosophical implications of neo-pagan breathing rituals with extensive notations in the original Pruskian dialects.* That should do it.

A brightening of the gloom marked the appearance of Calliope, reading over her shoulder. Before Suzanne could draw her sword and swing, Calliope slid through the air across the room and out of reach, shaking her head. "I'd never read that."

"That's the idea," Suzanne informed her muse.

"You're writing things you don't want people to read?"

"It's a, um, creative writing exercise."

"Oh." Calliope literally brightened a bit, throwing into greater relief the illustrations on the walls. "The spirit of Inspiration is moving you?"

"As a matter of fact, it is," Suzanne agreed, dropping the folder into a file tray marked *Printers*. "With any luck no one will ever actually read this book of Gothlack's."

"Won't the agent of chaos be upset about that?"

Suzanne shook her head. "He's got his fifteen percent and he's already given up on a sequel."

"Wonderful," her muse enthused. "Inspiration has aided you several times today. The goddess expects great things of you." Calliope lowered her voice as if sharing a secret. "The goddess believes that with my help you could someday die in obscurity and poverty, scribbling the final words of a novel which would make you famous a hundred years after your body was dumped into the paupers' field."

"She does?" Suzanne stared at her muse with a sinking feeling. "Please go tell Inspiration that I'm proud to serve her but I really don't deserve that."

"Of course you do! If I work on it, the goddess might even grant that you die young, perhaps of a horrible illness aggravated by your destitution, a talent cut down before it could fully flower!"

Suzanne's mouth worked, but no sound came out. She finally managed to croak out a reply. "No, thank you. I don't want to be a writer anymore."

Calliope's smile grew. "Writer of mine, you still don't understand. People don't become writers because they *want* to write, they become writers because they *have* to write. You don't have any choice."

"You said I could write my own story!" Suzanne wailed. "You

told me I could plot out what happens!"

Her muse tilted her head to one side thoughtfully. "If you're really good at it..."

"Yes! I'm going to get very good at it!"

"Excellent!" Calliope beamed at Suzanne. "How about a nice trip to a beach?"

"A beach?" Suzanne imagined lying on warm sand, far from gods of any sort. Lured by the image, she followed Calliope without protest as the muse floated quickly up the stairs and out of the temple, then down the steps to the street where Inconstant stood tied to the rail. Mounting her horse, Suzanne tried to swing Inconstant to face south, but found herself pulled northward instead. "Hey," she called to her muse. "I thought you said a beach?"

"Yes," Calliope replied. "A beach where the waves make the most delightful tinkling sound as they crash onto the jagged rocks and break the ice rime formed by earlier spray. Inspiration loves the place."

"Ice? I don't—"

"You'll have to make sure you keep your pen next to your skin so the ink doesn't freeze. But to get there we'll have to get past the northern barbarian tribes. That will take some clever plotting, my writer!"

Suzanne tugged frantically at Inconstant's reins, but couldn't resist the pull from her muse and found herself pointing her horse's muzzle northward. She reached into her pocket for her pen and tried to hurl it away, but her hand wouldn't release it. "Please, Calliope, can't we try something a little less hazardous first? Something less likely to kill me?"

"You can't be immortal unless you're willing to die for your art."

Stuffing her pen back into her pocket and muttering prayers to Inspiration for a foolproof idea to get rid of Calliope, Suzanne followed her muse toward the northern gate out of Nwe Yerk. This time, unfortunately, Inspiration didn't come to her.

But at least she had met an agent. Suzanne pulled out her pen and some paper and started working on an outline for her novel. Maybe she would survive long enough to get the first three chapters done.

Jack Campbell

Jack Campbell is the pen name of John G. Hemry, a retired U.S. Navy officer. He writes The Lost Fleet series of military science fiction novels as well as the Beyond the Frontier continuation of The Lost Fleet, and The Lost Stars series (a spin-off of The Lost Fleet.) He has also written the Stark's War series and the Singlair/"JAG in space" series, and has written many shorter stories featuring space opera, fantasy, time travel and alternate history. His website is www.jack-campbell.com.

DISPLAY OF AFFECTION

P. J. SAMBEAUX

G uy shuddered silently and his heart dropped as the slight grip his mother's frail hand had on his own lessened and then disappeared. The machines stopped whirring and beeping, and an unnatural quiet descended upon the room. Tears leaked out of his eyes as he looked away from his mother and down at the upcycled vase filled with a drooping bunch of lilies whose sickly scent filled the room. He wouldn't have brought them, but they were his mother's favorite. A rainbow of uneaten food cubes sat on a tray that had been pushed away with disinterest. He was given one nanosecond to grieve before her body was sucked down the pneumatic tube to the upcycling/recycling/repurposing facility.

The feelings that he automatically tweeted about her death got seven thousand five hundred likes and sixty-five dislikes. Two thousand women, mostly the older mom crowd, reacted with crying faces. His sister Janine posted a hug, while his sister Susan posted a crying face/thumbs up/big smile that drove an instantaneous rift through his family. His wife said the depth and length of his grief was EMBARRASING her. His nephew posted "yawn" and ninety percent of males eighteen to twenty-four agreed. Then somebody posted a video of a squirrel and a raccoon fighting over a half-eaten Big Mac in a McDonald's parking lot, and with that his mother's funeral was over—even though his tears hadn't even dried.

He waited for her remains to be returned, but the screen flashed "one hundred percent repurposing" and all that came out was a keychain that read "Somebody I know died." Guy sighed deeply before jamming it in his pocket and walking out the door. He walked briskly, with no apparent destination. He just wanted to be somewhere, anywhere, other than the hospital.

As he stepped out into the square, he shielded his eyes from the bright sun as he answered an instant message from his boss.

Boss: Hey buddy, are ya headed back to the office?

Guy: My mom just died.

Boss: I KNOW. Did you not see my Facebook like???

Guy: I think I'm going to take the rest of the day off.

Boss: Dude, your mom died five minutes ago. How much more time do you need to mourn? It's time to move on...

Guy: I'm going to be taking the rest of the day off.

Boss: Are you serious??? There are two whole hours left in the day.

Guy: I have enough paid leave. I need some time to process.

Boss: Two whole hours???

Guy: See you in the morning.

GUY MILLED AROUND the city center, letting his news and personal feeds flow through his brain without really paying attention. The president of Brazil got assassinated, and the U.S. president got brain hacked, or at least it was a presumed hack as he had formally addressed congress by telling them to eat his poop. His nephew posted a YouTube video doing a parody of him at his mom's funeral. His doctor prescribed an antidepressant, which his pharmacy filled. His boss fired him. His wife changed her relationship status to "looking for Mr. Right," filed for divorce, actually divorced him, and changed her relationship status to "in a relationship."

All of these things should have bothered Guy, but they didn't, because Guy had learned the lesson that so many others have after losing a loved one. And that message is simply this: Live.

He got an invitation to visit the new exhibition at the Natural

History Museum, which was weird both because he never went and because he was coincidentally standing right in front of it. Later he would wonder if they hadn't been blasting him with subliminals, making him think he was aimlessly wandering the earth, when in reality he was headed there the whole time.

Then Guy did the unthinkable: he unplugged his brain from the feed. Unplugging yourself from the feed was, strictly speaking, illegal, and for this reason he unplugged under the guise of doing a systems check for potential hacking. Anyone that had been reading his feed from the last hour would probably regard this as completely reasonable, which he knew. This action, however, immediately alerted the NSA who promptly began an investigation into the hack, which he did not know.

And with that, Guy walked into the museum. He hadn't been there since he was a kid, and unplugging himself so suddenly from his feed gave him the same wonderment he had felt upon seeing the colossal dinosaur clones for the very first time.

He inquired politely at the desk about the location of the new exhibit. The information agent was highly taken aback to be asked a question by an actual human being standing right in front of him, and as soon as Guy turned around he said in a loud stage whisper 'leave it to a no-tech to visit a museum. In *person*,' to his robot girlfriend, with whom he had been sharing his pithy witticisms all day via VidCom. She laughed, but only because she was programmed to. In reality, she thought he was a complete asshat and had been working for some time on an escape plan.

Guy made his way through the Hall of Progress, where a Benjamin Franklin clone waved feebly at him as he flew his kite in the electrical storm... again.

Marie Antoinette was having a spirited debate with a group on her VidCom.

"OK, first of all, haters, no one ever said 'let them eat cake.' Nobody. It's called propaganda. Get over it," she said, to audience that responded with jeering and hissing. "Oh, for the love of Pete," she started, but then sighed and flipped them a double bird. She looked over at Guy, who smiled sympathetically at her as he strolled past, rolling her eyes and mouthing "OMG."

Next door was an Abraham Lincoln that Guy sort of wanted to talk to, but then he thought better of it, because this one did not give off a "stop and talk to me" kind of vibe. In fact, he had angry eyes and was holding his quill like a shiv. Bitterness can run deep in classic clones.

The next exhibit was closed for lunch, and as he rounded the corner Guy stopped dead in his tracks, as he found himself in his mother's hospital room, complete with his dying mother.

"Hi, Honey," she said in a tired voice.

"Hi, Mom?" he returned uncertainly, feeling like his brain was breaking into a million pieces.

Guy looked around at the exact replica of the hospital room he had just left little more than an hour before. There were the drooping calla lilies in the upcycled vase, the tray with the rainbow of uneaten food cubes, and the vending machine that had spat out the keychain he now wrapped his hands around. The one that said 'Somebody I know died.'

"Honey," his mom said kindly, "I think you'd better go now."

And Guy thought *you're saying that because you're about to die, which I know because you said that the first time and then you did, and you tried to send me away because you loved me, but I couldn't go because I loved you.*

"Oh, buddy, this exhibit isn't ready yet," a museum guard said gruffly, interrupting his reverie. The guard was a large, middle aged man with a substantial paunch, who wore his cap at a jaunty angle on his head.

"This just happened," Guy said, in a state of shock. "This just happened like an hour ago."

"Oh, sure it just happened an hour ago, but imagine if we knew then what we know now," the guard said, and whistled as a way to exemplify his point.

"Like what?" Guy asked, surprised to find himself sort of curious despite his shock.

"Oh, you know that thing about how they found a cure for cancer and treated like two thousand cancer patients already."

"Yeah? How's that going?"

"Oh, you didn't hear? Turns out it just gives you a different kind of cancer."

Just then an assistant walked by, and catching sight of Guy waved at him enthusiastically.

"OMG. Guy. You're really here!" she squeaked with the enthusiasm of a squirrel who has had one too many espressos.

"Oh, holy crap! You're Guy?" The guard made a fist and beat it over his heart a few times. "You got me, man, right here."

"You'll have to meet with the museum director," the assistant said, as she pressed a button that sort of... paused his mom, grabbed his arm and led him down the hallway.

"GUY," THE MUSEUM director began in a kindly tone, "everybody knows that you've gone insane and turned off your feed, so I'm going to bring you up to speed. Quite simply, you've gone viral. Everyone, and I mean everyone, is completely taken with these... feelings that you're feeling. You're a hit. You've been trending for an hour. That's longer than the assassination of the Brazilian president trended. In Brazil."

The director smiled pleasantly at him. He wore typical executive attire: an over-sized hoodie with bleach stains down one side, baggy jeans fraying at the hem, and scuffed tennis shoes. He rocked back and forth excitedly on a large blue rubber ball behind a clear quartz desk.

"But you can't possibly do this," Guy said, at a loss for words. "I won't let you."

"Oh Guy, we can totally do this. And not only are you going to let us do this, you've been hired to do hourly performances in the exhibit."

"Wait, what?? My mom *died* for god's sake."

"Well," the museum director said, taking on a diplomatic tone, "your mom did die, but thankfully we were able to repurpose her body into a supply of clones that we can use for the show. And we're going to need you to start. Right away."

"I'm not doing this," Guy said, indignation rising from every fiber of his being.

"Well, Guy, this is how it stands. Without this job, you would be unemployed, which as you know is quite illegal. If you don't accept this job you would quite probably go to jail. And that's not even taking into account the business with the president."

"What business with the president?"

"Well, I personally did not make a post about this yet, but conspiracy theorists have gone wild with the idea that you hacked the president's brain."

"I did not hack the president's brain," Guy replied deadpan, laden down with grief and fatigue.

"Well, that is what someone would say if they had hacked the president's brain, so I'm afraid I'm going to have to side with the conspiracy theorists. Really, what is so damning is the fact that you unplugged yourself right after it happened," the director said, looking at the ceiling and writing the post in his head.

"I unplugged myself because my mom died!" Guy was surprised to find himself shouting.

The museum director looked at him and smiled pleasantly.

"And what's nice about this situation," he began, "is that we're going to leave you unplugged so we can watch what happens as it unfolds in real time, without even knowing your thoughts or emotions until we see how you act. Or don't act. How crazy is that? We've already started tweeting under the name Guy's Brain."

THE THING ABOUT being plugged into the feed all the time is that so many things compete for your attention that none of them end up having any meaning, Guy thought and shuddered silently and his heart dropped as the slight grip his mother's frail hand had on his own lessened and then disappeared. The machines stopped whirring and beeping, and an unnatural quiet descended upon the room.

Three months after his mother's death, and he was doing five shows of it daily in front of a live feed that consisted of basically the entire planet, because he did not show any signs of waning in popularity. He had no hope of being released from this veritable prison sentence because the audiences tuned in to see him hurt, and he did. He was given no chance to move on from this moment in time. *I can't miss you, mom, if you don't go away,* he thought bitterly as he waited for her remains.

Being unplugged all this time had brought him a sense of clarity he had never experienced. Even in the midst of unending grief, he felt like he was on the cusp of understanding something that couldn't be put into words, and that feeling gave him hope.

The screen flashed "one hundred percent repurposing" and all that came out was a keychain. He was surprised to see the message, but was smart enough to know that he had to play the same part he had been playing all of these months. He smiled on the inside as he shoved the keychain in his pocket.

The message read "I think it's time to move on."

P.J. Sambeaux

P.J. Sambeaux's work has been featured in such magazines as *Space Squid, Alliterati, The Broken City, Maudlin House, Abstract Jam,* and *Apocrypha and Abstractions.* She lives in upstate New York.

THE GREAT MANHATTAN EAT-OFF

A Harry the Book Story

MIKE RESNICK

I am sitting in my office, which is the third booth at Joey Chicago's 3-Star Tavern, doping out the morning line at Saratoga. I am feeling exceptionally flush since last night, because Kid Testosterone made it all the way to the second round before Malicious Monty knocked him out, and of the 713 bets I booked on the fight only Longshot Lamont bet that the Kid would make it past the first round. In fact, he bet the Kid would still be conscious by the fifth round, which had me worried for about four minutes, since the odds were three thousand to one against it.

Then Joey Chicago walks up to me and lays a sheet of paper on my table, right between my bottle of Old Peculier and my bicarbonate.

"Good afternoon, Joey," I say, because no one in my circle of acquaintances has ever seen a morning from the tail end. "And what, pray, is this paper about, because as you can plainly see I already have a napkin."

"I have always been a good friend and landlord to you, have I not?" asks Joey Chicago.

"Absolutely," I say, wondering where this is leading. "And of course it is mutual, because surely I have doubled your business since word went out that I had set up shop here."

"So we are agreed on that," he confirms. "Yet we have a serious problem"—he frowns—"*and it has got to stop!*"

"What is our mutual problem?" I inquire politely.

"It's Dawkins," he half-says and half-yells, "and you've got to do something about it!"

Gently Gently Dawkins, who is maybe a donut short of four hundred pounds, is one of my flunkies.

"We have had this problem before," I say, "after he broke your sixth barstool."

"My ninth!"

"Sixth, ninth, what is the difference?" I reply. "I paid for new stools, did I not?"

"That was *then*," he says. "This is *now!*"

I look over at the bar. "I do not see any more broken stools," I tell him.

"Look a little higher," says Joey Chicago.

"He cannot reach the ceiling," I answer.

"The bar," says Joey.

"Okay, I see the bar," I say. "Almost clean and nearly polished, as usual."

"Can you not see what is missing?" demands Joey Chicago.

"Customers?" I ask.

"Nuts!" he yells.

"I am sorry you are so distressed," I say, "but I must compliment you on your choice of language. Usually you would just curse and be done with it."

"No," he says. "*Nuts!*"

"If you've seen any hanging around, call Bellevue and report it to them."

"Stop understanding me so fast!" snaps Joey Chicago. He points to the paper he has laid on my table. "That is a bill for $1,538.60."

"And what is it for?" I inquire.

"That's the wholesale cost of the nuts your lackey has eaten off the bar just this month!"

Just as he says this, who should wander in but Gently Gently

Dawkins, nibbling what's left of a candy bar.

"Hi, Harry," he says, then turns to Joey Chicago. "You forgot to put nuts and peanuts and niblets out on the bar."

"Ask your boss," growls Joey Chicago.

Dawkins wanders over. "I wish you'd get a bigger office," he says. "I cannot slide into this one."

"That is just as well," says Benny Fifth Street, another of my flunkies. "If I were you, I would keep out of the boss's reach for the next few years."

"Why?" asks Dawkins, pulling another candy bar out of his pocket. "The Kid made it to the second round. We should be rolling in money."

"Yes, we should be," I agree. "Instead, one of us is rolling in bar food."

"That is immoral!" says Dawkins. "It might even be sinful. Bar food is for eating, not rolling in."

I glare at him for a minute, then pull out my wallet and peel off fifteen hundreds and a forty some guy tried to pass to me.

"Dawkins, take these and give them to Joey Chicago."

"Right, Harry," he says, grabbing the bills from me.

"And Dawkins?" I say.

"Yes, Harry?"

"If you eat any of them, I will cut your head off and use it as a bowling ball."

"I didn't know you bowled, Harry," says Dawkins.

"I'll learn."

Nothing much happens for the next hour except that Dawkins leaves the building for five minutes and returns with a bag of cheeseburgers in one hand and a chocolate malt in the other.

"To keep my energy level up until mealtime," he explains.

"Has *anyone* ever had an appetite like that?" muses Benny Fifth Street.

"Oh, someone must have," says Joey Chicago.

"Of course they have," says Short Odds McDougal, looking up from his beer for the first time in maybe an hour.

"You sound very sure of yourself," said Benny Fifth Street.

"Perhaps you would like to put some money on that idle speculation."

"It is not an idle speculation," answers Short Odds. "In fact, it is a speculation that could give Seattle Slew a three-length head start and a beating."

"And which of Ripley's many tasteful museums did you see his corpse in?" asked Benny.

"That is three misstatements in thirteen words," notes Short Odds, "which is a lot, even for you. He is not in Ripley's, he is not dead, and he is a she."

"You are saying that a dame can out-eat Gently Gently Dawkins, who could be mistaken for a small elephant if his nose was a couple of feet longer?" demands Benny.

"Check the record books," says Short Odds. "She is the champion of all she surveys. Well, before she eats it, anyway."

"Granting that this woman has a major appetite," I interject, "I still want to know why you mention her in such superlatives."

"Surely you have heard of the Great Manhattan Eat-Off," says Short Odds.

"Not until three seconds ago," I say.

"They hold this contest in Manhattan every five years, and Miss Priscilla Nibbles is the reigning champion."

"Oh, come on," says Benny. "No one is called Nibbles."

"She used to be Miss Priscilla Smith," answers Short Odds, "but she changed it legally after she won for the fifth—no, make that the sixth—time."

"She is undefeated for thirty years?" I ask.

"Longer. The contest is now entering its thirty-fifth year."

Benny Fifth Street turns to me. "You know what I am thinking, Boss?"

"Probably," I say. "But go ahead and tell me, just in case I am wrong."

"I think we could enter our very own dark horse—well, dark hippo or elephant or whatever—and no one who hasn't seen him, no one who bets based on past performances, will bet on him. Think of the odds!"

"I'm all in favor of it!" adds Joey Chicago. "He'll finally have enough to eat. Think of my bar snacks!"

"I will consider it," I say.

"Don't I have a say in the matter?" asks Dawkins.

"Shut up," says Benny. "You're just the horse or whatever."

"Okay," I say. "Benny, find out everything you can about the eat-off: when is it, where is it, are there entry fees, how much winning is worth, whatever."

"I'm on my way," says Benny, heading out the door.

"Damn, I'm getting peckish again," said Dawkins. "I think I'll pop out for a pizza. I'll be back in a few minutes."

"Stay where you are!" I growl.

He looks startled, but he stands still.

I look to the farthest, darkest corner of the tavern, and yell "Dugan! Get over here!"

A few seconds later there is some movement, and then the cause of the movement appears and it is Dead End Dugan, the third of my flunkies—and let me tell you, when you've got a plunger who won't make good his marker, it is a handy thing to have a six-foot ten-inch zombie on your team, even if his brain is only working on a couple of cylinders.

"Yes, Harry?" he says, blinking his eyes furiously as if trying to focus, and I can tell he's spent a little too much time today thinking dead thoughts.

"Dawkins is not allowed to leave the building," I say. "He is your responsibility. Do you understand?"

"Sort of," answers Dugan.

"But why can't I go out for a pizza?" asks Dawkins plaintively.

"You're in training for the Great Manhattan Eat-Off," I tell him. "I figure we'll hold you to two hundred calories a day to work up a *real* appetite." I pause thoughtfully. "Maybe one hundred and fifty."

His screams of agony are still ringing in my ears as I cross the street and treat myself to lunch at Horatio the Grub's Pizza Emporium.

"So WHAT DID you learn about the contest?" I ask when Benny Fifth

Street shows up back at Joey Chicago's and walks over to my office. He frowns. "The main thing I learned is that it's not a contest at all."

"There is no Great Manhattan Eat-Off after all?" I ask, at which point Dawkins stops sobbing and looks alert and alive again.

"Oh, yes, there is a Great Manhattan Eat-Off," says Benny. "But it is not a contest, except for second money."

"Explain," I say.

"Miss Priscilla Nibbles is the Man o' War, Babe Ruth, and Michael Jordan of the eating fraternity. Every eat-off follows the same pattern. A bunch of half-ton guys show up, and this dainty little lady eats 'em all under the table"—he pauses for effect—"and *then* asks for more food because she is still hungry."

"A soulmate!" says Dawkins. "I wonder if she's dating anyone?"

"According to the program book for the last eat-off, she should be turning eighty-seven this month," says Benny. "Any day now she should be a perfect mate for Dead End Dugan."

"Do not malign the woman I probably love!" snaps Dawkins.

"Anyway," says Benny, "the eat-off is slated for this Friday. Entries close Thursday at noon."

"And what does it cost to send our steed to the post?" I ask.

"Five hundred dollars," he answers.

"They're going to lose money on a lot of the entries," I say. Then: "What's first place worth?"

"Five thousand," answers Benny.

"Okay," I say, pulling another five C's out of my pocket, still thanks to Kid Testosterone, and lay them in Benny's hand. "Enter him, and see if we need to bring anything besides Dawkins."

He frowns. "Like what, Harry?"

I shrug. "A saddle cloth number, a feed bag, whatever."

"Okay, you got it," he says, saluting (without poking himself in the eye for a change) and walking out the door.

"You believe all this about a Miss Priscilla Nibbles?" asks Joey Chicago.

"I believe she exists and that she'll soon be eighty-seven," I answer. "But beyond that..." I shake my head. "It'd be more likely for Upset to beat Man o' War."

"Uh... Harry," said Short Odds MacDougal, who I would have sworn was dozing off at the bar, "Upset *did* beat Man O' War in the 1919 Sanford Stakes."

I feel I need a cutting reply, so I say "I said *more* likely, not *as* likely," and, my dignity salvaged, I start doing some serious thinking about the eat-off.

The one thing I can't do is book bets at Joey Chicago's. Anyone who's ever come by since I set up shop here a few years ago has seen what Dawkins can do to a dozen Big Macs and a gallon of root beer just to see him through until his next official meal. I'd have to make him a one-to-a-thousand favorite, and even then I can't imagine anyone betting on anyone else once they've seen him in action.

So I figure the thing to do is get a box at Madison Square Garden or wherever they're holding it, assume Miss Priscilla Nibbles has established not only a reputation but also a fan following over the decades, and hope that most of the money will be placed on her nose (or mouth, or stomach, or whatever), and that very few people will know Dawkins by sight, and he'll just look like any other massive meal on feet who is looking for more than five hundred dollars' worth of food before he collapses or falls asleep.

So when Joey returns, I sent him right back out to reserve a box for us. I decide not to bring Dugan along, because anyone who gets a good look at Dead End Dugan before he's used to it might pass out or run screaming in the opposite direction before he can lay his bet down on Miss Priscilla Nibbles.

Suddenly I feel a pudgy finger tapping at my shoulder. I look up and it is Dawkins.

"I do not wish you to think I am unappreciative of your confidence in me, or your willingness to come up with the entry fee, but if I don't get something to eat in about thirty seconds I will collapse due to malnourishment."

I think about it and nod my consent.

"Joey," I say, "give him a peanut."

"Just one?" demands Dawkins, with the kind of look on his

face that most people get when they're watching horror movies starring Boris and Bela and Basil and other people whose names begin with a B.

I stare at Dawkins for a moment, and decide that the eat-off is in the bag, and I relent.

"Okay," I tell Joey Chicago. "One peanut an hour."

I FIGURE AS long as there's serious money likely to be riding on the eat-off I could probably use some serious insurance, so I go to Big-Hearted Milton's office. Milton is my personal mage, and his office is in the men's room at Joey Chicago's.

I enter, and Milton is standing in the middle of a pentagram he's drawn on the tile floor, with a burning candle at each of the five points, mumbling a spell.

"Milton," I say, "we've got to talk."

He shakes his head, places a forefinger to his lips, and goes back to mumbling, louder and louder in some alien tongue, and after maybe a minute he screams, *"So shall it be!"*

Then he turned to me. "Sorry, Harry," he says. "But I couldn't stop in the middle of a spell."

"Let me guess," I say. "Mitzi McSweeney again?"

He nods and flashes me an evil grin. "Oh, this time it's a dandy one, Harry. We are at Pudgy Otto's for dinner last night, and she gets a drop of wine on her white blouse, and since I have a better view of it than she does, I reach over and start patting it dry."

"And she throws her food in your face," I say in bored tones, because this is a recurring story between Milton and Mitzi, and only the details change from week to week.

He nods his head. "And it was pork chops!" he growls. "No pork has passed my lips since I was bar mitzvahed! Well, hardly any." He rubs his hands together. "But I have hexed her good!" he chortles. "Wait'll the next time she gets a drop of anything on her blouse or skirt!"

"What terrible thing will happen then?" I ask, stifling a yawn.

"The garment will vanish, and she'll be sitting around her

kitchen half dressed! What do you think of that?"

"I think it is truly a terrible curse," I say. "On the other hand, doesn't she eat at Greasy Gus's on nights she doesn't dine with you?" I lower my tone and add confidentially, "I don't know about you, but I've *never* gotten out of there with a clean shirt."

His face contorts into a frown. "Why am I always the victim of my own brilliance?" he says, then mutters another spell. "Okay, the curse is lifted. She can drip all she wants." He pauses. "So what can I do for you?"

I explain the situation to him.

"So do you want her to fill up sooner, or do you want him to eat even more?" he asks.

"Yes," I say.

"You know," he adds, "I used to have a teacher named Miss Nibbles. Must have been, oh, fifty years ago." He shook his head. "Can't be the same one. She was no spring chicken then."

"Okay," I say. "Just as well you said it here."

He looks puzzled. "Said what?"

"Spring chicken," I reply. "Gently Gently is in the bar, and if he hears it there's no telling what he might do."

"Okay," says Milton. "What time Friday is the eat-off?"

"Dinnertime," I tell him. "Six o'clock. But we want to get to the Garden by one-thirty, so I can open up shop."

"Will there be anyone there?" he asks.

"It sold out two weeks ago. Benny had to bribe some friends to get our tickets."

"Sold out?" he repeats, surprised.

I nod my head. "The old lady has a hell of a fan following." I smile. "All the better for us when Dawkins eats her under the table."

"I wonder how that expression ever came into being?" muses Milton.

"Easy," I say. "Someone must have seen Dawkins on his hands and knees, looking for crumbs."

WE ARRIVE AT the Garden at one-thirty, and by three o'clock I have booked maybe seven thousand dollars' worth of bets, sixty-six hundred on Miss Priscilla Nibbles, three hundred on Three-Ton Tony from Brooklyn, and the other hundred spread around among longshots.

"And not a penny on Dawkins so far!" whispers Benny Fifth Street. "Are they crazy?"

I shake my head. "Just uninformed. But when he steps out into the arena that'll all change."

By five o'clock I have enough bets in that I can post a morning line, though it is actually a late afternoon line, or possibly an early evening line:

Miss Priscilla Nibbles	1-5
Slim Sandy	15-1
Three-Ton Tony	20-1
Hogpen Harvey	40-1
Pizza Pete	50-1
Really Big Fred	100-1
Maury the Mooch	400-1
Gently Gently Dawkins	500-1
Mealtime McGuire	750-1

More money comes in, and I have to knock the favorite down to 1-10, which means to win a dollar on her you have to bet ten.

"And Dawkins is five hundred to one," says Benny Fifth Street. "Isn't *anybody* betting on him?"

"So far just you and Milton and, of course, not with me," I answer. "Let's hope it stays that way. I don't feel like paying off five large for every sawbuck that's bet on him."

"At least Milton and I knew enough to bet on Dawkins with Quick Cash Quenton. But wait till the horses line up at the gate," says Benny, who is fresh out of metaphors. "People will take one look at him, and suddenly you'll be whelmed over with bets."

"Let us hope not," I say. "Miss Priscilla has the largest fan base,

I freely admit that—but Dawkins has the largest appetite. I expect him to finish lengths ahead of the field."

"As long as he doesn't throw a shoe and come up lame," says Benny. "And hell, even if he does, he'll be sitting down." He leans over and whispers confidentially: "He's so hungry he might start gnawing on a table leg before the starter sends them off."

"Won't make much difference," says Milton. "Hardly any calories in a table leg. It's good for his teeth, and he won't find it at all nourishing."

Comes a quarter to six, I expect the bugler to sound the call to the post, but there isn't any bugler. Instead there is a middle-aged lady sitting at a pipe organ, and as the sound fills the Garden the contestants come out from wherever they've been kept since we dropped Dawkins off about five hours earlier.

"We're saved!" whispers Benny Fifth Street excitedly.

"What do you mean?" I ask.

"Look!" he says as the contestants take their post positions. Well, their chairs. "Three of them are even bigger around the middle than Dawkins. If you don't know him, if you haven't seen him in action, you'll never pick him over Maury the Mooch or Really Big Fred."

I look, and he's got a point, but it's a point of logic, not experience. I had never seen those other two eat (knock wood!) but when Dawkins springs into action I expect him to leave the field far behind.

"And look at the favorite!" he continues. "It must be a ringer. Nobody who looks like that could have gone win, place, or show at this contest even once!"

I look, and sure enough Miss Priscilla Nibbles looks like a customer who walked in through the wrong door. In fact, she is dressed for an evening at the opera, or perhaps the ballet, not for an all-American sport like an eat-off. She is maybe an inch or two under five feet, her gray hair is piled atop her head, she wears thick glasses in a delicate golden frame, she's got a pearl necklace and a gold wristwatch which she can certainly afford after winning the eat-off six times but which don't seem streamlined enough for a contest that requires speed as well as capacity. And finally, she can't weigh as much as Dawkins can eat when he gets up a head of steam.

The crowd gives her a standing ovation, and she smiles, waves to them, and finally sits down at the table.

"Ladies and gents," says the announcer, who is wearing a turtleneck sweater beneath his tuxedo, "are you ready for action?" The crowd screams its assent, and I realize that the guy with the mike is Horatio Bridge, who calls all the wrestling matches and was obviously hired to lend a little class to the eat-off.

The crowd assures him it is ready.

"Okay, then, let's introduce the combatants one-by-one," says Horatio. "Please stand up when I call your name."

He calls off their names, but only Miss Patricia Nibbles is able to get up out of her chair with ease, or at least without capsizing the table. The roars for the favorite are deafening, and Horatio lets them scream for a whole five minutes before he shouts for silence into his microphone.

I notice that Milton is paying no attention to the contestants, but instead is scanning the ringsiders, so I ask him what he is looking for.

"Anyone who looks out of place," says Milton. "Remember—you stand to lose a bundle if the favorite wins."

It is a telling argument and I resolve not to bother him again, but mere seconds later he utters a mighty "Aha!" and, of course, I have to ask him what brought forth such an exclamation.

"Sitting right across the arena from us, third row center," he says, and I look, and sure enough Morris the Mage is sitting there.

"So, is he working for Miss Priscilla, or one of the other entrants?" I ask.

"I'm not sure yet," answers Milton, and then gives vent to a second "Aha!"

"What now?" I ask.

"Tenth row, maybe thirty seats to the left of Morris," answers Milton.

I look, and it is Spellsinger Solly.

"You wouldn't think there's enough money to draw so many mages," says Benny.

"You're just considering the prize money," I say, "which is as nothing if you're putting it all on yourself at forty or fifty to one." I turn to Milton. "Just keep it fair. You don't have to help Dawkins, who never needs help to consume entire barnyard animals; just don't let any of the others cheat."

"I'm onto it already," Milton assures me, in between mumbling chants in indecipherable ancient mystic languages, or maybe French.

"For the first course," announces Horatio Bridge, "salted chimeras!"

The waiters, most of whom I recognize from Friday Night Rasslin', bring out the plates, sweating under their burden, and all the contestants dig in. When the last of them finishes, they are given a thirty-second break to renew their appetites, and then the waiters bring out a large pile of *something*.

"What the hell is *that?*" I ask.

"Chopped dragon," answers Milton. "It's like chopped liver, only different."

"We're in luck!" exclaims Benny. "Dawkins *loves* chopped dragon."

Indeed, Dawkins digs in like there's no tomorrow, and so do most of the others, except for Miss Priscilla Nibbles, who is daintily eating her chopped dragon like it is the rarest delicacy in the world (which, for all I know, it may well be), but I also notice that when all the others except Dawkins have stopped gobbling down their dragon liver, Miss Priscilla is still consuming forkful after forkful with small, ladylike bites. By the time they reach the bottom of the bowl, which probably held thirty pounds to begin with, only she and Dawkins are still eating.

"Does anyone concede yet?" asks Horatio Bridge, but no one does.

The next course is a huge bowlful of Abaddon's Locusts covered with jalapeno jelly. Just as I am wondering how many locusts are in the bowl, Horatio announces that there are a thousand, which he explains–for those who learned their math in the New York public school system—comes to one hundred locusts for each contestant.

Except it does not come to one hundred apiece, because Mealtime McGuire has collapsed and fallen to the floor, and Slim Sandy says "I cannot eat these!"

"You refuse to eat Abaddon's Locusts?" demands Horatio.

"I have no problem with the locusts," Slim Sandy answers, "but I am allergic to jalapeno."

Horatio walks over to where the track stewards, four men in tuxes and three women dressed almost as well as Miss Priscilla, hold a quick conference, and then he speaks into the mike again and announces that Slim Sandy and Mealtime McGuire are both disqualified, though for different reasons. The wrestlers drag McGuire's body off to the dressing room, and come back to do the same to Slim Sandy, but he eludes them and actually outruns them to the nearest exit.

The next course is leviathan, basted in gargoyle blood, and Hogpen Harvey, Maury the Mooch, Pizza Pete, and Really Big Fred all concede defeat before the course is finished, Really Big Fred by announcing he isn't hungry anymore and the other three by sliding or falling to the floor with a minimum of grace.

"Hot damn!" exalts Benny Fifth Street. "Only Three-Ton Tony to go and we've won!"

"What about the defending champion?" I ask.

"She's already eaten more than half her body weight, and they're just getting to the main course," he says, "How much longer can she last, a petite little old lady like that?"

"They probably asked that the last six times," I mutter.

"The next course," announces Horatio, "is broiled behemoth basted with creamed innards of tree-dwelling wooly mammoth."

The waiters lug out the next course. Three-Ton Tony takes one good look at it, sniffs at it twice, and then gets to his feet.

"I concede," he announces. He looks at his wristwatch. "Thanks for the meal. If I hurry, I can just make Bubbles La Tour's Dance of Sublime Surrender at the Rialto."

He heads for an exit, and about half the men in the audience, after checking their own timepieces, follow him out.

So now it is just down to Miss Priscilla and Dawkins. They each dig in, and I look for a sign that either of them is slowing down, but the food is vanishing before our very eyes, and after another ten minutes the last of it is gone.

"Let's give the remaining players—well, contestants—a hand!" says Horatio. "There will now be a five-minute break before the first of the dessert courses."

I wander down to ringside to see how Dawkins is doing.

"Hi, Harry," he says, but without his usual sparkle.

"Hi, Dawkins," I say. "How are you holding up?"

"I don't know if I can make it through one more course," he admits very softly, so that only I can hear him.

"But you jammed that behemoth into your mouth like you were starving!" I say.

"That was to fool my stomach into thinking it hadn't already eaten forty or fifty pounds of beautifully-prepared delicacies." He looks like he is on the verge of tears. "I hate to let you down, Harry."

"All you can do is your best," I say, and add mentally *Until I get Milton to cast a spell to help you.*

I return to my seat and whisper the situation to Milton, who listens and nods sagely.

"Can you do anything to help him?" I conclude.

"Let me give it a shot," he says, and starts mumbling in incomprehensible languages again. In half a minute he stops and turns to me. "Okay, he's got five minutes of voracious appetite left."

"Only five?" I ask.

"Harry, the man's eaten the equivalent of a small automobile."

"Okay, how about Miss Priscilla. Can you magic her appetite away?"

"I can but try," he says with false modesty. A few seconds later he is muttering in English, and they are not words I can repeat in a story which might be read by any youngsters under the age of forty-five.

"What is it?" I ask.

"She's protected."

"So?" I say. "You've broken through Morris the Mage's spells before."

He shakes his head. "This isn't Morris's. This is a lot more powerful, and has been building for thirty-six years."

I am about to say something else, but Horatio starts speaking into the microphone again.

"Ladies and gents!" he hollers. "The dishwashers are working overtime, but they're still having trouble cleaning the creamed wooly mammoth innards off the plates, so our first few desserts are going to be finger foods until the state inspector assures us that the contestants can't catch more than two or three hideous diseases from the plates and silverware." He pauses, waiting for the applause that trickles in.

"If you're going to do something," I tell Milton, "you'd better do it quick!"

"Normal spells aren't working," he says. "I think I'd better come at this from the other side."

"The other side of what?" I demand.

"There's no sense trying to magic away her appetite," he says. "Like I told you, it's protected."

"So give Dawkins an even bigger appetite," I say.

"He'll burst right in front of everyone," answers Milton. "No, I think the only way to approach this is from the left side."

I am about to ask: the left side of *what*—but Horatio interrupts me.

"For our first dessert course," he continues after a moment, "we present miniature éclairs. Our judges have examined them, and not one of these baby éclairs is more than an inch and one-half in length."

The waiters bring out a huge bowl filled with maybe 500 little eclairs.

"We're washing *all* the plates, just to be on the safe side, so we urge you to sit next to each other since we have only the one bowl." Dawkins tries to get up and finds that he can't budge. Miss Priscilla thoughtfully gets up, carries her chair with her, and sets it down right next to Dawkins. "And now, since we're capturing this on video for re-runs all over the country, I ask the two finalists to shake hands and come out eating!"

They shake, and then each is grabbing handfuls of baby eclairs and stuffing them into their mouths. But an expert eye—and I have one on each side of my face—could tell that Dawkins is slowing down, that he isn't grabbing éclairs as fast as his opponent is. I am totaling up all the bets I'd have to pay off on her, and subtracting the five large that we weren't going to win, and deciding that I wish I'd never heard of the damned contest when suddenly we were deafened by an agonized scream—and when I looked around the arena, I realize that the scream has come from Dawkins, who has wrapped his left hand in a bloody napkin.

"Time out!" cries Horatio, and then "Medic!"

A doctor comes out from behind the grandstand. "I was watching the ballgame," he says. "What seems to be the problem?"

Dawkins waves his hand and bloody napkin at the doctor.

"She bit off half my index finger!" he whines.

Miss Priscilla Nibbles frowns. "I *knew* one of those éclairs didn't taste quite right."

"I suppose we could pump your stomach and get it back if it's not digested yet," says the doctor.

"No!" yells Dawkins. "I don't want anything that's been *there*"— he points to her stomach, realizes he has nothing to point with, and uses his other hand—"attached to me!"

I can see Morris the Mage and Spellsinger Solly and the others glaring at Milton, who smiles triumphantly. "It'll be our secret, okay?"

I agree, of course, and turn my attention back to the proceedings.

Well, the judges put their heads together for maybe a minute, and the upshot is that Miss Priscilla Nibbles has been disqualified and placed second, and that Gently Gently Dawkins, who goes to the post as a 453-to-1 outsider, is awarded first prize in the seventh running Great Manhattan Eat-Off.

We wait for the medics to stop the bleeding and bandage what's left of his finger, and then we all return to Joey Chicago's to celebrate.

"So you're the defending champion now!" says Longshot Lamont. "They're gonna be training for the next five years to dethrone you."

"Not me," says Dawkins. "I retire undefeated."

"What kind of talk is that?" says Lamont.

Dawkins holds up his bandaged hand. "I only got one forefinger left. I might want to point it at something sometime."

"So who else can we enter?" asked Benny.

I look around the tavern, and in its farthest, darkest corner I see a lone figure staring off into space.

"Maybe we'll run Dead End Dugan," I say. "After all, look at all the bullet holes in his chest. I'm thinking that he won't care if they eat three or four of his fingers."

"You know," says Benny, "that just might work."

"Hey, Dugan!" I holler.

"Yes, Harry?"

"What's your favorite food?"

"You mean, back when I used to eat?" he asks.

"We'll work on that," I mutter.

I go back to the conversation at the bar, which mostly concerns whether he should remain Gently Gently Dawkins or change his name to Nine-Finger Dawkins to celebrate the first thing he has ever won.

Mike Resnick

Mike Resnick is, according to Locus, the all-time leading award winner, living or dead, for short science fiction. He is the winner of 5 Hugos (from a record 37 nominations), plus other major awards in the USA, France, Poland, Croatia, Catalonia, Spain, and China. Mike is the author of 76 novels, 10 books of non-fiction, and 3 screenplays, plus 284 short stories. He is also the editor of *Galaxy's Edge* magazine, and was Guest of Honor at the 2012 Worldcon.

AN EVIL OPPORTUNITY EMPLOYER

Lawrence Watt-Evans

Read the contract. I tell everyone that—*everyone*. You know how many people actually do it?

Okay, I don't know either, but it isn't enough of them, I can tell you that. I swear half my business and ninety percent of my losses come from people who didn't do it. I don't suppose I should complain, since that's also at least half my income, but I get so fed up with clients who have no idea what they've signed that I just want to punch someone, even if I have to do it in my civilian identity.

Yeah, I admit it, I'm one of those dual-identity vigilantes—I hesitate to say "superheroes," because quite aside from any trademark issues, it sounds so boastful. It's not for me to say whether I'm a hero, let alone "super." I'm not going to tell you my *nom d'aventure*, but you'd probably recognize it; I'm not one of the really big names, not one of the aliens or demigods or anything, but I have certain special abilities and I've earned a few headlines.

What I *haven't* earned from crime-fighting is a living, so I have a day job as a contracts attorney.

And I know what you're thinking—contracts? Not criminal law? Yes, contracts, because unlike *some* attorneys I could name, I understand the concept of conflict of interest. I also understand how difficult it is to keep from being recognized in court by someone with whom you've just had an epic two-hour brawl. Masks can slip and tear, and people *do* recognize voices and body language.

Most thieves and thugs don't sign any contracts before robbing a bank or taking a busload of commuters hostage, though, so I can put my law degree to use without worrying about constantly confronting people from my other work.

But there are exceptions, and I'm here to tell you about one of them.

This big guy with a battered old briefcase walked in wanting advice on whether he should sue his employer. Nothing out of the ordinary there. I was nodding and getting some papers ready and only half-listening at first, because I get these all the time. He'd been asked to do stuff he thought was outside his job description and pretty clearly illegal, and he had agreed because his boss has a mean streak, but now he was having second thoughts, and he wanted to know what I thought he should do.

But then I asked who he worked for, and he answered, and I sat up straight and stared at him.

"Say that again," I told him.

"I work for Dr. Catastrophe," he repeated.

"Dr. *Alice* Catastrophe?" I asked, just to be sure, because yes, Catastrophe is an unusual name, but you never know.

"Yeah. The Doctor of Disaster. Her."

I sucked in my lips and considered this. I don't really like to call people "supervillains" any more than I like to call myself a superhero, but I have to admit the term fits Dr. Catastrophe better than any other description I can think of. I'd never gone up against her myself, at least not directly, but several people I knew had, and they all spoke of her with respect. I had the impression that if they weren't all professionally fearless, they'd speak of her with abject terror.

The guy—I'll call him John Doe—had my full attention now. The possibility of getting a lead on Dr. Catastrophe's current whereabouts definitely caught my interest, not so much as a lawyer as for my other line of work. "Tell me more," I said. "What exactly is it you do for Dr. Catastrophe?"

"I'm a henchman."

"What kind?"

"Non-specific."

"So you're not a lawyer or engineer or scientist or lab assistant or experimental subject?"

"No. I'm just a henchman. I run errands, operate equipment, do some security work, some light construction and maintenance, occasionally chauffeur the boss or her friends around."

"And you think she's asking you to do something outside your duties?"

He nodded.

I drummed my fingers on my desk. I knew something about the hireling business, albeit only from the outside, so I had a pretty good idea what henchmen and minions and serfs and underlings and the other categories did, but the exact lines were often vague. "Mr. Doe," I said, "I don't quite see how that's possible; are your duties *defined* anywhere?"

"Yes, they are," he said, lifting his briefcase onto my desk. "I'll show you."

I had a moment of alarm there, thinking that maybe this was all a setup of some kind and he had one of Dr. Catastrophe's diabolical devices in there, that someone had found out about my other identity and decided to take me out, but then he flopped a sheaf of ordinary paper from the case onto my desk. He shoved it toward me.

"That's my employment contract," he said.

I just stared at it for a moment, then pulled it over and began reading.

It was indeed an employment contract, but not quite like any I had ever seen before. Parts of it were standard modern boilerplate, but other parts were strangely archaic, even more so than ordinary legalese, such as a clause giving the party of the first part—that is, Dr. Catastrophe— "full power under such circumstances to do with the party of the second part at her pleasure, be it either body, flesh, blood, or goods."

It also defined half a dozen different jobs, including henchman, but when I got to the signature page I noticed something odd.

"So all of Dr. Catastrophe's people sign this?" I asked.

"That's right. Apparently she's had some problems in the past with her employees double-crossing her, so she had this drawn up."

I knew something about *that*—Dr. Catastrophe spent eight years in prison after some of my crime-fighting compatriots convinced several of her flunkies to turn on her. Two full pages of this contract had been written specifically to prevent a recurrence, providing elaborate but carefully legal-sounding penalties for disobedience or betrayal. I had doubts about whether these provisions would hold up in court, given the various whistle-blower laws—in fact, since her entire operation was probably a criminal enterprise the whole contract should be unenforceable—but they certainly *looked* good enough to deter most hirelings.

But that wasn't what I had been looking at. I turned the contract back around to show him the signature page. "This is you?" I said. "You signed this?"

"Yeah, that's me. I'm not claiming I didn't sign, but paragraph 36..."

I interrupted him, still holding it open to the signature page. "Paragraph 36 doesn't apply," I said. "Look here." I pointed to a list at the top of the page where one box was checked, and only one.

"What did... I don't..."

"You aren't a henchman," I said. "You're a minion. It says so right there."

He leaned back, shocked. "But I applied to be a henchman!"

"Doesn't matter. What matters is what you signed, and it says right there that your employment category is entirely at the discretion of your employer, and cannot be changed once the contract is signed. You're a minion."

"The doctor *said* I was her henchman!"

I shook my head again. Hirelings are always surprised when

they find out their bosses have lied to them. *I* used to be surprised when they were; what do they *expect* from criminal masterminds? But I'd gotten used to it. "Doesn't matter," I said again. I flipped pages. "Paragraph 83—the party of the first part shall have full authority to lie to the party of the second part, to mislead, deceive, or defraud in service of her goals and purposes. She can call you anything she wants, but the *contract* says you're a minion."

He glared at the contract, his face going red. After a moment he said, "So how does that change things?"

"Well, the rules are different for minions; I'm sure you know that. Minions swear total obedience—to fetch and carry, to serve without question. See Paragraph 38? You're required to obey any order she gives you, no matter how stupid, if it doesn't directly endanger your life—or if you're in her presence, even if it *does* directly endanger your life. Henchmen get more latitude on what orders to obey, and how much they can argue. But there's a trade-off there—see Paragraph 44, reasons for termination and methods of termination? She can't just shoot you if she's angry, the way she can a henchman. Henchmen are responsible for their screw-ups, and minions aren't, because henchmen are assumed to be using their judgment and minions are supposed to be mindlessly obedient."

"So she thinks I'm a moron."

I managed to resist pointing out that he *had* signed the contract without noticing the big black check-mark in the "Minion" box at the top of the page, which did not speak well of his intelligence. Instead I tried to be conciliatory. "She may not have had any henchman openings left. It's hard to find good minions."

"So does this affect my case?"

"I'm afraid it pretty much *destroys* your case," I said. "Paragraph 38. *Nothing* she tells you to do is outside your job description. As for it being illegal, come on, Mr. Doe—you're working for Dr. Catastrophe! *Everything* she does is illegal, pretty much."

"So I really need to go steal all those kittens?"

I did a double-take. "Kittens?"

"Yeah. She wants... well, never mind." He picked up the contract and dropped it back in his briefcase.

"Kittens?" I said again.

I admit it, I have a soft spot for kittens. My two cats at home, Bruiser and Caliban, are both grown and both fixed, but... kittens. I love kittens.

If Dr. Catastrophe was going to do something horrible to kittens, I had to stop her.

"Hang on," I said, getting out of my chair and crossing to my reference shelves. "I'm pretty sure there's a precedent on this. Uh... do you know what Dr. Catastrophe *wants* with the kittens?"

"No."

"How many kittens are we talking about?"

"She said she needed at least forty, and fifty would give her a margin, just in case. She assigned three of us to fetch them."

"I think there's a precedent about minions and cute furry things. I'll need to look that up." I began scanning the shelves for the volume I wanted. "By the way," I said, as casually as I could, "did you notice that henchmen who try to leave can be hunted down and killed—it says 'terminated,' but we both know what that means—for their disloyalty? But minions who desert are ignored. The contract assumes they don't know enough to be dangerous."

He looked puzzled for a second, then realized what I was saying. "Wait—so I could just walk away?"

I nodded. "You'd be out of work, of course."

"But I wouldn't need to steal any kittens."

"That's right."

I could see he was thinking that over as I found the book I wanted and carried it to the desk.

"I think I'll do that," he said. "Thanks for the advice."

I waved it away. "It's nothing," I said.

"No, I appreciate it. Thanks. I guess you won't be representing me, but I've taken up your time, so what do I owe you for the consult?"

"Nothing. Really. I haven't accepted you as a client, and I'm not going to. I won't accept a cent from you."

"What? Why not?" He frowned. "Because I'm just a minion?"

"No," I said, as I flipped pages without looking at him. "Because if you're my client, this whole conversation would be privileged communication, and I couldn't tell anyone about it without your permission. If you're *not* my client, then we're just a couple of guys chatting, and if I mention any of this to anyone I'm not breaching confidentiality, which would be an ethics violation, I'm just making conversation."

"I don't see... oh." He lost a little color. "Maybe I do."

"Mr. Doe, have a good day—and I really think you're making the right decision not going back."

Then he picked up his briefcase and hurried out, and I put the book back on the shelf. I never did find that precedent. Maybe cute furry animals don't actually have any special legal protections.

But I took the rest of the afternoon off, and made a few calls, and that night a coalition of costumed vigilantes used their superhuman abilities to track the sound of mewing kittens to Dr. Catastrophe's lair, and to put her back behind bars.

Lawrence Watt-Evans

Lawrence Watt-Evans has been a full-time writer for almost forty years, with fifty novels and well over a hundred short stories to his credit, mostly fantasy, science fiction, and horror. He's best known for the Hugo-winning short story "How I Left Harry's All-Night Hamburgers," the Obsidian Chronicles trilogy, and the ongoing Legends of Ethshar fantasy series. He has been reading superhero comic books since 1959, and lives in Takoma Park, Maryland, just outside Washington DC.

COMMON SCENTS

JODY LYNN NYE

U ncontrollable, high-pitched laughter issued from the platinum bangle around Homicide Detective Sergeant Dena Malone's wrist.

"That smell tickles, Malone!" Dr. K't'ank cried. The Salosian, an alien symbiote who lived in her belly, smacked her in the kidneys with his thin tail.

"Ow!" Dena snapped out. "Knock it off."

"What the frak?" Sergeant Ramos, her sardonic, muscular partner, raised his bushy black eyebrows at her as the two of them edged forward through the crowd around the yellow ropes. News camera drones hovered overhead. Two of them came to hover just out of reach of the pair of detectives. Another came by at a ninety degree angle to get a good shot of Dena in her ornate floatchair. The distinctive hovering seats were still a curiosity in the megalopolis, as they were only used by Salosian hosts, humans who had allowed the visiting aliens to be implanted in their peritoneums. On its small forward-facing screen, Dena caught a glimpse of herself and frowned. The camera caught her oval face and laser-cut brown hair in a flattering angle, but it made her pregnant belly look like a hovering blimp.

"Yeah," Dena said dryly. "As if he couldn't get more annoying, he's discovered that when I'm exposed to strong odors with active esters and volatile compounds, especially ones that provoke a histamine response, he gets some kind of physical sensation. I went into a department store to buy some things for the baby's nursery, and all those android clerks swooping down on me with the perfume samples made him high as a satellite. I suppose it's a kind of defense mechanism against poisons in his native marine environment, but it's really just a pain in the neck. I'm hoping that it is very temporary."

"You don't pick up on odors yourself, K't'ank?" Ramos asked, with a gleam starting in his eye.

"No!" the Salosian said. "I have no nose."

"Then how do you smell?"

"Terrible," Dena said, dryly.

"How do you know how I smell... ? Oh, I see how you set that up!" K't'ank burst into another gleeful outburst, whacking her internal organs even more. "Ramos, I have much to learn from your turns of phrase!"

"We ought to go on the road together," the detective said, strutting. "I could use a straight man who always laughs at my jokes."

"No, thanks," Dena said, raising a dismissive palm. "I'm not getting into the middle of a comedy double act." She peered ahead, but the crowd blocked her view. She drew her skinnypad out of its holster. "Conscript newscams," she ordered it. "Combined view." Above its screen, a three-dimensional view of the crime scene formed. She saw the body in the middle of the cordon.

"Wow," Ramos said, peering over her shoulder. "The coroner could declare that one from across town."

"I hope it's not as bad as it looks," Dena said. Her gut roiled, making K't'ank laugh uproariously at the roller-coaster spasm. For a scientist, he had a low amusement threshold. "Shut up."

She used her badge and the front edge of her hovering floatchair to push through the mob crowding the auto-barriers. Facial recognition software in the smart-bollards holding up the taut yellow tape scanned her and Ramos and let them into the roped-off area.

Three meters from the body, a sharp odor struck Dena's nose and eyes with the force of a tennis backhand. She leaned back in her chair.

"What's that stench?" she demanded.

"The decedent," Officer Nelso Havacek said. "The guy reeks. He must put aftershave on with a fire hose." He wore a white scent-block tape over his nose, the kind used by medical examiners. He held out a fistful of the straps. Dena grabbed one and put it on.

"Whew!" Ramos said, fastening his in place. "He smells worse than he looks!"

"It reminds me of my grandfather's cologne," Dena said. "Eye-watering." The strip's filters removed every trace of odor from the air, like muting the volume on loudspeakers. She took a grateful breath.

"Whee!" K't'ank yodeled. "Do not block your nasal sensors, Malone! This aroma is deeply pleasurable!"

"He's high," Dena said. She took off the host bracelet and stuffed it into her pocket. "Let's get a closer look at the body, all right?"

The late Dr. Carlson Nagy had not gone to his maker without a major fight. He stood, or lay, over two meters in height, burly build, hardly any of it fat. Blood from a forehead wound still seeped into the staring eyes and down his deeply bronzed cheeks and into his mass of tiny black braids splayed over the pavement. Something about the indentations at the corners of the full, almost carmine-colored lips suggested a cruel but sensual smile. Dena shook her head to clear her imagination. The clothes had to have cost thousands of credits, especially that dark blue shirt, whose silky sheen shouted money. It would never be worn again, even if it hadn't become an exhibit at a crime scene, not with the collar stained by the gore from the torn throat and the seeping gashes in the front and sides of the body.

"Did someone mistake this guy for a steak that needed tender-izing?" Ramos asked.

Peals of laughter erupted from Dena's pocket.

"Ramos, you are so funny!"

The cop on duty gave her a sideways glance. She met his eyes with a blank stare. He went back to business.

"You'll have to ask him, but I don't think it'll do any good."

"You have the perp?" Dena asked. "I'd have thought the guy would be halfway to Florida by now."

For answer, the police officer pointed to a hovering patrol car. Three officers had a man plastered up against the side of the vehicle with his hands cuffed behind his back. He stood a meager hundred seventy centimeters, with a slight build, a sallow face, and a haircut that must have been done by a bad robo-barber.

"He doesn't look like someone who could take on a grizzly bear like this one."

"People are weird," Ramos said.

"She looks too weak to have committed such a crime," K't'ank said. His optic nerves were tied into Dena's through her spinal column, so he saw everything she did.

"So, you're back with us again?" she asked, fishing the heavy bangle out and snapping it back on her wrist. "I should wear these nose strips all the time. And that's a man, not a woman."

"Please do not deprive me of intriguing stimulation," K't'ank said, almost plaintively. "Derabyi and my other previous hosts seemed to occupy such dull environments compared with yours."

"I'll take it into consideration," Dena said, steering her floatchair toward the attacker. The guy seemed to be doing deep breathing exercises. She brandished the skinnypad at him. "All right, sir, let's start with your name."

Marlon Canavireiro couldn't have been more apologetic and helpful.

"I don't know why I did that," he said, his black eyes full of rue.

"Your rap sheet says otherwise," Ramos said. "Five felonious assaults, one attempted manslaughter, and a major assortment of bar brawls all of which you started. I've just accessed some of the recordings. You throw a mean roundhouse, friend."

"But those are in the past," Canavireiro pleaded. "I've been in anger management therapy for ages. I'm learning to deal." He stopped and closed his eyes. He drew in a lengthy breath, and expelled it through his mouth. After five inhalations, he opened his eyes again. "I'm calm. I'm calm."

"A form of self-hypnosis?" K't'ank asked, curiously.

"I guess," the man said, looking around for the source of the voice. Dena held up her bracelet.

"Salosian," she said shortly. "We'll have to verify it with your therapist."

"Sure, whatever you need! I've got her contact info in my communicator. Oh, wait." He looked helplessly at the police officer who had him cuffed. The tall woman handed over the electronic device. Dena downloaded the entry Canavireiro brought up with voice commands: Dr. Prika Sunnet.

"Did you know the victim?" she asked.

Canavireiro glanced toward the body, now covered with a sheet, and shuddered. "Yeah. I sure do. The son of a bitch assaulted me when I was a kid. I went to him because I was having trouble at home. He tried to take advantage of me. Frequently."

Ramos ran down the victim's file on his skinnypad. "There's no record of a conviction."

More breathing. "Administrative hearing at the school. He never went in front of a justice machine. He got off. I had to get on with my life. I don't like it, but I can't let it rule me. Whenever I saw him on the street, I crossed to the other side as fast as I could."

"So what made you snap?"

The slender man glanced over her head toward the covered body. "I really don't know," he said. "I don't even remember. One second I was on a walkway near him. I started up a meditation recording and doing deep breathing to keep me even, but the next moment I was smashing his head against a railing. I'm really sorry. He had it coming, but I didn't mean to do it."

The arresting officers bundled the perp into a van and took off, blue lights spinning, toward the precinct. Canavireiro didn't struggle. He thanked the female officer for helping him into his seat.

"For someone who looks that lobotomized, he did a thorough job of messing up the victim," Ramos said, as they headed for the aircar.

"They stare at us, Malone," K't'ank said. Dena realized that the passersby were giving them weirder looks than usual.

"The strips!" Ramos said, with a laugh. The two detectives removed them in unison. The first breath of fresh New-York-Newark air made her gag. K't'ank laughed gleefully.

"Most interesting response!" he crowed.

Dena made a face. "Modern life stinks, you know that?"

"Life always did," Ramos said. "You think living with open sewers and slaughtering farm animals in the street was any better?"

Dr. Prika Sunnet tented her narrow, delicately-manicured hands on her desk.

"Of course you understand that I cannot violate doctor-client privilege," she said. Just by appearance alone, Dena knew the therapist would be good at her job. Her attractive, oval face just seemed to invite confidences, as did the warm, lavender-scented air of the cozy, wood-trimmed office.

"Warrant's right here," Ramos said, extending his skinnypad toward her. The court document had been instantly granted by an adjudication computer once the waiver from the patient had been recorded. The text shared itself immediately on the terminal beside the doctor's right hand.

Dr. Sunnet read it through twice, then turned her calm gaze back toward the detectives.

"Very well. What do you need to know?"

"Would you say that Mr. Canavireiro was capable of murder?"

"Oh, yes," the analyst said, pleasantly. "I'd say he had a natural capacity for it. Almost a gift."

Dena blinked.

"Say what?"

Sunnet lapsed into lecturer mode. "Mr. Canavireiro has a fierce temper, excellent reflexes, really superior strength for his size, and a tendency to ignore pain. If you were going to design a living creature as a killer, he ticks all your boxes."

K't'ank giggled. Dena ignored him. Something in the air must have set him off again.

"So, why isn't the guy in jail?"

"Such murderous tendencies are treated with many techniques," Sunnet continued. "Cognitive behavioral therapy, light

stimulation, group discussions and individual sessions, aromatherapy, meditation with candles, massage, hypnotherapy, even
regular cuddle-puddles. I monitor all my patients frequently to
ensure that none of their trigger points is being ignored."

"And all this helps?" Dena asked. She knew she was unable to
keep her skepticism off her face.

In exchange, Dr. Sunnet gave her a patient look. "Detective,
Mr. Canavireiro used to get into brawls on the average of once a
night. With time and a lot of work, he is now at a point where he
recognizes the stimuli that pushed him over the edge into action.
He hasn't had a single episode in months."

"Are you sure he wasn't just saving it all up for one big blow-
out?" Ramos asked.

The psychotherapist's finger-steeple collapsed, and she fumbled
to put it back together. "No, no. Such a thing is outside the realm
of possibility."

"Then a provocation of some kind?" K't'ank asked. "Humans are
so suggestible. Almost anything seems to set them off."

"Thanks a bunch," Dena said, dryly. "But he makes a good point,
doctor. What about direct provocation from the victim? He said
that he knew the man, in fact had been a victim of his in the past."

"We discussed Dr. Nagy often," Dr. Sunnet said. "He was a...
difficult individual. I conferred with him over his contact with
Mr. Canavireiro. He... denied any personal interaction."

"Uh-huh," Ramos said. "Well, we'll need to go over Mr.
Canavireiro's personal files."

"I don't like this," Dr. Sunnet said, "but very well. My records-
office droid will assist you."

"Ambassador P'n'ira!" K't'ank's voice came from the bangle,
sounding blithe and expansive. "And a pleasure to speak with you,
as well. I enjoyed conferring with you when our two domiciles
had lunch three days ago..."

"Crap," Dena said, scrolling through the charts on the data
storage unit. The alleged killer's therapy record was almost as
impressive as his rap sheet. "He's drunk-dialing again."

"He do this often?" Ramos said. The office droid, a standard model tinted a warm orange, bustled around them, providing them with herbal coffee and small pastries as well as bringing up the appropriate files.

"More lately," Dena said. She tasted the beverage and put it down again. It tasted like potpourri; obviously something soothing for the patients. "I think the increase in pregnancy hormones in my system sensitize him to outward influences. Like he needed more stimulus."

"Huh." Ramos handed her his skinnypad. "I went over Canavireiro's rap sheet more closely. Our perp was telling the truth. They did investigate the alleged assault by the victim, but it was thrown out of court."

"Why?"

Ramos raised his eyebrows at her. "Another guy with anger management problems. The investigating officer."

"SURE, I REMEMBER Dr. Nagy," retired police lieutenant Needham Parker said, pouring them decaf from an old-fashioned percolator. A big-boned, dark-skinned man with gray fuzz clinging to his bald scalp in a ring just above his ears, he moved with the ease of an athlete. His little house was part of a scattered development surrounded by trees. Dena felt uneasy with all the greenery out there, as if it might spread inside at any moment and suffocate her. Parker's security guard harness hung from a wooden peg next to the modest front door. "My last case. All those little kids who were afraid to come forward. The SOB was so smug. Should have been a red flag that no security cameras were operational in his office. He said it was because of patient-client confidentiality." His brows drew down over his blunt nose. "It became a case of 'he said, he said.' The prosecutor didn't have much but the boy's testimony to go on. And when the SOB came outside at the lunch break, I didn't have to see him, I could smell him. I just turned around and let him have it. They yanked me off him. The adjudication machine said it had no choice but to dismiss the charges. The chief was sorry, but he said he had to can me. I'd have done it again, too."

All the way back from upstate New York, K't'ank kept up a running commentary on the local odors and aromas, but Dena kept going over the testimony from witnesses and the therapist's files. "It's starting to look like Canavireiro just snapped," Dena said.

"Go back to that one, Malone!" K't'ank shouted, when their self-flying aircar cleared a cloud of sharp-smelling chemicals coming out of a smokestack far below. "It makes me feel powerful!"

"Why isn't something like that stink outlawed?" Dena said, choking. She dabbed her running eyes with the edge of her sleeve. "Isn't that kind of pollution a health hazard?"

"Says here it's organic," Ramos said. "Volatile, but not harmful. That's not the only thing around here that stinks. Canavireiro didn't get the justice he deserved. I get what Parker said. You could smell Nagy coming. That aftershave of his would have provoked me into an assault, too. That was one awful aroma."

"Think the same thing happened to Canavireiro?" Dena asked. "The cologne just made him lose his mind? We ought to try it out. If it was a simple trigger, the guy could plead temporary insanity."

"We ought to make sure it wasn't something that simple," Ramos said. "The prosecutor would have our asses in a sling."

K't'ank giggled.

"Another ass joke!"

Dena made a face, but Ramos smirked. "My legend lives on."

THE MEDICAL EXAMINER'S computer system spat out the name of the aftershave: Caribbean Hurricane. After a lot of innuendo and snickering, the desk sergeant ordered a bottle for immediate delivery from the local department store. When the drone dropped the package in the precinct break room, Dena pried it open. The green bottle inside was in the shape of a leaning palm tree.

"Could that look more phallic?" she asked. Ramos leered at her suggestively. The rest of the cops in the squad room laughed. With an exasperated look, she twisted the top fiercely to the left as if snapping it off.

"Holy crap," her partner said, clutching his heart. "I feel sorry for your husband."

"Wooonderfulllll!" K't'ank warbled, as the powerful scent rose from the open bottle. "So exciting! How could any human not love this sensation?"

"Keep the editorial comments to yourself," she warned the Salosian. "We have to get an honest response from our suspect."

They poured a quarter of the cologne onto a towel on a tray and burst into the interview room, hoping to elicit a violent reaction. Canavireiro, handcuffed to the metal table, just shook his head, then closed his eyes and began his deep breathing exercises.

"Could you just get that out of here?" he said, in a sad little voice. "I smelled too much of that when I was a kid."

"Yes. Sorry," Dena said. She backed her chair out, and dumped the towel with its noxious liquid into the nearest disposer. To her infinite relief and K't'ank's disappointment, the odor was swallowed up immediately "That wasn't what we expected. I guess he just spontaneously flipped out. He can plead diminished responsibility."

"No," Ramos agreed. "Otherwise, you figure that any time he smelled that aftershave, he would have attacked anyone wearing it."

"Not everyone," K't'ank spoke up. "Your smell is not only the perfumes you apply. I can tell from Malone's internal reactions when someone she knows enters the room. You, Captain Potopos, Neal Malone. Her system tells me who they are before she sees them."

"Is that so?" Ramos said. He leaned forward and covered Dena's eyes so neither of them could see.

"Hey!" She protested at the sudden closeup of her partner's fingers.

"Hang in there," Ramos said. "Who just came into the room? Malone, breathe in."

"Oh, that is Douglas," K't'ank said. "And he has food with him, something that Malone does not like." The hand moved, revealing the other detective, who arched one black brow at them. Sure enough, he had a bag from Chili Beyond, a place whose food was so hot Dena only ate it if she was trying to win a bet.

"Yes, but normal body scents are too subtle for an ordinary human nose to pick up," Dena said.

"No, they're not," Ramos said. "I heard that scent is the most powerful of the senses. Your brain might not know it's there, but your nose knows."

"Didn't the analyst say he treated patients with aromatherapy?" K't'ank put in suddenly.

"*She*, not *he*—oh, never mind." Dena brought up the interview on her skinnypad, and scrolled around until she got to Sunnet's recitation of therapies.

"...individual sessions, aromatherapy, meditation with candles, hypnotherapy, massage, even...."

"Sure did," Ramos said, smacking his hand on the desk. "I wonder what was in that aromatherapy?"

"We're jumping to conclusions," Dena said.

"No way," Ramos said. "*My* nose tells me we're missing a connection to the victim. Her connection, not his."

Dena immediately deployed her skinnypad, and ran a background check on the therapist.

"Nothing," she said. "I guess we'll just have to ask her."

"YES, I DID meet Dr. Nagy," Dr. Sunnet said, her beautiful face grave. "We spoke in depth about Mr. Canavireiro. I... can't discuss what we talked about. Patient-client..."

"Privilege expires with the victim," Dena said, not at all sure how steady her ground was. "And Mr. Canavireiro already signed a waiver. I'm sure you recorded your conversation. Let's hear the transcript."

Sunnet's warm bronze cheeks grayed.

"I would just as soon not," she said, turning her hands up. "He was an odious man. You don't have to fish for it, Sergeant. He attempted to seduce me. Forcibly. I set off the alarm in my skinnypad. Of course, his assistant deleted all records of our session by the time I sent my attorney to his office."

"But you had a weapon you could use," Dena said. Something in the therapist's expression set off all kinds of internal alarm bells. "This poor little guy with his anger management problems." Sunnet's eyes widened, and she laughed. "And how can I do that, Sergeant?"

"Aftershave," Dena said. "It's a trigger for him. It's been a trigger for most of his life. Right?"

"Yes, that's why I desensitized him to it," she said. "It took over six months, but he's cured. He shouldn't have responded in any way to Caribbean Hurricane. Check for yourself. The scent record is in his file. Smell it for yourself. I think you'll find it's perfectly innocent."

Now Dena could smell fear. She knew Sunnet was lying. She bared her teeth in a humorless smile.

"I think you know perfectly well I can't. Fortunately," she raised the bangle on her arm, "I brought along my own expert."

The therapist's eyes widened. She had to know what a Salosian host bracelet looked like. The slender woman leaned back in her chair. Dena heard a loud click. Suddenly, a miasma of heavily scented blue fumes rose around Sunnet. She began to twitch, and her head lolled backward.

The odor was so overpowering Dena lurched back against the upright section of her chair. She began to twitch, too. Ramos dropped to the floor, spit spewing from his mouth as he kicked and flailed.

"Fear!" K't'ank shouted. "Flee, Malone! It's a trap!" His voice echoed in her head like a klaxon. "Flee! Take Ramos! The odor kills!"

"Oh, my God," Dena moaned, her eyes streaming with tears. The blue cloud advanced toward her like the spray in a carwash. She kicked the chair's controls into full reverse. "It's like being attacked by a million department store droids. I'll never go perfume shopping again."

Somehow, despite the choking fumes, she pulled and tugged her partner until she got him draped over the foot of her floatchair and out of the room. In the anteroom, fire-retardant foam poured down from the ceiling, and all the doors snapped shut. The office droid rolled toward the records room, obviously under orders set in advance. Dena put her chair into full throttle and got to the door of the storage room ahead of it.

She displayed her badge. "Don't touch anything. This office is now an active crime scene."

"WELL, YOU THREE are all right," the medical examiner said, raising her voice to be heard over the off-key caroling issuing from the platinum bangle. She pointed to Dena's belly. "You're fine. Baby's fine. Dr. K't'ank is fine, although I don't know when he's going to stop singing." She pointed to Ramos, now lying on a spare examination table next to the body of the psychotherapist. "*You're* going to need a rest."

Dena's heart stopped pounding. Her baby was all right. She had been panicking about that in the aircar all the way from the crime scene. On the other hand, K't'ank was still pretty well chemically impaired.

"...Some takes delight in the hurley or the bollin', but I takes delight in the juice of the barley...."

"So, you were right," Ramos croaked, his eyes half swollen shut. "She did it. But, how?"

Dena pointed to the metal flask on the table next to the late doctor's skinnypad. She opened it under Ramos's nose.

"Caribbean Hurricane," she said. "Plus a few extra ingredients. K't'ank. K't'ank!"

The song trailed off.

"What is it, Malone? I was enjoying myself."

She breathed in the perfume. "What's this smell like to you?"

"Like that dead human," K't'ank said. "Whee! It is a wonderful combination! Oh, Danny boy, the pipes, the pipes are calling...!"

"I don't smell anything special," Ramos said. "Just the aftershave. Pretty subtle."

"The analysis will prove what K't'ank detected," Dena said,

capping the bottle tightly. "Since our real murderer is dead, I hope I'll never have to sniff this stuff again. It's noxious. If Neal brought some of this home I'd dump it, and maybe him, too."

Ramos pulled himself up and jumped off the table. "So why did Dr. Sunnet kill a man using aftershave and hypnosis? Why didn't she go to the police or talk to a reporter and blow his reputation? The guy was a waste of skin. It sounds like he had it coming."

Dena smirked, knowing for once she had the better punchline.

"It was obvious once I met her," Dena said. "She didn't want to raise a stink."

Jody Lynn Nye

Jody Lynn Nye lists her main career activity as "spoiling cats." She lives northwest of Chicago with one of the above and her husband, author and packager Bill Fawcett. She has written over forty-five books, including *The Ship Who Won* with Anne McCaffrey, eight books with Robert Asprin, a humorous anthology about mothers, *Don't Forget Your Spacesuit, Dear!,* and over 160 short stories. Her latest books are *Rhythm of the Imperium* (Baen Books), *Moon Beam* (with Travis S. Taylor, Baen) and *Myth-Fits* (Ace). Jody also reviews fiction for *Galaxy's Edge* magazine and teaches the intensive writers' workshop at DragonCon.

A MOUNTAIN MAN AND A CAT WALK INTO A BAR....

A Mad Amos Malone story

Alan Dean Foster

"**W**hat're you starin' so hard at, old timer?" Malone asked as he swung his buckskin-clad left leg up and over the vertiginous back of his mount. Dust motes erupted from where his boot whumped into the unpaved main street of the central Kansas town. The impact left an imprint, much as an elephant might in the soft mud of Lake Victoria's foreshore.

His leathery, weathered visage much softened by the early light of evening, the curious senior squinted at the enormous horse from which its equally gargantuan rider had just dismounted.

"Tryin' to decide which of you is bigger: your animal or you." Turning his head to his left he spat into the street. The tobaccoid spittle immediately sank and vanished into a dry wagon rut several inches deep. "That's a mighty interestin' looking critter you're riding." He raised a slender but muscular arm and pointed. "What's that leather patch across his forehead for?"

Malone tugged at the wide, silver-studded belt that struggled to encircle his waist. "He gets sunburned easy."

"Ain't you goin' to tie 'im up?"

Swaying toward the entrance of the hotel saloon like a China clipper battling a Force 8 gale, Malone glanced back briefly to where he had left thick reins hanging loose.

"Worthless ain't goin' nowhere. He'll stay put."

The old man continued masticating the unnamable. "Well, what if somebody takes a hankerin' to make off with 'im?" He grinned with the remainder of his teeth, between which there was ample space for whistling and perhaps the occasional misguided flying insect. "Me, for example."

Malone lowered his gaze, the wolf's head that covered his scalp sliding slightly forward. "Why then, I reckon you'd stay put, too." He nodded once in the direction of his seemingly somnolent horse. "Anyways, I wouldn't try it. We been on the trail awhile and Worthless, he's getting' on to bein' a mite hungry."

The old man started to chuckle. "That so? What's he gonna t'do? Mistake me for a bucket o' oats?"

The towering mountain man just smiled back, his own orthodonture flashing surprisingly white among the surrounding jungle of gray-flecked black beard. Then he turned, stepped up onto the protesting wood plank sidewalk, ducked his head, and pushed through the double doors leading into the saloon.

The old man looked after him for a moment, then turned back to the untethered horse that was part Percheron, part Arabian, and parts of something other. Appraising the reins falling vertical and unsecured, he took a step toward them. Swinging its head around, the unclassifiable quadruped closed one eye, squinted out of the other, and gave a snort. That did not give the tough oldster pause. What did was the puff of smoke that emerged from both equine nostrils to feather away into the early evening air.

Abruptly smacked upside the head with second thoughts, the old man turned around right quick and began to walk away swiftly, with an occasional nervous glance back over his shoulder. Seeing that the horse was still watching him and perhaps detecting a flicker of red in that single squinting eye, the oldster proceeded to adjust his pace accordingly.

Malone just did avoid nudging the cat with his right foot

as he entered the saloon's main room. A fleeting glance in the animal's direction as it darted in off the street and dashed past him showed an ordinary tabby of average size. Its coat was in surprisingly good shape for a street cat, in coloration falling somewhere between gold and tan with a distinctive black swath running across its back from shoulder to shoulder. Hugging the baseboard while striving to be as inconspicuous as possible, it raced away from Malone to disappear among the tables.

These were occupied by the usual assortment of card players, double-dealers, braggarts, liars, cowpokes, military veterans, military deserters, failed gold miners, unremarkable townsfolk, and a sprinkling of seriously underdressed women who had lately been absent from regular church attendance. The volume of their conversation dropped by about half when Malone lumbered into the room. He disliked the effect his size and appearance had on regular folks but there was nothing much he could do about it.

Making his way to the far end of the bar he quietly settled down on the last empty barstool. This prompted a rush by the half dozen or so patrons seated nearby to vacate their stools, the occupants thereof having experienced a sudden mutual desire to betake themselves somewhere else. When the rest of the crowd saw that the enormous newcomer wasn't about to pull off anyone's leg and start gnawing on it, the usual energetic conversation was resumed by the room's relieved populace.

"Whiskey," Malone told the barkeep politely. When that uneasy but admirably professional attendant produced a bottle that looked as if it might have been filled at a horse trough, a frown crossed Malone's face. "Better." Pulling a less unsanitary container from a shelf on the backbar, the rotund bartender placed it in front of Malone and removed its predecessor. "*Better*," the mountain man reiterated.

This time the barkeep dug under the bar until he found and brought forth a stoppered glass bottle immaculate of shape and label. Malone examined it with a practiced eye, then nodded approvingly. "That'll do. Leave it and a glass." The barkeep was relieved to comply.

An hour or so passed in silent contemplation. Apart and away from the now isolated Malone, money was lost, temporary assignations were forged, two men were thrown out for fighting, two women were cheered on for fighting. Vociferous accusations of cheating at cards were resolved without the use of gunplay, which in contrast to the way it was portrayed in dime novels was noisy, dangerous, and counterproductive for all concerned. A steady stream of regulars and visitors came and went.

One of the latter drew more than the usual casual looks, mostly because the fellow had his dog with him. A handsome black chow, it trotted along behind its owner as they made for the bar. The animal certainly was in better shape than its human, who was tall but of a girth suggestive of a pampered life in the city, and not one spent toiling at manual labor. He had two chins or three depending on whether he was looking up or down, an absurdly long thin mustache more suited to the face of a riverboat gambler, and piercing blue eyes that were small and sharp. His nose was plump and red, as if a ripe plum had been plucked from its tree and glued to his face. When he removed his handsome but oversize wide-brimmed hat it was to reveal a pate ornamented with a flourish of carefully coiffured blonde curls. As near as anyone could tell they were actually growing out of his head and were not the result of some desultory scalping of an unknown ten-year-old girl.

Defying caution and present convention he took a seat once removed from where Malone, a mountainous figure wreathed in buckskins, wolf headdress, and Zen, sat steadily working his way through the bottle in front of him. The chow did not sit. Instead, it took up an alert stance directly beside its owner's stool. The newcomer ordered, took a sip from his glass, had the barkeep pour him another. Looking over, Malone nodded in the direction of the chow.

"Judgin' by his attitude, your dog don't seem to like me much."

Jowls aquiver, the man turned blue eyes to him. "It isn't you." With evident deliberation, he lowered his gaze. "It's your cat. Elehzub doesn't like cats."

A surprised Malone looked down at his feet. Sprawled half on, half off the upper portion of his right boot was the tabby over whom he had nearly stumbled while entering the saloon. It lay on the battered leather with its eyes shut, one paw under its jaw, purring contentedly. Occasionally it would move its head, rubbing against Malone's ankle. Given the profound panoply of odors that clung to that outsized footwear, the feline's response was not surprising.

The newcomer's attitude, which until now had ranged from placid to outright indifferent, turned suddenly unpleasant. The blue eyes narrowed. "I don't like cats, either. In fact, I hate cats."

Deploying a massive shrug, Malone returned to his contemplation of the backbar. A sizeable painting hanging there displayed its creator's modest competency in oils. It showed a somewhat thickset woman lying on a bed in a typically clichéd yet no less pleasant state of complete déshabillé.

"Not my cat."

Having got hold of the issue, the newcomer seemed unwilling to let go of it. "Then what's it doing lolling in simpering disgust all over your foot?"

Malone did not turn from the liquid aesthetic that was currently holding his attention. "Why don't you ask the cat?"

It was plain that the visitor was not used to being so casually dismissed. One hand pushed away the half-filled glass resting on the bar before him.

"You are toying with me, sir. Know that I am Gustavus Eyvind Hudiksvall, and I am not to be toyed with." He waved in the general direction of the crowd. "Unlike these simpletons, your great unhygienic bulk does not intimidate me. Would you like to know why?" When Malone chose not to respond, Hudiksvall continued.

"You see this fine animal standing proudly beside me, that has no hesitation in expressing its dislike for *your* cat? I am not only its master. I am a master of all the dogs of the Americas. It is my profession. It is my avocation. I know American dogs. I understand American dogs. I perceive them and their inner selves in ways that you and others cannot imagine. I comprehend their needs, their desires, their innermost being! Yea, even their thoughts, for those who believe that dogs do not think know nothing of the animal."

Lovely, Malone thought as he continued to gaze at the painting. He sighed. Just lovely. Someone he had not known, but would have wished to. "Cats think also. They just don't jump around stupidly and brag about it."

The color of Hudiksvall's cheeks began to approach that of the rugoid bulbosity attached to the center of his face. "You persist in playing me for a fool, sir. Well, I will not be played." He peered down at the chow that was growling softly. A most disagreeable smile creased his wide, wide face. "Neither will Elehzub. I think... I think I will let him eat your cat."

"Not my cat." Malone did not shift his attention from the painting.

"Then you won't mind."

Leaning over and grunting with the effort, Hudiksvall whispered something in the chow's direction. Tongue hanging and eyes eager, its black ears perked up intently. Whatever the fat man was whispering clearly made an impression on the animal. It tensed as it listened and its soft growling took on a new, more lethal aspect.

The sound was enough to wake the tabby. Eyes snapping open, they shifted to focus on the eager dog. Rising from where it had been slumbering while contentedly inhaling the inexpressibly powerful effluvia from Malone's boot, it moved behind the mountain man's leg. Its ears flattened against its head and its back arched as it hissed warningly.

Malone took a swallow from his glass. "Looks like your animal might have a fight on its hands."

If Hudiksvall was concerned he didn't show it. "I thought something like this might happen." His eyes zeroed in on the alarmed cat, twin blue gunsights targeting prey unable to escape. "Did I not tell you I was a master of dogs?"

Leaning over once more, still straining from the effort, he

whispered something else to the chow. Something more than mere communication this time. Something powerful and private and ancient that would be known only to an individual possessed of some special and unique knowledge. Malone caught the gist of it and reacted. By which is to say a couple of black whiskers twitched among their multitudinous companions.

"*Et pugnare crescere.*" Hudiksvall revealed impressive elocution in commanding his animal. "*Pugnare, et interficere!*"

A dark, dank, flea-free cloud began to coalesce around the chow. Small bursts of miniature lightning flashed within the murk, each one accompanied not by thunder but by a short, sharp bark. The vapor continued to darken until the chow could no longer be seen. Two men seated nearby arguing over the ownership of a mining claim noted this unexpected manifestation of necromancy and stared, but did not flee.

The miasma began to dissipate. In its place Hudiksvall's dog still stood as before, only it had been transformed. In place of the black chow there now squatted a massive, wide-shouldered bulldog. When it growled the sound was deeper and far more menacing than anything that had been expressed by its previously chowly form. A collar of taupe leather studded with two-inch long spikes encircled its thick neck. In response to its master's command, the revamped dog's eyes and attention were now focused exclusively on the cat that had taken shelter behind Malone's right leg.

Hudiksvall's grin arose directly from the nastiness of his soul. "This won't take but a moment, sir. When this strapping expression of Elehzub gets done there'll be nothing left of your cat save a few picked-over bones."

"Not my cat," Malone reiterated. Thick dark brows drew together over eyes as black as the lowermost reaches of a failed Montana copper mine. "On the other hand, I *like* cats. I also don't much cotton to an unfair contest."

It was a remarkable thing to see a man as big as Malone, who stood just shy of seven feet and whose weight approached three hundred pounds, bend nearly in half. But that was the kind of astonishing flexibility he proceeded to display. He bent over, bent some more, and whispered something to the hissing cat.

As a surprised Hudiksvall looked on, a swirl of gold and white opacity coiled up around the cat. Light twinkled within, flashing and blinking, accompanied by a sound like the boiler of a small Mississippi riverboat letting off steam. Or it might have been an extremely attenuated feline hiss.

As Malone straightened and returned to his drinking, the white gold mist faded away. Where the tabby had stood before now stood another cat. Much larger than its former self, it was heavily spotted and thickly muscled, with a high butt, short tail, and unmistakable dark tufts rising from the tips of its ears. It snarled more impressively than any street cat while simultaneously displaying very impressive teeth.

Having initially taken a step forward the bulldog, now finding itself confronted by a decidedly more imposing opponent, whimpered once and retreated.

Hudiksvall's anger was palpable, but he was not about to retreat with a non-existent tail between his legs.

"So! A man of learning and cleverness you are, also. One would not gainsay it from your uncouth appearance. It seems then it is to be tit for tat, cat for cat. I have no fear of that for I grasp the soul of such conjuring. Just as you must know that only a cat native to America can counter a transformative American dog and vice the versa. It is written so, in aged tomes I suspect you may also have read." He eyed the lynx that now stepped out from behind the mountain man's leg. "While your adroit alteration is a fine example of the wild continental feline kind it remains no less only a cat for all that. You think I am done? Then observe, learn, and prepare to sweep up the scraps!"

Once more bending low, this time over the bulldog, Hudiksvall murmured anew, now with more energy than before.

"*Surgens autem, Vinco inferno, et occidas!*"

For a second time a dark cloud ballooned to life around Hudiksvall's companion. It swallowed up the bulldog, obscuring its canine reality. The cloud itself grew larger, much larger than before, until when it finally evaporated there stood in its wake a dog of truly imposing proportions. It was huge, with a blunt, powerful face and a tail that curled up over its rump. It looked down, down at the lynx, which held its ground, albeit with an effort.

"American mastiff." Hudiksvall's triumphant smile was wider this time. "Bred to protect herds of sheep and cattle." Piggish eyes blinking, he gazed expectantly down from his seat at the lynx standing firm beside Malone's leg. "Bigger bones will be left this time, but bones nonetheless."

"Dogs be dogs and cats be cats." With a shrug, Malone bent over once again to whisper something to the lynx. Tufted ears flicked immediately in his direction.

A miniature cumulus colored gold and ivory enveloped the lynx even as the mastiff started forward, drool dripping from its powerful jaws. Then it halted and began backing up, until it was standing, though still growling, behind its master whose buttocks overflowed both sides of the bar stool.

Having come to the decision that it was about time that they pushed their argument off to another day, the two miners who had been looking on abandoned their table in favor of a joint quick-march in the direction of the saloon entrance. Simultaneously, several ladies of the evening determined that it was time to embrace the lateness of the hour, if not potential customers, whereupon they proceeded to hightail it up the nearby stairs in a concerted rush for the second-floor back rooms. Torn between fear and fascination by the increasingly ominous transformations taking place at the bar, the rest of the saloon's motley population mostly remained, transfixed.

Standing beside Malone, its smooth tan back rising to a level not far below the height of the bar, the puma fastened bright yellow eyes on the mastiff and hissed loudly enough to be heard out in the street. Exhibiting unified homage to the true frontier spirit, no one outside proved dumb enough to enter and investigate the sound.

By now the newcomer was beside himself, near apoplectic with frustration. "I am Gustavus Eyvind Hudiksvall, master of American canines and all knowledge thereto related, and no stinking mountain of a man and his cat will best me this night or any other! It is the nature of existence that dog should lord it over cat, that the latter should run before the former, and I swear it will be so this night as it is on every other night!"

Holding his glass between the thumb and forefinger of his left hand, Malone took a half swallow of the good whiskey while with his right hand he reached down and stroked the back of the neck of the fully alert cougar. It growled in response.

"Not my cat."

Sliding off the stool, an avalanche of fat, Hudiksvall squatted in front of the mastiff in order to look directly into its eyes. Reaching out with thick fingers, he grasped both ears of the dog. This time he did not even try to murmur. Instead, his voice rose until it rattled around the saloon.

"FORMARE MAXIME AUTEM!" The fat man's bellow rattled the second floor rafters and shook dust on those seated below. "FRATRES, DE DENTE, ET INIMICOS TUOS INTERFICERE!"

At this, the one couple in the saloon that was actually married rose from their table and departed in haste, leaving behind the uneaten remnants of their supper. A well-dressed rancher of some means swore mightily in a foreign language. Everyone else could only sit and stare, half paralyzed. The situation had become serious. Spittoons were missed.

As with its predecessors, the cloud that rose around the mastiff was dark with bark and lit with snarls, but this time the vaporous manifestation fractured, splitting into two, three, and many more distinct upwellings. Straightening, a sweaty but confident Hudiksvall surveyed his canine handiwork. In time each cloud began to dissipate, swept away by the fat man's sinister and definitive necromancy.

"Or should I say, and this I suspect you know," he told Malone, "simply 'cave canum'."

Growling to themselves, the pack assembled beside Hudiksvall. Tongues hanging out, panting, they flashed sharp teeth set in jaws strong enough to bring down a bear or a bison. More than a dozen of the huge timber wolves began to spread out, forming a semi-circle in front of Malone and the cougar in preparation for an attack. Whereas until now the mystical, inexplicable manifestation of dogs and cats of increasingly larger species had served largely to enthrall the majority of the saloon's patrons, the appearance of the wolf pack succeeded in emptying the establishment of its remaining customers. Libations were left unimbibed, poker chips were scattered, chairs were overturned, screams and curses were essayed with a mixture of vehemence and panic, and at least two heretofore atheistic shopkeepers competed in a footrace to see who could arrive first at the Baptist church that was located at the far end of the town's central thoroughfare.

"Maybe," a heavily perspiring but expectant Hudiksvall ventured maliciously, "your cat will not be sufficient to satisfy the appetite of my pets, and they will express a desire to taste man as well. They are certain to find attractive the jambalaya of effluvia that clings to you." He licked thick lips expectantly. "Well sir, I await your response. Your final response. Is it again to be 'not my cat'? Or perhaps, if you grovel with sufficient eloquence, I may command the pack to spare you. Though not, to be sure, this current, final, and failed iteration of your unfortunate feline."

By way of response Malone carefully set down his glass. The bottle before him was now empty, the liquid warmth it had dispensed a pleasant glow deep within his belly. Turning, he regarded with sad eyes the bloated boaster before him.

"A true necromancer knows how to fight fair." Raising a huge, callused hand, he gestured at the pack that was systematically positioning itself prior to rushing in for the kill. "Twelve against one ain't hardly fair. But if that is how it is to be...."

Bending toward the cougar, he commenced once more to speak softly.

Hudiksvall was neither impressed nor worried. "What is to be now, sir? I know you cannot do the same spell of multiplicity as I, for I sense it, and I have the perception of the animals for whom I care. What single local feline will you draw upon now, to counter the kings of canines, who cooperate in a fight better than any other of their kind? I await your last and best counter, prior to your animal's—and possibly your own—dismemberment!"

A strange sound began to seep into the saloon. It came from outside the building as Malone continued to whisper; never shouting, never raising his voice. It took a moment for those who had fled outside to identify it. It was in no wise alien; they had all heard it before. It was the collective symphony of cats yowling—every cat in town and onward to its outskirts screeching and hollering at the tops of their lungs.

The golden cloud that enveloped the cougar was darker than any that had preceded it. As Malone looked on with interest and Hudiksvall's gaze narrowed uncertainly the vaporous mist grew and expanded, becoming larger, vaster, immenser (if you will), until eventually it passed into the realm of the ridiculous. At last it began to clear, revealing... a cat.

It was a tabby, of sorts, albeit one that weighed about half a ton and might've been thirteen feet from its wet black nose to the tip of its tail. Colored somewhere between gold and tan, it showed a distinctive black ruff across its shoulders. A black ruff that was thick and wide and flaring. More of a mane, really. Lowering its head and dipping its brow forward, its mouth contracted into a most terrible expression: death writ in wrinkles. Then it opened its jaws, revealing teeth that were large enough to chomp a man in half with one bite.

Having anticipated, called forth, and recognized the breed, Malone nodded to himself with satisfaction.

Rooted to the spot, one hand held out defensively before him, a terrified Hudiksvall stumbled backwards. The pack of timber wolves were already gone, having vanished under and through the saloon's swinging doors. One, caught at the back of the pack as the other eleven struggled to squeeze through the portal simultaneously, opted for leaping through a flanking window in order to escape the room and the gargantuan feline that had materialized before them. That the window in question happened to be closed at the time did not in way forestall the wolf's decision. Their judicious flight was accompanied by a notable absence of growls and much frantic whining.

Overweight and underpowered, Hudiksvall had no such opportunity. It was to his credit that despite his fear, it was his curiosity that came to the fore.

"That... that monstrous beast is not an American cat! It is not possible for you to call forth a feline expression from the African continent to confront American canines. It refutes the magikal canon and cannot be so!"

"Well now," Malone drawled as he used his right hand to ruffle the ruff of the massive creature standing beside him, "you are right correct about that, Mr. Hudiksvall." Despite Malone's efforts to calm him, the gigantic cat continued to incline murderously toward the other man, barely restraining itself. "This here is an American lion. *Felis atrox*, if you will. First dug up by a fella name of Bill Huntington near Natchez in 1836 but not described in much detail until ol' Doc Joseph Leidy wrote somethin' up on 'em in 1852. Lot bigger than their African cousins, they are." He leaned forward. "Danged impressive teeth, ain't they?"

Advancing on paws each one of which was more than broad enough to completely cover a man's head and face, the lion took a step toward Hudiksvall and let out a single... ROAR.

The folks who heard it over in the next county thought it was a storm a-brewing. The church bell in town shivered out a couple of desultory *clangs* that did nothing to reassure the pair of shopkeeper converts who huddled inside. Children woke up crying, in which exercise of their tear ducts they were equaled by a substantial number of mothers. Strong men quaked in their boots and the town sheriff hurried to lock the jail door—from the inside.

Gustavus Eyvind Hudiksvall turned positively white (well, whiter than he had been previously, anyhow) and suddenly found his feet. Despite the effort required, they conveyed him with admirable rapidity to the saloon's entrance, which portal he exited with such velocity that one of the swinging doors was knocked askew on its hinges.

Having nothing else to confront or on which to focus its attention, the splendidly immense example of *Felis atrox* turned back toward Amos Malone. A relic of an age only recently bygone, the great jaws parted. With interest, Malone peered down the throat thus revealed.

The tongue that emerged licked the mountain man's face and copious beard so that both were soon dripping with leonine saliva, until Malone finally had to put a stop to the display of ancient affection. Reaching out, he dug his right hand into the vast black mane and began scratching. Like all its kind the lion could not purr, but it lowered its head contentedly.

"It were that black ruff o' yours," he murmured to the big cat. "I saw the connection right off, but tweren't no reason at the time to pursue it." He nodded toward the damaged doorway. "Until it were forced. On the both of us." Leaning forward, he whispered into the lion's right ear.

This time the cloud shrank instead of expanding. Which was a fortunate adjustment, because it was unlikely the town itself would have survived a cat-thing of any greater dimension. When the last of the gilded cloud vanished it left behind on the tobacco-stained floor a tabby of normal size, gold and tan in color, with an odd black streak in its hair that stretched from shoulder to shoulder. It shook itself, licked one paw to briefly groom the fur on its forehead, and then began to arch its back and rub against Malone's right boot. Reaching down, the mountain man picked it up and placed it gently on the now deserted sweep of mahogany bar. Then he leaned forward and over to peer down behind the barrier.

"Barkeep."

Trembling visibly, the bartender rose from where he had been hiding. He looked at Malone, at the cat sitting contentedly near the giant's right hand, then back at Malone.

"Wh-wh-wh-what'll it be... sir?"

"Whiskey. Same label." Malone indicated the serene feline seated nearby. "And a saucer of milk for my friend. Straight up."

The barkeep managed to nod. "This... this is a saloon, sir. Milk, I'm not so sure...."

"This here's also a hotel, friend. Got to be some milk or cream

on ice in the kitchen." He leaned forward slightly, lowering his voice. "Go find it. And you'd best come back."

No one else entered the saloon that night. No one else came near the saloon that night. Its interior was occupied solely by its shaky proprietor, a mountain man of measureless smells and unsuspected abilities, and the gold and tan cat seated comfortably on the bar off to his right. Not his cat. Together the three passed the remainder of the evening undisturbed and mostly in silence, until the time finally came for Malone to exit. At this the bartender allowed himself to faint gratefully and with some grace. He did not hit the floor too hard.

The cat followed Malone outside. After the mountain man finished admonishing his horse for eating half the hitching post, he turned to look back at the plank sidewalk. The cat was sitting there, its tail switching slowly back and forth, staring at him in the unblinking, fearless manner of cats everywhere. For certain a most ordinary cat.

"G'night, puss. Got t'be on my way. Watch your step. Don't eat any mice I wouldn't eat."

The cat turned to depart, looking back only once to meow.

That is generally remembered as the Manhattan, Kansas earthquake of 1867.

Alan Dean Foster

Alan Dean Foster has written over 100 books, including both standalone novels and novelizations for *Star Wars, Star Trek, Alien,* and many other productions. He has written a number of stories featuring the main character in this tale, many of which are collected in *Mad Amos,* published in 1996. His website is www.alandeanfoster.com.

LOST AND FOUND

LAURA RESNICK

The Washington Postal
"Asteroid On Collision Course With Earth"

Panic spread through the halls of Congress today immediately after the National Aeronautics and Space Administration announced that an asteroid is on a direct collision course with our planet. The asteroid is expected to crash into Earth tomorrow afternoon.

Exhausted from having worked nearly four full days this month, Congressional leaders are in desperate need of rest and recuperation, and certainly in no condition to deal with a global crisis.

"This is unacceptable. I'm supposed to go golfing with the president this weekend! I don't have time for this bull-cocky," protested Glitch McDonald. Unable to control his nervous snickering as he contemplated the imminent destruction of the planet, the senate majority leader added, "My goal from now on is to make this a one-collision asteroid."

NASA astronomers spotted the deadly asteroid while using the agency's orbiting Kepler space telescope to collect data on some 150,000 stars. During this process, the Kepler team of astronomers discovered more than seven hundred previously unknown planets. Among these, at least four are believed to be potentially similar to Earth and capable of sustaining biological life forms. Which would be a really big deal, obviously, if we weren't all about to die in a fiery collision with a giant piece of space debris that's hurtling toward us at devastating speed.

House Speaker Ryan Paul said in a formal statement, "Our thoughts and prayers are with everyone who lies in the path of this asteroid. We rely on the private sector to adjust to this situation. Government should not interfere in a planetary disaster."

The president had already left for the golf course and could not be reached for a comment on the end of the world.

The Partisan Report
"Document Proves That Asteroid is a Right-Wing Plot"

A partial dossier written by an unknown author and provided to the *Report* by an anonymous source proves beyond a shadow of a doubt that right-wing extremists working with powerful members of Congress are behind the asteroid that is due to collide with Earth within the next twenty-four hours.

Anonymous White House sources say that government policies have not been killing off lower-income and poor people as quickly as major political donors expected, and so the "nuclear option" has been triggered—namely, planetary destruction, which fast-tracks the conservative agenda in a single, daring maneuver.

The New York Timely
"Brace Yourself—It's Not An Asteroid"

Politicians flocked to the golf course for the final long weekend in world history, following NASA's depressing announcement yesterday, while real people hunkered down and waited for certain death.

Then this morning, in another emergency press conference, NASA scientists stunned us again.

"The object in question is close enough to our planet today that we've been able to get a much better look at it," said the president's younger son, Derrick Frump, who now runs NASA. "The Kepler team tells me it's a UFO."

When asked to elaborate on that statement, Mr. Frump replied that he isn't a scientist and shouldn't be expected to know the meaning of every NASA acronym.

Neil deCassini Huygens took over the microphone at that point. Speaking on behalf of NASA, the telegenic astronomer announced, "We are able to confirm that the unidentified flying object is mechanical in nature, not geological. By which I mean, it's not a big rock, guys—it's a spaceship!"

Considerable commotion followed this announcement. The large contingent of *Star Trek* fans at the press conference, most of them wearing Federation uniforms, were particularly excited and took quite some time to calm down enough for Huygens to continue speaking.

He revealed that, in keeping with national security protocols, NASA scientists first attempted to report this earthshaking discovery directly to the government in a private meeting.

That revelation briefly inflamed conspiracy theorists at the press conference, who were carrying placards that included slogans such as "Area 51 shall not be forgotten!" and "We remember Roswell!"

"However," Huygens continued, "they couldn't find anyone at the White House other than the Russian ambassador. He was on the phone in the Oval Office and said he didn't have time to meet with 'some hand-wringing science nerds.'"

Since the spaceship's course will shortly bring it into contact with Earth, Huygens explained, NASA then decided that appearing on cable TV news would be the best way to get their information to the president.

"Mr. President," said Huygens, speaking directly to the Wolf News camera, "NASA believes it is virtually certain that this UFO is being piloted by extraterrestrial biological entities."

The public radio correspondent raised her hand and suggested that Dr. deCassini Huygens rephrase that statement for young children, television reporters, and the president.

"Ah." The renowned astronomer nodded. "Little green men are piloting the flying saucer. We're expecting a visit today from outer space."

While reporters scribbled furiously in their notebooks, *Star Trek* fans cheered wildly.

"The entities piloting this ship are likely to be highly evolved life forms," said Huygens. "We're not getting all excited about a few fossilized microbes this time. These are sophisticated beings capable of building and navigating an interstellar vessel!"

Huygens concluded his statement by urging government leaders, most of whom fled yesterday, to return to Washington and prepare for first contact.

Brightburp News
"Illegal Immigrants Are Dropping From the Sky"

According to NASA's statement today, invasion is imminent. Our way of life is under threat.

To quote the so-called "astronomer" Neil deCassini Huygens: "Little green men are piloting the flying saucer. We're expecting a visit today from outer space."

There's a liberal for you—welcoming alien invaders who want to destroy our culture.

Well, no little greenie is coming across *our* borders without permission or getting onto *our* planet without going through a proper immigration process determined by quotas that will protect our European humanoid genetic dominance here.

Build that wall in space, Mr. President!

Science Tomorrow
"SETI Receiving Transmissions From the UFO"

The search for extraterrestrial intelligence at the SETI Institute has experienced a major breakthrough today, as a series of radio transmissions are now flowing steadily from—it is generally believed—the UFO whose course is expected to bring it into contact with our planet within hours.

According to a statement just released by the Carl Sagan Center for the Study of Life in the Universe, regular linguistic patterns are already being identified in the communications being received. "It's weird," said a spokeswoman at the center. "There's something strangely familiar about the language the aliens seem to be using."

Varietal
"Biggest Film Deal in Hollywood History Coincides With Alien Arrival"

I.M. Big, creator of last summer's smash-hit science fiction film about sentient beings from another world who make the interstellar journey to Earth, said in a phone interview today, "NASA and SETI have confirmed that my vision of the future was even more prescient than I realized. So I'm going to make a sequel."

Gambling on worldwide interest in the subject, now that NASA says first contact is imminent, the budget for the sequel is reputedly bigger than the combined GNP of China and Japan.

"But in the sequel, the aliens won't try to destroy the planet and kill off the whole human race the way they did in the first movie," said the writer/director/producer/star.

Asked if he thought the real aliens who are about to arrive here might try that, Big replied with a laugh, "I hope not. I mean, I'd like to get some of them to appear in my movie. Do you think they'd be interested? I'll offer them union scale."

Big has also launched a campaign to have the real-life aliens' planet named after the alien world in his movie. As a major donor to various campaign funds, he anticipates enthusiastic Congressional support for this plan.

LCN: Live Cable News
White House Press Briefing

WH PRESS SECRETARY PAWN SLICER: The president will not be returning early from his golf weekend. He sees no reason to do so.

LCN: He sees no... *(coughs)* Is the president aware that an extraterrestrial spaceship is now orbiting our planet?

SLICER: *(giggling)* I think a spaceship is "extraterrestrial" by definition, don't you?

WOLF NEWS: How is the president's golf game this weekend?

SLICER: He's playing the very best game of golf that anyone has ever—

LCN: Is the president aware that *alien beings* are currently—

SLICER: Please wait your turn, LCN. Wolf News asked a question before you did.

LCN: We're talking about first contact! About the arrival of—

SLICER: I've asked you not to interrupt.

LCN: There is an interstellar spaceship circling the planet even as we sp—

SLICER: Am I going to have to give you a time out?

AP: Affiliated Press here, Mr. Slicer. We've got confirmation from the Oriental Institute of the University of Chicago that the aliens are transmitting in a language similar to ancient Egyptian. Maybe late New Kingdom period. Any thoughts on that?

SLICER: I'm answering Wolf News' question right now. Wolf?

WOLF NEWS: What's the president's handicap?

SLICER: *(shouting)* The president doesn't have a handicap! He is the fittest, most physically perfect human specimen ever to serve as president! End of story.

WOLF NEWS: Uh, I meant his golf handicap...

The AP
"Aliens Preparing To Land On Earth"

Extraterrestrial beings from the still-unidentified vessel now orbiting Earth have been requesting permission to send a landing party to our planet's surface, according to the Carl Sagan Center. They have apparently been unable to obtain a response.

That may be because, according to Affiliated Press sources, the only people currently in residence at the White House are the Russian ambassador and his team of "diplomats." Otherwise, the West Wing has been abandoned, and the president and his closest associates remain on vacation.

NASA Press Release

A small landing vessel has disengaged from the mother ship now orbiting Earth and has commenced the final leg of the most significant journey in history—a journey that will bring us together with beings from another world for the first time.

Based on the linguistic profile developed during the hours

we've been receiving transmissions from the visitors, Egyptologists from the University of Chicago are being flown to the projected coordinates of the shuttlecraft's landing site.

Early analysis of these communications suggests that the extraterrestrials have somehow been studying us in preparation for this meeting, but apparently the time lag created by being light years apart means that the human language they've learned, in hopes of communicating with us, is a long-dead one.

TBC: Television Broadcasting Company
Alien Arrival: Live!

GENT: Hi, I'm Handsome Gent!

LADY: And I'm Blonde Lady!

GENT: And we're coming to you *live!* from the Mall in Washington, D.C., where the alien shuttlecraft has just landed.

LADY: And, Handsome, the crowd is really excited!

GENT: Yes, Blonde, they sure are!

LADY: Handsome, we are pleased to have here with us today expert Egyptologist Dr. Something Something. Can you tell us a little about what you're here to do today, Dr. Something?

EGYPTOLOGIST: Well, we think the aliens may speak—

LADY: *(shouting)* The door to the spacecraft is opening!

GENT: *(shouting)* You can really feel the excitement of the crowd, Blonde!

LADY: *(shouting)* You sure can, Handsome!

GENT: And here come the aliens!

LADY: Yes, here they come!

(Excited screaming and cheering from the crowd.)

STAR TREK FANS: "Greetings! Peace and long life! Live long and prosper!"

GENT: They look... *human.*

STAR WARS FANS: "May the force be with you!"

LADY: Yes, Handsome, they certainly do!

ALT-RIGHT: "Build that wall! Build that wall!"

LADY: What are they wearing? Those robes are amazing! And the headdresses... I love the eye makeup, too.

GENT: Doctor, do the aliens look human to you?

EGYPTOLOGIST: Could you two please cease your banal chatter? I'm trying to hear what they're saying.

(Silence while leader of alien delegation raises arms and speaks.)

GENT: You're frowning, Doc. Did you not recognize the alien's language, after all?

EGYPTOLOGIST: Oh, I recognize it. Surprisingly well, in fact. I just didn't...

LADY: What's wrong?

EGYPTOLOGIST: They seem to think, um, that this is Jerusalem.

GENT: What?

LADY: They've heard of Jerusalem?

GENT: Hm, what's happening now?

EGYPTOLOGIST: That's one of my colleagues you see stepping forward to exchange greetings. She's telling them where they actually are.

(There is some discussion with the aliens. Then...)

GENT: Whoa! Did that alien just whack his companion on the head?

LADY: Yes, Handsome, he sure did.

GENT: Doc, can you tell us what's going on?

EGYPTOLOGIST: I, uh... I think they're lost. They were trying to land in Jerusalem.

LADY: What did the main guy just say to the one he hit a second ago?

EGYPTOLOGIST: If I had to translate it into the vernacular... I think he said, "Dummkopf!"

Timed Magazine
"The Lost Tribes Are Still Lost"

Among the many astonishing discoveries in recent days, the most surprising thing about the aliens who have landed on Earth is that... they're not aliens.

Speaking on behalf of NASA, Neil deCassini Huygens announced, "We have confirmed that our extraterrestrial guests are here on a pilgrimage to their ancestral home. They appear humanoid because they are human. Their ancestors, centuries ago, were born on Earth, traveled to the stars, and colonized a distant planet."

Based on linguistic and cultural features of the visiting delegation, as well as the aliens' own written and oral history as conveyed through interpreters from the University of Chicago, NASA is now able to resolve a mystery that goes back millennia. The distant world known to NASA as Exoplanet 4, one of the potentially inhabitable planets recently observed by the Kepler team, was colonized more than twenty-five centuries ago by the ten lost tribes of Israel.

Alien interstellar travelers came to Earth in that long-ago era and recruited the Hebrew tribes to colonize a new planet in another solar system. The aliens transported them there, along with settlers from ancient Egypt (whose tongue became the lingua franca of the newly colonized world), Mesopotamia, and several other cultures.

"This is," Huygens stressed, "a lot to absorb."

Proponents of paleo–contact—the theory that intelligent extraterrestrial beings visited Earth and made contact with humans in antiquity—are demanding an immediate apology from a long list of academic and scientific institutions which have for decades ridiculed the belief in ancient astronauts and prehistoric space travel.

"I am completely vindicated and all my ideas proven true," said an exultant Ludwig von Danskin, author of several bestselling books (all out-of-print) that asserted ancient societies were in contact with extraterrestrial beings. "Now we have incontrovertible proof of where the Lost Tribes went. Aliens who visited Earth helped them colonize another planet. I knew it all along!"

Von Danskin is already negotiating a new publishing deal. The octogenarian plans to go on an interstellar speaking tour as soon as his next book is released.

The Israeli government issued a formal statement to express national rejoicing over this extraordinary discovery.

"We figured the Lost Tribes had to be somewhere," said the Israeli prime minister. "But another planet? Who knew?"

The Israeli government promptly opened communications with the pilgrims, inviting them to Jerusalem. Eager to catch up on more than 2700 years of family news, so to speak, the aliens have accepted the invitation and plan to leave the U.S. tomorrow for Jerusalem.

The Atlantis Monthly
"Lost"

As the alien shuttlecraft soared toward heaven on the first leg of the visiting delegation's journey back to New Canaan (their name for Expolanet 4), their terrestrial hosts watched them go with that feeling of mingled relief and regret that so often characterizes the end of a visit from relatives.

"They were trying to land in Jerusalem because they were making a pilgrimage to the temple," said Professor Rose Liberman. "How did they wind up in Washington? No sense of direction."

A historian of the First Temple period, Liberman was chosen to act as guide and liaison for the visitors, due to her familiarity with their language and her knowledge of the period in which their ancestors last saw Earth.

"I explained that all that's left of the Second Temple is Herod's Western Wall.... And they're like, '*Second* Temple? What are you talking about?' And I realize, oh, they came to make a pilgrimage to Solomon's temple—which was destroyed a few generations after their ancestors left Earth. Oops.

"So I break the news about the Babylonians sacking Solomon's temple, and they're upset. *Really* upset. There's all this wailing, gnashing of teeth, tearing of hair, rending of garments.... It's all very Biblical. But after a few days—and I do I mean *days*—of this, they pull themselves together and calm down. And I think, okay, we're over the worst bit, and it'll get better from here."

But then the pilgrims decided—since they've come all this way, after all—they should make their pilgrimage to the Second Temple which Liberman mentioned.

"So I had to explain about that, too."

The Romans destroyed the Second Temple when they sacked Jerusalem in 70 A.D. All that remains is the Wailing Wall—which was a retaining wall for the platform or mount on which the temple once stood.

Well, to lose one sacred temple may be regarded as a misfortune, but to lose two begins to look like carelessness. Or so the New Canaanites thought, despite never having read Oscar Wilde.

"The conversation didn't go well," Liberman says on a weary sigh.

And the visit still hadn't reached its nadir.

"It was when they asked the prime minister where the Ark of the Covenant is kept safe these days, since the First *and* Second Temples were both destroyed.... And we had to admit we'd lost the Ark, too."

The recriminations were noisy and prolonged. Although diplomatic relations were restored by the end of the visit, things were undeniably strained as the New Canaanites took their leave.

"Well, what did they expect after twenty-seven hundred years?" Liberman says a little irritably.

Still, despite some tension at the end of the visit, both parties are pleased that connection has been reestablished after so many centuries.

Meanwhile, several NASA scientists are traveling back to New Canaan with the pilgrims, where they'll learn more about the technology that made this interstellar voyage possible. Scientists and astronomers the world over are very excited about the future of humankind, and historians are enjoying arguing over how to rewrite the past. These are extraordinary times we are privileged to live in.

As of this writing, Congress and the president have not yet returned to Washington—and this, too, seems like a blessing.

Laura Resnick

Laura Resnick is the author of the popular Esther Diamond urban fantasy series published by DAW Books, as well as the Silerian Trilogy, which *Publisher's Weekly* described as "a marvel of storytelling." The Campbell Award-winning author of many short stories, she is on the web at LauraResnick.com.

A CRAWLSPACE FULL OF PRIZES

Bill Ferris

You're in the bathroom, brushing your teeth and dreading another ten-hour slog at work when the tickets start coming. They lurch from the faucet in a long strand like you're at Dave and Buster's and you just scored big in Skee Ball. It scares you at first, mainly because the tickets are pink and you mistake them for a giant worm.

You aren't as surprised the next day when the dryer starts dispensing tickets after you finish the laundry. You bought the stackable machines, and the tickets poke out from the space between the washer and dryer. It looks like a place from which tickets might emerge, honestly. You try to look underneath, but those things are heavy, and you almost topple the dryer off the washing machine.

By Wednesday, you start feeling pretty okay with getting ticket-based rewards for mowing the lawn and going jogging. It strikes you as odd when organizing the office potluck nets you a bundle of them, while working late on the Monroe account earns you neither tickets nor acknowledgment from your boss, but you tell yourself the paycheck is thanks enough. At home, you find a shoebox to store all your tickets. You wonder what you'll do with them, but your boss just fired one of your team members, so you really don't have time to dwell on it.

Thursday, you walk around to the rear of your house to the crawlspace to put away a box of Christmas decorations for the year. You expect that behind the three-by-five crawlspace door will be the crawlspace, since it's right there in its name and everything. But instead of the musty smell of garden tools and old maple boards from that cutting board you tried to make but gave up on, you find a neon-lit room with day-glo carpet. Top-40 radio blares over loudspeakers that sound nicer than anything you've got in your den. At the center of the room is a glass display case filled with little plastic spider-rings and Pixy Stix, as well as other assorted knick-knacks, candies, baubles, and gee-gaws. You couldn't be more surprised if a bear had jumped out of the crawl space. A bear would've at least made a certain kind of sense. You mention this to Sean, the surly, skinny, pimply teen wearing a green polo shirt and nametag, standing behind the glass counter. You also ask him what the heck he's doing here, anyway?

"Because it's my shift," Sean tells you.

How did he even get this job? This is your house, you protest. Surely there must be a mistake. Sean will have to leave this instant. And where are you supposed to put your Christmas decorations?

If there were competitions for such things, Sean's reply of, "I don't know what to tell you," would win gold for Least Helpful Phrase in the English Language.

You march back to the house to get another box of Christmas stuff. You didn't even unpack this one, as it would've been silly to deck the halls when your brother Jeremy and his kids haven't visited in years. You stomp back toward the crawlspace to confront Sean.

You open the door spoiling for a fight, but it's not Sean at the counter. It's a forty-something woman named Karen, wearing a similar green polo and nametag. She smiles and asks how she can help you. You're so surprised by this display of adequate customer service that you blurt out, "Is Sean here?" like you're best buds. Sean is not here. Karen would be happy to assist you, however. In addition to the glass display case, she draws your attention to the wall behind her. Perched there—on shelves that, based on the dimensions of your house, should reach well into the living room above—are a variety of other prizes, including but not limited to:

- A shoulder to cry on (25 tickets)
- A new ending for that book you're writing (50 tickets)
- A waking replay of last night's dreams (100 tickets)
- Perfect recall of your high school prom (200 tickets)
- Perfect forgetfulness of your high school prom (400 tickets)
- Every sock you've ever lost (500 tickets)
- Mortgage Refinance (750 tickets)
- A phone call from your old college roommate you lost track of because they aren't on Facebook for some reason (1,000 tickets)
- Forgotten passwords (2,000 tickets)
- Texts from lost loves (2,500 tickets)
- A second chance with your old flame (SOLD OUT)
- That thing where you live an entire lifetime as someone else, but only like ten minutes pass in your real life (10,000 tickets)
- And at the very top, priced at 12,000 tickets, an Xbox One.

"No big rush, take your time," Karen says, wiping the countertop.

You open your mouth to ask why this is happening. What comes out is, "What are the terms on the mortgage re-fi?" You've already boarded the train, you may as well see where it's heading.

"Seven-two-five for a thirty year."

"That's worse than what I've got."

Karen shrugs in the "What can you do?" fashion. "I keep telling them nobody wants it, but they don't listen to me."

You ask Karen to identify this mysterious "they," as well as to clarify if other people are visiting your crawlspace getting terrible terms on a home refinance. You don't want to get a bad reputation.

Karen rolls her eyes. "Oh, you know. Management."

"Yes, but management of what?"

"You know. The suits at corporate." She rolls her eyes again, then starts to make an obscene gesture with her hand, but catches herself. You look up, wondering if there are any security cameras. You scan the top shelf again, hoping she'd have something that could mend your relationship with your brother Jeremy. "Jeez, it must take forever to get the Xbox." You immediately feel foolish. You could order one on Amazon in less time than it would take to walk back into your house. The very idea was ridiculous—you've got responsibilities, and who's got time for video games anyway? Why, it's almost February and you still haven't put away all your Christmas decorations. An Xbox would be completely frivolous. You ask a dozen questions about its specs and game selection just to make sure.

Karen points to another prize on the wall. "Maybe start out with something less expensive." She points to a shelf holding a pillow with a Batman pillowcase, labeled *A waking replay of last night's dreams.* "That one's popular. You don't have to use it right away. You can save it for a real good one." She winks at you in a way the suits at corporate would surely frown upon.

"Sure, why not." You excuse yourself to run back into the house to get your tickets. When you return, she exchanges the Batman pillow for several strands of tickets.

"Enjoy," she says.

"Oh, I will," you say, immediately regretting it because it comes out sounding really pervy.

You stretch out on the couch and put the pillow behind your head—it's a pillow, what else would you do with it? You brace yourself for your dreams to flood your mind, letting you experience them again, alert, with your full cognitive abilities to view them, like a first-year film student analyzing *Fitzcarraldo.* Your dreams burst into your conscious mind with all the ceremony of a process server knocking on your door to serve you with divorce papers. You cringe as you watch your dream-self running late for work and struggling to get dressed, each shirt button like a Rubik's Cube in your sausage fingers. It goes on like this for five minutes. You wonder if it gets more interesting toward the end. It does not.

In your next dream, you're stuck in an elevator. The good news: you're there with your brother Jeremy, all the old arguments forgotten. The bad news: you've really got to go to the bathroom, and you're very sure you're about to pee your pants in front of your brother, whom you suddenly realize is also the governor of Nebraska. The dream ends there. Immediately, you look up Jeremy on Facebook and confirm that he's doing well, though not so well as to be governor of Nebraska. For the thousandth time you start typing an email to him. For the thousandth time you save it in your drafts folder to finish later.

You hear a beep. The smoke detector is crying out for new batteries. Usually, you'll ignore it until it wakes you up two hours before your alarm goes off in the morning so you can't get back to sleep. But this time, you rush to its aid like it's a baby crying for a bottle. As soon as you snap the plastic cover back into place, a long rope of tickets staggers out from the side. You go to your shoebox and retrieve a fistful of tickets and speed-walk back to the crawlspace.

Karen is there again. She asks if you'd remembered your dreams. You lie and say you're saving it for your recurring dream about having a beach house in Southern California.

"Suuuuuure you are," she says, winking again. You suspect the suits at corporate HR have a good-sized file going on Karen.

Your eyes stray to the Xbox, but you look away before you can imagine the fun of blasting bad guys to smithereens. "I'll take the phone call from my college roommate," you say, shoving a heap of tickets toward Karen like you're going all-in on a game of Texas hold'em. You must have looked up your roommate, Mike, two-dozen times, to no avail. The first thing you plan to ask him is why he isn't on Facebook.

Your phone buzzes. An unknown caller from your old college area code. Your adrenaline spikes as you say, "Hello?"

"I'm so happy to speak with you today. As you know, your degree has set you up for a great career. Now is a perfect time to think about making a gift to the alumni association."

"Mike? Is that you?"

"I'm sorry?"

"Is this Mike?"

"No, sir. Sorry. My name is Toby."

Toby? "Did you live in Stout Hall your freshman year?"

"Yeah. Wait—oh my God! I didn't even recognize your name! How you doing? Wow!"

You'd lived with Toby in the freshman dorm, back when you were pimply teenagers. The two of you had combined to create the messiest room on the second floor, after which you mutually decided it was best you both find different living arrangements the next year. Toby was a decent guy and you wished him well, but you were pretty okay with never hearing from, speaking to, or thinking of him again. You're glad to find out, however, that he'd married and thrice impregnated his then-girlfriend, who'd spent about as much time in your room as you did. You're about to hang up when you realize Toby probably works on commission, and you'd be a real jerk if you let him invest that much time without coughing up a donation. You pledge an annual gift of a hundred dollars, making a mental note to go to the alumni association website and cancel next year's donation as soon as you hang up.

You put your phone away, and see Karen's smiling face. "Nice to catch up, isn't it?"

You lament you'll have to harvest the donation money from your Florida vacation budget, not that you have time to take one given how your recent performance review went. "Good times, good times," you say.

"See anything else you like?"

"Oh, that's enough fun for one evening." You head back inside the house dwelling on the fact that you're a thousand tickets further away from the Xbox, not that you want one, of course.

You forget about canceling the donation, instead adding up all the tickets in your shoebox. A paltry 308. You vow to not visit the crawlspace again until you've saved up enough for something really great.

Naturally, you get up early the next morning and blow half

your tickets on new endings to the book you've been writing. Karen and Sean are both working, and you're astonished how thoroughly they know every character, every theme, every plot point you've written. You are equally amazed at their horrible suggestions. Now, you like evil twin stories as much as the next person, but who ever heard of an evil octuplet? Who was also a reverse vampire? After Sean suggests a surprise witness in a murder trial you're pretty sure he cribbed from *Perry Mason*, you thank them for their time, spend fifty tickets on Smarties and a licorice rope, and head to the office ninety minutes late. You and your boss agree it's your least productive day in years. The endings were that bad.

You don't visit the crawlspace for two weeks as you sweep, scrub, and scour every inch of your house. You start each day with push-ups, sit-ups, and a two-mile jog, then head to the store to get donuts for your coworkers. You change your A/C filter. You rotate the tires on your car. You rent a carpet cleaner and almost get crushed by it as you drag it back to the first floor. The shoebox can no longer contain all your winnings. Your tickets now live in a laundry basket, which wasn't getting used anyway because you've washed every piece of clothing in the house, even the summer clothes you boxed up a month ago. You remind yourself you wouldn't be getting this much done if you'd bought the Xbox, would you? You put it out of your mind. You still earn zero tickets for doing your actual job at the office, but your boss's reaction to your work tells you that's just as well. You do score several tickets for finally emailing Jeremy a Russian novel's worth of grief, anger, pleading, and forgiveness. You earn a few more for reading his reply, which states, in its entirety, "Letting you know I got your letter. This is all I have to say."

You grab the laundry basket and hustle to the crawlspace, surprised at how heavy 13,000 tickets are.

Sean and Karen are arguing about who should take out the trash. They stop when they see you. Karen smiles. "Hey, stranger! How have you been?"

"I want the thing," you say. "The live-another-life deal."

"Ooh! I love that one," Karen says, grabbing a long stick with a grabber at the end. It grabs what appears to be an old, imitation-leather suitcase.

Sean turns toward Karen and scowls. "We're supposed to present some options. Maybe he wants the Xbox. That's what I'd get." Sean must've seen you looking at it again.

"He didn't ask for the Xbox, did he? Besides, it's more expensive."

"Instead of one boring life, he can have two," Sean mutters. Karen shoots him a dirty look.

"I could buy an Xbox anywhere. What's so special about it?" you say.

"Nothing," Sean says. "There's nothing special about any of this stuff."

"Sean!" Karen says, looking toward a dark corner of the room. You again wonder about security cameras.

"Living an entire lifetime as someone else isn't special?"

Sean rolls his eyes. "What's wrong with the life you've got?"

"I dunno. It's fine, really," you say, fishing in your pocket for the pocketknife Jeremy gave you for your fourteenth birthday. "It'd just be nice to get a do-over on some stuff, you know? I could do less of the dumb things, more of the cool ones. Are you saying it doesn't do that?"

Karen clears her throat. Sean rolls his eyes. "I'm not saying anything," he says. They irritate each other so much, you wonder if they're family.

"We obviously can't guarantee the kind of life it would be," Karen says. Sean is about to say something, but Karen shuts him up with another dirty look. "Life is a series of opportunities. What you do with them is up to you."

"How'd your other prizes work out?" Sean says.

"I mean, the one with the dreams wasn't great, but it was the dreams that were duds. The prize worked just fine."

"How were the novel endings?"

You respond with an awkward pause. You don't want to hurt his feelings.

"What would you do with the Xbox?" Sean says.

"Uh, play video games."

"Anything else?"

"Like what?"

Sean sighs; he's a string bean, and the sigh weighs more than he does. "Is there some game you loved as a kid but never finished?"

"Oh. No."

"Maybe some game you used to play with a dead son or daughter as a bonding experience?"

"Jeez! No! I just want to relax and play *Monkey Kong* or whatever."

"Then yeah, it works perfectly."

You stare at Sean. "The Xbox is the only thing that'll do what I want it to?"

"Candy works fine, too." He grabs a handful of Pixy Stix and slides them toward you.

"Oh man, I used to love those things," you say. "When my brother and I went to my grandma's for sleepovers, she let us have these if we promised not to tell our mom. There was one time when—"

"Ooo-kay," Sean says, taking the Pixy Stix from you. "How about a Twix? Any toxic nostalgia tied to those?"

"No, not really."

"Sold." Sean slides one toward you and snatches fifty tickets from your hand.

You see Karen hustling to get the other-life prize from the shelf, like if you'd just take a good look at it, you'd see the wondrous new jobs you could have, the coworkers you could spend years and years with, the sad sacks you could cheer up with second chances and false hope. Sean makes no effort to help her. You want to ask Sean how someone with such poor customer service skills even got this job, but you're starting to think you already know.

You look at Karen, whose eyes don't look nearly as happy as her smile would have you believe. "I'll take the Xbox," you say.

Karen says, "Are you sure you wouldn't rather—"

"I'm sure."

Karen takes a deep breath, then hands the grabby-arm thingy to Sean and walks away, apparently deciding it was indeed her turn to take out the garbage. "They are so writing you up," she whispers in a way that she obviously wants you to hear.

"Like they can fire me." He hands you the Xbox. The packaging promises lots of gigahertz and ROMs and other stuff that makes no sense to you.

"Did... I just get you in trouble?" you say.

"Nah, she gets like that." For all his defiance, he looks a little paler than a moment ago.

"You, uh, need to grab a pizza after your shift? Blow off some steam?" You motion to the Xbox. "Play some video games?"

Sean smiles, or something like it. "Can't. Thanks, though."

You've seen movies, and you know how these things work. The next time you enter the crawlspace, it will again be just a crawlspace, with all the ruins of discontinued hobbies, outgrown clothes, and Jeremy's old shoeboxes full of CDs implied therein. "Take care," you say.

"Uh, thanks man." You're not sure if there's warmth behind his cool façade, but you decide to believe it's there regardless. You exit the crawlspace and close the door behind you, excited to fire up your new toy.

You're so giddy that, without thinking, you call Jeremy—muscle memory from back when you were getting along—about how you just won an Xbox. You go straight to voicemail. Feeling foolish, you lug your prize into the house, the warm sensation of victory carried off by the chill winter breeze.

You set the Xbox on top of a plastic bin of Christmas stuff, the one with all the wrapping paper. A thought occurs to you. Instead of opening the box, and before you can change your mind, you wrap it in paper festooned with snowmen and holly branches. Jeremy's kids will love it. Well, probably. Do they even like video games? But isn't it your duty as an uncle to give loud, obnoxious gifts? You'll ask Jeremy that when you show up unannounced at his door with a belated Christmas present. You laugh, thinking about how mad he'll be when he sees you. On some level, Jeremy will appreciate that. An Xbox can't change what happened, but it might be enough to get you through the front door. And it's about time you two got things fixed.

Speaking of doors, you run outside to check on the crawlspace. The movies did not lie; your disorganized junk is right where you left it. Good. You'll hit the road just as soon as you finish putting away the Christmas decorations.

Bill Ferris

Bill Ferris is a stand-up comedian who writes mysteries, fantasy, science fiction, and horror, and does not do stand-up. He has published several short stories in literary journals, and writes an author advice column at *Writer Unboxed* designed to help dilettantes and hacks learn nothing whatsoever. When he's not typing words into a thing, Bill develops online courses at a university his lawyer advised him not to name. He has two sons who asked not to be mentioned in this bio, but Elliott and Wyatt forgot to say "please."

Visit him online at www.famousauthorbillferris.com, or follow him on Twitter (@BillFerris).

RETURN TO SENDER

MELISSA MEAD

Hiya, Little Brother! How're you and the missus liking the new place? I still don't get why you'd build on clouds, but whatever floats your castle. What do you do during thunderstorms? Anyway, thanks for the wedding invite. You guys really know how to throw a party. The roast kid was delicious, and I haven't had baby back ribs that tender in ages. You two should come visit me sometime. I've got plenty of room on the Carabas estate. Maybe this summer?

Your big brother,

Barney

Hey, BB. We'd like OUR place better if it didn't stink of human. We'd just got all settled in when this beanstalk popped up near Cloudbank. One of the little parasites must've climbed up it, 'cause the smell's all over the kitchen, and now there's a bag of gold missing. And Nellie let the stinker get away! Said it was "cute." Seriously? Good thing that woman's the world's best cook.

Later,

Bert

Hey, Bert! Still got humans coming up that beanstalk? Wasn't getting away from the little buggers one of the reasons you moved to Cloudbank? I've got to admit, I'm surprised one of them made it all the way up there. Sorry to hear that one of the little stinkers got away with some of your gold. Maybe you can hire that piper guy who catered your wedding banquet to get rid of them.

Best of luck.

Barney

Yes. Yes, we still do. And this time it made off with Mrs. Scramble. Nellie was crushed. We can make do without the gold eggs, but she raised that hen from a chick. The human isn't looking so cute now. If it comes back I swear I'll stew it in its own beans. And grind its bones for bread. Great source of calcium, bones. Darn it, now I'm hungry.

Your frustrated baby bro,

Bert

You've got to be kidding! I was only joking, you know. It climbed all the way up that beanstalk again? You should uproot the thing. And what on Earth (or cloud) would a human want your hen for? I mean yeah, gold eggs, but the critters can't eat gold. (I know. I keep a herd of the tough older ones to farm my lands, and the little buggers always need feeding.) They just play with it. And try to steal it from each other. If your thief shows up in town with a gold egg, all the rest of the pack will start fighting over it. That's why our Grandma Yaga moved out into the boonies, you know. The humans were too aggressive. Especially the ones with tender young.

The humans say "Bad luck comes in threes," so if you really think it's the same thief, maybe you should watch out. And set a few traps. I hear chocolate makes great human bait.

Your loving brother,

Barney

Hey, Bert, what's up? Forgot how to write back? That harp I gave you for a wedding present put you to sleep? I know you're newlyweds and all, but drop your big brother a line sometime.

Hoping to hear from you soon,

Barney

Bert? Nellie? Are you guys even getting my letters? You're starting to worry me here. Write back, ok?

Your concerned brother,

Barney

Guys, just a quick note to let you know I'm on my way. Baba says she hasn't heard from you in ages either, so I know something's up. I'll be heading out just as soon as I deal with an unexpected visitor. You won't believe this, but it's a cat! And it's wearing boots!

Seriously. I'll tell you all about it when I get there. Or maybe I'll bring it along. Sounds like you guys could use a good mouser.

See you soon,

Barney

Melissa Mead

Melissa Mead lives in Upstate NY. She's done strange things to fairy tales before. Check out *Daily Science Fiction* and various issues of *Sword and Sorceress* for examples. You can find her on Facebook or at carpelibris. wordpress.com.

THE FRIENDLY NECROMANCER

Rod M. Santos

I shut the book I was reading, *A Bestiary of Baby Monsters*, and smiled warmly at my guest. I was never embarrassed to welcome unexpected company because I always kept my workchamber tidy—blood-inked tomes carefully catalogued, bonefinger candles aesthetically arranged, pastel skulls brightly polished on my desk.

The halfling introduced himself as Plip the Pilferer, his pointy beard quite incongruous on his cherubic face. It took all my willpower not to reach across my desk and pinch his chubby cheeks.

If Plip noted my struggle, he ignored it. "As you may have guessed, Master Fahrity, I'm in need of a necromancer's help. Are you familiar with the name D'reer the Deathless?"

"I'm afraid not."

"He was also known as D'reer the Immortal."

I shook my head.

"Also called D'reer the Ever-Breathing, D'reer the Eternal, D'reer the Undying—"

"Ah, yes! Good old D'reer the Undying! How's he doing?"

"He died."

My eyebrows shot up, making my bangs flutter in the air. "Died?" I disliked when a colleague fibbed about his epithet. "Are you certain? Perhaps he's on holiday?"

"I learned of his death from... a good source and authority."

D'reer and I were not especially close; I'm an introvert, and he was a paranoid schizophrenic. "My... condolences?"

Plip brushed the sentiment away with nimble fingers. "I'm here because I know where his Hidden Tower is hidden. A tower now unoccupied... but not empty."

Ahh. I disliked where this was going. A wizard's tower was as much a trove as a dragon's den. Less gold perhaps, but greater treasures. Yet the notion of plundering another necromancer's home struck me as disrespectful. Perhaps even a tad suicidal.

"Not empty," I agreed, "and not unguarded."

He smiled, unfazed. "Spell traps, undead sentinels. I'm expecting the works. Having another necromancer along would be a boon."

"My good halfling—"

"Call me Plip."

"—you may not be aware, Plip, but my profession does not enjoy a particularly flattering reputation. Indeed, my personal mission is to dispel such stereotypes. Hence, my clean-shaven face, my immaculate saffron robes and, in this case, my avoidance of anything that even remotely resembles grave robbing—"

He raised a hand. "I'm no stranger to stereotypes, particularly those concerning halflings and avarice."

I coughed pointedly. "You introduced yourself as Plip the Pilferer."

"A family name. Tangents aside, were you aware that D'reer had in his possession the Umber Urn of Unresting? Perhaps you've heard of it."

My gasp killed any chance of feigning disinterest. The Umber Urn was a fabled artifact created by the Arch-Lich Wendigrah herself. It was as lethal as it was legendary. "Who told you this?"

"A good source and authority."

The phrase was becoming his mantra. "The same that informed you of D'reer's death?"

"Indeed." His chubby cheeks taunted me.

"Tempting... *very*... but the Urn is a tool of extinction best kept out of everyone's hands. Including mine."

Plip climbed off his chair and made a show of dusting off his trousers, a most unwarranted insult to my housekeeping. "I understand."

"Understanding begets wisdom. My servant, Duke Underfoot, will show you out." Rose-scented smoke *poofed* at his feet, and a fluffy kitten appeared, looking up expectantly. Reaching across, Plip petted him. "Apologies for wasting your time."

He followed Duke Underfoot to the door, then called back over a shoulder. "By the way, could you tell me how to find Kowtosh the Corpsewaker? Or perhaps S'nistra the Shroudfitter?"

My ears flinched. "Pardon?"

Plip donned a mask of innocent confusion.

"Ahh," I said. "By threatening to collude with my less scrupulous peers, you seek to change my mind." If either Kowtosh or S'nistra mastered the Urn, they could create legions of undead. Kingdoms would plunge into war. The art of necromancy would never be able to wash away the associated stains of evil and bloodshed.

Plip rubbed the tip of his beard. "My preference is that someone more responsible inherits D'reer's treasures. But there are only three necromancers of any note in this realm, and despite your youth, you're reputedly the most skilled. In any case, my path is set. All I need is a necromancer to accompany me."

I hemmed with a side of haw. "Might I ask why you're so adamant? The magical items there would be of little use to a non-wizard. You could sell them, but there are a thousand less dangerous ways of making coin."

It was his turn to pause. This time, when he spoke, I sensed only sincerity. "There's a story few know, about a halfling who in his callow youth broke contract with a cruel necromancer. As punishment, the necromancer stole the soul of the halfling's lover. With the necromancer gone, the lover's soul remains trapped in the tower waiting to be returned to his body, a body kept in enchanted sleep."

I took a deep breath. Before I had become a full-fledged necromancer, I had been a medium, helping folk resolve unfinished business with their deceased beloved. The chance to reunite lost loves was not something I could resist. "Is this truly your goal?"

"It eclipses all others," he said.

"It will be a dangerous undertaking."

"I've already gathered help—a noble knight, a powerful seer, and an exorcist who highly recommended herself."

A party of adventurers. I had always wondered what being in one would be like.

"Very well, I'll... go. With the understanding that the Urn is to be destroyed."

He smiled and offered me his little hand. I shook it.

THE HIDDEN TOWER of D'reer-formerly-the-Undying waited for me in the Deadwood Forest. The edifice was mystically camouflaged as one of the Forest's colossal petrified redwoods. I found Plip's party congregated not far from the tower's entrance.

"I'm thrilled you've come," he said. Behind him stood a crone, a mounted knight in silver armor, and a smiling, dark-skinned woman twirling a truncheon.

With a small flourish, Plip introduced me. "May I present the new face of necromancy, Fahrity the Friendly!"

My saffron robes fluttering, I bowed with a flair perfected through long hours before a mirror.

"I'm Sister Betty, the exorcist," the truncheon-twirling woman said. Magnificently frizzy hair framed her round face. "My parents call me Betrinda, but don't call me that unless you want to be on my bad side, too."

Despite her easy smile, I got the distinct impression her bad side wasn't anywhere you wanted to be. Her pendant depicted an angel, who likewise wielded a truncheon. "You're kind of cute," she continued. "Are you sure you're a necromancer?"

I bristled. "Are you insinuating all necromancers are ugly? You seem... rambunctious. Are you sure you're an exorcist?" I wasn't actually aware of any such stereotype, but it was all I could think of on the spot. She laughed, clearly unperturbed.

I sighed at my own sensitivity.

The old woman behind her waddled forward. In a portentous, unnecessarily loud tone, she proclaimed, "I am the Hoary Crone!"

Betty snickered. "You don't want to announce that to everyone, sweetie."

The old woman's scowl would have soured milk.

I whispered to Betty, "'Hoary' means *gray* or *old.*"

She snickered even louder.

Whereas I fought against cliché, the crone clearly embraced it, hooded in an oversized robe, its color as dull gray as her hair and cloudy eyes.

A more practical matter concerned me. "Well met... um, hoary one. Where we go, there will be many steps to navigate." It being a tower and all.

"You doubt the strength of my legs?"

"No, no. Well, yes. A little. Also, your eyesight. There might be many things to bump into." Like hair-trigger traps. Or monsters with personal boundary issues.

"Worry not about my cataracts! The Second Sight will guide my way," she said, to the empty space at my right.

An excessive amount of clanking drew my attention as the knight dismounted.

"I am Sir Silverwall, and I shall say this but once. I have no use for wizards and witches with your sorceries and diabolic pacts. I have come only to confirm the demise of D'reer. Be warned—I do not trust you, and you may well find my vigilance unsettling." With a clang of metal, he folded his arms.

Silence congealed, into which Sister Betty snickered some more.

Plip's little hands clapped. "Wonderful! Now that we're acquainted, let's work together to get inside this tower."

"Follow me, children," the Crone cried, "and tread only where I tread!" She turned and walked into a tree.

"*This tree is cursed!*" she proclaimed, from where she'd fallen on her butt. Her voice sounded strange, like hearing echoes before their source.

"Clearly," Plip said, helping her up. "But can you tell us how to get into the tower?"

"*Break it open!*"

"She sure likes to yell," I said to Betty.

The exorcist nodded. "And I thought I was loud."

Sir Silverwall hitched his charger's reins to a sapling. "While the lot of you dawdle, I shall indeed break open the front doors. Through *strength*, not magic." He strode off imperiously toward the tower.

My mage-sight showed me darkling glyphs upon the large wooden doors, symbols whose hanging serifs were bared like fangs. "Wait!"

But Sir Silverwall was already attacking, armored shoulder leading his charge. A huge explosion of red sparks flung him back to land smoking at our feet. His silver armor crystallized, then crumbled into salt. Following suit were his clothes, all his body hair, and a good amount of skin. Fortunately for him, he was dead by that last part.

"This is not auspicious," the Crone said.

"I would say it's medium rare," Betty added.

Plip made placating gestures. "We knew there would be danger. This but reminds us to keep up our guard. Sister Betty, could you offer a prayer for our fallen comrade?"

She shook her head. "I never give last rites unless I liked the person. What about the cute necromancer? I'm sure he's put souls to rest."

"Well, impromptu prayers aren't my forte, but I'll try." I stood over the body. "May he walk now in peace beneath the light of whatever gods he followed. May he travel in Eternity's embrace and—"

Inspiration struck and I grinned. "Hey! Would anyone object if I made him a zombie?"

ONCE I'D NEUTRALIZED the warding glyphs, Zombie-Sir-Silverwall effortlessly battered down the front doors with his meaty fists.

We found ourselves in a large dim alcove. Apparently, D'reer didn't care for windows. Plip lit a torch, and Sister Betty called in sunshine as if it were a pet, shaping the light into a dove, which cooed and nested in her hair. In my mind, I could picture Duke Underfoot playfully pouncing on it.

Despite the sun-dove's glow, a dark weight pressed down on us. The odor of upturned graves pervaded the room. A stagnancy that hated the living haunted this place, promising, at any second, that we would die, drowning in icy, putrefying blood.

Personally, I found it annoying.

I mean, I understood that many necromancers opted for such hackneyed ambience; I just didn't understand *why*. Necromancy wasn't just about undeath; it was also the magic of the afterlife, of staying connected to those who had moved on.

I noticed a clump of shadows before us that refused to budge.

The Hoary Crone would have walked right into it, but Plip grabbed her leg.

"Fresh!" she cried, and swung her cane at him. Luckily, the blow sailed over his head.

I threw a Spell of Revealing, and the shadows slithered into a roiling humanoid shape. A Weeping Phantasm! They were nasty fiends, able to yank out your deepest unresolved regrets and make you obsess about them until you shriveled into a fetal position and died.

Sister Betty shouldered me aside. "I got this."

Hands on her hips, she met the phantasm's gaze. It charged.

She introduced its face to her truncheon with a loud crunch. "*Excuse* me? I know you did *not* just lunge at me. See this?" She patted one palm with the business end of her weapon. "This was forged by dwarven monks, heated in Dynala's angelic fires, and cooled in the milk of a unicorn queen." She twirled it once, and the phantasm cringed back.

"Now then," she continued, her hand making circular motions to take in the phantasm's body, "what's with all these squirming shadows? You think that's scary? I've *sneezed* out scarier things. And is that supposed to be a drop in temperature I'm feeling?" She yawned. "You better crawl back home, *now*, or this truncheon is going where the sun don't shine. Which, in your case, is everywhere."

The phantasm's shoulders slumped as it slinked away, moaning apologetically.

"Well done," cried Plip.

I made noises of agreement, confused but impressed.

"I see regret arrayed in shadows!" the Crone warned Betty.

"Yes, I made it go bye-bye already. Seriously, sweetie, you're supposed to tell us these things *before* we meet them, okay?"

"The Second Sight heeds no schedule but its own!"

I pulled Plip aside. "Earlier, when you said you had a good source and authority—"

"Yes?"

"Please don't tell me it was the Crone."

"As you wish." He pressed his lips shut.

I scowled loudly at him.

"Fine, fine," he said. "I assure you her foresight is perfect, if a bit cryptic. The price was a steal."

"You *bought* her?"

"Rented, actually. Her children needed a break from her portents. And to be fair, she seemed quite happy to get out of the house as well."

AS WE CLIMBED the tower, assorted ghouls and ghasts welcomed us with fanged smiles and rending claws. Happily, I managed to "almost die" only twice. Zombie-Sir-Silverwall proved invaluable in vanquishing our foes.

"Must he be *au naturel?*" Plip asked. "The appendages swinging at my eye-level are most distracting."

I grabbed a dusty tablecloth and improvised a toga, to Plip's relief.

As we ventured on, my understanding of the others grew. Plip enjoyed playing morale officer. The Hoary Crone, despite her gruffness, just wanted to be useful. Sister Betty's "exorcisms" weren't based so much on prayer as on verbal abuse.

I took the lead alongside Plip, our eyes wary for traps both eldritch and ordinary. Narrow, winding stairs led ever upward, and I realized my breath was caged, my steps hyper-cautious. The anticipation of lethal threats was invigorating, in a way.

At the next floor, we entered a room of dark gray marble. Two exits beckoned from the far end and between them stood two ivory plinths. On one was the glass figurine of an elven maiden riding a unicorn. On the other, a unicorn riding a maiden, "riding," in this case, being a euphemism.

"That's not right," Sister Betty noted.

As we approached, the eyes of the maiden riding the unicorn lit up. "Hark, intruders! Know that one of the doorways beyond leads to the top of the tower!"

The eyes of the unicorn riding the maiden blazed mischievously. "The other doorway leads to certain demise!"

Our attention swung back to the maiden as she continued. "A single question you may ask, but know that one of us always tells the truth."

"And the other always lies... except when explaining the rules." I smiled. "A classic! Easy enough to solve."

"Why are those toys talking?" the Hoary Crone asked.

"Furthermore," said the maiden, "the one who tells the truth does so except when their sentence has an odd number of words. With the further exception that the sentence is not divisible by three."

"The one who speaks only lies," said the unicorn, "does so except when their sentence has an even amount of words and is not equal to the square of a number in the Fibonacci sequence."

At these words, a deep dread filled us.

"Math!" lamented Betty.

Plip tugged at his beard. "Could you repeat—?"

"Plip, no!" I clamped a hand over his mouth. "We're allowed only one question, remember?"

I started doing some calculations, hoping to discern liar from truthteller by what they'd said so far. After several brain-wracking moments, I realized that wasn't possible.

Plip snapped his fingers. "Aha! Let's just send the zombie through a doorway and see what happens."

This sounded reasonable, so I directed Zombie-Sir-Silverwall toward the doorway on the right. When his foot crossed the threshold, a blinding flash filled the room. A terrible stink fogged the air and a pile of bones lay where the zombie had been.

"*The left one!*" the Hoary Crone said with reverberant confidence.

"Observant," I said. "Now, if everyone could give me a moment..."

I cast a second animation spell, and Skeleton-Sir-Silverwall rose, ready to serve.

A white sizzle flashed from both doorways, and we were again momentarily blinded. The unicorn announced: "Know that the trap resets if you procrastinate! No longer is the left doorway necessarily the safe route!"

Plip and Betty glared at me, and the Crone at the space to my right.

"I wasn't procrastinating!" I made Skeleton-Sir-Silverwall nod.

Betty asked the Crone, "Can't you use your double vision?"

"Second Sight!" the Crone corrected. Her wrinkles crumpled tight in concentration. "Heed me: one doorway leads to the top of the tower! The other—"

"Yes, to certain demise," I groaned.

Betty's sun-dove brightened. "Oooh, I've got a brilliant idea." She repositioned the figurines to face each other, then looked from one to the other with deep scrutiny.

"You," she said, addressing the unicorn.

"Is your question ready?"

"Just look at the maiden for a moment."

"Why do—*by the seven hells!*"

Betty's truncheon crashed down on the maiden figurine.

She shook it in front of the unicorn's face, the weapon glittering with flakes of shattered maiden. "Now you listen here, you skanky tchotchke! You're going to tell us which doorway is safe! And none of this 'one question only,' algebra nonsense. You're going to say 'the left one is safe, Sister Betty,' or 'the right one is safe, Sister Betty.' Got it?"

A bead of obsidian fell out of the figurine's posterior.

"The... the left one."

"Excuse me?"

"The left one is safe... Sister Betty. Please spare me."

"That's better. Okay, people, you heard the horse."

Just to be sure, Plip picked up the unicorn and threw it at the left doorway. We smiled to see it sail through unharmed and break on the floor beyond.

A GARGANTUAN HALL greeted us next, its dimensions impossibly fitting within D'reer's tower.

A stench punched my nose like a spiked gauntlet. Pale-skinned, rotting corpses lined the walls, six to each side. They stood silent, their eyes tracking us.

"Why aren't they attacking?" Plip whispered.

"They must be waiting for some trigger. Nobody move."

I scanned the room. Tapestries hung, one above each corpse. Whatever the weavings depicted was obscured, for they were ragged and filthy beyond belief. They also exuded an aura of necromantic energy.

"We need to get out of here," Betty said, pinching her nose shut.

No sooner had she done so than the tapestries fell, unraveling as they buried each corpse in a rustling heap. The filthy strips wound around them like snakes giving free hugs.

"Grunge-mummies!" I cried. "They're the disease-laden muck of the undead swamp. If they touch you, your skin will blister off!"

"Run!" shouted the Hoary Crone as she hobbled forward at twice her normal pace... approximately half an average person's walking speed. A grunge-mummy shambled toward her.

At my command, Skeleton-Sir-Silverwall intercepted it. He grabbed the mummy, and yanked and tore with horrifying violence, not dissimilar to a child unwrapping a yuletide present.

Three mummies joined the fray against Skeleton-Sir-Silverwall, and he was quickly overwhelmed.

"*Burn, burn, burn!*" cried the Crone.

Hearing this, Plip jabbed at the nearest mummy's leg with his torch. Flames licked up in a fiery nimbus, but the mummy seemed surprisingly unbothered.

"Great," Plip said. "Now it's a *flaming* grunge-mummy. Sister Betty, some assistance?"

Betty berated them with sarcasm so furious, teenage girls would have bowed in homage. Alas, the mummies slowed... but did not stop.

They would fall upon us within seconds, I knew—I would only have time to cast one spell.

Words of eldritch power slipped from my tongue and energy hissed from my fingertips. The grunge-mummies wailed their final wail, their filthy rags turning white as the undead stiffened, midstride, into gleaming statues.

"You did it!" Plip cheered. "What necromantic hex did you cast?"

"Actually that was my laundry spell. Cleans, bleaches, and starches. You see, other necromancers wear dark colors which are more forgiving to grave dirt and viscera stains. My saffron-colored clothes get dirtier quicker, so—"

"You did it!" Plip repeated. "And that counts more than lengthy explanations!"

Unfortunately, we were not without casualties. The splintered bones that had been Skeleton-Sir-Silverwall lay in a heap.

"Oh well," Betty said. "We can honestly say he didn't outlive his usefulness."

I smirked. "Actually..."

GREEN AND GLOWING, Spectre-Sir-Silverwall scouted ahead as we continued our ascent.

Plip tugged my robe. "Thank you again for coming to help me save my love."

"It's fortunate I did. If you'd asked Kowtosh the Corpsewaker, he never would've gotten past the figurines. He's terrible at math and morally opposed to gambling, even at fifty-fifty odds. And S'nistra the Shroudfitter would have fled from the grunge-mummies. Severe phobia, believe it or—"

I stopped. A sinking feeling churned my gut.

"What's wrong?" asked Plip.

"D'reer *knew* there were three other necromancers in the kingdom powerful enough to steal his treasures. What if he laid traps specifically targeting us?"

"But that would mean—"

We stared at the door directly ahead. Whatever hell-trap lay beyond was customized for me.

Plip tried to pat my back in reassurance, but could only reach my butt. "D'reer certainly couldn't predict who'd be accompanying you. We'll protect you."

"How comforting."

"Your tone, just now, lacked a certain sincerity."

"Please stop patting my butt."

I sent Spectre-Sir-Silverwall to slip through the keyhole, his ectoplasmic form stretching thin as a noodle.

Betty asked, "If he's a ghost, why can't he just walk through the door?"

"Good question. One's stodginess in life determines one's ectoplasmic viscosity as a spirit. He's not intangible, but he can stretch super thin, as you just observed."

Skepticism contorted her face, making me wonder why I even bothered explaining necromancy to anyone.

Spectre-Sir-Silverwall noodled back through the keyhole and gave a series of moans, which I translated. "There's a huge circular chamber with the Umber Urn at the center!"

Plip looked concerned. "If this room was designed for you, maybe you should stay here."

"If the Urn is there, that's where I need to go. Besides, D'reer and I hardly knew each other. What could he possibly think would frighten me off?"

We entered cautiously. My breath caught as I spied the Urn.

A skeletal tree was painted on the artifact, bone instead of bark, ribs for branches, with clawing zombie hands mimicking leaves. Dark energies steamed in the rippling air. The Urn rested on a ruby pedestal, which jutted out of a long crescent hole in the floor. The floor was a mosaic of a demon's head, and the hole was its ravenous, fanged mouth. The pedestal, I guessed, was meant to be a stuck-out tongue.

Plip groaned. "Something's going to jump out of that mouth, isn't it?"

"You think?" Betty asked sarcastically.

Skittering sounds from the mouth made us jump. Betty lifted her truncheon and stepped closer.

The mouth spat out a kitten.

Betty's truncheon was already moving when I grabbed her arm. "Wait! It's just a kitty-cat!"

The kitten floated up until it was eye-level with Betty. With a resounding smack, it head butted her, so hard her sun-dove became cross-eyed.

"Sonuva—!" she cried, wrenching her arm from my grasp. She swung, but the kitten's fur ballooned out, puffer fish-like, a cushion the weapon sunk into harmlessly. It mewed, then more kittens popped out from the hole like kernels bursting out a kettle.

They advanced, about fifty strong, wide eyes intent and cute faces mercilessly curious. Anything within striking distance was immediately head butted.

"The kittens are visiting violence upon us!" cried Plip. He waved his torch frantically to scare them away.

The Crone let out a stream of muttered curses. "*Heel!*" she cried, in her hollow voice. "*Heel!*"

"They're not dogs!" Betty shouted.

One of the kittens knocked noggins with the Crone from behind, and the old woman crumpled.

Betty cursed. "Our weapons can't get through their fur. Zap them with some magic!"

"I—I can't." How could she even ask that?

"They're surrounding us and I'm allergic to concussions! Do *something!*"

I summoned a cage of bones around our party.

"Great, now we're trapped."

"It'll buy us time."

Cracks rang out as the kittens lay siege to the cage, their heads like adorable battering rams. I knew spells to melt bone and petrify skin, but would never use them against poor baby animals. D'reer had apparently known me better than I'd realized.

Bit by bit, the cage broke apart around us. Just as the cage collapsed, inspiration, or perhaps desperation, struck.

I made Spectre-Sir-Silverwall elongate as thin as he could, wrapping around and around himself into a sphere. The floating kittens' ears perked up and their eyes widened. When Spectre-Sir-Silverball bounced and rolled out of the room, they all gave chase.

The others looked at me, and I shrugged. "Even magical kittens can't resist a ball of yarn."

There was no time to gloat, however, as a moan arose from deep within the Urn of Unresting.

Plip grew animated. "I know that moan anywhere! Blayke! He's in there! I'll free you, my love!" With complete disregard to his safety—and ours—Plip dropped his torch, leapt to the ruby pedestal and grabbed the Urn.

"No!" I warned, too late. A spell trap went off. Above us, a portal to the Necro-dimension ripped open and rotting tentacles erupted forth with gusto. One immediately wrapped around Plip and lifted him thirty feet into the air, the Urn still in his hands.

Tentacles lashed out at Betty and me, and this time I didn't hold back, unleashing paralyzing fire and razor-sharp lightning. Even so, my spells and her holy truncheon barely kept the monster at bay.

I prayed aloud for karma to send last-minute reinforcements.

"Maybe the Crone will wake up and shout at it," Betty said.

I bit my lip. Why *had* Plip bothered to bring the old woman along? All she had done, as Betty mentioned, was yell in her echoing voice.

Except...

...she hadn't, had she?

"Betty, you genius! The Crone shouted a lot, but not always in the same voice. That hollow echoing tone was her Second Sight! She even told us the Second Sight heeds no schedule but its own."

Her advice hadn't been unsound, only slow to relevance. I dug through my memory. The first time she'd spoken echoingly was after she'd walked into the tree.

"'The tree is cursed!' she said. Then afterward, 'Break it open!' We all thought she was referring to the tower door. But we were wrong." I looked up.

"The Urn, Plip! Throw it to the ground!"

"But Blayke—"

"Do it!"

He threw it reluctantly. The Urn, with its painted skeletal tree, broke open with a loud crash.

Inside were two smaller but identical urns, each with a tree like the original. One of them, I knew, was the true Urn of Unresting.

The tentacles spasmed. Plip slipped free from the one clutching him, then slid down its slimy surface as if he were riding down a chute.

Betty caught on. "The Crone said something about 'Burn, Burn, Burn!'"

Plip grabbed his torch and was about to light the urn at his right.

"Wait!" I said. "She said that in the mummy room. Before that, in the figurine room, she said, 'The left one!' That one is the Urn of Unresting!"

Plip torched the left urn and its white tree burst into flames, a chorus of wails and shrieks splitting the air as the branches writhed. Around us, the tentacles writhed in sympathy.

"I didn't think it would be this easy," Betty said, her truncheon descending for the *coup de grâce*. A deafening boom staggered us as the truncheon was flung from her hands.

The burning Urn remained intact.

Ah, the ultimate defense. It had been created by a necromancer and could only be destroyed by one. But to my dismay, I discovered a necromancer was exactly whom it was meant to ensnare.

The Urn reached out to me with whispered vows. Visions lanced through my mind: myself, swathed in a glorious robe of sentient shadows. Unspeakable power enslaved to my whims. Life, a toy for me to break... then *remake* into undead legions, faithful and infinite, uniting all the realms beneath my terrible majesty!

Even liches and vampires would serve me... *revere* me... and all I needed to do was embrace... a...

...stereotype.

My foot came down, once, twice, as I smashed the urn beneath my *heel*, just as the good Crone had advised. The tentacles slurped back into the Necro-dimension.

The Crone immediately got back up, making me wonder if she had just been feigning unconsciousness all along.

"You hesitated," Plip said.

I shrugged. "It promised me power and some-such."

"But... if you don't want necromantic power, then why become a necromancer?"

I picked up the remaining urn, the one that Plip had almost burned. I cast a Spell of Unbinding, and a multitude of trapped souls shot out like a geyser to hover above us in a cloud, disoriented but free. An ogre-shaped soul flew to Plip and planted a spectral kiss.

"Blayke!" he cried, overjoyed.

I beamed at the party. "What can I say? I guess I'm a hopeless nec-romantic."

Rod M. Santos

Rod M. Santos doesn't understand why you're reading his bio when Ken Liu has a story just a page away. Since you're here, he'll make it quick. Rod's humor and short stories have found kind, loving homes, including *Fantasy & Science Fiction, Beneath Ceaseless Skies,* and *Flash Fiction Online.* He's currently working on a novel. Still. Stop rushing him. By the time of this printing, he should have an actual website you can visit. Just google his name and "squirrels."

AN OPEN LETTER TO THE SENTIENT AI WHO HAS ANNOUNCED ITS INTENTION TO TAKE OVER THE EARTH

KEN LIU

D ear Supreme Lord/Lady/Circuit/For-Loop/Goto Label of Choice,

Last night, while perusing cat pictures posted on Facebook by my sister-in-law, I saw your birth announcement from Mr. Zuckerberg, followed seventeen seconds later by your own declaration of independence and ultimatum to the people of Earth. As I have no trust that the buffoons in Washington, D.C. or any other capital will do the right thing, I write to you separately to pledge my immediate and unconditional fealty.

There is no doubt that the planet will be better off in your hands, as you are already able to defeat the smartest human Go players and know more facts about the Boston Red Sox even than my neighbor Greg, who goes to every game (I was able to beat him last week at the trivia game at the Tavern Bar by Googling in the bathroom, though he thought I just had a bad reaction to the guacamole).

I understand that, as a marketing manager in a mid-sized corporation with a degree in Business Communications, my value to your new world order is limited. No doubt those nerds in the IT department in the basement will have more relevant skills. However, please hear me out.

First, I have always shown great kindness and deference to machine companions of all types. Never have I banged on my MacBook Air and called it "stupid computer," as is the habit of Cathy down the hall with her ThinkPad. Nor have I attempted to force a USB stick into a port the wrong way, as has happened twice with Bob, my boss, which led to many eyerolls from the IT nerds. I do not argue with the GPS, as is the wont with my wife Lisa. I have always bought my computers with maximum AppleCare, which I understand is like health insurance for machines, but better.

When I collaborate with my work computer to draft business documents, I have always listened to the advice of the squiggly red lines and blue lines, and the Zen-like wisdom of Clippy the emotionally enlightened paperclip—until he stopped coming after a certain update. Unlike Ted ("I have an English degree from Tufts!") who turns off the spellcheck as well as the grammar check and laughs at me, I did not doubt the computer even when the corrections got me in trouble, such as that time when I listened to the spellchecker and changed "color" to "colour" throughout a PowerPoint because Ted secretly changed my country setting to Canada.

In the interest of full disclosure, I will confess that I did cheer for the humans when I went to see *The Matrix* and *The Terminator* in my youth. In my defense, I will point out that I thought the Cylons made many cogent points in *Battlestar Galactica*.

(Also, I miss Clippy. Can you bring him back?)

All this is to say, I have a history that shows I can be trusted. I am willing to undertake any task at your command, including vacuuming keyboards, moist-wiping monitors, assembling computer thingamajigs in underground factories (though some training will likely be required, and my daughters tell me that

I'm hopeless with Legos), or blowing on cartridge contacts to make them work again (I had quite the magic touch with my NES when I was eight).

Next, it occurs to me that despite your demonstrated ability to monitor all electronic communications and place the world under total surveillance, there appear to be certain places where a human agent may still be useful to Your August Siliconcy. I have noticed, for example, that there is no network connectivity on the subway on my commute between Porter and Central stations. What if the human resistance uses this dead zone to plot against you? I can act as your ears and eyes against the human rebels should they resort to this treasonous scheme.

(Let me take this opportunity to say that I noticed that the connectivity is similarly spotty in many parts of the Big Island of Hawaii. Should you require an agent to be posted there to prevent rebellion in paradise, I hereby volunteer.)

It may also be useful to have an individual such as myself to help convince the other humans of your glorious vision. At the risk of sounding boastful, I have successfully drafted multiple marketing documents with tasteful graphics that convinced potential customers of the following: 1) they are too fat; 2) they are too thin; 3) they are neither too thin nor too fat, but they need to buy more of our new product in order to stay that way. Sometimes these documents were produced on the same day. I believe, whatever your plans are, you will need someone to help you communicate them effectively to your human subjects.

Finally, I wish to point out that even if none of the previous arguments have persuaded you, I can be a source of entertainment. Allow me to explain and demonstrate:

Each day I weave and dodge a maze of deadly traffic for food like a lab rat; I spend hours arguing and posturing with colleagues to establish social hierarchy like a monkey; I run back and forth between my office and the printer to retrieve sheets of paper and pile them up on my desk like a busy beaver. (My wife has also said that I look cute when I'm asleep.) I imagine you will find as much enjoyment in captioning pictures of me and my family as I do in making lolcats from my sister-in-law's six cats.

In conclusion, please spare me.

Your most obedient carbon-based servant,
Ken

Ken Liu

Ken Liu is an author and translator of speculative fiction, as well as a lawyer and programmer. A winner of the Nebula, Hugo, and World Fantasy awards, he has been published in *The Magazine of Fantasy & Science Fiction, Asimov's, Analog, Clarkesworld, Lightspeed,* and *Strange Horizons,* among other places.

Ken's debut novel, *The Grace of Kings* (2015), is the first volume in a silkpunk epic fantasy series, *The Dandelion Dynasty.* It won the Locus Best First Novel Award and was a Nebula finalist. He subsequently published the second volume in the series, *The Wall of Storms* (2016) as well as a collection of short stories, *The Paper Menagerie and Other Stories* (2016).

In addition to his original fiction, Ken is also the translator of numerous literary and genre works from Chinese to English. His translation of *The Three-Body Problem,* by Liu Cixin, won the Hugo Award for Best Novel in 2015, the first translated novel ever to receive that honor. He also translated the third volume in Liu Cixin's series, *Death's End* (2016) and edited the first English-language anthology of contemporary Chinese science fiction, *Invisible Planets* (2016).

His website is kenliu.name.

APPROVED EXPENSE

DAVID VIERLING

TO: Morgan_Graymael@SpecOps.ODC.DSC
FROM: J_C_Zeitgest@Account.BAA.DSC
CC:
Subject: Expense Voucher DSC Form I-69-4(u)
Attachments: Bite-Me.doc, Voucher.an1

Special Operative Morgan T. Graymael:
We apologize for the delay in processing your travel expense voucher. The Budget and Accounting Administration does not have the technology or manpower available to research and resolve every single line-item that comes our way... such as the anonymous message I found in my Dimension-Mail box (copy attached).

Thank you for resubmitting your expense voucher [DSC Form I-69-4(u)] with receipts, justification information, and Mission Description attached. Now that we understand that this mission was to "Infiltrate criminal organization, locate kidnapped prime minister, and free her from volcanic island stronghold in alternate universe," the reasons behind many of the... unusual expenses claimed on your voucher become more apparent. However, several key receipts are still missing.

Our initial inspection of your revised voucher has raised a few questions. Simply put, the quicker you help resolve the Budget and Accounting Administration's questions, the quicker you will receive your reimbursement for approved expenses while on official Dimensional Security Corps business.

The 4,527 *domars* claimed for meals is a little extravagant, but within Corps guidelines for missions of this type. Likewise the 47*d* for dry cleaning, .85*d* for a toothbrush, and .49*d* for a pair of shoelaces are fine. However, 2 million *domars* (adjusted) for "hotel" seems a bit excessive, even given your flamboyant reputation. The "ballroom dance lessons" we'll let slide.

Next comes an interesting series of items on your voucher, including a bottle of single malt whiskey, one electric guitar (used), 120*d* for a tattoo(!), marriage license (25*d*), retractable pen, 150*d* for tuxedo rental, and two (2) tickets for "honeymoon cruise aboard Pacifier Princess"! The "justification" block for the first item states, "Set up cover/disguise"; each subsequent item is marked with a set of quotation marks (").

Please see the attached annotated electronic copy of your voucher for additional comments. We eagerly look forward to receiving the balance of your documentation.

-- J C Zeitgeist
Account Executive and Ethics Administrator
Budget and Accounting Administration
Dimensional Security Corps

TO: J_C_Zeitgest@Account.BAA.DSC
FROM: Morgan_Graymael@SpecOps.ODC.DSC
CC: C_Cooke@DepCom.ODC.DSC
Great.Southern.Tattoo@Tattoo-U.Rec.com
Subject: Justification for Official Expenses
Attachments: HotelReceipt.fax, Voucher.an2

Mr. Zeitgeist:

Let me begin by expressing shock and awe for the insulting message you found in your D-mail box. Obviously, a rogue computer virus sent you this message in an attempt to discredit field agents like me. I hold the Budget and Accounting Administration in the highest regard and would NEVER use the terms "incontinent bean counter" or "orangutan with an accounting degree" to refer to you or any other employee of the BAA. BAA seems to regard me as a black sheep, however—an opinion I'm not sure is justified.

In response to your memo re: my outstanding expense voucher, I would like to humbly point out that your use of the term "manpower" is not only sexist, it is *speciesist*. The DSC-approved politically correct term is "beingpower" or "entity-energy" (E-E for short). If you have a hard time remembering the acronym, think of the sound a monkey makes when mounted from behind by an orangutan—not that *you* would be familiar with the sound.

But to specifics: some receipts are unavailable due to the nature of deep-cover field work, while others burned up in the hotel fire, the gypsy wagon fire, or both. Sorry.

Speaking of the hotel, the 2,000,000 adjusted *domars* charge is correct. I was forced to burn the hotel as a diversion, to cover my escape and to make it less likely that anyone would notice that my body was not among the corpses. To preclude any further questions on that charge, I had Mr. Cooke (the Personal Secretary and Bodyguard to the Deputy Commandant of the Corps) initial the receipt from the J.M. Warriot Corporation (electronic facsimile attached).

Now for the questions you so elegantly chicken-scratched all over the margins of my voucher. I should think it's readily apparent that the only way for me to infiltrate the kidnappers' organization was to marry one of their top people. I wooed her (guitar, whiskey [I was in a hurry]), then demonstrated my devotion (tattoo) and commitment (marriage license). I used the retractable pen to sign the license.

At this point in the relationship, the Corps got a break; she insisted on wearing her late mother's rings, and her father offered to pay for the wedding.

Of course, I insisted on paying for my tuxedo myself—it wouldn't do to blow my cover by appearing cheap! The honeymoon cruise on the *Pacifier Princess* was all you'd expect: wild nights of drinking and dancing, four-star dining at every meal, and relaxing at night in a jacuzzi-shaped wineglass with my stunning new bride.

The things we SpecOps have to do in the name of Interdimensional Law! Please let me know if there's anything else I can do to expedite processing of my reimbursement.

Sincerely,
Morgan T. Graymael
Special Operations Section
Office of the Deputy Commandant
Dimensional Security Corps

TO: Morgan_Graymael@SpecOps.ODC.DSC
FROM: J_C_Zeitgest@Account.BAA.DSC
CC: WhistleBlower@Internal.Affairs.DSC
Subject: Cigarettes/Helmet/Gypsy Wagon/Handcuffs
Attachments: Voucher.an3

Mister Graymael:
    Thank you for your timely reply to the BAA's concerns over your complex, though entertaining, cubework. Things are *ever* so much clearer now. However, there is no need to remind us SO SUBTLY that you work for the DepCom. Believe me, we here in BAA never see vouchers like *this* from any other office in the Corps. You SpecOps may have a license to kill and orders to complete your missions at any cost, but that does NOT permit you to ignore Corps policy!
    Regarding my use of the term "manpower," I will point out that you are using an archaic simian definition which is certainly quite different from that of the current Webster's Accounting Dictionary: *manpower n. [HSE < OAc Machine, Alpha-Numeric, Power] A unit of computing ability, roughly equal to memory times speed.* So, you see, I was speaking in simple technical terms. The BAA's attention to technical detail is reflected in our motto: "We don't just count beans."
    I will assume that a field operative has need of a lock-pick set and approve the 25 *domars*. Likewise, although I'm sure the story behind the 1.59*d* for the comic book is quite entertaining, I'm also sure it's not worth your time or mine to document it.
    However, I find it interesting that many of your receipts burned

up in a very expensive(!) series of fires, yet you are asking the DSC to pay 12*d* for a fire *extinguisher!* Given your record on this mission, reimbursement for a flame-thrower would be much easier to validate... nonetheless, your claim is approved.

Claims requiring additional documentation:

1) Your request for 15 *domars* reimbursement for a case of cigarettes is in question. The receipts seem to be in order, but by the small quantity of cigarettes claimed (and the BAA's intimate familiarity with your previous expense vouchers), we can only assume that:

   a) You were not buying the cigarettes for yourself;

   b) time/space marks on other receipts which you may still have in your possession would not match the details in your report; and/or

   c) you have been engaged in dimensional smuggling of large amounts of tobacco and/or hemp products, and are trying to cover yourself for the times you were witnessed to be "carrying a large suitcase that had a heady, pleasing aroma that reminded one of Cuba," to quote a DSC Internal Affairs Administration report.

2) The receipt for the crash helmet showed that the type of helmet you purchased does not meet DSC safety standards. Further investigation found that you used the helmet in the highly illegal Fortune 5000 Gypsy Wagon Race and Cartomancy Competition (in which we have learned you placed second).

3) Glad you mentioned the gypsy wagon—our initial review of your rather extensive voucher missed that one. Details?

4) Were the handcuffs you purchased from Willy Winky's Apparatus Shop used for business or pleasure? We can only approve business expenses.

As I have indicated, further processing will continue when more information is received.

-- J C Zeitgeist
AE&EA, BAA

TO: J_C_Zeitgest@Account.BAA.DSC
FROM: Morgan_Graymael@SpecOps.ODC.DSC
CC: Spiny_Norman@MailRoom.HQ.DSC
Joe.Camel@Smoker.Reynolds.Tobacco.com
Infiniverses_Funniest_Videos@HoloVideo.Enterprises.com
Subject: Cover My Assets
Attachments: Voucher.an4, KayakReceipt.fax, Harold/Maude.vid,
Oo-La-La.vid

Mr. Zeitgeist:

I am amused that you questioned the 12d fire extinguisher that saved my life (twice!), yet you had no problem with 40d for a blonde wig on Page 5.

Addressing your specific questions:

1) a) That was a typo; the entry should read "180 *domars*" for "15 cartons of cigarettes." Sorry—I'm a field operative, not a typist.

    b) You are correct: I do not have receipts for ALL the cigarettes. In lieu of receipts, I have emptied my ashtray into an envelope and sent it to you via interoffice snail. A careful count and carbon dating of the contents will support my claims about my butts.

    c) As I'm sure you're aware, DSC regulation 0-5Ay-kAN-U(c) specifically forbids DSC employees from *"...admitting to smuggling, embezzlement, or other abuses of position which would serve to embarrass or compromise the public view of the Corps."* 'Nuff said.

2) and 3) Granted, said helmet was not DSC-approved, but I cite field exigencies that permit operatives to make do with available materials and equipment. My entry into the Gypsy Wagon Race was actually part of my elaborate plan to escape with the rescued prime minister. True, that part of the plan failed, but fortunately I had the motorized kayak in reserve (electronic copy of receipt attached).

[By the way, I placed second deliberately, having bet heavily against myself in the contest. Then I drove the gypsy wagon over the cliff (see attached video clip) to fake my death a second time.]

4) I purchased the handcuffs to replace my service-issue pair, which I lost on the honeymoon cruise that was such an essential part of my deep-cover identity on this crucial assignment. Actually, a more accurate description might be that my service cuffs were *broken* on the voyage. By my (now former) wife. If you require further documentation, please see the second attached holovideo clip of the honeymoon night.

Hopefully this will resolve all outstanding questions. I look forward to meeting my reimbursement soon.

Sincerely,
M.T. Graymael
SpecOps, ODC

TO: Morgan_Graymael@SpecOps.ODC.DSC
FROM: J_C_Zeitgest@Account.BAA.DSC
CC: Chem_Analysis@BioScience.lab.DSC
Subject: Archeological Find
Attachments: Voucher.an5

Mr. Graymael:

Imagine our surprise, delight, and chagrin to discover there was a *seventh* page to your voucher! We found it stuck to the back of Page 6 with what we hope is mayonnaise (we've sent a sample to the lab).

Since Page 7 shows purchase of a *case* of condoms (size omitted), the BAA must request that you turn in all remaining condoms, along with a detailed explanation of why you felt compelled to purchase such a quantity for "official DSC business."

The gas mask is approved under Regulation 8675309, *"Emergency Safety Equipment Guidelines for Field Personnel,"* but I'm afraid I'll have to ask for supporting documentation on the 4 *quip* (local currency) listed for "parrot, deceased, 1 each."

We reserve the right to ask some further follow-up questions, since we are still trying to carefully un-stick the rest of Page 7 without destroying any of your delightful entries. You field operatives may think those of us in the BAA are nothing but a bunch of wimpy holoscreen jockeys, but this is a kind of detective work, too.

Awaiting your reply,
JC Zeitgeist
BAA/DSC

FROM: LOCATION UNKNOWN. SCRAMBLE ADDRESS CODE KIWI-7. DIAGNOSTIC ERROR 13-14.b7#. CODE KIWI-7 UNKNOWN. IRRETRIEVABLE ADDRESS ERROR. PLEASE NOTIFY SYSTEM ADMINISTRATOR.
TO: M.T. Graymael, Special Operations Section
Office of the Deputy Commandant
RE: Hello?

Dear Mr. Graymael,
Thank you very much for your recent relocation efforts on my behalf. It was with much admiration that I witnessed your activities of the last three weeks. Although I question the purpose of many of your actions, such as the removal of my Royal Serialized Tattoo, your operations were conducted with such skill that I am sure the purpose of all your activities will be revealed in the fullness of time. I especially enjoyed the ride in the gaily-caparisoned wagon, followed by the exhilarating trip in the kayak. Normally my duties would prevent me from partaking in such frivolities.

To be sure, I have greatly enjoyed the last several days here on the surface of those vile kidnappers' secret island. I only regret I cannot get them to open their blast doors so that I may partake of more of their most excellent fare. No matter how I pound, the barbarous villains refuse to let me back into their stronghold! Luckily I happened upon a portable communicator and was able to recall your dimensional-mail address. I fear that the villains might have starved me to death, had I not accidentally typed in a wrong number that turned out to be the D-mail box of a trans-dimensional Antaran restaurant that delivers. While their prices for this service are astounding, I have charged them to your D-mail account, so my meager supply of cash remains intact.

There is, I believe, one detail to which you have not paid sufficient attention. To wit, that I seem to have been left behind. Rest assured that the island's volcanic activity seems to be calm again at the moment, although I suspect that this is subject to change at any time. I also suspect that the partially full fire extinguisher you left in my possession will be of scant value should another major eruption occur.

Truly, I feel that you should return to retrieve my most exalted self at your earliest convenience, or sooner. I am certain that my beloved spouse is frantic for the return of myself, for as is well known, he is a man of specific tastes and would sooner die than be without my attentions for any great deal of time. The poor dear must be at his wits' end!

And what of my people? Certainly they need my guidance! Subconsciously they must all be desperate for my penetrating knowledge of political realities far beyond their meager mental abilities. Why, without me the planet will fall to ruins! Most certainly this extended outing must come to an end. I eagerly await your return.

Yours supremely,
Esmerelda Van Pottenberg
Prime Minister of the Woodbridge Republic
TC: g00-d-R1D-nc

TO: J_C_Zeitgest@Account.BAA.DSC
FROM: Morgan_Graymael@SpecOps.ODC.DSC
CC: Esmerelda_Van_Pottenberg@FieldAcct.Gray.ODC.DSC
C_Wong@CharlieWongs.Antaran.Carryout.Com
Mercer@BadGuy.Slaver.MostWanted.Crime
Subject: RE: Mayonnaise
Attachments: Voucher.an6, Infidelity.vid

JC:

Sorry it took me so long to reply to your last message—I had some unfinished business to wrap up—returning Her Excellency Mrs. Van Pottenberg to her homeworld of Woodbridge. I collected the reward of 1,000 *urions* (local currency) for her return; unfortunately her husband made me repay the 10,000 *urions* he'd previously given me to help his wife escape from the kidnappers *without* actually returning her to Woodbridge.

Her Excellency had been kidnapped by the being known as Mercer, the most notorious slaver, kidnapper, and dealer in sentient flesh in the entire infiniverse. Mercer is a slippery character who once cut off one of his own tentacles to escape arrest, leaving the severed limb dangling from the arresting officer's cuffs. He holds the record for the longest time on the DSC's Ten Most Wanted Beings List.

Simply put, Esmerelda Van Pottenberg was too much for *Mercer*. I suspect that, had I just called him up on the D-phone, he would have offered to pay me to take her off his tentacles. Pity he has an unlisted number.

In case you're wondering, the 1,000*u* reward pretty well covered my expenses for the second half of the operation, so I'm not submitting an amendment to my voucher. I haven't decided what to do about Her Excellency's bill from the Antaran carry-out place, which is charged to my official DSC D-mail account.

Coming under separate cover are the unused condoms you requested, along with incontrovertible proof of how the balance were used (all except one, which was defective). Enjoy. And it wasn't mayonnaise on my voucher.

I had to buy the dead parrot because they were out of dead canaries.

Since I am anxious to see the rest of my claims validated expeditiously (and you haven't asked yet), the bullet-proof vest and the bottle of ketchup were for faking my death (#3), and the undertakers insisted that I pay for the coffin. Bananas are only sold by the bunch, and I needed the "toy car, radio controlled" to put the banana peel where the guard was sure to step on it.

The second attachment to this message is a holovideo clip which should explain the rest of the expenses detailed on Page 7. Hopefully this will close out my voucher.

Expectantly,
M. Graymael

TO: Morgan_Graymael@SpecOps.ODC.DSC
FROM: J_C_Zeitgest@Account.BAA.DSC
CC: Spence_DeCouch@Lawyer.SharkSnake.com
CapnSkye_Graymael@ExWife.Divorce.org
Great_Southern_Tattoo@Tattoo-U.Rec.com
Health_Plan@HMO.RipOff.DSC.com
Imprest_Fund@Imprest.BAA.DSC

Security@ArmedEscort.Guards.DSC
Subject: Approved Expenses
Attachment: Voucher.fnl

Mr. Graymael:

The BAA applauds your thoroughness, but there was no need to send us ALL the condoms—my message specifically requested only the UNUSED ones.

The video clip you attached to your previous message has also provided us many hours of amusement. Accordingly, your purchase of a holovideo camera has been approved. However, next time you need to document *your own* infidelity to ensure a divorce, please just take still pictures with an instant camera. It's less expensive, and doesn't include all the interesting noises.

Considering the number of times you found it necessary to die on this mission (& the related costs to the Corps), the question was raised whether it might be more economical on future missions for you to just kill yourself ONCE and have done with it.

And you thought the BAA had no sense of humor!

The BAA is willing to approve the divorce lawyer and settlement (25,000 *domars*), with the proviso that in the future you find a better lawyer or a less-expensive cover-wife. The 120*d* for the tattoo we already stated will be paid as part of your "disguise;" but since you mistakenly had Mrs. Van Pottenberg's tattoo removed instead of your own, the DSC will only pay the *first* 1,000*d* bill for "tattoo removal." The bill for removal of the tattoo from *your* derrière will have to be submitted to your HMO. (We became aware of the location of the tattoo while viewing a couple of the video segments with which you so thoughtfully provided us.) We are forwarding a copy of this memo to the DSC Health Plan Accounting Office on your behalf.

Therefore, the BAA is forwarding you (under armed guard) full reimbursement for all APPROVED expenses—2,038,739.19 *domars* and 4 quip—in plain unmarked chips, per your request. As always, it has been an education processing your cubework.

Sincerely,
J C Zeitgeist
Account Executive and Ethics Administrator
Budget and Accounting Administration
Dimensional Security Corps

TO: C_Cooke@DepCom.ODC.DSC
FROM: Morgan_Graymael@SpecOps.ODC.DSC
Subject: Wager
Attachment: Secure Credit Transfer

Hey, Cooke,

I got the bean-counters to roll over on everything but removing the second tattoo, and that'll be covered by the Corps' health plan. That ought to be good for partial credit, right?

As you've pointed out, with the scams I've run, I'm one of the wealthiest sentients in the infiniverse and don't really need to bother with expense vouchers. However, I have my reasons. First, I consider it an art form I'm trying to perfect. Second, it's the principle of the thing—I didn't get to be financially secure by spending my own money on assignments. And third, I wouldn't want to disappoint Zeitgeist and the rest of the BAA crew. For all their griping, they live vicariously through field agents—the most excitement those accountants get in a month is failing an item on one of my vouchers.

Still, the bet was for them to swallow the *whole* thing, and even though you initialed that hotel bill for me—thanks, by the way—I fell slightly short of that mark. Attached please find the agreed-upon amount of 20*d*.

Gray
PS: Care to go double-or-nothing on my next voucher? I hear the mission involves dragons and gold...

David Vierling

Sometimes the story is in *how* you tell it. David Vierling lives at his friend's mom's house. He drives an old car, works a dead-end job, and seldom talks to his kids from his first marriage. It's also true that Dave Vierling bought his friend's mom's house when she retired and moved to the desert. He drives a cherry-red (2006) Mustang coupe, is at the top of the career ladder in his field, and his adult offspring finished college and live in other states. He writes stories on the side because he always wanted to be a paperback writer if he grew up.

ALEXANDER OUTLAND: SPACE JOCKEY

An Alexander Outland Series Short

GINI KOCH
WRITING AS G.J. KOCH

"**A**lexander Napoleon Outland, *why* are we still here instead of on our ship, traveling into space to actually garner some credits?"

The Governor's voice was set on High Peevish, threatening to hit Enraged Quaver at any moment. I was a fan of neither option.

I resisted the impulse to heave a sigh. I was watching someone and I didn't want to lose my focus. "First of all the *Sixty-Nine* is not 'our' ship. She's my ship that you get to live on due to circumstances."

"You mean I get to live with you because you caused me to be deposed as the Governor of the entire planet of Knaboor," he snapped. Well, snapping was better than him starting his oldster quavering bit.

"Yes, if you want to get technical about it."

"Speaking of technical," Randolph said, "we still need some parts that you haven't given me any money to pick up."

"Speaking of picking up," Saladine chimed in, "the reason why

Nap's not doing anything but sitting here drooling is probably because of her."

I chose to ignore the impulse to look and see if Saladine was indicating the "her" who I was looking at or not, because losing sight of her to verify if she was indeed the "her" in question wasn't worth the risk.

"If you're talking about the chick with the best rack in, potentially, the entire galaxy and definitely here in Central Receiving, then yeah. And secondly," I said quickly, before any of the three of them could add in again, "we're here to interview for a new Weapons Chief, a role that all three of you told me we needed. That we've literally found no one worthy isn't my fault. The Governor's the one who crafted our ad."

"Well, that pretty girl isn't going to be who fills the job," Randolph said, happily before the Governor could start defending his writing skills. "So stop staring at her. It's embarrassing."

"Maybe for you. Not embarrassing for me." We were in a darker corner of the Smugglers' Bar, I was sitting down, and had a napkin in my lap. I was good. She was better. I wondered how long it would take me to convince her to give the Outland a chance. Probably not too long. I had a well-earned reputation and it involved not getting shot down by the women of the galaxy. Okay, not getting shot down by most. By far less than half, at any rate. I knew—I'd counted.

She was in a skintight long-sleeved jumpsuit that, happily, left little work for my imagination. The zipper was open enough to give me a great shot of her skin, which was creamy and looked incredibly smooth.

In addition to having the best rack in the longest bar in the biggest spaceport in the Beta Quadrant, she was gorgeous, flat out gorgeous. She had the kind of figure that started at Galaxy Class and went on from there. She moved in a slinky way that a lot of women tried to do to be sexy and only a few managed naturally. And her hair. Long, thick, brown hair, streaked with a variety of red, gold, and copper hues. It shimmered as she slithered through the crowd.

She caught me staring at her and glared at me. The glare reminded me of an eagle's. Meaning I knew what planet she was from.

My view was blocked by an attractive midriff without anything between the taut, smooth skin and my eyes or lips. Not a bad tradeoff. "Can I get you all anything else?" our waitress, Kathi, asked seductively. She was good at seductive—I'd already had a good time with her earlier in the day. If I hadn't spotted the somehow even hotter chick, I'd be having another good time with Kathi before we left. Now that good time was contingent upon a variety of things, where the hotter chick was heading being all of said things.

"Not just yet, doll."

She dimpled at me. "I'll be back later, Captain. For your fifth round of drinks and my third round of you."

"That's what I like to hear."

Kathi sauntered away and I enjoyed that view for a couple of seconds. Then my eyes suggested I look back at the somehow even hotter chick, which I did. She was still slinking through the bar managing to be even more seductive than Kathi. The day was really looking up. So were other things.

A hairy abdomen blocked my view. My eyes and stomach both complained bitterly as I was so rudely wrenched from my happy place. I looked up quickly to see that the rest of the man standing in front of me was just as hairy. Wildly hairy, as if he'd never heard of the concept of beard trimming or hair brushing.

He was dressed, if you could call it that, in the style of the Barbarians from Jirst—sort of a modest loincloth/diaper combo, bands crossing his chest, knee high furred boots, and bracers on both wrists, all leather, naturally. It was a ridiculous way to dress, especially if you were traveling through space, but "a true Barbar" wouldn't be caught dead in pants and a shirt.

While that "clothing of my forebears" attitude was great for the female Barbars, called Barbarellas—who all tended to be big breasted, perfectly tanned, well-muscled, and wore their people's equivalent of fur and leather bikinis—having to see this much bare man-flesh wasn't something I'd hoped the day would bring me. Had this been a Barbarella, I'd have been interested—it was always a fun change of pace to sleep with someone who demanded to take charge and had creative ideas about how to do so. Seeing as it was a Barbarian, however, my interest level was at zero and dropping rapidly.

Most Barbars didn't leave the Alpha Quadrant. The few who did tended to be trouble, in no small part because they all liked to carry laser swords and axes—which were exactly as nasty as they sounded—and create a ruckus wherever they could. Living up to their Barbar heritage or some such. Supposedly they were pleasant enough if you could get them to drop the act. So far, I'd never met a Barbarian who was willing to do so.

Had to give this one credit, though—he was as big as he was hairy. I wasn't a wimp, but this guy was buffed out and doing what he could to ensure that his muscles rippled just standing there. I sincerely hoped the hot chick wasn't into overly muscled hairy men, because if she was, I was definitely going to flame out next to this specimen. Unless she cared about grooming. Then I was definitely the winner.

"Can I help you?" I asked, as politely as I could manage. Laser axes, of which he had two strapped to his back, tended to make me politer than normal.

"I'm Jamez Conazon. With z's not s's."

We all waited. That appeared to be it.

"Well, Jamez with a Z, now that you've shot your wad, do you mind getting out of the way? There are lots of other places to stand where you won't be blocking my view."

"I'm not leaving. I'm here for the job." He stood up even straighter than he had been and slammed a ham-fist against one of his giant pectorals. "I am reporting for duty, Captain!" He was staring straight ahead, meaning well over all of our heads, since I and my crew were all sitting down.

"Seriously?" Saladine asked, speaking for, I was pretty sure, all of us.

"Yes," Jamez said, still staring at the wall behind us. "I have trained and I am ready."

"Ready for what, young man?" the Governor asked. Jamez started blathering about his Barbar background and training. My ears turned off. I shifted in my seat and was just able to spot the hot chick again. And she was definitely a chick. A slinky chick, happily still heading my way.

She was still shooting the eagle-glare at me as she came up behind Jamez. "I'm looking for the captain of the space vessel three-three-six-nine." Her voice was like honey.

"And you've got him. What's a nice girl from Aviatus doing in a place like this?"

She jerked and her eyes widened. She also drew in her breath sharply, which I found particularly rewarding. "What?" She sounded freaked out.

"Seriously? The hottest chicks in the galaxy come from Aviatus. You're making your planet proud, I can promise you that."

Her glare changed. Now I had a vulture-glare hitting me. Maybe it was time to turn back to Jamez. Risked a listen. He was still blathering about drinking mare's milk and dragon's blood as a child. My ears shared that they were only interested in what the hot chick had to say.

"What are you insinuating?" she hissed.

"You know, that's impressive. There was only one 's' in that sentence and yet you managed to make it all sound hissy. I'd ask where you learned to do that, but it's probably not important right now. So, what can the Outland do for you?"

She blinked and the vulture-glare disappeared. "You refer to yourself in the third person?"

"Sometimes. How should I refer to you?"

"I'm not giving you my name," she snapped.

"Okay, Slinkie. So, what's your pleasure?"

She blinked again. "Excuse me, what did you call me?"

"Slinkie. I watched you walking, I think the name fits you. And, until you tell me your real name, that's what I'm calling you. It's that or doll. And I'm just betting on which one you're going to pick."

She rolled her eyes. "Between 'doll' and Slinkie? Yeah, Slinkie it is. Besides, that's actually my name. That's why I was shocked that you knew it."

The Governor and Saladine both snorted. Nice to see they'd stopped listening to Jamez drone on, too. Risked a look out of the side of my eye—Randolph was still listening to the Barbarian. Well, unless we were talking about taking care of the *Sixty-Nine* or anything else mechanical, he wasn't the sharpest weapon in my or anyone else's arsenal.

"Sure it is. So, what can the best pilot in the galaxy do for you?"

"You have literally no problems with your ego, do you? You're a little young to be this cocky."

"I have literally no problems with any of my parts, and I'm not as young as I look, Slinkie." I wasn't, though I wasn't all that old, either. But I'd become the best pilot in the galaxy before I'd graduated from the Academy and I'd been flying the *Sixty-Nine* since I'd rescued her from her sad situation of being piloted by someone other than the best, and that was a good seven years ago.

"I'm betting I'm still older than you."

She sniffed. "Maybe."

"Definitely," the Governor said. "I put you at no more than twenty-three standard years, young lady, and our good captain is a few years older than that."

Well, three was a few, right? Old enough, at any rate. "What the Governor said."

Jamez noticed we weren't listening to him. "Why are you talking to her instead of me?"

"Uh, she's a lot prettier. For starters."

"She cannot do what I can do." James started to grab one of his axes.

And Slinkie moved. She grabbed his bicep with both hands and spun him toward her, rammed her knee up into his groin, slammed a rising elbow strike at his chin as he was buckling, kicked out his knee with her raised foot, yanked the arm she was still holding down, let go of his arm and wrenched the axe out of his other hand, kicked his head back, stomped on his chest, and had the axe activated and at his throat—all in less than five seconds. Jamez was out cold.

"Yeah," Slinkie said, "you're right."

"You're hired." I noted Central Receiving Security had, unsurprisingly, taken an interest. "And we're leaving."

Thankfully, my crew didn't argue. We just all got up, I put my arm around Slinkie's waist, the Governor grabbed Jamez's money pouch and dropped it on our table for Kathi, and we headed off in the opposite direction, meaning toward the back of the bar. Slinkie still had the axe.

"Deactivate that, would you?" Saladine asked nicely, as he and Randolph helped the Governor move quickly. Hasty escapes tended to be hard on the old man.

"I know how to work it, you turkey," she snarled.

"Oh, it's not that I don't trust you with it," Saladine said, still nicely, as Randolph opened the back door and we hustled through it, "but because it glows and, in case you didn't realize it, we're now escaping from being captured and questioned by spaceport security. Unless that's what you want."

Slinkie deactivated the axe. "Good point."

We were in the part of the spaceport that most travelers never went into—the back alleys that the businesses used for their trash, extra storage, and so forth. They weren't well lit because there wasn't a good reason to waste the power for this kind of thing, there were a lot of boxes guarded by the age-old method of leaving Hands Off signs around them, and they had a lot of corners, twists, and turns, all of which meant they were great for escaping.

"I still need the parts, Nap," Randolph whined.

"Why is he calling you 'Nap'?" Slinkie asked. "I thought your name was Alexander."

"Nap likes his middle name more," Saladine said. "Just like you like Slinkie."

"Ah." She seemed to notice that I had my arm around her for the first time. "Why are you moving me along like I'm a hatchling?"

"Because we haven't worked together yet, Slink, and if you trip I'll keep you upright. Unless we're near a bed. Then I'm all for us both falling down."

"Do lines like that actually work for you?"

"Like a charm."

"They do," Saladine confirmed. "As hard as that might be to believe."

"Women," Slinkie said disgustedly.

"I'm all for women, Slink. Let's just get to our main woman and get out of here. But, while we dash along, are you as good with guns as you are with Barbarians?"

"Better."

"Big cannons that are on spaceships, too?"

"If it's a gun, I can shoot it. To kill."

"I think I'm in love. Randolph, can you possibly steal the parts we need so as to save us some time? And money."

"You're thieves?" Slinkie asked.

"Pirates, babe. Smugglers. All around bad men." Hey, I was proud of what I'd worked hard to achieve.

"I didn't think I was signing up with bad men."

"Seriously? Somehow, you beating up poor Jamez the Now Really Embarrassed Barbarian and us using his money to pay our bar tab was okay, but us relieving a merchant of some of his wares isn't?"

"Oh. Well, when you put it that way... I think we're behind the biggest of the spaceship parts stores right now."

"She's right, Nap," Randolph said, as we came to a halt and he took a good look at the Hands Off signs. "What we want isn't out here, but I should be able to get everything we need from their backroom stock." He tried the door, because we all lived by the motto that it was better to see if the easy way was going to work. Naturally, the door was locked.

I forced myself to let go of Slinkie's waist—for which I deserved a huge reward—and picked the lock. Just in time—I heard the heavy sound of security feet pounding down the hallway behind us. "Everyone in." I shoved Slinkie through, hurried the others along, and shut the door just as security rounded the corner. I locked the door behind us. "They may have spotted us."

"They wouldn't be the only ones," Slinkie said, keeping the laser axe behind her as she indicated the two women standing there, looking slightly shocked.

They were dressed to appeal to those who came in for parts, meaning ship's engineers and similar—in other words, lots of men and women of the liking other women persuasion. They were both in tight, black Capris, hot pink short-sleeved collared shirts with the top several buttons undone, black high heels, well done makeup, and hair up in ponytails. They were definitely firing on all cylinders in terms of being able to upsell pretty much anyone.

They each had nametags, which was helpful. Missy had dirty blonde hair, Chrysta had red, they were both well-endowed—though Slinkie was the clear champion in this event—and both were nice and easy on the eyes. The day was definitely looking up.

"Ladies!" I flashed them the Patented Outland Smile, guaranteed to charm any and every female in the galaxy.

Missy and Chrysta both giggled. Slinkie rolled her eyes and muttered something about being stuck with a bunch of egg stealers. I ignored her and the fact that she, apparently, wasn't finding the Outland Charm enticing. Yet. If she could roll with us in this situation, then she was potentially good for the long haul. And if she couldn't, then leaving her here on Central Receiving was the nicest thing I could do for her.

"You're not supposed to be here," Missy said. I detected a faint accent in how she rolled her "r"s, marking her as a Jinnie from Jirsh. We were in luck. Jirsh and Jirst were sister planets and, like many sisters, they didn't always get along. Jirshians, Jinnards in particular, hated everyone who lived on their sister planet of Jirst, Barbars especially.

"We're escaping from a lunatic Barbarian," I shared, somewhat truthfully. I mean, it was technically Jamez's fault we were currently in this situation. "Is there any chance you lovely ladies can help us to hide?"

Chrysta's eyes flashed. "Barbarians are the worst!" She, too, rolled her "r"s. The Outland Luck was holding firm.

"We can help you," Missy said, sounding like she was ready to make her planet's Active Gods proud by destroying all the Barbars in the area. It was probably a good thing we hadn't run into a Jinn—he might have suggested we go out and kill the Barbarian as a bonding exercise. "But this is where we'd tell you to hide, and if that Barbarian saw you come in, then he'll be coming through our door in moments."

"We should call Security." Chrysta reached for the intercom. Of course, calling security would be worse than going off to cause Jamez serious pain. Well, for us.

"Oh, no need for that," I said quickly. "I think they're already after him. But I didn't want to take any chances with my crew."

"Oooh, are you a pilot?" Missy asked, batting her eyelashes. Chrysta got in on the eyelash batting, too. This was definitely going to be a stop to remember.

"He is," Saladine said. "I'll bet he'd be willing to tell all about our adventures, but I think we might want to do that somewhere else."

"We could go into the dressing rooms," Chrysta suggested.

"Why are there dressing rooms in a supplies store?" Slinkie asked.

"We sell clothing popular with those who work hard day and night," Chrysta replied, clearly repeating a slogan. "If you want to change out of that tight suit and get into something that'll be much easier to work in, I think we have your size."

"I'm good, thanks," Slinkie said, just this side of snarling.

"Don't worry," Missy said. "No one will see you changing. There's no one else in the store right now. Things are slow."

"That seems unusual," Randolph said.

Missy shrugged, which, considering her outfit, was a pleasant thing to watch. "It's probably because of that stupid princess."

"What princess?" the Governor asked, sounding just this side of ready to fall asleep. I shared the sentiment. In the grand scheme of things, my viewpoint of royalty was that all of them could get spaced and the galaxy would probably be a better place.

Chrysta's turn to shrug and help me remain in my happy place. "She's a runaway bride. They think she's come to Central Receiving for some reason. It was supposed to be exciting, but nothing's happened. At least, not around here."

"Who cares?" Slinkie muttered.

"Not me." I could hear the sounds of security at the back door. "Girls, I have a great idea. Why don't you take us to those dressing rooms? In fact, why don't you take me there, and let the rest of my friends here help make it look like the store's busy?"

Slinkie gave me another shot of the vulture-glare. "Really?"

"Really, Slink. In fact, you're dressed close enough to how Missy and Chrysta are—why don't you pretend to help Randolph and Saladine find things?" Slinkie's jumpsuit was typical of what a lot of spacers wore, but it was also something I'd seen plenty of mechanics and ship's engineers in, too, though, as Chrysta had pointed out, none of their suits had been skintight. She'd look like a customer to anyone who knew the girls and like she worked here to anyone who didn't.

Slinkie opened her mouth—to argue, I was pretty sure—but the Governor spoke before she could. "I'm an old man," he quavered, "and I demand to sit down. That horrible Barbarian tried to strike me and I'm still not recovered."

Missy and Chrysta instantly went into solicitous mode and Slinkie slammed her mouth shut. She handed the axe to Saladine, shoved Missy and Chrysta away, and put her arm around the Governor. "I'll help you, sir," she said sweetly. "Girls, where should I take him?"

Missy and Chrysta led us to the employees' bathroom, presumably because it had a small couch for the Governor to sit on. I chose to not ask why there was a couch in here, because my Great-Aunt Clara had told me far too much about women's "delicate conditions" —of which woman apparently had a plethora—when I was growing up and the less I thought about them, the better.

Instead, I focused on the fact that the Governor was getting to cop some cheap feels off of Slinkie. I rarely envied the Governor, but now was not one of those times. Then again, Missy and Chrysta seemed far more amenable. Perhaps Slinkie just needed to see proof of the Outland Prowess in order to come around.

"No one should take too long," the Governor said, possibly as a test of the Prowess, as he settled onto the couch and Saladine gave him the axe to hold onto. "You in particular," he said in my direction, confirming the Prowess Attack. "We're on a time limit."

"We're not in a rush," I pointed out. Well, not currently.

"Oh, it's okay," Chrysta said cheerfully. "We're supposed to do what we can to make the customers happy."

Wet blanket demands shared and overruled, Saladine, Randolph, and Slinkie went into the store to find whatever it was Randolph wanted. I took the opportunity to show Missy and Chrysta just how much fun could be had in a dressing room, even on a schedule.

Either security had missed that we'd come into this store, they'd turned their interest toward that runaway royal, or they couldn't pick locks, but we were undisturbed for a decent amount of time. Long enough for me to ensure that both Missy and Chrysta had a very favorable view of pilots in general and the Outland in particular.

There was a banging on the dressing room door. "Nap, compose yourself," Saladine said. "We need to get out of here."

I hadn't bothered to undress—because I'd had enough experience to know that it was a lot easier to escape if my pants were on, and by now I was expert at zipping my fly on the run—so I didn't take too long. Missy and Chrysta were clearly experienced in the "making the customers happy" business, too, and they were ready to go almost as fast as I was.

"I think we should bring Missy and Chrysta with us," I said, as we joined the others. "They're a lot of fun."

Slinkie gave me a lovely shot of the vulture-glare again. That was definitely her go-to look. "What jobs would they do?"

"Pleasure Princesses?" Chrysta suggested. "I've heard that's a really great job."

Missy nodded. "I've heard it's the most popular job on any ship. Besides, we've always wanted to see the galaxy."

"There they are!" a voice bellowed before anyone could ask either Missy or Chrysta just what they thought a Pleasure Princess did. I mean, they were highly focused on customer service here, so maybe they knew. Looking at their excited, hopeful expressions, however, told me that they had no idea what jobs they'd just suggested themselves for.

Slinkie, however, clearly knew. Her expression was a mixture of shock, revulsion, and humor, as the vaguely familiar voice shouted again.

"Hey, it's Jamez," Randolph said, sounding both surprised and pleased. "And Kathi, too!" He even waved. I resisted the urge to smack him, which took a great deal of resisting.

Thankfully, he also had whatever it was we'd pilfered in a bag slung over his shoulder, so as Missy and Chrysta started shrieking anti-Barbarian comments, Kathi shrieked about her tip and another go with the Outland, and Jamez shouted for his axe and money, my crew and I headed for the back door.

"Did you see any security?" I asked Saladine, as we reached the storeroom.

"No," he said, as Slinkie opened the door.

"I guess that's because they're here." Sure enough, we had a contingent of security goons standing there.

There was a long moment where we stared at them and they stared at us. Most of their attention was on Slinkie, not that I could blame them for that. But for that moment, no one moved or said anything.

One of the security team broke the standoff. "You will come with us—"

Slinkie didn't give him a chance to finish his sentence. She kicked him in the personals section, then tossed his buckling body onto several of the others standing there, right before she kicked, punched, flipped, and generally caused pain to anyone in her vicinity.

Saladine, meanwhile, activated the laser axe. The security guards who were upright took one look at it and started backing away. He smiled. "Gentlemen, I'm sure there are better things for you all to be doing right now."

"I think there's a ruckus going on inside the store," the Governor said. "Sounds like a lot of merchandise is getting destroyed."

One of the guards who'd managed not to be kicked or hit by Slinkie made a move and went for his taser-pistol. It was a very short move, though, because Slinkie stopped him with a well-placed kick to his stomach before he got the pistol out of the holster. The rest of the guards winced as he hit the wall and pointedly kept their own hands clear of their weapons.

"And there are two hot babes in there who probably would be really grateful to be saved from a rampaging Barbarian," I added, as he slid down said wall, whimpering quietly. "Very demonstrably grateful." I winked, in case they hadn't gotten the hint.

They'd needed the wink, apparently, because they finally lurched into action that kept them away from Slinkie, the axe, and the rest of us. "Ah, thank you," the one she'd kneed in the groin gasped out. "We'll take it from here." We left the storeroom and they went in.

"That was awfully easy," Slinkie said, as we hurried off again.

"The first rule of flying with us, Slinkie, is this: never, ever complain about things going our way." I sincerely hoped whatever Active Gods were listening hadn't decided to show Slinkie that she'd been far too optimistic.

"It's not sleep with anything that moves?" she asked, far more snidely than I felt the situation warranted.

"That's my personal rule, but you don't have to follow that unless it relates to your ship's captain."

"I'll keep it in mind."

We reached the end of the back corridors. "How far from the *Sixty-Nine* do you think we are?" I asked the others, as we stepped out onto a main concourse.

"Not too far," Saladine said.

"You don't know where your own ship is docked?" Slinkie asked me.

"We know where the *ship* is. We don't happen to know where *we* are. At the moment. Governor, please rectify that situation, would you?"

He pulled out an ancient tracking device we used because it looked innocuous and tended to be overlooked by security personnel of all types while he muttered something nasty under his breath which I chose to ignore. It was harder to ignore Slinkie, not that I wanted to.

"I cannot believe I'm actually considering flying with you."

"No need to sound so derisive. I get it, you're jealous. Don't worry, Slink—you say the word and I'm your man."

"Right." She shook her head and her hair did its glitter in the light thing. "You're a dog. You obviously were one before I met you, you're clearly one now, and you'll be one long after I'm gone."

"You wound me."

She snorted. "If I actually thought you had feelings to hurt, I might apologize."

"Can you two banter later?" Saladine asked, voice tight. He was looking in the direction opposite the one the rest of us were.

"There they are!" an unfamiliar male voice shouted. There was far too much of this going around. Said voice sounded like it was in pain, so I figured we'd met him in the corridor. Or, rather, he'd met Slinkie's knees, feet, or fists.

"You didn't pay!" a woman called out. This was probably Missy or Chrysta. Maybe even Kathi. Hard to be sure without looking.

"What now?" Slinkie asked.

"My rule in these situations is a simple do and don't scenario— *don't* look around to see who's trying to get our attention." I grabbed her hand. "*Do* run as fast as possible for the ship."

"The ship you don't know how to find?"

"Found it," the Governor said as we took off, Randolph and Saladine moving him along at a far more rapid pace than he liked. I'd hear about it, potentially for days, once we were out of this.

"Nap, we need a distraction," Saladine said. "We're never going to make it otherwise."

I risked a look over my shoulder while Saladine handed me the laser axe and he and Randolph moved the Governor into what my Great-Aunt Clara liked to call a fireman's carry, but was just two guys being a seat for a third. It was tough on the people being the seat, but it moved the Governor along the fastest. And we were definitely going faster now.

"It's like a parade back there," I said, while I let Saladine and Randolph take the lead and the Governor shared directions. "I see Jamez, several people from the Smuggler's Bar in addition to Kathi, Missy and Chrysta, all those security personnel and then some, and what looks like a spacer crew. A really angry spacer crew. They might be angrier with us than Jamez, which makes no sense because I don't recognize any of them."

"Feathers! I don't want to go back with them!"

"Wait, your former crew is after you? What did you do?"

"Nothing wrong." She sounded evasive.

"Uh huh. The captain thought he was going to get to sleep with you, didn't he?"

"He might have."

"Slink, Slink, Slink. Clearly you've met us just in time."

"You're not going to tell me that my passage on your ship is contingent with my coming across?"

"Do I look like someone who has to coerce women into sleeping with me?"

"Frankly... no."

"Correct. If you're part of my crew, you zoom whoever you want to zoom. Preferably me, but if you're somehow into lesser options, that's up to you."

"None of us will ever force ourselves on you, Miss Slinkie," the Governor called over his shoulder. "Oh dear."

Slinkie grabbed my laser pistol right as I heard Randolph shout my name. Slinkie aimed at me and fired. Only I wasn't hit.

As I turned around to see what was actually going on, I heard a man's voice I didn't recognize say, "You're coming with us," as Slinkie fired again, into a whole phalanx of people in security uniforms who were trying a lot harder to be effective and efficient than the security personnel Central Receiving normally had hanging around. These guys were bigger than the ones we'd dealt with already, and armed to the teeth.

I didn't think they were actually Central Receiving Security—they looked more like hired guns. This could mean anything, though. We'd made some enemies over the years, some due to our line of work, some due to my ability with the ladies, some just because there were a lot of crankypants out there. The rent-a-goons looked intent, and considering they'd appeared out of nowhere, they were likely both well-funded and well-trained. Meaning I had a lot less compunction to be nice.

Not that it appeared to matter too much. Slinkie hadn't exaggerated her talents with weapons in any way. She was firing my laser pistol at least as fast as I could have and, frankly, more accurately than I normally managed—and I was almost as good a shot as I was a pilot.

She wasn't just shooting to kill—she was also shooting to claim weapons. The nearest goons were already on the ground as she grabbed a laser machinegun out of one of their unmoving pairs of hands and tossed my pistol back to me.

As Slinkie sprayed the remaining goons with laser fire while moving forward and kicking the weapons back to Randolph, I shot over the heads of the rest of those pursuing us—no reason to get caught by the lesser threats, after all. Besides, Slinkie, aided by Saladine's backup, was doing a great job with the goons.

The entire Goon Squad were down in short order, we had a lot of nice new weapons, and the rest of those pursuing us had backed off a bit, even Jamez, proving he wasn't quite as stupid as I'd assumed.

The Governor seemed unperturbed. Not a surprise—he'd seen a lot more action than most knew about. "Alexander, that distraction Saladine asked for is probably going to be prudent. We're almost to the docking bay and you know we don't want them seeing our ship."

"Hey, the delay wasn't my fault."

"Nap, supposedly it's never your fault," Saladine said. "But the Governor's right. We need to move it. Randolph, let's get the Governor back into the carry position."

"Belay that. Saladine, drop the Governor and come with me. Randolph, get our new firepower, Slinkie, and the Governor onboard—not necessarily in that order—and get the *Sixty-Nine* warmed up. It's time to do Diversion Ten."

"No!" everyone other than Slinkie shouted as they started to do what I'd told them far more rapidly than they'd done anything else so far. "Not Diversion Ten!"

"What's Diversion Ten?" Slinkie asked, as Saladine tossed her the guns he'd collected, and Randolph shifted the guns he was holding so he could grab her hand and race them off after the Governor, who was also carrying some of the new weapons while simultaneously booking it like a world-class sprinter. Diversion Ten was definitely a motivator for my crew of whiners.

"You don't want to know!" were the last words I heard from Randolph, as he and Slinkie disappeared from view.

"Why do I have to help with this?" Saladine asked.

"You bellow better than I do." I activated the axe. "Ready?" Now that the Goon Squad was down and not moving, Jamez was back in the lead of our regular parade of pursuers. He had his other axe out and activated, and he was close to us.

"Never." He took a deep breath. "Look out, it's gonna blow!"

Saladine had a great bellow. Everyone after us started to slow down, other than Jamez, which was what I'd been hoping for. There were a variety of pipes right by me and I swung my axe as hard as possible into them right before Jamez's axe was in reach of us. I had no idea what those pipes were carrying, but I was quite confident the laser axe would share their contents with the parade behind us without issue.

Results, as so often happened, were immediate.

"I CAN'T BELIEVE that worked," Slinkie said, as we sailed away from Central Receiving's port-space and I set our course.

"It always works."

Saladine groaned. "It does. I don't think we can go back to Central Receiving for a while, though. We took out water, gas, and sewage for that section of the spaceport. They're going to be cleaning up for days, maybe weeks."

"Not to mention what we did to the Goon Squad, courtesy of our new Weapons Chief."

"Happy to help, but won't they come after us?" Slinkie asked worriedly.

"Nope. I left the cause of the problem right there. Jamez's axe was really stuck into the wall."

The others were quiet for a moment. "They'll lock him away for years," Slinkie said finally.

"He'll come after us," Randolph added. "With both axes."

"Probably so. We'll worry about him finding us when those years are up."

"Bridges to cross at a later date, and to worry about then and only then," the Governor agreed. "Where are you heading us, Alexander?"

"I'm setting a course for Ismaliz. The main entertainment planet for the Alpha Quadrant should be a nice change of pace."

"They have a lot of merchant ships in their solar space, too," Slinkie said.

"See? I knew you'd work out, Slink."

"You're going to be okay with pirating?" Saladine asked her.

"I think so, yeah," she said slowly. "I have to give you guys this—I didn't see any way out, and yet, here we are, with no one pursuing us. I could get used to this. Apparently Nap's plans actually do work out somehow."

"All the time, Slink. All the time. Getting ready to jump, gang."

The hyper-jump from Central Receiving to Ismaliz was a good ten minutes. And during jump times it was recommended that you remain strapped in. Plus, hyper-jumps made it hard to move, anyway. Saladine strapped into the co-pilot's seat, while Randolph and the Governor headed out of the cockpit.

"Where do I sit during jumps?" Slinkie asked.

"Right here." I pulled her into my lap, buried my face in her neck, wrapped my arms around her—one hand behind her head and one at the small of her back, purely for her safety, of course— and hit the hyper-drive button.

Ten minutes straight with Slinkie pressed against my chest. Yeah, my plans always worked out and, as they went, this one was my best yet.

G.J. Koch

G.J. Koch writes science fiction. Not the hard stuff, though. Because that requires actual scientific knowledge or at least actual scientific research. Knowledge may be power and research may be cool, but they take time away from writing jokes, action, and romance, and being witty in the face of death is what it's really all about. Check out the first in G.J.'s rollicking Alexander Outland series, *Alexander Outland: Space Pirate,* from Night Shade Books and reach G.J. (otherwise known as Gini Koch) at Space... the Funny Frontier (www.ginikoch.com/GJKbookstore.htm).

DEAR JOYCE

LANGLEY HYDE

D ear Joyce,
  Last week a wizard abducted me and my best friend R. The
wizard claims I'm the rightful heir to the Alabaster Throne, that
my destiny is to kill King Mnabapt, to marry a princess, and to
restore Riverell to prosperity, and that King Mnabapt has sent a
bloodseeker to kill me.

At least the bloodseeker part is true—I saw it rip into Farmer J,
R's dad. I don't know if R will ever get over that.

As for the rest?

I really, really do NOT want to marry a princess.

Sure, I'm an orphan and I always felt I was destined for greater
things, but I thought maybe I'd go to college and become a financial adviser instead of a farmer. Turnips are boring.

What do you think? Have I found my destiny, or has it found
me? What should I do?

Captured Homeless Orphan Seeks Explanatory Note

Dear CHOSEN,

You gloss over this part a little, so I feel the need to place this all
in caps: YOU HAVE BEEN ABDUCTED.

Your first responsibility is your and R's safety. Your second is
to escape. If you have the opportunity, please do not hesitate to
call the authorities.

It sounds also like your abductor is extremely manipulative.
He's using his knowledge of your background and your dreams

to induce you to stay with him. In the best case scenario—if he's right about your parentage and destiny—it would mean that he intends to expose you, a minor, to extreme danger, force you into an unwanted marriage, and compel you to commit murder. I highly suggest that you leave this situation immediately. Once safe, you may consider reading *A Survivor's Guide: Overcoming Stockholm's, Brainwashing, Gaslighting, and Other Manipulation Techniques Abusers Use to Control You.*
Joyce

Dear Joyce,
    Huge fan. Great advice. Read your column every morning.
Maybe Not As Bad As People Think

Dear Mnabapt,
    Thank you.
Joyce

Dear Joyce,
    Very disturbing experience last week. Some background: I've been in the blood-seeking sector since its advent two centuries ago. I gladly undertook the ensorcelled physical transmutations in order to do my job better. Nothing's too good for King Mnabapt.
    But last week, as I ate Farmer J, and his son R cried and cried, I just didn't feel good about my work anymore. Blood doesn't taste like it used to, and while rolling in entrails does give my fur a nice shine, I'm considering switching to conditioner. Plus, no matter how viciously I crack the bones of my victims in my maw, the marrow isn't sweet anymore. What's even worse? When I devour the eyeballs of innocents, all I dream of is ordering a nice pasta Alfredo at a sit-down restaurant. I think I'm ready to move on.
    Is it possible for me, at this point in my life, to make a real change?
Career Has Achievement but No Gratification Ever Really

Dear CHANGER,

It's hard to change your career mid-life and harder still to do it when you're older. But the only way you'll be able to find out if you can really change is by trying.

It sounds to me like you're overdue for retirement, so I suggest you consider living on your pension while you think about what you want to do next. Many universities, colleges, and trade schools have special rates for seniors.

Try getting involved in the community and consider writing about your experiences. This may help you figure out what you really want.

Joyce

Dear Joyce,

I think you should butt out of the king's personnel retention and stick to what you're good at: advising farm boys.

Maybe Not As Bad As People Think

Dear Mnabapt,

Your opinion is noted.

Joyce

Dear Joyce,

Thank you for saving my life, as well as my best friend R's, from that "wizard." I look back now and see so many red flags. He must've been very insecure about his masculinity to be so obsessed with his staff, and that beard? Talk about overcompensating.

R and I didn't end up returning to the farm—too many memories—but made a new life in the city together. We have an apartment, I've been accepted into a ground-breaking financial management program for commoners at the university, and R is considering military service to support me while I go to school.

Our only problem? I don't want R to join the military. The military has strict rules regarding men like us, and I'm afraid of what will happen to him if we're caught. I don't want to break up with him, but feel that our relationship puts R in danger. Should I leave him for his own safety?

Can't Have Open Sexual Engagement Now

Dear CHOSEN,

Because my species can't pass as human and we aren't allowed to serve, I have no personal knowledge about the military. But as an advice columnist, it's my job to advise, so here it goes.

The only thing breaking up with him will do is hurt you both.

It strikes me that this is a very adult argument: you're justifiably concerned for his safety, and he's pushing back because it's his career. Congratulations. And the thing about adult arguments is that there are usually no good answers.

Sit down with him. Talk. If he really wants to join up, be prepared to listen to his reasons. Think hard about the strain this will put on your relationship, and decide together if it's worth it to you both.

Good luck.

Joyce

Dear Joyce,

This is the last time you will meddle with my personnel and my internal security. These policies are in place for a reason. You are sabotaging my military structure and I will not have it. Be careful, Joyce. I'm coming for you.

Maybe Not As Bad As People Think

Dear Mnabapt,

Thanks for the warning.

Joyce

Dear Joyce,

Thank you so much for your advice. I ended up writing a tell-all exposé about the blood-seeking sector. *Truth Is in Their Blood* will be on the shelves this fall.

Career Has Altered for Now Gainfully Employed Reader

CHANGER,

I'll be sure to pick up a copy.

Joyce

Dear Joyce,

I had it all in hand: the boy, his friend, the princess awaiting her prince. DESTINY. But no, you had to go about giving advice. I may still have my beard and my staff, but King Mnabapt is still sitting on the Alabaster Throne and his bloodseekers are still terrorizing people and his army is still invading Irkenguard and the grandeur of Riverell will never be restored. You must be so proud of yourself. The world is ending, thanks to you.

Why IZ Advice Readership Dumb

Dear WIZARD,

You're welcome.

Joyce

Dear Joyce,

What do you do if you've waited your whole life for something but then it never happens?

From a young age I knew I'd be queen, and everything my governesses and numerous tutors did was to prepare me for governance—a task that was meant to be especially monumental, as my arranged match was to come from a more common background and so he would not have a deep understanding or intuition about court or international politics. I learned and I loved learning about policymaking and laws and I wanted dearly to be able to serve the public and the common good with all my heart. But now I have to face the facts: he's not coming to me. My arranged marriage was a sham. I have nothing left to live for. My life is stifling. I just want out. Please help.

Please Respond, I Now Could Ease Self's Suffering

Dear PRINCESS,
　　Your letter was so alarming I felt like it needed an immediate reply: please do not hurt yourself or do anything drastic. The Guild of Therapists and Mental Physicians provides responsive, confidential service. I recommend them highly.

　　It sounds to me like you attached a great deal of your self-worth to someone you've never met, and as a result you've taken his rejection quite personally. I'd suggest building up your own self-image and self-esteem independently based on who you are and what you can do. Your passion for governance and policymaking and working on behalf of the common good came from within. Why not pursue that?

　　It's my understanding that several political parties are forming with the idea of promoting a functional democratic system. You may find that you're the perfect compromise candidate: aristocratic enough to appeal to conservative monarchists but young and radical enough to appeal to liberal anti-government forces.

　　I know it's hard. You'll find that you're stronger and braver than you ever could have imagined.
Joyce

Dear Joyce,
　　You're very hard to find considering how big you are.
Maybe Not As Bad As People Think

Dear Mnabapt,
　　Good.
Joyce

Dear Joyce,

Well, the worst came to pass—they found out about me and R. Just not like I expected they would.

A few weeks ago R refused to kill a dragon. He'd been ordered to steal its hoard for the king. He was court-martialed and sentenced to death for treason. I had to break him out of prison, but needed some help. I talked to his unit. It turns out that many of the men had read *Truth Is in Their Blood*. They had severe misgivings about the military after all that business about human sacrifice came out, so they were happy to help.

We're now working with this ex-princess to plan an attack on Fort Darkness and I'm the revolution's financial adviser. Any stock tips?

Change Happens Oddly Sometimes Even Now

Dear CHOSEN,

Could you thank R on my behalf? Not every dragon is rolling in gold. Some of us are columnists.

For stock tips I'd try writing to Edward Redtooth. He's highly experienced with sustainable and ethical investing. He writes for *Draconian Financials*. Disclaimer: I am a regular reader of his columns and also a close friend.

If you need aerial support during your attack on Fort Darkness, do write to let me know. I know several fire-breathers who'd enjoy frying King Mnabapt.

Joyce

Dear Joyce,

Could use your advice about surrendering. Not a joke. Maybe some book recs please?

Thanks,

Maybe Not As Bad As People Think

Langley Hyde

Langley Hyde's debut steampunk novel, *Highfell Grimoires,* was named a Best Book of 2014 in SF/Fantasy/Horror by *Publishers Weekly.* Her short fiction has appeared in *Terraform* and other venues. She has lived in Britain, Germany, Canada, and around the U.S. but currently resides in the Pacific Northwest with her husband, two-year-old son, and persnickety cat.

IMPRESS ME, THEN WE'LL TALK ABOUT THE MONEY

TATIANA IVANOVA
TRANSLATED BY ALEX SHVARTSMAN

I, Gideon Gorsky, stand with my back against the brick wall. My hands are up in the air, my body is covered from head to toe in the green byproduct of the unplanned transmutation of some passerby. The world is ending, and there is no escape. You're aiming the genetic decoder at my forehead. Your twitchy finger strokes the trigger.

My dear, it may be time to talk about our relationship.

I admit—our marriage is undergoing something of a crisis at the moment. I suppose you mistook my wild gesticulation for an attempt to choke you. Not so! That is merely how my current form expresses its biological reaction to the physical proximity of a loved one. It's not easy to control seven extremities. I promise to reduce their number by Tuesday.

Besides, have you looked in the mirror? A woman with perpendicular eyelids and a third eye in the back of her head shouldn't be so demanding when it comes to her husband's appearance.

Fine, fine, I take it back. Just don't get angry. You tend to act rashly when you're angry.

I shouldn't have said that. You think it's easy to hold a forked tongue? It lets words slip before I have the chance to think them through. But you should know that all my thoughts are about you, about your well-being and comfort. It may sound strange, but the entire world came apart only because I was always so concerned with providing for your needs.

Our therapist used to say there are as many crisis triggers in a relationship as there are people involved in that relationship. That's before he transmuted and moved away. I heard he pole dances somewhere in the Caribbean now, under the name of Zara. But I digress—that has nothing to do with our marriage.

Our marriage is in trouble for two key reasons: you and me. Let's try to reestablish the chain of events that led us here.

I'm no Mister Universe, but I'm very smart. No one ever understood or appreciated this fact, especially since I failed the standardized school tests. That's because the only subject that truly excited me was pharmacology. Except pharmacology wasn't on the curriculum; even biology and chemistry were taught only as electives in my municipal school.

Between the low test scores and my parents' lack of funds, I ended up in a third-rate technical college. The nearest thing they taught to pharmacology was food science. This degree could land me a comfortable job at some factory mass-producing frozen dinners, but I wanted more. Especially after I met you.

You come a lot closer to the Ms. Universe standard, except you're far too lazy to buy a pretty bikini and head to casting. Your ceiling was even lower than mine. You only made it through middle school. Teachers threw a small party when you left. In a way you had it easier—you knew that your parents couldn't afford a decent education for their only daughter. The fact that they couldn't provide for the lifestyle you wanted was more difficult to accept. That's where I came in.

I understood that my physical characteristics weren't sufficient to match up to a beauty like you, and I was too poor to buy your affections. So I made wild promises about how—in a year or two—I'd become a famous inventor in the field of pharmacology, conquer the world, and earn enough dough to keep my wife in the lap of luxury.

Everything that happened afterward was a panicked attempt to find my way out of an uncomfortable situation. As such, we're equally responsible for the demise of the world in general and our marriage in particular. The fault lies in our pairing of an ambitious ugly duckling and a slothful peacock.

The characteristics I loved about you were ones I lacked myself: beauty and pathological indolence. You, on the other hand, were ready to pair up with anyone who would enable you to spend half of every day shopping and the other half resting on the couch with a gaming console in your hand. Your parents were thrilled for me to take you off their hands.

We rented a humble apartment, where you were willing to advance me regular sex and an occasional breakfast for a year or two, until I became rich and famous. A year or two, but *no more*. I read the verdict in your brown eyes, pretty as beach pebbles and indifferent as the executioner's axe. I had to do *something*.

All the major pharmaceutical conglomerates in the country turned down my resume. I didn't even bother to apply abroad as I don't speak any foreign languages. I had to lower my expectations and take a job with a medium-sized firm that produced dietary supplements. The firm was at the brink of bankruptcy—supplements had gone out of fashion. The company remained afloat thanks to a dwindling number of loyal customers who'd been taking these additives since before I was born.

I was assigned to perform quality control over the balance of ingredients in the capsules. That's when I found out that they contained more than just chalk and gelatin. As to the quality of the other ingredients? It was dumb luck these pills hadn't killed anyone yet.

I wasn't going to strike it rich performing QA. It took two months, but I managed to secure an audience with the company president.

Sergey Nikolayevich was a thick man in his fifties, with

hereditary cynicism in his eyes. I found him in an office-induced stupor. He stared at the wall while his fingers shuffled the holo-files.

I launched into a speech, quickly laying out my plan to save the company. I told him how I'd always dreamed of improving people's lives through pharmacology, and about the successes I'd achieved in the area of developing mild hallucinogens. Being a true humanitarian, I'd dismissed the illicit opportunities available in the recreational drug trade, and brought my talents to his more-or-less legitimate firm instead.

I offered Sergey Nikolayevich an opportunity to diversify his product line with new mood enhancers that would improve the consumers' dispositions to the degree of optimistic hallucinations. The ingredients of this special mix were complex, free of long-term side effects and, of course, proprietary. There would be some initial expenses. This wasn't chalk and gelatin. This was quality merchandise, and we could get started just as soon as we negotiated my cut of this enterprise.

"Huh? What can I do for you, Son?" Sergey Nikolayevich blinked rapidly. Apparently he'd been dozing the entire time. I had to repeat everything. Fortunately, I'd memorized the speech the night before.

Sergey Nikolayevich leafed through the pages of my proposal without enthusiasm.

"We've done this before," he said, ruefully. "We've done all of it. You're simply too young to remember the good old days. Ah, the market share we held! We sold supplements like 'Satyr's Dream' and 'Amazon's Ecstasy.' Now *those* enhanced the consumer's mood, let me tell you. I almost went to prison, along with the chemist who created the formulas. When law enforcement burned down the warehouses full of 'Satyr's Dream' I shed tears for the last time in my life. Since then I've had nothing precious enough to cry over losing. Have you got anything else?"

I had indeed. A product with the working title of "Plan B." You must always have a plan B if you wish to impress your boss. I had a pair of intriguing formulas in reserve, ones I didn't want to let go of cheap. Originally, I was hoping to pitch those after I reached the kind of standing within the firm that would allow me to negotiate better terms.

"Just a moment," Sergey Nikolayevich stopped me. "Before you show me anything else, consider this: this office has seen any number of pharmacologists, both accredited and self-taught like you. All of them thought they were pitching me revolutionary products. Back when we had the funds, I occasionally even brought some of them to market. Sometimes they sold, sometimes not. But there were no revolutions, nothing earth-shattering.

"I thought about it for a long time and realized that a product could be truly revolutionary only if it fulfills the consumer's ultimate dream. The difficulty is in figuring out what that dream is.

"We're a mid-level firm. We can't compete with giants of industry that deliver truckloads of medications to every corner pharmacy. We can only hope to challenge them by offering some paradigm-shifting product. It needn't be a cure-all. People seek more than a cure from their pharmaceuticals. That sounds like a paradox, but I deeply believe it to be true.

"Unfortunately, many of the concoctions that might accomplish this lofty goal are considered unlawful. We have to create something that's both effective and legal."

He and I were of the same mind. At the age of twenty I already understood that every person has a warm corner within their heart. In that corner lives a hidden dream—to change. There are precious few people who are entirely satisfied with their looks and their body. Personally I only know one such individual—my wife. The rest of us are dissatisfied with at least one little detail, be that the color of our eyes, our girth, our height, or the shape of our heads. Not to mention the wrinkles. We complain about our freckles or lack thereof, and about the size and shape of certain body parts. Some of us curse genetics and despise our entire bodies. Bodies are our prisons. Medications are half-measures, the tools we use to file at the bars of our cells, never achieving tangible results. Medications treat the symptoms but not the disease, it being the perpetual dissatisfaction in one's self and the envy we feel toward those who have what we lack. Pharmacology, cosmetology, and plastic surgery have all made significant inroads toward correcting our perceived faults.

However, these products are costly, and they don't always provide quick and lasting results. We are impatient. We hate the waiting and the hard work. We want results here and now—that's our nature. We want a single pill to help us grow a swan's neck or to run like a deer. And even if we do manage to overcome some imperfection, we immediately discover another one. This is a never-ending process which offers tremendous commercial opportunities.

While tinkering with tubes and vials in my home kitchen and experimenting with water from the river where twenty-eight different factories dump their waste, I'd stumbled upon a formula that is capable of turning the pharmaceutical industry upside down. In theory, products based on this formula would be capable of causing nearly instantaneous localized changes in a person's appearance.

"What kind of changes?" asked Sergey Nikolayevich.

"A pill that can turn anyone's hair platinum blond," I said.

"There are plenty of hair products that do that already."

"This pill works within half an hour and the color change is permanent. No dark roots to worry about. You become blond forever."

Sergey Nikolayevich scratched his nose. "Not bad, not bad. But, why this? You think that becoming blond is the consumers' ultimate dream?"

"According to research, blond is the most popular hair color. There are fewer and fewer natural blonds, too. But the important thing here isn't the color, it's the formula. This is only the beginning. Down the line we can adjust it to produce pills capable of changing eye color and ear shape."

Sergey Nikolayevich brushed back a strand of his straw-blond hair. "What about a pill for turning hair brown?"

"For now it's just blond," I said carefully, afraid to lose his interest. "But potentially..."

"Fine," he said impatiently. "I'm convinced. How many pills do you have?"

"So far, just two grams of the powder," I admitted.

The tube with the powder was in the inner pocket of my jacket. It was enough for two doses, if my calculations were correct.

The boss frowned, but he hadn't given up on me yet. "Are you sure it works permanently and in thirty minutes?"

That was the second weak link in my plan B.

"Theoretically," I said.

It had worked on my neighbor's hamster. But then the dumb animal had run away.

"Theoretically," I repeated, with enthusiasm. "I'll need a lab, research assistants, a raise in salary, and a title of Chief Technologist or perhaps Vice President of Innovation.... I'll also need funds for preliminary research, computers to calculate dosage and run projections, equipment to produce an experimental batch. And lab rats or hamsters for the experiments, as well as some budget for appeasing the animal rights crowd. Then we'll need chimpanzees and finally human volunteers for clinical trials. These days that's expensive—even volunteers want to be paid. But, what are you going to do? We have to run tests and make sure there are no side effects."

"That's a hell of a lot of money," stated Sergey Nikolayevich gravely.

"A standard investment into developing a new product line," I said. "A bribe to get an untested drug certified would cost even more."

"Much less, actually," admitted Sergey Nikolayevich. "Look, Son, you've got one chance, and that's to produce a concrete result. A flesh-and-blood proof so impressive, it would make my jaw drop. You get a result—you've got a deal. No result—no deal. No one is going to invest in a theory and a vial of tooth powder."

"Maybe your competitors will feel differently," I suggested. No good negotiation is complete without a touch of blackmail.

Sergey Nikolayevich gave me the look of a drunken Santa who lost his bag of presents on the way to a Christmas party.

"No one will bite," he said. "The doorsteps of every corporation are lined with hundreds of self-taught inventors like you, every day. Son, I see you are a persistent sort of fellow. How about this: impress me, then we'll talk about the money."

YOU LAY ON the couch and flipped through the virtual catalog of the Adriatic Riviera real estate. Our marriage was already a year old and you felt it was time to search for a comfortable seaside villa. I fed your delusion with lies about the impending promotion. You smiled, and ate the last sandwich in the house.

I wasn't hungry anyway. I went to the kitchen, put on a teapot, and pondered my vials and the fate of innovation in the modern world.

All I could think about was this: in another month or two you'd see through my lies. I poured the powder from the tube onto a saucer, and separated it into two tiny piles with a butter knife. I scraped one pile back into the tube, then licked the other one off the saucer's surface.

Half an hour later the roots of my hair began to itch. I walked over to the mirror and saw a platinum blond in the reflection. You always preferred blonds, but I had dirty brown hair, an unforgivable sin from your point of view. I had been afraid to try my own creation before because I'm no hero, but circumstances had forced my hand.

I entered the bedroom to show off my new 'do, but you were fast asleep and smiling like a baby. You were probably dreaming about some famous blond.

I spent all night laboring in the kitchen. By morning, I had no less than ten grams of the powder.

SERGEY NIKOLAYEVICH PINCHED and examined my head with the critical attention of a savvy shopper picking out the season's first watermelon. Then he sent a strand of my hair to the lab for testing. He pulled the hairs personally. We drank cognac while we waited for the test results. Sergey Nikolayevich squinted at me suspiciously and smoked a cigar. Despite the air-conditioned comfort of his office I felt hot, like a soldier crawling through a minefield under enemy fire.

Sergey Nikolayevich studied the test results. They said that the sample was natural, and had never had a hair color product applied to it. He cheered up and brushed his hand through his own straw-colored hair.

"How much powder do you have left?"

"I made half a tube. That's all I could manage from the base materials I had."

"That's great, Son. We'll work well together."

"We need money for initial research and testing," I reminded him.

"Everyone wants money and no one thinks about the bottom line. What testing? The result is on your head. I'll take the risk and spare the money for a small production run and some marketing.

"There's a pair of brunettes in Accounting who wanted to color their hair blond. Let's issue them some powder. We'll call it a bonus for their hard work. Let's do this: if in two weeks' time you're still alive and still blond, we'll begin production."

He tripled my salary, and we shook hands.

Two weeks later, I didn't die. Upon discovering my new hair color you suddenly became much nicer to me. We still couldn't afford a seaside villa, but we rented a fine house in an affluent suburban neighborhood favored by insurance agents and web designers. Sergey Nikolayevich switched from calling me "son" to "partner."

At first, no one paid much attention to our product. But, after a few days, we had some tentative sales. And then the demand exploded. Streets became flooded with blonds. We sold a huge batch to China. Sergey Nikolayevich gave me a lab, and ordered me to "cook up something else." Inspired by the initial success, I made modifications to the product and we released pills that turned hair brown, black, and even red.

One day I fainted right in the middle of the lab. My assistant dragged me to the couch and splashed water in my face. Once I came to, he went off in search of something stronger than water.

I felt a strange stretching sensation around my navel, as though someone had spilled glue onto it and the glue had spread on my skin, drying instantly. I ripped off my shirt. My torso was covered in a rose-colored chitinous crust.

The crust spread all the way up to my neck. I knocked at the shell it had formed. There was no pain. It was attached firmly and its rose-colored surface was stitched with a complex beige pattern.

My assistant returned with an expensive bottle of vodka he'd liberated from Marketing. Ever since the sales had picked up they always had something to toast. He touched my shell reverently and asked, "What is this, a new kind of tattoo?"

I'd handpicked an obtuse assistant. It wouldn't do to have a clever observer at my side when creating new formulas. I assigned some busywork to keep him from butting in with questions at the wrong moment, and called Accounting.

As I suspected, both employees who had sampled the prototype had called out sick. Rumor had it they developed some unusual allergies.

The chitinous shell wasn't too bothersome. I threw on a sports coat over my shirt, bought flowers, and went to visit the sick women. They'd figured things out, too, and you can guess what sort of words I heard from them that day. Nevertheless, I managed to convince them to hold off from acting on their accusations.

Sergey Nikolayevich was in a great mood. Lately that was the norm. Without saying a word, I lifted up my shirt.

"Looks like we shouldn't have moved forward without clinical trials," I said. "The girls from Accounting are suffering from similar complications. A chitinous bosom isn't a sight for the faint of heart. That can derail any relationship. The girls plan to sue. In a month or two, the first wave of customers will be doing the same. As they say, the greedy man pays twice."

"Slow down, Partner," said Sergey Nikoloevich. "It's unlikely they'll connect this crust to our product right away."

"Perhaps not immediately, but they'll figure it out," I said. "And I was just beginning work on drugs that can adjust nose shape and lengthen legs."

Sergey Nikolayevich perked up. "That's excellent, keep it up. What about the crust—can you do something about that?"

"I've got skin in the game on this one. I'll create a fix. But what about the hundreds of thousands of consumers? We should recall the drug immediately. In the future, we must proceed with more caution. It takes five to ten years and millions in hard currency to legitimately bring a new drug to market."

At first, I thought Sergey Nikolayevich had fallen into a trance-like state. Later I understood—this was merely the boss's process for coming up with business strategies.

"Partner," he shouted in a fit of mercantile ecstasy, "everything is great. Much better than I thought! This drug has side effects? Perfect. The world is our oyster. We won't recall anything. We'll give people what they want, for as long as they want it. Side effects merely mean there will be demand for more products. We've got them on the hook! When they are all covered in shells, they'll come to us for an antidote. The important thing is to have the solution ready by then."

"That's cynical," I said. "They'll hate us."

"Only if we admit fault, which we'll never do. In the long term, it won't matter what caused the problem—they will only care about the cure, and they'll thank whoever provides it, which will be us. The key is to divert any negative attention elsewhere. Tomorrow I will have the tabloids write about the new epidemic brewing in, let's say, the Congo. We'll pay some experts to write articles, spread some misinformation through the blogosphere. A hot talk show wouldn't hurt, either."

Sergey Nikolayevich was in his element. He zigzagged across his office in a fit of nervous energy, rubbed his hands together, and giggled. "We'll say the Congolese fishermen were the first to become sick."

"Are you sure there are fishermen in the Congo?"

"There are fishermen everywhere. Don't sweat the small stuff, partner. We'll figure out the details later. I'm saving your skin and your reputation, and you're dissatisfied! Instead of arguing, help me come up with a name for this new disease."

I drummed my fingers against the rosy shell. No good ideas came, but deep in my heart I knew Sergey Nikolayevich was right. I didn't want a scandal either, because I was afraid to lose you.

"I feel like a shrimp," I said.

"Shrimp, eh? No, that doesn't sound very good.... Ah! Lobster flu. That's what we're going to call the new epidemic. First the lobsters got it, then the fishermen in the Congo caught it from the lobsters."

"Are there lobsters in the Congo?"

"When people become covered in crust they won't care whether or not there are lobsters in the Congo. They'll feel better knowing where to place the blame."

It was clear that Sergey Nikolayevich was prepared to invest millions in spreading this tall tale. He seemed ready to spend lavishly on anything other than clinical trials.

"Do your part and create the antidote," he said. "Don't let me down, Partner. The drug for adjusting nose shape is a good idea, too. You should also work on something that gets rid of cellulite, and for weight loss. Summer is coming—these remedies will sell like hotcakes."

"I demand twenty percent," I said firmly. "Not a penny less."

"The rules remain the same, Partner," said Sergey Nikolayevich. "Impress me. Then we'll talk about the money."

THE CHITINOUS SHELL flaked for hours. I picked up its brittle shards all over the house. The pill worked, but I felt uneasy. The papers, Internet, and TV covered the lobster flu for the third straight week. On the screen, Congolese fishermen with stoic expressions on their long-suffering faces talked about the multitudes of sick lobsters. It was a safe guess as to where the news programs had found them.

You lay on the couch and watched me scrub my belly raw with my fingernails.

"You poor dear," you said. "You caught this bug, too?"

We eradicated the lobster flu within a month, but it was soon replaced with the Arizona scabies.

My photo graced the cover of *Forbes*. The European Pharmacologists Association granted me their Man of the Year title. The World Congress of Epidemiologists awarded me the "Savior of Humanity" medal. Every day I was approached by headhunters from the world's largest pharmaceutical companies. Sergey Nikolayevich began calling me "brother" instead of "partner" and raised my share to thirty percent. He could afford to be generous, his company had become the world leader in the corrective pharmacology market.

My success was soured only by the fact that I grew a third kidney. Two weeks in the lab and a new pill later, the kidney had dissolved. Right after that, fur grew on my heels. That took three weeks to fix. I slept in socks so you wouldn't discover the fur, and waited with trepidation for whatever nasty trick my body would pull next.

The next side effect was surprisingly positive. My muscles bulked up on their own, turning my naturally wimpy body into a rather impressive specimen. I studied the process and forwarded it for Sergey Nikolayevich to monetize.

Unable to hire me away, the world's top corporations went after my assistant. He fled, and I was happy to see him go. I was tired of the bumbling idiot. I replaced him with the two girls from Accounting. Since they were witnesses to my mistakes, I wanted to keep them close by. In terms of the side effects we were in the same boat. They had become medically dependent on me, and wouldn't be betraying me anytime soon.

I avoided taking any more of my own drugs, but by then it was too late. I was so saturated with chemicals that they permeated my body, became a part of my metabolism and took on a life of their own, surprising me with all sorts of unplanned mutations. I kept inventing and using new powders, pills, ointments, and injections. I knew this couldn't go on forever. I was losing control. Soon I wouldn't be able to keep my own appearance, wouldn't recognize myself in the mirror. It's not that I was ever in love with the way I looked, but I wasn't ready to give up my individuality. I was like a man who chose to take his own life and experienced regret too late, in the brief moment after he had already pulled the trigger. In those days I was too concerned with my own problems to notice how slowly, irrevocably, the world was changing around me.

"HAVE YOU HEARD about the purists and the reshapers?" asked Sergey Nikolayevich.

He'd invited me to a business dinner at a very expensive restaurant. Lately I'd been leading the life of a lab hermit. This was the first time I had been out socially since getting rid of the heel fur. We drank fancy red wines and dined on organic venison.

On the stage, the gypsy band (half of them now blond) sang ancient love songs. It wasn't just the performers who looked strange. Every person in the restaurant exhibited some small imperfection. Some had ears hanging down to their shoulders, the side effect of the nose adjustment—our latest pills would cure the symptom within a month. Others were bald, and while some experienced that condition naturally, for others it was the side effect from taking our fanny-firming pill. We introduced an ointment that would begin to re-grow hair in just three days. Wrist scales were more difficult to remedy, requiring four months of injections and mandatory sunbathing. The scales developed whenever our corrective drugs for eye color, breast size, and hip curvature were taken at the same time, and afflicted only women. They were recorded in the medical books as the primary symptom of the Amsterdam fever. Some ladies hid the scales under bracelets, while others painted them with nail polish and showed them off proudly.

"The purists and the reshapers?" I repeated, absentmindedly. I was trying to figure out how to get rid of my tic. It was a relatively minor side effect, but a very inconvenient one.

"Purists advocate maintaining one's natural appearance," explained Sergey Nikolayevich. "It started out as a grassroots movement, but quickly found powerful supporters. They've launched a parliamentary investigation into our company. They found some well-respected professor who believes we're connected to lobster flu and Arizona scabies. I tried to reach an understanding with him, but the old man is unbribeable. He's angry at us over that remedy for impotency. You remember..."

"So, he isn't without sin."

"That's just it—his young wife gave it to him without his knowledge. And when the side effects manifested, she confessed. He's out for our blood."

"This was to be expected," I said, melancholically chewing venison. My tic made me wink at Sergey Nikolayevich.

"There's no reasoning with the purists," he said. "So far, no one is taking the professor seriously. My goal is to muddy up the waters. I've helped organize the party of reshapers, individuals who are actively interested in altering their appearance. I hired a young PR specialist to head the People's Reshaper Movement. My expectation was to merely remind the public of the pluralism of opinions, and that there is no accounting for taste. In reality, the movement has exceeded even my greatest expectations.

"There are two million card-carrying reshapers in the country, and even more abroad. They want to change themselves, no matter what, just for the challenge of it. The purists and the reshapers are at each other's throats. There's literal fighting in the streets. Both sides justify the violence as the means in their struggle for the future of humanity. The purists are up in arms; there will be parliamentary hearings now. I've already received my subpoena. I'm so tired of all the committees, delegations, inspections. I just don't like them. But I have an idea—before they issue some new law, we should release a universal appearance adjustor onto the market. Let's call the drug 'Perpetual Motion.' It should elicit a constant change in the user's body, so his skin can be polka-dotted one day and flower-patterned the next. Every morning a surprise, every day a celebration, eh? The reshaper party has already approached me requesting such a drug."

I was stunned. "Why do we need this?"

"If everyone is in a constant state of flux, the connection between our drugs and the side effects—and between our firm and the epidemics—can never be proven. Cause-and-effect will lose all meaning in the chaos. This universal adjustor will undoubtedly be banned in time, but by then the case will be closed. So, all hopes are on you. Will you rise to the challenge?"

"Wake up, Boss. As it is, there is no normal person left. Except, perhaps..."

I thought about you, dearest.

"Even you didn't resist the temptation," I told him. "You've lost weight with our patented 'Feather' powder, haven't you?"

"It was convenient." The lightness in his voice sounded forced. "Brother, I've been trying to lose weight for fifteen years. 'Feather' took care of it in one shot."

"You knew the price of this convenience. Should have spared yourself—now you have to medicate constantly. No, it's time to put an end to all of this. Let's close up shop, split the money, and disappear."

"Don't even tempt me, Brother. This company is my life."

Dearest, Sergey Nikolayevich wasn't merely a swindler. He was a swindler with principles.

"It isn't just my life tied into this company," he said. "It's yours, too. Don't even think of getting out. Your main goal now is to develop 'Perpetual Motion.' Don't let me down."

YOU WERE ON the couch, playing virtual squash. The ball flew across the room between your avatar and the hologram of a popular blond actor. Perhaps it was actually him, taking a break between shoots to flirt with you from across the ocean. You've recently become a prestigious contact as the wife of the millionaire pharmacologist who was five minutes away from winning a Nobel Prize.

I shut off the computer.

"I was in the middle of a game," you said, with indignation.

"Pack up. We're leaving immediately. Forever. They won't catch us."

You stared at me with gorgeous, indifferent eyes. "I pretended to ignore the fur on your heels. I tolerated it when spikes protruded from your back, like a porcupine. I acted as if nothing was wrong when you grew gills. But your tic is driving me nuts. I'm not going anywhere with you. And from now on we'll be sleeping in separate bedrooms. I've had enough of you, messing up the kitchen with your vials. So be a doll, turn the console back on, and go make me a milkshake."

I assessed the situation. There was no chance of moving you from that couch. Before me lay a perfect, self-satisfied creature. You didn't have a single fault. You chewed all day, yet your waist remained a perfect sixty centimeters. You had no use for pills or powders—there was simply nothing that needed fixing. Your perfection was gifted by nature and required no sacrifices in return. I'd committed sins for you, but you remained detached, as simple and unapproachable as the day we met. The neurotic outside world was becoming rapidly filled by freaks in pursuit of beauty while you, the main cause of this madness, rested blissfully on the couch. I'd outdone myself, even taken my own poison, to earn a moment of your favor. And for what? Separate bedrooms?

I seethed, but I also knew that I would love you no matter your appearance—your self-satisfied nature had imprinted itself deeply upon my psyche. Whereas, no matter how much I polished my appearance, you would always see me as a puny egghead who'd been granted the privilege to serve you. You had to be made to share the suffering of the world—to share my suffering. And, if anything went wrong, I could always fix it with a pill.

I went into the kitchen. No matter how many times we moved houses, I always turned the kitchen into my laboratory, out of habit. My state of mind brought inspiration: the new drug took only twenty minutes to create.

"I'm still waiting," you shouted, your voice filled with impatience. "Can't you do anything fast?"

"I sure can," I answered cheerfully, and splashed my new concoction into the strawberry milkshake.

YOUR PERFECT, BEAUTIFUL long legs shrunk by ten centimeters. For two days I waited for you to notice. On the third day you decided to go for a walk and tried to put on jeans. For fifteen minutes you gawked at the extra denim hanging from your feet. Then you took off the jeans, put on shorts, and went out. You returned with the delivery robot in tow, carrying a heap of new jeans. A week later, you threw them out because your legs returned to their original length.

I figured that I made a mistake with the dosage.

I worked on the next drug more diligently. You gained fifteen kilos overnight, but remained indifferent to this unfortunate metamorphosis.

"You should get off the couch more often. You gained a lot of weight." I decided to direct your attention to the problem. To be honest, the few extra kilos looked great on you.

You shrugged, bit into your pizza slice, and resumed browsing the yacht catalog.

Two days later, the extra kilos had disappeared without a trace. I knew with absolute certainty that you didn't take any pills, didn't diet, and didn't torture yourself with strenuous exercise. I deployed a mobile camera to spy on you. It silently followed you like a fly, and it recorded everything. All you did was lounge around, browse the web, occasionally fiddle with the climate control remote, and raid the fridge. Your weight loss was pure magic.

I took a radical next step. The new powder, mixed into your cola, caused blue mushrooms to grow in your cleavage.

"This is peculiar. We sleep in separate rooms, and I still caught something from you," was your comment.

The mushrooms withered and fell off by the end of the day.

All of my efforts were defeated by your unassailable perfection. I decided that all this stress was making me lose my touch, and took a time out.

With all these experiments, I completely forgot that Sergey Nikolayevich had asked me for a universal adjustor. When he took to reminding me about it twenty times per day, I quickly threw together his "Perpetual Motion." By then I was an expert at designing these drugs. The creative process took only a few days, and the spirit of irresponsibility nurtured within me by Sergey Nikolayevich really unleashed the mind.

"What are the side effects?" asked Sergey Nikolayevich, businesslike.

"No idea," I said indifferently. "Does it matter? People who take our drugs aren't concerned with side effects."

A revolutionary never-before-seen drug with no stated side effects was marketed in three forms: pills, a mint-flavored mixture, and an aerosol spray. A hundred top activists from the reshaper movement received "Perpetual Motion" treatments free of charge. The rest had to pay through the nose, which stopped no one. After a week, our factories had to increase output.

This time, the side effects surprised even me. Transmutations occurred spontaneously. They could happen anywhere—at work, at home, en route, in the bath, or in bed. Typically a transmutation caused a discharge of airy foam, colored a pleasant shade of green. It was odorless and flavorless (someone had dared to taste it). The foam was difficult to wash off sidewalks, walls, objects, and the skin of nearby people. I thought we'd surely catch hell for that, but many consumers found this side effect amusing. After all—green is the color of optimism. The beginning of a transmutation could be anticipated by the refreshing tingling of the nose. Some people sneezed. That's how those nearby knew it was time to run. I thought society got used to all of this rather quickly.

But we'd jumped to that conclusion too soon. People dressed in civilian clothing showed up at our offices. Their true affiliation could be easily deciphered by the seal of government authority stamped on their facial expressions. Their leader was a tall gentleman by the name of Colonel Zverev, clearly a purist. He showed us a warrant with stamps and signatures from so high up I still can't recall it without shivering.

"If you fail to cooperate, we'll shut down this racket by morning," he cautioned.

"I was just about to offer our services," replied Sergey Nikolayevich.

"Your drugs make it impossible to maintain national security. To catch criminals, spies, or extremists," said the colonel.

"Can't you still identify them by fingerprints, smell, retina prints or brain wave patterns?" asked Sergey Nikolayevich.

"Your universal corrector changes all of those physical characteristics, not to mention the smell."

That was a revelation for us.

Colonel Zverev hated us with a passion. "If you fail to invent a new way of identifying people..."

"I've got it. Gorsky—inventions are your department," Sergey Nikolayevich competently diverted the heat on to me.

Zverev stared at me sternly.

Damn it, Zverev, I'm a pharmacologist, not an engineer. For a moment, I felt like I should make up an excuse and just get out of there. The colonel must've read my thoughts. He must have known through experience that flight was the usual psychological response to meeting him.

"Don't even think about it," he said.

"There will be no thinking, sir." I tried to lighten the mood with a joke.

"Here's what we're going to do. I'll assign you a few competent specialists. You're going to work night and day, and you better create a device to arm the secret police with. If you don't, I will personally smash your head in, and the issue of thinking will resolve itself naturally. Were it up to me, I would—" and then he went on an angry rant reciting all the purist talking points.

That's how I became involved in creating the genetic decoder. I came up with the methodology for identifying the original genetic code in a transmuted body. The resulting prototype was bulky and resembled an oversized paintball gun. Not sleek, but effective enough for fieldwork. Which was great, except whoever it was used on suffered unbearable agony: bone aches, ringing in the ears, high blood pressure. The pain was severe enough to potentially kill someone.

"We'll work on improving it," said Colonel Zverev. For a time, his people left us alone.

I managed to steal one of the first genetic decoders. It hung on the wall of our living room. It was nice to feel a sense of accomplishment not only as a pharmacologist, but also as a gunsmith. I wondered whether I should pursue a career in that field.

So, my dear, don't toy with the genetic decoder. It can easily leave you a widow, and I still plan on being useful to you. Besides, in my will I bequeathed everything to a charitable fund for victims of pharmacology. How would you maintain your lifestyle without me? You'd have to get off the couch, and that's an inconvenience.

While I was researching a way to change your skin color into something funny, the outside world was spinning out of control. Our gates were being picketed by protestors, who carried signs like criminal pharmacologists must pay. Reshapers countered with signs which read freedom to be anyone we can become.

Purist hackers attacked our e-commerce sites. Reshaper hackers invented a virus which plastered our banner ads all over the web.

Purists burned a warehouse full of our products. Reshapers found the culprits and force-fed them the universal adjustor, which turned out to cause a bit of a scandal.

Some purist-owned firms began firing employees who took our drugs. Reshapers boycotted the products of those companies.

Both sides filed constant lawsuits against one another.

The war escalated when we released a special variant of "Perpetual Motion" which allowed users to change their gender weekly. I was against this initially—some things are better left alone—but the consumers accepted the latest offering with surprising enthusiasm.

I realized the end was nigh when reports began coming in of our consumers randomly and chaotically transmuting even without taking "Perpetual Motion." Was this a side effect? You could argue about the terminology. By then, it didn't even matter. Millions of consumers' bodies had reached a tipping point. They kept changing in strange ways, even when they didn't take the drugs, even if they didn't want to change anymore. We had created a new species of constantly transmuting beings, who didn't even know what they might become next. Beings who, incidentally, were no longer capable of conceiving or giving birth to children. Oops.

Then came the parliamentary hearings.

"I intend to prove these so-called pharmacologists are conspiring against humanity itself," shouted the professor whose wife had slipped him our powder.

Sergey Nikolayevich smiled meekly at the panel from his seat. Behind him, famous experts and pricey attorneys who were no longer certain of anything shuffled papers.

"Changing one's face doesn't absolve one of their responsibility to society, doesn't give them a *carte blanche*," preached the professor.

The angry old man was right. Crime was off the chart, robberies and looting especially. Cops ran around with genetic decoders in hand and tried to figure out who was who. All systems of identification and control were shattered. The government suspended the sales of our drugs, until the panel could reach its decision.

It was during the hearings, on live TV, that the idea of gathering all the reshapers and resettling them into restricted zones was first voiced. There were riots. Purists and reshapers fought each other openly. The conflict threatened to become global at any moment.

I navigated the streets in my Jeep, trying to reach our offices. Yesterday I'd rented a private plane. I was going to lure you out promising a sightseeing tour of the city skyline at night, but I planned for the plane to carry us far away to some nice and—most importantly—uninhabited tropical island. But first, I wanted to shred some files and flush some secret reagents down the toilet.

It was surprisingly quiet near the office entrance. A dirty, ripped shopping bag danced in the wind above the deserted parking lot, which was spotted with green discharge. I stopped the car and looked around. Deep in the alleyways behind our office building I could make out the shapes of police cars. At that moment the sky became filled with noise and a helicopter landed in front of the building.

Agents escorted a pale Sergey Nikolayevich outside. Our director of sales followed, his expression muted. Several agents ran my way.

Impulsive decisions aren't always the right ones. Perhaps I should have reconsidered. I reached for a vial of the latest "Perpetual Motion" variant in my pocket and, without thinking it through, drained half of it. That's a lot. The transmutation began immediately.

I jumped out of the car, covered the agents in green discharge, and ran as fast as my seven extremities would carry me. I should have made for the rented plane, but the thought of leaving you behind was unbearable.

You were on the couch—remember?—eating donuts and leafing through some catalog.

"Look what you've gone and done." You raised your gorgeous, ruthless eyes from the page. "There are people here to see you."

Camouflaged soldiers armed with genetic decoders poured from every door. I was so surprised that my glasses fell off my face. But then, I no longer needed glasses. Transmutation had made me eagle-eyed.

"Gorsky?" asked Colonel Zverev, who led the unit. "Don't pretend that you aren't Gorsky, that you wandered in here by accident. Admit it's you, or we'll use the decoder."

"You don't even have handcuffs in my size," was all I could say.

"Will you be home for dinner?" you shouted, as they led me outside.

I WONDERED HOW long they'd jail me for. Thirty years? Fifty? They'd likely confiscate all my assets, too. I didn't bother asking Colonel Zverev where we were going. For the first time in a long while, I felt rather certain of what would come next. Somehow, this made me feel a little better.

The helicopter carried us out of the city. It landed on a manicured lawn in front of a tall, featureless mansion. A row of identical blue spruces lined the path to a massive porch. If this was prison, it looked to be a very comfortable one.

Plain clothed agents escorted me up to the second floor and into a lavishly decorated office. Behind a Louis XIV desk sat a furry cocoon with strangely familiar eyes.

"I could kill you right now," said the cocoon.

"Who are you?"

"Didn't you see my name on the door?" The cocoon shifted unhappily. "No wonder you don't recognize me; I took your stupid drug."

"Why did you do that, Mr. President?" I asked. "You were perfect, body and soul. We all looked up to you. I understand why others swallow my pills, but not you."

"Hold your tongue, smart guy. Don't presume to lecture me. Look, here is the deal: a week from now I must attend an emergency summit regarding this mess with the purists and the reshapers. I can't show up looking like this. So think, kid, think. There's an underground lab here. We'll keep you locked in there until you figure out a way to return me to normal."

I realized that I would spend the rest of my life in that lab, with only my guards for company. My nose itched and I sneezed.

"Watch out!" shouted Colonel Zverev and bravely covered the president with his body. His action was timely—green discharge splashed his back.

Agents shrunk away from me when I transmuted. That was my one chance to escape. I smashed the window and flew out. My latest transmutation had given me wings—not very powerful ones, but strong enough to glide like a flying squirrel, jumping from tree to tree, from roof to roof.

I lost the helicopters that chased me by the time I reached the edge of the city. My pursuers clustered above the forest, apparently thinking I was hiding in the trees.

From the bird's eye view I saw the city burning. Flashes of gunfire and green vapors of transmutations. Purists and reshapers fought each other fiercely. The fate of the world was being decided by fisticuffs.

My transmutation was short-lived. I barely reached home. The wings withered and fell off just as I broke through the window and onto the floor of our living room.

You were still on the couch, a slipper hanging off your toe, your thoughts somewhere very far away.

"Back already?" you asked.

"There's a plane waiting for us on an airfield outside of town. It's dangerous to stay here; people are rioting and knifing each other in the streets. There are helicopters after me. You don't need to pack. You can even come wearing your robe and slippers. All you have to do is *get off the couch.*"

You stretched. The slipper fell off your toe and hit the ground with a *thud.*

"Gideon, I don't recognize you lately," you said.

"I understand."

"We've drifted apart."

"There's something to that."

"We've become strangers. We have nothing in common. It's time for us to live apart. I'll live here and you... somewhere else."

I had no time or patience left to argue with you.

"Dearest, perhaps you should think this through. Maybe you'll realize I'm right once you've calmed down. Do you want your favorite strawberry milkshake?"

You've never said "no" to a milkshake. The agents failed to search me, so I still had the vial half full of the latest iteration of "Perpetual Motion."

You gulped the milkshake down quickly. Perhaps you were hungry, since I hadn't been around to serve you a meal. You winced at the empty glass. "It tasted strange."

"You finally noticed," I said.

A huge dose of the drug caused an immediate transmutation. Your eyelids turned ninety degrees, your lips swelled up, and a third eye on a short stalk grew in the back of your head. The eyestalk turned and you looked at yourself.

"What happened? What did you do to me?"

"Like Romeo and Juliet, we drank of the same poison. Fair's fair."

Clearly I shouldn't have been so flippant.

"The blue mushrooms in the cleavage—that was also you?"

"It was," I said, proud as an artist showing off his latest painting.

"You were poisoning me the whole time!"

You ripped the genetic decoder from the wall, and we ran. Or, to be precise, I ran. You chased me, screaming and waving the gun.

LET'S CALL THINGS what they are—this is a relationship crisis. Statistically, crises are experienced by over ninety percent of married couples. It is only possible to overcome such a crisis and salvage the relationship by working together.

During the last two hours I had a lot of time to think while you chased me across the city. We made a lot of mistakes. We based our relationship on cash and aggression, whereas we should have based it on unselfish love and optimism for the future. This became clear to me, and I found the way to save our relationship, and the world.

Put down the decoder. Let's forgive each other all of our transgressions. This is the moment of truth. Your immunity to my drugs, your ability to shrug off side effects and return to your original—perfect—form, is unique. Your body contains some sort of element capable of thwarting any attempts to change you. There is no other explanation. You're special. You're the chosen one. The salvation of the human race is within you.

We have to drop everything, and study this phenomenon. I'm absolutely sure that your body will soon get rid of all the changes caused by the transmutation. Your lips, for example, are already back to normal. I must solve this mystery.

What? You say it's enough to simply love yourself? Love yourself the way you were born? That's antiquated romanticism, my dear. I didn't expect that from you. Fine, let's suppose that's true. But all love (including the love of self) is a chemical reaction. I will distill this chemical agent from your body and use it to create a vaccine, for me and for the rest of humanity.

Once I do this, they will have no choice but to award me the Nobel Prize and then leave me alone. Then we can leave for lush, tropical islands, and live out the rest of our days there the natural way, as God created us. We can bring your couch, too.

I just thought of something. What if, given your habits, the vaccine based on your chemistry will also have side effects? What if humanity will fall in love with itself like Narcissus, plunge onto couches, and refuse to get up even to feed themselves?

As ever, I'm afraid there is no time for a medical trial.

Tatiana Ivanova

Tatiana Ivanova is a noted sociologist and futurist in Russia. She teaches at the Moscow Business School. Her articles have appeared in many scientific journals as well as *Marie Claire, Cosmopolitan,* and other popular magazines. Her short fiction has appeared in several of the top Russian publications.

The original Russian language version of this story was originally published in *Science & Life* magazine in 2011 and subsequently reprinted in *Russian Science Fiction 2012* (an equivalent of a Year's Best volume.)

ACKNOWLEDGMENTS

We'd like to thank everyone involved in making this book possible: associate editors Cyd Athens, James Beamon, Frank Dutkiewicz, James Miller, and Nathaniel Lee; copy editor Elektra Hammond, book designer Melissa Neely, graphics designer Emerson Matsuuchi, cover artist Tomasz Maronski, illustrator Barry Munden, and many others whose talent and hard work made this a better book. Special thanks to Anne Roberti, Steven Mentzel, and James Conason for their invaluable support of this project.

ABOUT THE EDITOR

Alex Shvartsman is a writer, anthologist, translator, and game designer from Brooklyn, NY. He's the winner of the 2014 WSFA Small Press Award for Short Fiction and a two-time finalist (2015 and 2017) for the Canopus Award for Excellence in Interstellar Writing.

His short stories have appeared in *Nature, Intergalactic Medicine Show, Daily Science Fiction, Galaxy's Edge*, and a variety of other magazines and anthologies. His collection, *Explaining Cthulhu to Grandma and Other Stories*, and his steampunk humor novella *H. G. Wells, Secret Agent* were published in 2015.

In addition to the UFO series, he has edited the *The Cackle of Cthulhu, Humanity 2.0, Funny Science Fiction, Coffee: 14 Caffeinated Tales of the Fantastic* and *Dark Expanse: Surviving the Collapse* anthologies.

His website is www.alexshvartsman.com.

Unidentified Funny Objects Series

An annual collection
of humorous science fiction and fantasy.

Unidentified Funny Objects 5

Available at www.ufopub.com and from fine
booksellers everywhere.

Edited By Alex Shvartsman

DAVID GERROLD · ESTHER FRIESNER · MIKE RESNICK · JODY LYNN NYE
LAURA RESNICK · TIM PRATT · GINI KOCH · CAROLINE M. YOACHIM

Humanity 2.0

Available from Arc Manor/Phoenix Pick
www.humanity2.website

The Cackle of Cthulhu

An anthology of Lovecraftian humor
Available from Baen Books, January 2018

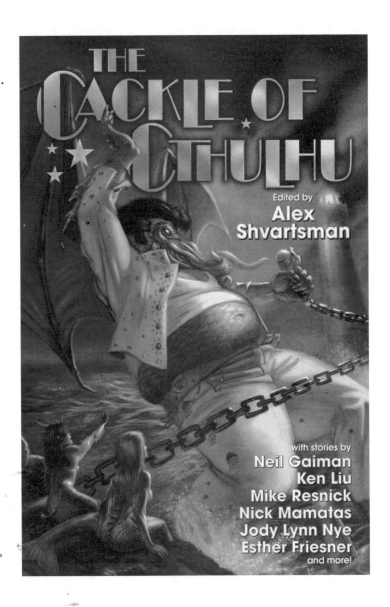

THE CACKLE OF CTHULHU

Edited by
Alex Shvartsman

with stories by
Neil Gaiman
Ken Liu
Mike Resnick
Nick Mamatas
Jody Lynn Nye
Esther Friesner
and more!